THE YELLOW SUITCASE

L.W. CLARK

ISBN: 978-1-09837-424-2 (print)

ISBN: 978-1-09837-425-9 (eBook)

For my friend, lover & husband

CONTENTS

ONE

JANUARY 1995, EASTERN EUROPE

It was New Year's Day around noon when I woke up. The air was cold, my body was sweating and my mouth was dry. I didn't want to see the world that day. I had a major hangover and was feeling so embarrassed that I just wanted to disappear from this place and the people around me.

I know it sounds dramatic but that's the way I felt. I was sick, moody and angry. All negative stuff. It started when a few of my girlfriends and I decided to celebrate New Year's Eve together. No brothers, sisters, cousins or any other relatives. Every other celebration followed the same tradition—lots of food and drinks with family, relatives and close friends. Every year we'd go to someone's home or rent a place. These were good times. But now we were older and (somehow) still single; we thought we should break with the tradition and go out to a club, do some dancing, and maybe meet someone interesting.

The four of us were best friends and neighbors, and our parents, brothers and sisters were close as well. We were all pretty and charming (if I do say so myself). All of us were coming from traditional families where there was lots of love and support for each other. "Traditional family" also means that one day you're supposed to have your own family, which meant getting married and having kids.

Back then it was almost tragic if you were twenty-one or something and still not married. To make it worse, most of our other friends were already married and even had one or two kids. Some even got married when they were eighteen. It was that kind of lifestyle. There was nothing else to do, so getting married was one of the fun parts of life, especially if it came with a big wedding. Most parents would throw a wedding no matter what. If they were tight with money, they would borrow some. I guess the parents wanted to have some fun too.

We all graduated from college and had jobs, but no matter what kind of work you did at that age, you never had enough money, unless your parents gave you some. Most parents would support their kids financially if they needed it, even though they were adults, and even if they were married.

I think it was a bit much, but the parents didn't have much to do either. I think some of them liked having their children dependent on them, so they could still have control, and so they wouldn't move away from them. We're all a little selfish, right? So, this "support each other" thing seemed to work pretty well.

After asking around, we found a nightclub where there was going to be a New Year's Eve party with a DJ and that was affordable. Since I was the only one in my family with a job at that moment, I supported everyone, and I rarely had any extra money to indulge myself with things and doing stuff. But what I did have was a lot of friends in the city. I mean, I was well connected with many people. So even if I couldn't afford many things, I was always invited to parties, concerts and events, and my friends would take care of me.

It was a time when many people couldn't find work and families were struggling with money. Mine was one of them. Every day was difficult. The economy was really bad in the country. It wasn't that people didn't want to work. They weren't lazy. It was just really hard to find even some elementary work. I was lucky. I had a job, sometimes two. But when it came time to buy an event ticket, I barely had enough money.

We got the tickets but kept our New Year's Eve plans a secret until the last minute, to avoid all the questions about why everyone wasn't going to be together. And what was the most important reason for the four of us to go out on our own? You can't flirt with guys and be free to do whatever you want if you're out with an older brother or sister.

Let's say you're feeling good and want to go a little crazy. You can't do that with family there. You'll hear a lot of criticism, which I hated. We weren't bad girls. We wouldn't do something stupid or unacceptable. I guess we just wanted our freedom.

Yes, that's it. Freedom. Parents are great, and so are brothers and sisters. But sometimes they can drive you crazy. Especially Moms. Most Dads couldn't care less what their kids are wearing or what their hair looks like. But Moms? They care about all of it. They want you to look, dress and do your hair just the way they want, so they can be so proud of you. What can you do? Even if I didn't want to go out looking the way she wanted, in the end I would, so I could make her happy.

The party tickets only got us in the door. Food or drinks weren't included. We couldn't afford the drinks, so we brought a bottle of vodka. One of my friends hid the bottle in her coat. That worked, and we all got so excited as we made our entrance into the room. The club was small, with only two rooms. One was with a bar and a couple of couches. The other was a bigger space with the DJ. They said there was a DJ, but I never saw one.

It was black inside. We could barely see each other. Every so often you could see because of some kind of disco lighting, which I guess was pretty cool. When it was dark we would sip a little vodka so we could get a buzz and some liquid courage to break free from being shy and insecure. Then we could dance and flirt with ease. I sipped a few times and sat down on the couch to wait for a buzz.

I'm not feeling a thing. Hmmm ... maybe I didn't drink enough? I should have some more.

I went back to the dark room and drank some more as I watched all my girlfriends feeling buzzed and happy. I wanted that buzz too, and I was in a hurry. I had another drink and then another. I stayed there with my friends and danced and finally started to feel this nice buzz as the music played. As I looked around, the room was packed. Everybody was dancing, happy and drunk.

I feel happy too. But I don't like this spinning disco light. It's making me dizzy. I'm going to take a break. Oh ... uh oh.

Suddenly I felt buzzed, and not in a fun way, but in a sick way, when you want to find a bathroom—fast. I went to the bathroom. I felt sweaty and dizzy. I stayed in the bathroom for a while, just sitting on the toilet hoping the sick feeling would go away. It didn't, but I made myself believe I was all right. I forced myself to get up. I didn't want to miss all the action out there. I went back to the dance floor and pretended everything was just fine, but it hit me again. I didn't feel right and went back to the bathroom.

Then I threw up. I thought it would help get rid of the alcohol in my body, but nope. I felt even worse. I sat down on the toilet and couldn't move. I couldn't even open my eyes. I tried but I just couldn't do it.

I stayed in the bathroom sitting on the toilet and leaning my head on the wall. I don't remember how long I was in there, but it seemed like all night. Every once in a while, one of my girlfriends would come into the bathroom and yell to be heard above the pounding music.

"Alyssa!! Are you OK?"

"Yes, I'm OK. I'll be right out."

The girls were having a good time, and since they were taking turns looking for me, I don't think they realized I was in the bathroom for so long. I guess I bought the New Year's Eve ticket to use the bathroom all night.

After what seemed like forever, one of my girlfriends came in again. She already knew which stall I was in and told me that we were leaving the club. One of our friends was on his way to pick us up so we could go to some other place. I had no choice now. I needed to force my eyes open, get up and pretend that I was doing just fine.

When I got out of the bathroom and walked through the club, it seemed like there were fewer people: Some drunk people, a few boys and girls standing by the bar. A few couples were having pointless conversations. You know: the kind of passionate, drunken discussions that have no meaning whatsoever, if you can even remember them.

It seemed very late. My girlfriends were pretty buzzed, and they couldn't figure out how long they had been dancing and chatting with others. I got my coat and went straight to our friend's car. I sat in the back seat by the window so I could put my head on something. My head was so heavy I had trouble keeping it up.

As soon as we took off, I closed my eyes. It was night and dark in the car so no one could see my face. The girls were so loud and so was the music playing on the radio. The car was going so fast, but I didn't care about any of that.

All I cared about was getting home without them noticing how drunk I was. The strange thing is, I remembered everything that happened that night, every single moment. I think I was poisoned by the vodka. I just got sick from it. Maybe it's because I didn't eat much before going out, but whatever the reason, it was a really bad feeling. It was a long time before I had another vodka.

We soon approached another place to continue partying. Everybody got out of the car and I was next, but I just couldn't move. I couldn't even say hello to some other friends as they approached the car. They were knocking on my window and kept saying, hey, get out, hurry let's go. I tried really hard to open my eyes, but it was impossible.

"Hey Ivan," I said to my friend who drove us. "Can you do me a big favor and take me home? I'm really tired."

"Sure," he said.

"Great, thanks," I said.

"Hey guys," he said, "I'm going to drop Alyssa off. I'll be right back."

"Oh, OK. We'll take a ride, so you won't be alone on the way back," some said, and they all piled into the car.

Great, now there are even more boys in the car. More people around so I can be even more embarrassed.

I know it's not a big deal to get drunk or sick. So what? But I've always been a proud person and maybe a little insecure. I thought this was such a big deal that the next day the whole city would talk about me and laugh. I was so ashamed and mad at myself for having even drunk the stupid vodka. It's just not cool or sexy for girls to drink like that. I understand having a cocktail at the bar, sipping it slowly, and being all feminine, which was the way I was, mostly. That's why I was disgusted with how I behaved at the club. I criticized myself all the time.

The guys in the car were as loud as the girls. They were buzzed too, so they didn't pay much attention to me. I would open one eye once in a while to see how far we had to go. Finally, we had approached my house.

I got out, said thank you, and pretended everything was fine. I went into the building, pushed the elevator bottom and guess what? It wasn't working. Of course. Out of order. Typical. It took me a long time to walk up to the seventh floor. I was struggling with the steps and trying hard not to fall. I couldn't even keep my head up. I eventually made it and went straight to my room and crashed.

Now I'm (barely) awake, wearing the same clothes from the night before and I stink.

Even before I opened my eyes, I knew I hated everything. I hated myself, my life, my home. Everything. This was one of the biggest moments of my life. I made a major decision. And what was it? Let's go back.

TWO

I was 21 and single. I had a decent job with just enough income to support my entire family. I had a relationship with a guy. I thought we were in love. But after some kind of silly conversation, we broke up. Just like that. No reason.

That kind of break up is the worst. When you don't even know what happened or why. There are so many questions and doubts spinning in your head. It drives you nuts. Somewhere you have some glimmer of hope that you might get back together one day. And that hope makes you so impatient and distracted. I thought my life was over and I'd never fall in love again. I thought he was the one and no one else. I guess I wasn't happy with my life. That's why everything was so dramatic.

My family's lifestyle changed when my father died unexpectedly from a heart attack. He was forty-four years old. I was twelve. He was highly educated and a well-known, prosperous businessman. Before he died, my siblings and I lived an upper-class life and didn't want for anything. As we grew up, we were given the best education and were taught the right manners and etiquette. We had a summer house in the country and a private house in the city. Our family was the center of attention for many people in the city.

We had caviar for breakfast and high-quality meats for dinner. We had a private tailor for clothes and shopped for the best shoes. We even had a car with a private driver. We had fun and a love for sharing with others. My mother never worked. She stayed at home and took care of us, with love and attention. We had it all, until my father died. And we quickly went from an easy life to a difficult one.

Back then in my country, no one had life insurance or much savings. Why bother? What could possibly go wrong, right? Well, all the income died with my father. Once he was gone, so was everything else. Even his well-connected friends and the people he had done so much for slowly faded away from us. People are like that. When you have power, everybody's your friend. Once you don't? They forget about you. At least that was my experience.

It's really hard when your life suddenly transitions from comfort to fear. Instead of a carefree life, we lived day to day, making sure we had a place to live, food to eat and decent clothes to wear. We sold everything we could—the house, furniture, clothes, jewelry, silverware, dishes—for living money. I no longer lived in a nice house, with my own room and nice clothes. I remember once my mother wanted to take the bus and I started crying, begging her to call a taxi. I wasn't used to public transportation.

But through it all, we always had each other and love. I had a great family and great friends. Some of my friends came from families with money. They would always invite me wherever they were going, so at least I had something of a social life.

As I grew up, I became more and more ambitious to get back to the same safe, nice life that I had before. I wanted more, but I wanted to get it on my own and not from my friends. I wanted to be the person who paid for my friends and not the other way around.

So, what was my major decision that New Year's morning, when I was tired and disgusted with myself and my life? I was going to do something about it. Continuing to live like that was not an option. I spent a lot of time over the next few days doing some serious soul searching.

What do I really want? How can I make my life better? What options do I have? I need to be honest about money. Let's face it, money is power and freedom. It will let me do what I want, when I want. I can study for a career or open a business. I can improve my image with the right clothes and styles. Even if I get sad I can just go away for a while, to snap out of it. I need money, but not just for myself. I need enough to help others. Not only for my family, neighbors and friends, but also for people I don't even know. I want to give back—to society and to people who struggle. To be so financially stable that I can do whatever I want, and to make others happy, which would bring me happiness.

All these thoughts were racing through my head, but I couldn't see any path to my dreams. This country didn't provide opportunities to break through and succeed. The most common way was to get married to some rich guy, but even that wasn't easy. Even if I could find him, it couldn't be just anyone. I had to have feelings for him. I wasn't lucky to find love and money at the same time. Besides, even when life was easy, somewhere inside, I had doubts that I belonged here. I didn't like the traditions, the old-school mentality or atmosphere. I'm not saying it was bad for everyone. It just wasn't my cup of tea, that's all.

While I struggled to find a way forward, I always believed that once you start searching for something, somehow people, things and opportunities come to you, no matter what it is. You are what you think, so I changed my mind. I thought about how to make my life easier, pleasurable and more interesting. I thought about it day and night, and I waited. Then one hot summer evening in 1995, I got a call.

"Hi Alyssa," my friend Niki said. "What are you up to?"

"Not much. Just finished dinner, doing the dishes. How about you?"

"Same, but I did have an interesting chat with my relative Blanka. I think you met her once? She said she met a woman who could help get a U.S. invitation letter to apply for a visa. Isn't that cool?"

I had thought about going somewhere, but I wasn't sure where. Maybe work in another country? If I go to America, I could learn English, which is always useful in business. Come back with a little savings and experience so I could get a better job or even start a business. I could help my family and myself.

"That is interesting," I said.

"I would love to go to America."

"Me too, especially to New York. I'm sure it's fantastic. Well, at least based on the movies we've seen."

We laughed and continued chatting into the night. When I went to bed, I thought about the conversation. Niki said if you got the visa, the lady could also help you find a job when you got to the U.S. But getting a visa from the American consulate was challenging. There were always a lot of applications and they only approved a few, so the odds were against you. But there was always a chance.

I called Niki the next morning. We were both thinking the same thing. We wanted a change, and maybe this was the opportunity. She wasn't happy here either. She was single, in a low paying job, and she lived with her parents, her brother and his wife and her niece. But at least her father had a job that paid well.

"We should meet the lady," I said. "We have nothing to lose by listening to what she has to say."

"That's true," said Niki. "But are you really serious about this? We'd be leaving our family and all our friends."

"I know, but I am serious. I'm becoming more serious the more I think about it. If you are too, maybe we can meet her together."

"Yes, let's do that. Let's get together for coffee this morning so we can talk some more."

The lady's name was Margo. I got her phone number and gave her a call.

"I'm really, really busy but I can try to find time for you next week," Margo said.

"That would be great. Thanks so much," I said.

"Yes, yes. Come meet me next Tuesday, July 11th at 12:30 in my office. See you then," and she hung up.

Well she certainly sounds busy. And she has an office, so that seems to make it more legit. Having an office is a big deal these days.

Niki and I were so excited, with hope and fear. Where were we going? What if this didn't work out well? What if this or that? It's hard to leave friends and family, even if life sucks. I guess I was used to this everyday crap life, so it was still hard to imagine a change. Changes are tough for most people, but that's because they're lazy. It is easier to stay where you are with what you have because of the comfort of routine. Even if we know it's a change for the better, we might still be too lazy to do it. This is our weak human mentality. We're afraid to take a chance because of all the "what if" questions.

And I'm just like everyone else. I've got all these "what if" thoughts in my head. But come on. I've made absolutely no progress in my life. I don't see any good coming to me in the future if I stay here. And anyway, I'm not going to miss much if I leave here for a year or so. Maybe I'll miss all the gossip, but not much more. The pace of life here is about as fast as a turtle. I'm sure I'll catch up quickly when I come back. And what's wrong with going to a better country, one that's safer and more civilized? It's not like I'm going to a war zone or a violent place where things could be dangerous.

These positive thoughts are making me feel better, but still … still … I'm worried. It can be frightening. A new culture, new people, and I don't even know the language. If I'm so frightened, why not just stay here? Carry on, with the same life? That's even more frightening. Staying here without any hope for the future? Yes, change is hard and risky, but at least there's hope for the future.

As these thoughts raced through my head, I became more determined to meet busy Margo, who even had an office. Niki and I were always great friends, but now we had a chance to get even closer. It would be great to go through this journey together. We made ourselves believe our plan would come true, and that it would be awesome. The next day I shared my idea with my family. Their reactions?

"What?"

"Are you crazy?"

"Where are you going?"

"What busy lady?"

"What did she say?"

"Who the hell is Margo?"

And finally, "No." My mom said, "I will not let you go."

She's not taking my idea seriously. No one is. Who can blame them? Sometimes, even I don't take my idea too seriously. There's still a lot to do. I'm not going to argue with them. When things become more real I'll bring it up again, and tell them what I'm going to do.

Niki said we should bring one of our parents with us to meet Margo so she wouldn't screw us out of our money. Of course, Margo would want to get paid for her services, but we didn't know if we could trust her. Maybe she would make all these promises, take the money and disappear. That happened a lot.

So, Niki asked her father, Bernard, to come with us. Her father was an easygoing, quiet person. All he ever did was work to support his family and then went home. Day after day. I'm sure he was exhausted at some point. Doing so much hard work without any rest. It's kind of boring from my perspective, but maybe that's all he wanted. Niki knew her father would say yes. Just one word. He never talked much, but he did like the idea, and he agreed to go with us to meet Margo.

Maybe he liked this plan because it would mean supporting one less person in the family. He was worried that Niki was still single. I know men usually don't care about that stuff, but I knew he did, since I saw him so often. And Niki was the kind of daughter who would talk about everything with her parents. She would bitch about still being single and the relationships with guys that wouldn't last long. Bernard was probably tired of hearing about that over and over again. Or, maybe he wanted to see Margo the business lady, because he imagined she would be sexy?

Being a business lady was unusual in our city. Most women were married and stayed at home, taking care of the family and the house. You know those kinds of housewives, who don't really care about how they look anymore? They don't put any makeup on or dress sexy for their husbands. They think they're already in this marriage thing so why even bother with any extra efforts. They already have lots to do in the laundry room, the kitchen and so on. But men? They always like a woman with makeup or in a sexy dress while wearing high heels. It doesn't matter how long they've been married. They always like it. I'm sure Bernard was enjoying his "business lady" imagination. Men like those kinds of fantasies. I'm just saying.

Niki's father left work at lunchtime and picked us up to go to the meeting. As we approached the address, it looked like a residential building. We went into the building to the second floor where there were two doors. The left door was where (hopefully) all the magic happened.

What if this is all a joke? Maybe she isn't even in there. What if we ring the bell and no one opens the door? Or someone opens the door and says, "Margo who?" I'm so skeptical. I just want to see this lady. It would be embarrassing if we asked Bernard to leave work and take us here, all for nothing.

We buzzed the door and heard a female voice.

"Come in, the door is open."

Oh, thank God. At least someone's in there.

"The office" was obviously somebody's apartment, you could tell. Well, I could tell. I saw everything, all the details. I can scan an entire space in a second. But it was fine. There wasn't any desk with work papers or a phone. It was just one big, dark room. Old walls, high ceiling, with nice furniture.

Margo was sitting on a couch near a couple of chairs and a coffee table. She greeted us, and we all sat down. She looked like a business lady, which made me feel a little better. She had olive skin with bleached blond hair and puffy but small, sexy eyes. With her deep voice, you could tell she was a smoker.

I don't know why some women think if they bleach their hair blond, they can get more attention from people, to attract men or have a more believable business look. I guess she was one of those ladies. But maybe it does work sometimes, because the minute she started to reach for her cigarette box on the coffee table, Bernard was up with his lighter on. He calmly lit her cigarette.

"Thanks … thank you," Margo said, looking at him with a slight smile.

"Of course," Bernard said as he sat back down.

It's kind of funny watching them. Regardless of the circumstances, every woman likes a gentleman and every man likes a woman's attention.

"We understand you're able to get invitation letters from the United States. Is that right?" I asked.

"Yes, yes I can," Margo said. "I have very good connections in America. I've known them for a long time. They can send notarized invitation letters."

"That's great," Niki said.

"Yes," Margo said, exhaling smoke. "With this letter, you can apply to the American consulate for a visa. There's no guarantee you'll get one, but without the letter, you can't even apply."

We weren't there long. We left content and got in the car. We couldn't wait to hear Bernard's opinion. But he was quiet. He turned to the back of the car and looked at us, but he didn't say anything.

This guy seems to move in slow motion. It can really get on my nerves, especially when I'm impatient. I can't imagine dealing with him every day. No wonder Niki's mother is always screaming at him. I've heard that a few times. She's such an emotional person. Fast and loud, and the complete opposite of him. And yet they still live together after twenty-some years. Go figure.

Bernard lit his cigarette, inhaled deeply, twice, and while blowing the smoke right into our faces he finally said, "I think you girls should go for it." Again, he inhaled, even deeper. "She seems like the real deal."

That's exactly what I wanted to hear.

Margo said when she got the money, she'd start working on the papers, which might take a few weeks since she was super busy. After receiving the papers, we'd apply for the visa. She also told us that the people inviting us to America could buy the airline tickets for us. Once we got there, we could stay with them and they would help us find jobs. We would pay them back at triple the amount of the airline ticket.

Triple the amount was kind of steep but overall it seemed like a win-win situation. I liked it because there was no way I could afford the airline ticket. The hardest part was getting approved for the visa. I heard from others that so many people had tried to get one but without any luck. Maybe one in one hundred were approved. Maybe.

I didn't expect Niki's excitement. Her eyes got big as she hugged her father and thanked him. Then she grabbed me, shook me, and we started bouncing up and down in the back seat of the car.

I wanted to continue talking about this plan, in part to make myself more confident.

Niki said we should give Margo the money as soon as we could, so she could start working on the invitation letters. Niki's father agreed and he promised her he would give her the money tomorrow. We decided not to talk about it to anyone until things moved along. We thought people might get jealous, and we didn't want any evil eyes from them.

The second hardest part? I didn't have any money.

THREE

That evening I went home happy, but impatient. I just wanted all the paperwork done, to pack and get out of there. I was in a hurry. It was going to be really hard to endure the process of getting this letter.

I knew I needed to find a way to get the money, but I had no idea how. Where or who would it come from? It was a few hundred dollars, which was a decent amount back then, especially for me. I was thinking and thinking, to find some way to make this happen. Nothing was coming to mind, but I was sure I'd find a way.

I just wanted to run away from this city, the city that I loved and hated. The city I grew up in and was mine. The city where I had so many memories. This was the only place I knew, and I knew everything about it. I knew each street, every building. This city and I were excellent friends and I thought I would never abandon it. When I was outside of the city, I would miss it so much. As soon as I approached the city after being away, my heart would start beating fast. It was always an exciting and happy feeling coming back to the city.

This was the city of my family, my friends, my first love, my second, the boys who loved and respected me. The city where I knew so many people. When I walked down the street, I would randomly see so many of the people I knew, and we would greet each other, embrace, chat or maybe gossip a little. We loved to gossip. We loved to hear something new about something or someone. It was usually spicy.

I wasn't even sure how I knew some people. I just did. We were all connected. The person could be anyone—from school, mutual friends, a relative's friend or a coworker. These were the people I grew up with, the people who I saw so often. They were everywhere, when you went outside, when you visited your friend. You saw them at birthday parties, weddings and funerals. It was one big life in one small place. This was the place where I didn't want to be anymore.

Is this true? What's happening to me? What's happening is I want more. I want a progressive life and growth. I want independence, to be free and strong. None of which is possible here. There aren't enough opportunities. So many people are unemployed. Thank God people help each other survive, and I give them credit. But those people don't need or want more. They're happy as long as they have bread on the table every day and hang out. But that's not me. I don't want to just survive.

We can't be independent here because our families won't let us move out and do whatever we want. We can't be strong because they won't let us. I want to be free. And by free, I mean free inside, in my soul. No judgment, no criticism, no everyday worries about who said what to whom and how often. No mandatory cultural things like getting married before I'm twenty or being home before 11:00 at night.

There were so many reasons I needed a change. A big one being that I didn't see any way to make financial progress. I was tired of counting every penny. My paycheck was divided up for so many things. There was never enough. Most of it would be gone in a couple of days, to pay the bills, for food and other stuff. The rest of the 28 days we'd have small amounts for transportation, some bread and minor necessities. While it was fun to live in this city, with its lunatic lifestyle and even nuttier people, I just didn't feel like I belonged there anymore. Maybe I never did, and I finally just had had enough. One night I went to bed and couldn't sleep. I kept thinking about my plan. My head was spinning with so many worries. I was having doubts.

Why do I want to do this? To escape from the many problems that make me unhappy? What's the point of that? There are problems everywhere, right? Where was I going, where I didn't even know anybody? Going to a foreign country, where I don't even speak the language? Well, at least I'm going with Niki. That gives me some comfort. But I'm still afraid. At least I have a home here. I have my family and friends. People I can trust. I feel I'm more protected here. I could just stay, get married and have my own family. That is probably the best choice. Yes, this makes sense. There are a few boys around who love me, and I could consider marrying one of them. I seem to always have someone in love with me. But somehow, it never ends with marriage.

I was engaged once, in 1990, when I was 16. But I broke it off. Now and then I think about him. He had an attractive personality and a great sense of humor, which I loved. We went to the same high school and he was a year older than me. We would see each other every day at school, and after. He would walk me home after school or wherever I would go. He was so in love with me, and the feeling was mutual.

After school as we neared my home, he would beg me to stay outside for 15 minutes. I'd agree, and after he would beg me for another 15 minutes, and another and another until my mom would yell from the window to come inside. We would laugh uncontrollably.

He would walk with me any time he had a chance. I took music classes twice a week. I hated the classes because the teacher was so mean. But going to class became exciting because he'd go with me. We also saw each other when my high school friends had birthdays, and there were a lot. He knew all my classmates and since he was older, everybody respected him.

He was part of my life, and we were both so attached. We used to go to movies with other friends. Watching the movie wasn't as exciting as sitting right next to each other in the dark. It felt so intimate and sexy. Not much we could do there, just kissing or touching each other. He would just put his arm over my shoulder, and I would lay my head against him. This was so exciting that my heart would start beating so loud I was worried I wouldn't hear anything. I often blushed. I could feel my face get warm. But at least the room was dark so he couldn't see it.

These moments were like having sex for us. It felt so exciting. I guess our blood pressure would skyrocket as we held back our desires. It was torture. Besides loving me so much I think his sexual desire drove him crazy. He was so young, and at that age the desire to have sex is intense.

When he graduated from high school, he wanted me to quit my last year of school and marry him, but I couldn't do that. My mother would kill me. I also wanted to continue studying after I graduated, to become more knowledgeable. College was free, once you passed an entrance exam, and I wanted to take advantage of that. I never answered him, but he went ahead and told his parents about the wedding plans anyway. But his parents didn't take his plans seriously. They told him he couldn't get married.

He got so depressed. You know, at that age every little thing seems so dramatic. His parents started to worry about him because he was so unhappy. So, they gave in and agreed to meet with him and my family about an engagement. His parents asked my mother if I would marry their son—they even brought an engagement ring.

He was going into the army for two years and he was worried about leaving me. I promised him I'd wait for him, but he wanted more than words, so I said yes to his offer and accepted the ring. My mother didn't resist at all. She liked the idea. My family knew and liked him. His parents were nice people. They were both book smart, intelligent and classy. High-quality people. His mother was a housewife and his father worked in the Ministry of Foreign Affairs.

I was happy with the way it worked out. I was able to graduate from high school and continue studying at the university. But after an exciting and successful freshman year, I met someone else.

I went crazy having fun and enjoying the full attention of my new boyfriend. I don't even know why I did it or how it happened. I guess girls need attention from boys all the time. They can't be without it, like a fish can't be without water. I think it's in the female DNA.

But most of us are confused at that age anyway. Nothing special really happened, and it's a typical thing. People under the age of twenty-five are immature, inexperienced and quick to make decisions, and not always good ones. They see the world as easy and light. It's just a time when we live carefree, observe situations and gain experience, so one day we can make the right decisions. I'm not sure any love is real at that age. You think it's real at the time, but it's mostly about attraction, excitement and butterfly feelings, which come and go, just like butterflies.

"I'm so sorry, but I don't think we can see each other anymore," I told my fiancée when he came back.

"I knew this was what you wanted to talk about," he said. "My friend Alex told me you were with someone new. But I wanted to hear it from you."

Awkward silence. I feel so bad, and very sad. Besides losing someone I love, I'm losing my best friend. But what can I do, considering my behavior?

"This is really hard," he finally said.

"It is," I said.

Another long pause as he stared at the ground. He took a deep breath, got up and just left. I watched him walk away from the window. I sat down and cried and cried. Until I had no more tears. A few months later he had army leave for a week and came home for Christmas.

"You know, I saw your old boyfriend at a party last night," one of my friends told me.

"Really? How is he?" I asked.

"He's fine," she said. "He's looking forward to the end of his army service. He brought a date to the party. She seemed nice."

I wonder why he hasn't called me? At least to see how I'm doing and say happy holidays.

"Hi," I said. "I heard you were in the city so I thought I'd call to say Merry Christmas."

"Thanks," he said.

"How are you?"

"You know Alyssa? I really can't be bothered with the small talk."

"I just thought …"

"Yeah, yeah, I know. But I'd rather not hear from you. And you know, if we happen to come across each other on the street, just make sure you cross to the other side."

And he hung up. I had heard that his entire family had moved to a different country. After he completed his army service, he moved in with them. But I did see him once more, at a mutual friend's wedding in the city. I had no idea he'd be there. I was speaking with one of his friends when he came over and stood next to us. He smiled and seemed to want to say something, but I just ignored him. His eyes seemed to follow me all night, or maybe it was just my imagination. Anyway, it was getting uncomfortable, so I left the wedding early. He called me that night.

"It was nice to see you at the wedding," he said. "You look well."

"Thanks."

Silence, again.

"Listen Allyssa, I've had a lot of time to think. I know we've grown apart, but I want you to know, I still love you. I always will. One day, you'll get married, and so will I. Maybe even more than once. Perhaps we'll both have children. But no matter how long it takes, or where we are, I believe we'll be together, in love. There will come a day when I will marry you."

I was speechless. I just sat there, with the phone in my hand, tears welling up inside. It was one of those painful and sad life experiences that you never forget. He said goodbye and hung up, and I cried a thousand tears, again. His name was Maximillian.

I laid in bed with all these thoughts and emotions swirling around in my head about my life when the phone rang and startled me. It was another boy who loved me. He was one year younger than me, which I didn't like. I never liked boys my age or less. I think women mature earlier than men. And this boy? He had a car, some kind of job and a rich father, who I'm sure helped him out financially.

He lived in a big house with his parents. His mother wasn't friendly when I met her for the first time. She was unattractive, with a tight-lipped smile, and the boy looked just like her! It was kind of freaky. But he was well-mannered and a gentleman. He seemed like a good choice. The only thing was, if I married him, I knew I'd have to live in that big house, too, with his entire family, including his younger sister and grandmother.

In this country, people didn't live separately from their parents, even if they're married. Not because they couldn't afford it or anything. It was a cultural thing, which I never, ever understood. But who was I to talk? I lived with my mother, brother and two sisters, just like everyone else. But I was living with my immediate family, who I grew up with. Moving in with another family? That was life changing. You needed to learn their personalities, adapt to their traditions or lifestyle. And on top of that, you had to see them every day. Morning, noon and night. Share the kitchen and bathroom. Share life with them, all the time. That didn't seem so glamorous to me.

I spoke with him for a while and agreed to go out with him the next night. I thought maybe I'd start liking him and take a more traditional step, instead of this disruptive move to another country.

It was late when I finally fell asleep. I slept so deeply, probably because I was exhausted from thinking. I slept until I heard my mother's voice, yelling. She couldn't believe I was still in bed. It was only noon, but she kept saying it was already 2 p.m. She liked to exaggerate. It was Sunday and I wasn't in a hurry. Why couldn't I just sleep? I never understood that.

I woke up fresh and energized. My mind was serene, which I didn't expect. All the thoughts I had last night that gave me insomnia were gone. Last night my thoughts were like a messy bookshelf. Now, they're well organized, like someone cleaned, dusted and put things back where they belonged, nice and neat.

I loved the daytime at our house. It was peaceful. At night when everybody comes home, some of them could be grouchy or noisy, or the opposite—happy, drunk and loud. That evening, instead of meeting the boy, I met Niki. The previous night I had thought maybe I should just stay and marry someone. Now? I wasn't so sure.

It was already near the end of summer. I wanted to see her and once again talk about our plan. Niki said she could pay Margo, but she'd wait until I was ready. I didn't tell her I still had no idea how I would get the money. I just told her I was working on it and would let her know soon.

"Alyssa," she said, "This is important. I want us to promise each other we won't change our minds about this, no matter what. If we start, we finish. We go together. We cannot bail on each other."

"Yes, absolutely Niki. I promise. I swear to God. I would never do that to you."

"Me either," said Niki as we hugged.

The next day I just stayed home. While my Mom was out visiting someone in the hospital, I cleaned the house, washed the floors and did some ironing. My mother loved it when I surprised her with this housekeeping stuff. She usually did all of it, but I tried helping and surprising her now and then while she was out.

I was never into cooking dinner, but desserts? Making dessert was a lot of fun, especially baking a big cake. Most of the time I would make one when I got paid and I had money to buy the ingredients for it. But since I was home, I decided to bake something. Something nice and fancy. I used my weekly transportation money, which meant I was going to walk to work for the next few days. I hated getting up in the morning and walking for forty-five minutes, but I really wanted to do some baking.

I made a beautiful, creamy and fluffy napoleon. Everybody's favorite. The oven had some issues with heating. Sometimes it worked well, sometimes not at all. The heat would randomly go up or down. We used to call it the "moody oven". This time I got lucky. The oven was in a good mood.

My family usually came home for dinner so we could eat and chat together. They were in and out all day, every day. Who knows where, but they all loved coming home in the evening. It seemed like they were coming home from work, except that none of them had a job.

I couldn't wait for everyone to come home and sit down for dinner. I had so many surprises for them. My mother came home earlier than the others. She looked tired after being out all day.

"I took care of all the housework, including the laundry," I told her.

"That's a nice surprise. Thank you," she said.

"I also baked a fancy napoleon," I said. "I want to surprise everyone after dinner."

She frowned.

"How did you do that? We didn't have any ingredients for it did we?"

How does she always know what we have in the kitchen? Probably because there's not much in there.

"I bought stuff today," I said.

"Why would you do such a thing when you can't afford it?" she said, frowning even deeper.

"I wouldn't if I couldn't. I'm in a happy mood."

She just sighed and left the room.

Why can't people just enjoy the moment? Why must there always be worries? I already baked and that money is gone. It's already in the past. And soon, we'll have a wonderful dessert. I'm so tired of this relentless "worry thing". If there's good news and bad news, so many people here want to hear the bad news first, and they don't care about the good news. So much drama. It makes me want to go away even more.

Dinner was last night's leftover chicken soup with a loaf of bread. Not so appetizing, but I hinted to my brother and sisters about a surprise after dinner. None of us were big fans of soup, which always seemed mandatory.

"You've got to have soup," I've heard again and again since I was first able to hear.

"The body needs liquids."

"Soup helps with digestive problems."

"First soup and then anything else."

Why is it that whenever something becomes mandatory it also becomes less enjoyable? Only my mother liked the soup, any kind. She would finish all of it. I don't know if my father was a soup fan, but I know he was a meat lover, like most men. I remember once he ate his soup so fast. He probably wanted to get it over with so he could enjoy the next course, with meat.

We all indulged in the dessert. I hoped I could save a piece for Niki since she was coming over later, but I didn't have a chance. The whole cake was gone in no time. I was on the phone for a few minutes, came back, and the cake plate was empty, except for a few scattered flakes. But I saw a lot of satisfied faces.

"Tea anyone? I'm having one," I said.

"Yes, please."

"Me too."

"Oh, me too please."

"Well I wasn't going to but if everybody else is having tea, I'll have one too."

"Anyone want to help?" I smiled.

"No, we'll pass on that but thanks," they said laughing.

Having tea after dinner was always good. It calmed everyone down. I needed them calm and relaxed before starting the conversation. Usually they were loud and wouldn't let each other get a word in. If they were like that it would be way too confusing as I tried to speak.

While they were sipping tea there was silence. It was nice. I thought I was at an opera house, with that silence just before the performance starts. My performance was about to start, and I hoped they would find it exciting.

Showtime. I stood up, although I'm not sure why. Maybe to divert attention?

"I want to tell you all that I've decided to go to America for a few months, maybe a year."

Silence. I guess I said something interesting. They just stared at me with their mouths open, holding their tea cups. But it didn't last. They all became so loud, all at the same time. I heard a few laughs and so many questions at once that none of them made sense. I couldn't hear what the hell they were asking or understand how they all had so many questions when they didn't even know my plan! I said a few words; they said hundreds. It was chaos. Only my mother was quiet. She had heard this story before.

"Ok, people," I pleaded, "Please calm down. Let me talk, and then we can deal with the questions."

I sat down and told them everything. I tried to explain, so they would support and encourage me. We had a good conversation. First, there was the big reaction and push back, then after the discussion, there was excitement.

Then, I looked over at my Mom. She was just staring at me, shaking her head no.

"Mom," I said, "please let me do this."

After what seemed like forever she finally took a deep breath.

"How is this any different from when I said no last time?" she asked.

"What's different is I've given this a lot of thought," I said. "I'll be with people who will help me live there, and find a job so I can make some decent money. It's an opportunity not only for me but for everyone."

"But I'm afraid. You'll be going to another country where you don't know anyone, and you don't even speak the language. It will be hard. I'll be worried about you."

"I know, but Niki's coming with me. Together we'll be fine."

"Well that does make it a little better," she said as she took my hand and smiled. "OK then. I guess you're going to America."

Everyone cheered as I gave her a big hug.

She's making me feel even stronger, knowing that she supports me. I'm going to need that support for the next conversation, about money.

My grandmother was a sophisticated woman. She always loved to dress fashionably, and she had a lot of beautiful jewelry. She had given my mother a beautiful emerald ring. It was round, with the emerald in the center and diamonds around it. My mother told me that the ring was going to be mine when I got married. No one ever wore the ring, and she kept it in a safe place.

"Mom, what about selling grandma's ring, so I can pay Margo for the invitation letter and maybe the visa?"

"Really?" she asked.

I need a solution. What's the point of keeping this ring for years when I could use it now as a down payment on a better life? It's hard to say goodbye but it's just a thing.

"I know it's sad to sell it," I said, "especially since it's been in the family for so long. But it's the only valuable thing we have. Besides, there's nothing to worry about. I'll make a new life and buy an even better ring one day."

"You know," she smiled. "I really believe you. Well, the ring belongs to you, so sure, let's sell it."

It was already September. I quickly sold the ring at a reasonable price, and Niki and I paid Margo. She said it could take up to three months for the invitation letters to arrive.

I became more confident than ever. I knew this was just the first of many steps, but I felt like nothing could stop me now. I knew I was ready for it. Niki and I saw each other almost every day and talked about our future. We were so focused that sometimes we didn't even care about guys or flirting when we were out. Our behavior and attitude had changed. No one around us could figure out what was going on. Only we knew.

FOUR

It was a cold and cloudy day when the phone rang. The invitation letters had finally arrived from America. That was the day winter immediately turned to spring. Life was so good in those few seconds. The beautiful feeling of moving forward. For a second, I forgot that this was just the beginning. There was a lot more to do, but I didn't care. I felt once started, I would finish.

Visa interviews at the American consulate were the next step. Getting an American visa was more magnificent than anything else. The consulate accepted applications twice a week; no appointment needed. It was first come first serve so people would go very early in the morning to wait in line outside before the doors opened. When I say early, I mean like, 4 o'clock in the morning early.

Nicki was so nervous about the interview. She drove me crazy. She wanted to know what kind of questions they would ask. I was nervous too, but I knew I had to just go for it. My only concern was if I was rejected, it would all be for nothing. My money was already spent, and my ring sold, and neither of them was coming back.

She begged me to do the interview first so she could prepare herself better. Since I had a somewhat better job than her, she thought I was more qualified for a visa. If you had a decent job, you were more likely to come back. I had all my papers ready, so now I had to choose a morning to get up super-early to wait in line.

I immediately felt the cold air when my alarm woke me up in the middle of the night. It felt like my nose was frozen. I covered up with my comforter, where I felt warm and cozy in my bed. We only had one heater in the house, in the living room, so going to bed was quite a challenge. It was like going into a cave. Getting out of bed was even worse. It was brutal.

The first two times I didn't even make it into the building. There were limited acceptances, but at least they announced there weren't any more times available after a couple of hours, so we wouldn't waste time standing there. The third time I decided to go an hour earlier, to be on the line by 4:00 in the morning. I thought I'd be the first person in line but was surprised to find a few people there.

Did these people stay here all night? I live fairly close to this consulate. Where the hell did all these people come from? They were even more desperate for a visa than me!

It was pitch black and wicked cold, much worse than the other days I was there. This standing on line, outside, was so harsh. It made me so impatient that I thought about quitting and going home. But I never did.

I'm cold and sad. Standing outside with these people in the dark cold always makes me sad. It has broken my heart since I was a kid when I'd see people outside, cold and poor. What time is it? It seems like I've been here for an hour but the minute hand has barely moved. Maybe it's frozen too.

A few people in front of me became chatty. They were sharing some visa interview experiences or stories about people they knew who went to America. There were good and bad stories. No one knew if any of these stories were true, but the good stories gave them hope, which encouraged them to stay.

Some of these bad stories seem made up. Maybe it's a trick. They're telling the bad stories hoping others would give up and leave so they could get into the building faster. My skeptical mind.

After a while I got tired of listening to the stories. They started sounding like morning birds randomly chirping away. It was too early and I was in no mood.

I can't believe these people are so talkative at this hour. Can't they be quiet for just a little while? But no, they're mostly women, and they can talk nonstop, anytime, anywhere.

I took a look back and there was a long line of about forty people behind me. That made me feel good. I knew I was getting inside. I was on the line for five and a half hours.

It was so nice and warm inside. I gave my papers to the lady behind the first window and sat down, waiting to be called for the interview. While I was waiting, I got so warm, but I didn't want to take my fancy coat off. I had borrowed it from a friend and was having fun looking nice, pretending to be rich. I was freezing before but now I was freaking sweating. When I heard my name called, I got so nervous, but I stayed calm on the outside. The interview went so quick I have trouble remembering most of it.

I was one of the lucky girls that day. It was my day, my destiny. I got the visa. I was shocked and happy. I was so numb I couldn't even express myself, but it was just as well. The people surrounding me in the waiting area looked at me in desperation, with wide-open eyes. I thought they would attack me because they heard I got the visa. Their faces pretended to congratulate me but in reality, they were envious. I felt bad for them but there was nothing I could do. We all fight for something. Some win; some lose. That's life. I was the only one who was approved while I was there.

I couldn't wait to announce the news to everyone. My friends couldn't believe it. They had been saying that they wouldn't even try for a visa because it was almost impossible to be approved. It would just be a waste of money.

Now it was Niki's turn. I told her everything I could remember and gave her advice. I didn't tell her about the brutal long line thing. I didn't want her to freak out. She had something of a capricious personality. I even offered to go with her to cheer her up while waiting. I was becoming super-impatient. I wanted to make sure our trip happened right away.

"You can do this Niki," I said. "Just relax, smile and answer the questions directly."

"You're right. If you got lucky so can I right? We're the same. We're the same age, single, and have similar jobs, kind of."

"You're in even better shape than me. Your family's financial status is stable, so they'll think you'll come back."

"That's true," she said, as she gradually became more confident.

But Nicki's interview went south. She was refused. It was so upsetting I started to lose my happiness. But Niki became even more ambitious. She promised she would apply over and over again until she got it. She asked me to be patient and wait for her. Of course, I would wait for her. What else? I didn't have a choice. I couldn't go by myself, and that was our promise.

Meanwhile, life went on. I didn't care much about my future life there, or dates with the guys or getting a better job. All I knew was another door had opened and I needed to make an entrance, even if I wasn't sure where it would take me. I knew I was going.

And then, one of life's surprises: I randomly met a guy at a friend's birthday party. He was much older. He was financially stable, had his own business doing something or other, and seemed interesting. I got his attention right when I entered the room. At least that's what my friend told me. He asked my friend to introduce us.

We all had a good time. Even though I had been told that he liked me and that he was a good catch, I didn't care. I had my plan and I wouldn't change my mind for anybody, no matter what. I wasn't looking for a relationship. I was just socializing, that was all. He offered to drive me home and I agreed. A free ride was always good. He took a few of my friends home too. He was more than happy to give a ride to all of us.

His name was Tobi. He was one of those people who could be a pain in the ass when they wanted something. He could taunt you to death. He called me every day and begged to let him take me out to dinner or drinks. Anything I wanted. He had money and connections everywhere. He talked a lot too. I resisted the first few times. I explained I was leaving the city and wasn't going to date anybody. But he wouldn't leave me alone.

I finally agreed to go to dinner with him, with five of my girlfriends. That was a really good time. He agreed to take my girlfriends everywhere. I'm sure he was hoping eventually we'd have a one-on-one date. One night after he dropped everyone off and we were alone, he said he wanted to talk. We stayed in a car.

"I think you know Alyssa that I like you," he began, "and I'd like to have a relationship with you."

I just looked at him and stayed quiet.

"I know you have a visa and plan to leave the country, but I wonder why? Why do you want to leave?"

I shrugged and continued to stay quiet. I didn't feel like sharing the real reasons I wanted out.

"If you're doing this for financial reasons, please don't," he said. "I'll provide you with anything you need."

This is too funny. Where have you been? Why is this happening now? Is this some kind of test, from the universe? Who says God doesn't have a sense of humor?

"I'll only be gone for six months, maybe a year," I said. "I'm going to come back. Besides, you can always take a trip and visit me."

He ignored me, and continued, on and on.

"I travel a lot, even to America," he said. "I've been to New York several times."

"Really?" I asked. "Did you like it? What did it look like? Does it look like it does in the movies?"

He noticed how I perked up and suddenly became quiet.

"New York is a magical city," he said out of nowhere. "It's a city where dreams come true. I know if you go there, you'll never come back."

I laughed out loud. So dramatic. I definitely wanted to see New York but I didn't know what the hell he was talking about.

"I'm serious," he said. "You'll see."

I didn't believe what he said and thought it was just another attempt to get me to stay.

"Of course, I'll come back," I said. "I could never leave my city, family and friends forever."

It was early February with its usual cold, short days. Days and weeks flew by, and Niki wasn't making any progress with getting a visa. Over time she talked less and less about our plans, and I started to worry she would bail out.

"The promise. Do you remember?" I'd say with a smile.

"Of course, … of course. Are you kidding?" she'd reply.

And I'd be comforted, at least for a little while. Then I found out Niki had met a guy. I knew this guy, Luka. He was a player and liked flirting with the girls. She liked him physically and wanted to date him, for fun. She knew she couldn't expect a long-term relationship with him, which was fine, for now. But that doesn't always work for girls. She started having real feelings for him, which she was hiding from me. One day she called just to chat, like girls do.

"Hi Alyssa, how's it going?" Niki said. "Any plans for tonight?"

"None, just staying home and watching whatever movie is on TV. You?"

"Going out to a club with Luka. You should come."

"No, thanks. I'll pass. How's it going with the visa? When are you going to apply again?"

No response.

I knew the hesitation was about a decision. I hung up. I was devastated, confused and angry. I couldn't even think of going without her. How could I? I had begged my family to let me go. I sold the only thing I had, and now the ring and the money were gone. What about my visa? Could I just ignore it?

My best friend, Niki. We were so close and tight. We never got upset with each other. We literally shared life. A real relationship. Like when two people know each other's everyday moments, every detail, important or not. When they share good times and bad, when they call each other for no reason. When they listen to each other, and feel each other, with support and trust.

My long, wonderful friendship with Niki. It's over? Just like that? I love her. Maybe I never should've started this with her. If I didn't then this painful break up wouldn't be happening. What is she feeling? What's her reason? I hope it's not because of that Luka, because that's not going to last. I don't want to be upset with her. But I feel betrayed. Our plan has collapsed. I feel empty.

I never called her back or anything. I avoided her and she did the same. I needed some time to get through all this and think, without all the emotions. I lost my best friend. I mean, I lost trust in her. We could stay friends, but it would never be the same. It's impossible to rebuild things once they're broken. I hardly knew what to do next.

FIVE

MARCH 1996, EASTERN EUROPE

I decided not to give in or give up. I was going. I wasn't going to let someone else's choices dictate what I was going to do with my life. I reached out to Margo and asked if she knew anyone who received a visa through her and had plans to leave soon, so I could at least have a travel buddy for the flight.

I didn't care who it was. I was already going to a place where I didn't know anybody. I didn't want to be alone on the long flight. I'd never been on a plane before. Plus, there weren't any direct flights to New York. I had to change planes somewhere, and I was afraid of missing the connection. It was easy for others to say, oh, it's nothing, you'll figure it out, and I probably would. But when you've never done it before it's a big deal. I could be a brave girl, but I could also be timid.

No luck. Margo said she helped a few people with the papers but none of them received a visa approval. The bad news was I was going alone. The good news was I was going, because I was one of the chosen few.

One morning as I was getting dressed, I passed by the mirror. I stepped back and I saw this girl, staring at me. I stared back, observing from head to toe.

She's twenty-two, medium height with a slim, toned body. Slightly muscled calves and upper legs, that merged to an hourglass waist. A flat stomach and small pointed breasts, which fit well with this type of body. Long straight, light brunette-colored hair covered the shoulders. A small oval-shaped face with pouty lips and a small, slim nose. Her big, greenish-blue eyes were looking at me without blinking. I see her full, naked body, and facial features.

Why me? Here is this girly girl, and I'm torturing her. I'm asking her feminine mind and body to be a fearless, brave man.

I felt like I had two personalities, male and female. My body and real personality were feminine—fragile, delicate, with a quiet, good-tempered manner. But I could also force myself to be masculine—fearless, brave and tough—when I needed to be. I could drive myself crazy with this split personality sometimes. Why was I doing it to myself?

I had to leave soon. It was already March and the visa rules required that I visit the U.S. within three months. I asked Margo to reach out to the woman who sent the invitation letter, to ask if she was also willing to pay for my airfare, and I would pay her back at triple the amount. This would be a kind of contract through Margo. I needed to do this because I didn't have the money to pay for the flight.

When I went to pick up my airline ticket, it was an actual ticket, with my name on it. This was when I knew I was definitely on my way. I got goosebumps. I felt excited and proud of myself that I had made it this far. The past was starting to fade away, and I was so looking forward to living my future.

I had an early morning flight. The days before should've been emotional, but I was so busy preparing I didn't pay much attention to my emotions. I started to pack and realized I needed a suitcase. Nothing like the last minute. I guess I was a little distracted! We all sat down to figure out how to get a suitcase. All of a sudden my mom yelled.

"The yellow suitcase! Yes, we have one, it's in the closet!"

We looked at her as if she'd lost her mind.

"What are you talking about?" I asked. "What yellow suitcase?"

Turns out she kept a suitcase hidden away, behind the clothes and shoes. We never traveled so she used it for storing sheets and towels. It was like a "closet suitcase". We all rushed to the closet. It was a beautiful thing. We emptied it, cleaned it up and packed it for the trip.

If this suitcase had feelings and could talk, I'm sure it would've been so excited and happy. It had been stuck in a dark place for a long time, like a jail, and now it was free, and going on a trip! That's what suitcases are for right? But I'm glad the suitcase couldn't talk because there would be a lot of yelling at my mother.

When I first saw the suitcase, it was obvious why my mother called it yellow. You couldn't just call it a suitcase without mentioning the color. It was bright yellow. I mean, really, really bright yellow. I was hoping for a more muted color, but I rationalized that it would be easy to distinguish from the other suitcases. The suitcase was huge. It was one big fat suitcase. It was heavy even before it was packed. The outside of the suitcase was thick leather with rough stitches and two wide, heavy metal buckles, and the handle was hard.

But the best part? My yellow suitcase had no wheels! I'd have to carry this damn thing. Soon I'd have calloused man hands to go along with the male side of my personality.

My family threw a going away party. All my close relatives and most of my friends came, but not Niki. I thought she might stop by, but it was just as well she didn't. I didn't want any drama before the trip. It was a fun, warm and exciting evening. I was surrounded by my closest, most lovable people.

We had a big dinner with wine. We had meringue walnut cakes that my aunt made. After the cake we had dessert wine and cognac. As usual, after eating and drinking the crowd became noisier. Everybody talked so loudly and all at the same time. I couldn't tell who was saying what, but I was used to this kind of "conversation". These people knew how to talk loud and over each other. It was in their genes, I guess. They never seemed to listen or let someone finish a sentence. They just wanted to be heard, so the volume gradually increased.

Some music was playing but nobody cared. Fueled by alcohol, everybody thought they sounded intelligent and knowledgeable about anything and everything. Most of them were so excited for me. Some told me they hoped to imitate me one day.

"Hey, why don't you go now, figure out what's going on over there, and then we'll consider coming over," they kept telling me.

"We promise we will," they said as they became more excited about the idea.

I wished one of them actually would come with me.

"Hey, who wants to come with me the most? I have some room in my big suitcase!"

Silence. Then a burst of laughter.

It was getting late, but nobody wanted to leave. People started to go home around midnight, but my closest friends stayed overnight. They were all taking me to the airport. By the time we went to bed it was just after two. At least I could catch a few hours of sleep before the long journey ahead.

I crawled into bed. I was so tired. All day I had been running around and my feet hurt. My body was so sore, and my mind was full of thoughts. I tried to sleep but couldn't. My head was spinning. I'd have positive thoughts, and then all of a sudden, negative thoughts, again and again. My mixed emotions evolved into one big, paralyzing fear. My heart started beating faster and I started to sweat. I started second guessing myself. Thinking again about where I was going and why. I was leaving all these people I loved so much, and my home and city that I knew so well.

I was suddenly frightened. I sat up. One of my girlfriends slept right next to me so I tried not to wake her up. I stayed quiet, taking deep breaths. I felt tears rolling down my face. I wanted to cry out loud, but I didn't let myself. All I wanted to do was give up, just cancel the trip and stay here. I was having a panic attack.

Then, one of the weirdest feelings I ever had. I began thinking, deeper and deeper. I let my subconscious mind take control. I let all the fears come in and destroy me. That's what a panic attack does if you let it.

How do I escape this fear? How? How can I cancel this trip? Everyone is asleep. Should I wake them up? Should I wake up my friend next to me? Maybe she could help me? No, no. That won't be good. Maybe I can make up a story. Something reasonable and believable. What can it be? It's not just about the story. I'll have to lie. I'll be a good actress, so everyone will believe me. Am I good at acting? I'm not so sure but I'm so desperate, maybe I can fake it. I'm such a mess. I'm crying, and so sad. Maybe I should just be honest. They'll understand, won't they? They love me. They might be happy to hear that I want to stay. They don't really want me to go.

I felt good, for a second.

But wait. What about my plan and my promises to myself and my family? If I change my mind, what kind of person does that make me? No one would believe me anymore. I wouldn't even believe myself. What if I have regrets? Stop! These thoughts? They're disgusting and so unfair.

I took a deep breath. I became aware. I knew what a runaway mind could do to your body and soul. Slowly, I relaxed and slid back into bed, and covered myself with the blankets. My heartbeat slowed down. I closed my eyes, but the tears kept coming, so many they made my pillow wet. I tried to relax but I couldn't. Again, my subconscious mind took control, even stronger than before.

I don't want to listen to it anymore. But … but … what if this is my intuition, telling me not to go? What if something is telling me to stop, and all these thoughts are for a reason? I have to sit up and make a plan. I should make up a good story and act on it. That's it. I know. I'll make believe I'm really, really sick. I got food poisoning or something, with a major stomach problem. I could cry and groan in bed. I can pretend I can't even get out of bed. My face is so puffy from crying, that will definitely help me look sick. I can wake up my friend next to me first, and announce my illness, then she would wake the others. There wouldn't be enough time left for me to get better, so I would miss my flight.

I don't remember falling asleep. I woke suddenly with a pounding heart. It was 5:30 a.m. and I had to get up. I remembered my plan. I was still scared and sad, and now I was also exhausted. But I just couldn't do it. I couldn't put on some foolish performance because I was afraid. I couldn't do it to my friends and family, and more importantly, I couldn't do it to myself. I've never been a good liar, but that's probably a good thing, right? Besides, I suck at pretending to be sick.

Most of my relatives and many of my friends showed up at the airport. I felt like a celebrity probably does, with all these people staring at me for some special event. Who knew I was so important to so many people? They all wanted my attention. To chat and make some jokes, to make me feel better and cheerful. It gave me a headache.

It felt awkward, and harder and harder to say goodbye to every single person. I didn't want it to get emotional or cause my mother to worry. I didn't want to see anybody anymore, so I said I needed to go to the gate. I turned around quickly, climbed the stairs and didn't look back. As I reached the second floor, I sneaked a look down just for a second, and I saw Niki standing there, staring up at me. She was late, but she was there. I just turned and walked to the gate.

I got on the bus to the plane. There was no turning back now. I was leaving everything behind. I was completely numb and emotionally spent. I was going with the tide. The bus was full of people excited to travel. It felt nice.

"Hi," said a voice behind me. "I guess we're going to the same plane."

I turned to see a stranger.

"Yes, I guess we are," I said.

"This flight is quick," he said. "It won't be that bad."

He had no idea this was the first leg of my long journey.

"Yes indeed," I responded.

I don't want to have a conversation.

"This one is easy, but then I connect for the flight to New York, which is much longer."

"I'm sorry, where are you going?" I asked.

"New York," he said.

Now I was happy and couldn't help myself. I screamed and jumped in his arms with a big hug.

"Me too, me too! I'm going to New York too! Can we travel together?"

"Wow, I'm so glad I met you!" he said. "Of course, we can. We'll be stuck with each other for a while! My name is Zachary," as he came closer and put his hand out.

I smiled.

"I'm Alyssa," I said as we shook hands. "So nice to meet you. Now I feel much better."

"Don't worry, we'll find our way," he said with a big grin.

How great is this? I've found a father, brother and good friend all in one. I feel protected, with a stranger I just met. My heart feels peaceful and my mind has stopped thrashing. My trip is suddenly awesome.

I can honestly say we instantly became good friends. He was kind and a gentleman. He wasn't that attractive, but he was manly and polite. He was also a great storyteller, which I like. The flight was over quickly.

"We have six hours to kill before the next flight," he said. "How about I buy you a drink or two at the bar?"

"Thanks, that sounds good," I said.

I was glad he was buying. I only had a hundred dollars. I needed some spending money while I tried to find a job. I was lucky to have the hundred dollars since I had to borrow it. We had asked a few people, but they didn't have any money to spare. Finally, our neighbor lent it to me, but I had to pay it back quickly because she gave it to me without asking her husband. She took it from the safe, hoping he wouldn't notice that it was gone. She told me she needed it back within a month. I promised I'd pay her back as soon as I got paid. So, this one hundred dollars was really "non-spendable". It was only for emergencies.

We went to the airport bar and ordered Heineken. It felt really good. I needed that beer. It relaxed my body and mind completely, and I was friendlier to him. I'm not friendly with people when I first meet them. I need time to get to know them. I've heard many times from others that they thought I was mean and unfriendly. Once they get to know me better, they're surprised I'm actually friendly.

With Zachary I felt comfortable. We treated each other respectfully. The layover went by quickly, as it usually does with alcohol and good conversation. When we got on the plane, we had separate seats. I took my window seat and looked for Zachary. I saw him on the other side, in the front row. We looked at each other with sad faces, then I crashed.

I woke up as the food was being served. I almost forgot where I was. I looked around and saw Zachary sitting right next to me.

"Hey, how did that happen?" I smiled.

"I switched seats with the guy. I gave him a better seat so he couldn't refuse. And I got the best seat on the plane, sitting next to you," he said.

We didn't sleep for the rest of the flight. He was telling me so many anecdotes. We laughed and had a great time. He was moving to New York to be close to his mother who had lived there for years. He told me he had had some trouble back in our city. He was protecting his friend in some kind of fight and ended up punching a policeman. Not good. But it seemed he somehow got out of it all right.

Guys in my home city were always getting into trouble. They thought fighting proved how fearless and brave they could be. Sure, they were fearless, but they weren't thinking rationally. They were thinking emotionally. I've always thought there was nothing wrong with using your brain and walking away from a fight, but that rarely happened. So many young guys even died during these stupid fights because of their egos.

We finally landed. The airplane party was over. Time to enter my new life with new experiences. I went through immigration and went to get the yellow suitcase. I looked and saw Zachary still standing near the counter as the immigration officer checked his papers. It made me nervous since he was there for a while. Then I heard his voice.

"There you are," he said.

'What happened? Is everything ok?" I asked.

"Of course. All is well, always," he said. "Ah, there's my suitcase coming now. I'll wait with you until your luggage comes, so I can help you."

Oh no, I don't want him to see my big yellow suitcase without wheels. I'll be so embarrassed.

"Thanks, but that's ok," I said. "You shouldn't leave your mother waiting in the terminal."

"No, no, I insist," he said.

It took a while for the luggage to show up but he stayed and helped me. It was hard to say goodbye to Zachary. He was the only person I knew here. He asked to exchange phone numbers. He gave me his mother's number, but I couldn't give him mine because I had no idea where I would end up. We said goodbye and I promised to call him the next day, but I never did.

SIX

MARCH 1996, NEW YORK CITY

Viktor and Lora picked me up at the airport. They were the couple who sent me the invitation letter and bought the airline ticket. I was going to stay at their house until I found a job, so I could pay them back as promised. Viktor had a sign with my name on it, so I went over and introduced myself. Lora was waiting in the car.

"Hello Viktor," I said in English as we shook hands.

'Hello, Alyssa, nice to meet you. What took you so long?" he asked.

"I'm sorry, what?"

I didn't understand his question. I barely knew any English and I was tired from the flight. He tried a few more times in English, and then he resorted to body language, pointing to his watch.

"Oh," I said as I shrugged and pointed to the luggage.

I didn't mention my long goodbye with Zachary. It would take too long, and Viktor seemed cranky. We got in a car and I said hello to Lora. I knew some English, words like "thank you", "you are welcome", "I'm hungry" (an important one), "I am sleepy". The basics. I could also put together some sentences, but nothing complex.

I had just met them, but Viktor and Lora seemed strange. They weren't that friendly. I didn't really care since I was the same to them. Seemed like we all behaved like it was just a business transaction and nothing more.

It was dark when they picked me up from the airport. I had hoped to see something while we were driving, to get an idea of what this country looked like. What I saw in the movies looked wonderful. I wanted to see skyscrapers and a lot of bright lights. So far, I didn't see anything like that. All I saw were big wide roads, which were called highways, as Viktor explained while he was driving.

"You probably want to see something special right?" he said. "Well, there's nothing here. You see? It's nothing. In America, it's all about the roads."

That certainly seems true so far. This place isn't what I imagined. Is this really what America looks like? I thought America looked like Manhattan.

"Where is the city? Manhattan?" I asked. "The one I've seen in movies?"

He laughed.

"I don't know why everybody wants to see Manhattan. I don't like it. It's a crazy place."

What does he mean by crazy?

I went silent. I had no clue where we were, but we started going over a huge bridge.

"Look," he pointed out the window. "See all the buildings and lights? That's Manhattan."

In the distance I could make out some tall buildings shining brightly.

It looks magical. I want to go there right now. I want to see that sparkling place and what it looked like being "in" the city. But I'm not about to ask Viktor to take me. It's not like he's my uncle, who would do me a favor. He doesn't care what I want.

I continued looking out the back window until the city disappeared.

"Is Manhattan far from here?" I asked in my broken English.

"It's not too far," he said. "I take a bus there every day to go to work."

I almost asked him if it would be ok for me to go with him by bus the next morning but decided not to. Viktor and Lora lived in the middle of nowhere. A place called New Jersey. It was a silent, dark suburban town where there was hardly anything around. The house seemed brand new and clean, which was nice. It was a small, two-story house with a few pieces of furniture.

"So, Alyssa, I'll be off from work in a couple of days," Lora said. "I'll make some phone calls then, to help you find a job.

I'm sure she wants to make that happen quickly. To get me a job and the hell out of here so I could pay them back, with interest.

"Come with me," Viktor said. "I'll show you around the place. You'll be sleeping on the sofa bed downstairs. It has a TV and an open kitchen. Feel free to have something to eat whenever you want."

That's nice. I'm not comfortable opening up other people's refrigerators, but I'm sure I will when I get hungry.

"Thank you," I said. "Can I make a phone call to my family? I'd like to let them know I'm here."

"Sure," he said. "Let me help you dial long distance."

"I can pay for the call," I said, knowing that long distance calls were pricey.

"No, it's ok. I don't know exactly how much it'll be."

It felt so nice to hear my mother's voice, even though she sounded sad. I didn't want to have a long conversation because Viktor was paying. We spoke for a couple of minutes, which was enough. Any longer and it would get emotional. After the call Viktor went upstairs, and I was alone.

It was so quiet and dark outside. It was kind of spooky. I wasn't used to quiet places. I grew up in a bright, noisy city with loud people. It was around ten o'clock when they came downstairs to say goodnight. That was also different. I never saw anyone go to bed at ten, unless they were sick or something. Back home most people went to bed after midnight. And my family always had to eat something before going to bed. These people didn't even have a cup of tea or anything.

Well, I'm definitely in a different world and culture now. It makes me excited, to learn something new, and to see things I've never seen.

The next morning, I woke up before everyone else. I knew they would come downstairs so I fixed the sofa bed and made the room nice and neat. I didn't want to be in bed in case they came downstairs.

"Good morning," Lora said to me.

"Good morning," I said.

I'm not one for conversations first thing in the morning. But I didn't need to say a word because once Lora started talking, she was non-stop.

"We're going to leave soon for work. You just stay here, have some food, whatever you find," as she pointed to the refrigerator and smiled.

"Thank you, Lora."

I'm not so sure about staying in the house by myself. I wish one of them would take me with them.

"You can also watch TV if you want," she said.

She showed me how to turn on and use the TV remote. It seemed strange to me to have to push so many buttons to get the channel on. First push the TV button, then the cable button, then select from a hundred channels. I was pretending I understood it all, but I didn't. I missed my home TV. It was much easier with a big old TV with three channels.

It was hard to understand them. They spoke so fast that I was only catching a few words here and there. But the face and body language helped a lot. She made some coffee, which was excellent. I was starving for coffee.

Lora was in her forties. She was around medium height and in great shape, but with a rather cold looking face. But she wasn't as mean as she looked. She had pale skin with dirty blond hair, small eyes, thin lips, and a long thin nose. I guess those features are what gave her that cold look. She seemed to take care of her face. She had smooth, young girl skin.

Lora dressed very well. She wore a silk blouse with mashed up pastel colors, and straight light brown pants with medium size high heels. I had had a good sense of fashion since I was a little girl. I read and watched a lot of fashion shows. I always recognized high quality clothes and shoes, even if I never had them after my father died.

And Viktor? He wasn't much taller than her. He was a big-shouldered kind of guy. He had dark skin with dark hair. But he was a mess when it came to his fashion. He was sloppy. When he came downstairs, he looked like he had slept in his clothes and was still half asleep.

"Hi," he grunted.

"Good morning, Viktor," I said.

He wore some kind of old 1960s style shirt with a long collar and light blue, rough made jeans, which were wrinkled, and not as a fashion look. They looked like a cow had been chewing on them and he just snatched them right out of its mouth and put them on.

See, I don't get that. When a man doesn't know how to groom or dress, then he needs a woman's touch. I mean a good woman's touch. Viktor has one. He has a wife who knows how to take care of herself. But does she take care of Victor? Nope. Why is that? Doesn't she see? Or maybe she just doesn't care. Yeah, that's probably it … she doesn't care. A woman who treats herself well but doesn't care about her husband's look sends a clear message. Sorry dear, but we're out of love, so I've stopped caring. It's selfish. I'm more embarrassed for her than him. I feel sad for him.

They both left at the same time but in different cars. I said goodbye and went back into the living room.

Now what?

The bathroom was upstairs. I went up to take a shower. I stayed there for quite a while. It felt good and I wasn't in a hurry. I had nowhere to go and nothing to do.

After the shower I felt fresh and energized. It was like the water had rinsed away the tiredness from my body and mind. All my past, stressful life, and all my worries faded away. I felt like a newborn baby with a new start in life. I was going to learn everything, step by step, like a baby.

I had another cup of coffee and sat on the couch. I wished I could've called my family and friends. I had plenty of time to chat. I started playing with the remote to turn on the TV, but I couldn't remember what Lora told me, so I stopped before screwing something up.

So much for watching TV.

I had brought an English language book, so I decided to study to prepare for my job interview. I wanted to make sure it went well. I started studying but quickly fell asleep.

I slept deeply for a few hours and had several vivid dreams. They were so chaotic that my heart's pounding woke me up. It was still morning and there was a lot of time before Viktor and Lora returned. I wanted them at home, but I didn't know why. It wasn't like they were going to hang out with me, or we'd go out for drinks and dinner. I guess I just wanted someone around.

I ate, read, looked at magazines. Ate again, read again, looked out the windows. Time was going so slow. I was so bored I was going insane. I was processing being somewhere far away from my country and family. I heard the garage door open and got excited, like a little kid waiting for her parents. It was Lora.

"Hi, how was your day?" she asked.

"Good," I said.

"Good," she said as she grabbed an apple juice and disappeared upstairs.

I was alone again. About an hour later Viktor came home.

"Hi," he said.

"Hi," I said. "How was your day?"

His eyes got big as he looked surprised. I guess no one ever asked him that.

"Not too bad," he said. "There was some traffic because of an accident ..."

Then he went on and on. I didn't understand much but pretended I did. With his facial expressions, I could figure it out when there was some drama thing and I would scowl. When he smiled, I'd smile too. Then he went upstairs. They both came downstairs for dinner, but I wasn't hungry. Between the jetlag and excitement, I had zero appetite. I'm sure it had nothing to do with all the stuff I ate during the day.

"Do you want to watch some TV?" Lora asked. "Turn it on."

"No thank you."

"You've probably been watching all day and are tired of it right?" she smiled.

I can't lie and say yes. She might throw me some questions about TV shows.

"I don't watch much TV," I said. "I spent some time studying English."

I handed her the remote control so she wouldn't ask me to turn it on for her. They sat down for dinner. She didn't cook. She just heated some stuff and they ate as they chatted. She would ask him questions and he would respond with short sentences. I had no idea what the conversation was about, so I grabbed the English book and read.

Reading makes me so sleepy. I can't keep my eyes open. How long am I going to have to wait for them to finish and leave the kitchen so I can crash? This is torture. Every time I hear her voice and his response, I'm hoping that will be it. But no. It's going on and on. I don't like being so dependent on others. All I can do is wait. I have no control. It's like being held captive. Oh, good, they're done, finally.

The next morning was just like the day before. Same routine. I was so sleepy because I woke up in the middle of the night and couldn't get back to sleep. Then I fell asleep right before I had to get up. I hate when that happens. It feels like you have a hangover without the fun. I forced myself to get up and make the bed, even though I planned to go back to bed as soon as they left. But after they left I was wide awake.

This is even more boring than yesterday. I need to find a job, and fast. I want to get busy and make some money. These two days make me feel like a nobody, like I don't exist. I've been so inactive it's become rather disturbing. I wonder why Lora said no when I asked her if it would be ok if I took a walk. It was a firm no, without hesitation. She even shook her head and seemed irritated. She didn't even explain why. She can't be afraid I'd run away—they took my passport the first night, as security to make sure they got paid. I guess I could've asked her why, but with my weak English I wasn't so sure I'd say the right things. Maybe it was just a misunderstanding. Did I even ask her the right way? Maybe I didn't say something right and she heard it completely different and it scared her?

I smiled and laughed out loud. I was overthinking it and became so tired. I was thinking so much that I drove myself crazy. That's what happens when you have too much time. Thinking isn't a bad thing. But too much of it and your thoughts start to spin out of control and become useless. I took a shower to clear my mind.

After putting on some fresh clothes I started to head downstairs when I paused in the hallway. I saw the couple's bedroom door wide open. When I went to the bathroom the night before I noticed they were sleeping with the door open. I thought it was rather odd, sleeping with the door open when someone's in a house, but maybe they just forgot to close it.

Maybe they never close the door? Then why even have it? Maybe it's just broken. This is so silly, but it does make me curious. Maybe I should go into the room, just to see it. No, no, I shouldn't do that. It's not me. I'm not a nosey person. No, I'm not, but then again, I have nothing else to do. It doesn't matter. It's a bad idea. Inappropriate and rude. But … I still want to go inside. I know, I'll just sneak in and out. I won't touch anything. I'll just look.

I started walking in but stopped.

What is wrong with me? I can't do this. It's not right. It's not, but what's the harm? Why not go in? Just for fun. It's not a big deal. But what happens if I see something that I shouldn't? That could be uncomfortable. What could that possibly be? They seem like normal people, kind of. Yes, yes, it's fine. Besides, my intuition tells me there's some reason I should do this. Why is Lora so strict about me staying in the house? Maybe she doesn't want the neighbors to see me? When we came home from the airport, I don't think anybody saw us.

My heart started pounding.

Here we go, another something to worry about. Like I don't have enough already? I need to just go inside and see if everything is fine so I can stay calm and sleep well. Yes, that's right. That's the reason.

I went inside. Even though it was daylight, it looked like nighttime in the bedroom. The dark shades were down. I wanted the shades up so I could see better but I left them down. I was afraid to touch anything. I just wanted to look around. It was a simply decorated room. They had a large-sized bed that took up most of the room. There was one dresser, a standing floor mirror and one armchair. All the furniture was dark brown. It was a heavy and dramatic looking bedroom, which made me want to leave, quickly. I raced down the stairs, grabbed my English study book, and sat down on the couch.

It was good I left. There wasn't anything interesting to see there. I feel relieved. It's better to focus on my studying.

I opened the book to do some exercises. I kept reading but my mind was elsewhere. I was distracted and couldn't focus. I read the same page over and over again and couldn't remember anything.

I hate when this happens. I'm just wasting my time. Maybe I need to close my eyes and relax.

I closed my eyes. My thoughts went back to the time I looked in the mirror and saw myself as two people, when I discovered my dual male–female personalities inside the essential, feminine body.

I wonder if I'd see anything different now, since I've traveled into this unknown place. To fully see myself, I need a full mirror, like the one upstairs, in their bedroom. I need to go back. I just want to look at myself, that's all. Or, maybe I'm just trying to find a reason to go back in there?

I went back to the room, and straight to the mirror. I didn't look around this time since there was nothing to see. I could barely see myself because it was so dark. I could make out some features of my face and the silhouette of my body. I hadn't moved much the last few days, so I wanted to see if my shape was still good. I was a little obsessive about being in shape. Mirrors have always been my best friend. I love standing right in front of the mirror and spending quality time there.

"You know," my friend once told me. "I watched you, always checking yourself out in the mirror. You once told me you do that to make sure you didn't gain any weight. I started doing the same thing, and it motivated me to eat better and exercise. I've lost a lot of weight, thanks to you."

I'm happy I found this mirror. I can have some fun while checking myself out. I like the way I look, but then, maybe not so much. I look sad and tired. My eyes are puffy, cheerless.

I did a couple of turns, right and left, left and right. I looked straight and in profile, and I did it all over again, checking on my body from top to bottom.

I look fine. I am fine. My body looks the same. I just need some sleep and exercise. Wait, what's that?

I noticed something in the mirror. It was a door. I didn't see it when I went in the first time and I wondered how I missed it. The bedroom door was always open, but this door was closed. I walked towards the door.

Was it possible the bedroom is connected to another room? Now I definitely want to see inside. I'm not hesitating this time.

I opened the door and switched on the light. It was a walk-in closet. I had never seen one in person before. We didn't have them back home. Nobody did. This was fascinating to me.

How nice for your clothes and shoes to have a room of their own? It seems respectful to the things we wear and use every day. I love it. I hope I can have one someday.

The closet was divided in two, one side for her and one for him. His side was a mess, hers was organized. Her side looked colorful and fresh, with a lot of clothes. Not so much color on his side. I went to her side to take a closer look. I wasn't going to take any piece or try anything on. I checked them out, and went back and forth a few times, as I touched a few pieces to feel the fabric. I looked at them, over and over again.

I've never seen so many dresses with so many styles in one closet. Tops with long, short or no sleeves. Tight and loose pants in different colors. Skirts that were long and short. It looks like a store. I can only dream of having so many clothes. I'm astonished.

But this wasn't all. On the shelf above the clothes I saw so many boxes lined up side by side and stacked high, filled with shoes.

I'm in complete shock. I think I'm going to pass out. This is insane. Does she own a shoe company? No, that's not it. I think she said she's a pharmacist and he works at some real estate company. But how was this possible to have this many pairs of shoes? How many times could you possibly wear each one of them? I have two pairs of shoes. One for the warm weather and one for the cold. I have got to see these shoes. But there are so many, it might take too long to go through every box. I would freak out if one of them came home and caught me going through their stuff.

But I started looking, from the top box to the bottom. I just looked. I didn't take them out to try them on. She wasn't my size anyway, which somehow made me feel better. I opened the fourth box and saw my dream shoes. The kind I'd love to wear on a special day in my life. I loved them. They were leather, with a pastel beige color, five-inch-high heels, a rounded cut open toe, with a small-sized pearl on the right side. These shoes belonged to me. It was just my style. I couldn't stop myself.

I took them out and tried them on, even though they weren't my size. They barely fit. They were painful but enjoyable at the same time. I looked in the mirror and dreamed of having them one day. They looked so beautiful on me.

That's it. I have got to get things going here. I need to be more active and ambitious, so I can improve my situation and be free. So free that I can indulge myself and others without financial worries. But I've got to take these off. My feet are killing me.

I said goodbye and put them back where they belonged. I was just about to leave the goldmine, but I saw that it was still early, so I checked a few more boxes. And then more, and more, and more, until I was on the last row. I tried to slide the box out halfway, to open the top and sneak a peek, when the entire stack of boxes fell and landed right on my head.

Damn, that hurt! I just got punished. Good, I deserve this. I shouldn't be so nosey. I shouldn't be somewhere I don't belong. Now I'm pissed at myself.

I worked fast to put the boxes back up on the shelf. The problem was I didn't remember the exact order. I lined them up and switched a few boxes, stepped back and looked.

What if Lora has some way she organizes these boxes? If she does, I am so screwed. If she asks, how can I respond? And what would happen to me? Maybe she'll send me back home or somewhere else?

I focused on putting the boxes back the way I remembered. As I was finishing, I began to feel better. I sat down on the floor for a second. My knees were hurting from bending up and down. I looked around. My work was done. The boxes looked nice and organized. I was fairly confident that I put them back where they were supposed to be. As I sat there, I noticed three other boxes all the way in the back of the closet on the floor, slightly hidden by some hanging clothes.

Why not open them? I'm already guilty, I've already been punished. I might as well have a look.

I gathered all three together and tried to lift them out, but they were kind of heavy, so I pulled each box out individually. I opened the top of the first box, looked and closed it—fast. I opened the second and closed it even faster than the first. I became nervous. With the last one I opened the top slightly, peeked in with one eye, and closed it. I quickly put the three boxes back. As I stood up, my heart was pounding and my hands were shaking.

SEVEN

APRIL 1996, NEW JERSEY

I don't remember running from the closet, but I suddenly found myself downstairs, pacing around the living room. I was frantic.

What the hell was that? A different kind of gun in each box? That explains why they were heavy. Look at me, I'm sweating, confused and scared. Did I close the closet door? Maybe not, but who cares? I don't care about anything except how to escape from this house. I wish I could call someone, to tell them what happened and to ask for help. I remember my hesitation about going into that damn bedroom. My internal debate, back and forth. See? My intuition said don't go in, and it was right. Something bad is going to happen and I don't feel safe. I need to do something. I want to leave this place, but how?

And, who are these people anyway? Why did they want to help me out with money and get me over here? Maybe they're the kind people who just want some extra cash, but they certainly don't seem desperate for money. I should stay positive. Maybe everything is fine. But why did they have guns hidden in the house, and in shoeboxes? Do they collect them? Is it just a hobby? Is it that unsafe around here that people need guns for protection? How could that be? No one is ever around! OK, just calm down. Think … think … who … Zachary! My travel buddy, I should call him. He would help me out. I can explain my situation and I'm sure he'd come and rescue me.

I looked for his phone number in my purse. I grabbed the phone and called. After two rings I hung up.

Is this the right thing to do? Maybe I'm exaggerating the situation and he would even laugh at me. And how am I going to ask him to get me out of here when I don't even know where I am? I don't even know the address.

Lora came home early. She looked happy and was friendly.

"How was your day?" she asked with a smile.

"Good," I said.

"I had a good day too," she said, and she told me all about it.

I wish I could speak English well. I can understand more than I can speak. It's like I'm mute but not deaf.

"Well," she continued, "I'm off tomorrow so I can work on finding you a job. You understand?"

"Yes," I said.

But not really.

"I'll make some phone calls. The job market is pretty good for live-in help so hopefully it won't take too long. Do you understand what I'm saying?"

"Yes," I said with a smile.

I have no clue what she's trying to tell me. I get a word every now and then. All I can think about are the guns upstairs. But I can't show any emotions. She looks kind of different to me. Her face is slimmer and her nose is even longer. Her lips look like they've disappeared behind the red lipstick. It's funny what our imagination does. I liked her yesterday. Well, not that much, but I kind of liked her style and fresh look. But now I see her as a monster, with a small and unattractive face. She's a complete stranger to me. She was always strange, but now she was even stranger, and dangerous.

When she turned to go upstairs my heart started pounding so fast and hard that I thought it might pop out of my body. I became anxious. I had no idea how I would respond to her questions if she asked about her closet. I sat down and didn't move as I watched her climb the stairs. I listened to hear something, but it was silent for a long time. It was like sitting in a waiting room, waiting for your name to be called. I heard water running so I assumed she was showering. Time slowed down, like they say it does when your life is in danger. An hour passed and I was still sitting in the same position.

I hope Viktor shows up soon. And why would that help? I guess it wouldn't. My head hurts from thinking about what's going on here. I'm like some kind of filmmaker with all these different stories to choose from. What a messed-up movie.

Maybe she's going to kill me tonight. That's why she came home early, and why she's being so nice to me. Maybe they're both sick people and this is what they do. Invite foreigners in and then kill them, for pleasure. If they killed me, nobody would ever find me. Maybe no one around them knows they have a guest in the house. Maybe that's the reason she doesn't want me going outside for a walk. Who would come looking for me? No one in this country knows I'm even here, except Zachary, and who knows where he is. Even if someone asked where I was they can just say I left. They weren't responsible for me. My family is so far away they can't do anything to find me.

Or … maybe they want someone killed and they want me to do it. How evil would that be? I've never even thought about killing anyone. I even hate movies where people kill each other. And I'm really afraid of guns and knives. Geez, I pass out at even the sight of a few drops of blood. I remember crying once when a bandage got stuck on my skin and I was afraid to take it off because it might bleed.

Wait, hang on. What is up with all these thoughts? Am I going crazy? It's OK to have guns at home. People do it all the time, and it doesn't mean they kill people. Then again, why hide them in a shoebox?

Maybe they're not killers, but they've set a trap for me to find the guns, and now they're going to punish me by making me pay them even more money. Yes, this makes sense. I like this story the best. Those first two stories are more interesting. There's action, suspense and killing. The stuff a lot of people like. But I like this third story, since I still love myself.

The phone rang and startled me out of my private movie production. It rang a few times, but Lora didn't answer it. I wanted to hear her speak. Not that I would understand what she said, but at least I could hear the tone of her voice, to figure out her mood. Then the phone rang again. I stood up and went closer to the stairs to hear, but she wasn't answering. I didn't hear the shower running anymore. I waited for a little bit and went back to the couch. The phone rang once more, but still she didn't answer.

What happened to her? Did she kill herself? That's yet another interesting story!

I smiled. The singing of birds outside distracted me. I went to the window to see them. I needed a distraction. I had to stop thinking and scaring myself. I saw two small birds sitting on a branch. They looked so beautiful. They were lively and happy. I smiled as I watched them. I thought they were a couple and in love. One would tweet and the other would tweet back. They were nestled together. They didn't move except for their heads, which darted fitfully, left, right, up, down. I wondered if they could see me. Maybe they did. Who knows?

Life can be so beautiful when we stop to see the beauty. I mean really see beauty, without labeling anything. It's all around us. I saw those birds and they made me happy. It felt so wonderful. All we really need is love, and we should all have love. We should search for it, fight for it, to feel it, have it and enjoy it. We don't have time to waste time. We shouldn't let time-wasting activities dominate us. They make us invisible, and invisibility brings unhappiness, and when we're unhappy, we become empty.

"Alyssa!!!"

I jumped up quickly. I was all dreamy when suddenly I thought I heard someone scream my name loudly. My heart, serene a second ago, was now pounding so hard I could hear it in my head.

What the hell was that? Am I hallucinating?

"Alyssa!!!"

I'm not hallucinating. That came from the bedroom upstairs. It's Lora. Now I'm in trouble. I know something isn't right.

I slowly moved towards the stairs. I heard her call my name once again, not from the bedroom but from the hallway upstairs. She sounded desperate. In one second, so many thoughts passed by so fast, like bullets whizzing by.

"Yes Lora?" I asked, my voice shaking.

"Come on up here!"

She sounds like someone else. I hope it's her and not some stranger.

I slowly climbed the stairs. My knees were shaking as my heart accelerated. I couldn't control all this trembling.

I feel like I'm falling apart.

I went into her room, my head down. I didn't want to look her in the eyes.

"I'm sorry," I whispered.

"No, no. It's just that I'm in a hurry and I kept calling you. So?"

"No … I mean," and I looked up at her.

She was standing in front of me in a bra and panties, thigh high stockings and high heels, holding a different dress in each hand as she moved them up and down. Her eyes wide, eyebrows raised, waiting for an answer.

But I barely touched her clothes! Maybe I touched them lightly to feel the fabric, but I never took them down to try them on. Why did she think I did that? What about the shoeboxes? Did she notice them? I don't know what to say to her.

I looked at her in silent, wide-eyed wonder.

"So, what do you think?" she asked.

"I'm sorry, what?"

"What do you think about these two? Should I wear this, or this? I can't decide which one to wear with these high heels."

It took me a while to get it, then I got it, and I felt like an idiot. I was so relieved as I shook my head slowly.

"Are you OK?" she asked.

I want to hug her. The Lora I knew before is back. She's that fresh looking, well-groomed, but still a little bit weird, Lora.

"Come with me to the closet," she said.

I know that place. Just when I thought my paranoia was gone, it's back again. Why did she want to take me in there?

I followed her. She approached the shoeboxes, stood staring for a while, then finally grabbed one of them. She took out the pair of shoes and pointed to me.

"What do you think?" she asked. "Maybe these are better with this dress?"

"Yes, yes, nice, very nice," I said.

Is she trying to tell me I know you know?

As she bent down to reach the bottom boxes I said I needed to go to the bathroom. But instead of the bathroom I went to bed and crashed. I didn't care about the guns, what she was wearing or what they might do to me. I just dove into bed in my clothes and didn't move all night. The jet lag and my overactive imagination had caught up with me.

I woke up the next day as I heard her on the phone. I jumped out of the bed so fast that I got dizzy. She came downstairs and walked right by me, like nothing happened the night before. She gave me the same cold, frozen fish facial expression that I saw when we first met. Maybe she was hungover, who knows.

Lora went to the kitchen with her coffee mug. She didn't even offer me a cup of coffee as we sat down at the table to make some phone calls for my job. I was dying for coffee so I helped myself. I wanted to ask her how her night was, but she had that morning "don't even think about talking to me until I have my coffee" look, so I stayed quiet. She made some calls to a few agencies. In between calls, she talked to herself, but I had no idea what she was saying. She didn't tell me what she was doing, and it was all rather awkward.

Did I do something wrong? Is she mad at me for something? Is she mad that I left her closet and never came back? This is crazy. Why do I always think I did something wrong? She's probably just moody or cranky and doesn't want to communicate. It's not like I would understand her anyway. Maybe she doesn't want to do any of this, and she's frustrated. She's mumbling to herself again. This is getting weird.

One of the agents Lora called said she had several job opportunities working as a babysitter. She asked Lora a few questions about me. She lied to the agent that I had experience with kids.

"Does she speak English?" the agent asked.

"She does, a little bit," Lora said. "I think it's enough, especially for little kids."

"Ok, let's see. I want to meet her in person so we can talk more."

"How about today? I'm busy the rest of the week."

"Sure. Bring her here at 1:00 this afternoon."

'Go get dressed," Lora said to me. "We leave in an hour."

I got so excited. I wanted to start work as soon as I could to pay off my loans. I also wanted to leave this depressing and weird place. It's so uncomfortable staying in someone's house, doing nothing. I couldn't go anywhere without them driving. There weren't even sidewalks. When I looked out the window, there was just grass. It was like being in a high-end jail. And after the whole wardrobe review and the crazy "gun in a shoebox" thing I just wanted to get the hell out of there.

Since I was going to an interview I decided to dress in conservative chic. I wore a shapely, light wool fabric, solid gray dress that went to the bottom of the knee, with skin color tights, and my only pair of black, low-heeled shoes. I refreshed my nails with a light pinkish color. I put some makeup on with light pinkish-red lipstick and made a ponytail for a simple look. I was ready in 20 minutes. I sat on the couch and flipped through magazines I couldn't read while I waited. Lora came downstairs and looked at me.

"You look good," she said.

I feel much better when she says something nice to me. Maybe she's in a better mood. That's a good thing. She does have a good fashion sense and with many clothes and a seemingly unlimited number of shoes.

"Thank you," I said.

We got in the car. It felt so good to be outside. I felt energized. I rolled down the window to breathe in the fresh air, but she told me to close it. Seemed like I was still in jail, but a different one. She drove without talking. The radio played but you could hardly hear it.

It was a nice sunny day. It was my first trip outside the house, and I wanted to see something. Something that I never saw before, that would astonish me. I thought everything would be different here. The roads, lights, cars, trees, even people. I felt like a little kid who was going to get some candy or ice cream. I wanted to see some major attractions, so I could call home and astound them.

So far it was just one big, long road, with a lot of cars. It was a two-hour drive to the agency, which was a long time for me. I came from a small city where everything was so close, it took no more than ten to fifteen minutes to get anywhere. It felt like we were going on vacation to another country. She drove fast and confidently, like an experienced driver. She probably drove better than she walked. I already missed walking around the city streets. Sitting in the car for a long time wasn't my thing.

As we approached the office, she searched for parking close to the building. I hoped she wouldn't find a spot so we could walk a little. But she got lucky and found her spot, and that was fine. Whatever made her happy. I just didn't want to hear her mumbling again.

"Hello Julia, I'm Lora and this is Alyssa."

"Oh, hi. Please have a seat," Julia said. "I'll be with you in a minute. I just have to finish up this call."

This is a really small room. Just one desk and these two chairs in front. I'm guessing from the look of her desk, she's been working here for a long time. She has so many pictures in different kinds of frames. Her phone looks like it's a hundred years old, it's so bulky, with a rotary dial. Look at the mess on her desk. Newspapers, pads and pens everywhere. She looks like she should be retired. Maybe she likes to work. Or maybe she doesn't like to be at home. She does have a pleasant look. She seems to be checking me out through those tiny round glasses.

"How can I help you?" she asked as she hung up the phone.

Lora briefly explained my situation as Julia listened and glanced my way now and then.

"Ok, we can find her a job. I have plenty of opportunities. Alyssa, Lora said you understand some English?"

"Yes, a little," I said.

"Excellent. How old are you? How much education have you had?"

We mechanically went back and forth with simple questions and answers.

"Excellent. You do speak English rather well for a beginner," she said with a smile.

Really? I speak English well? I'm shocked that my English is acceptable for a job that could easily be filled by an American.

"Ok, excellent," Julia said.

Apparently everything is excellent.

"The only thing is your age."

Well, almost everything.

"You're young," Julia said, "and sometimes families don't like to hire someone your age. But we can work on that."

Her facial expression looks just like one of my old teachers back in high school. That probing look, trying to read my mind for some hidden problem. She even sounds like a teacher. Caring but suspicious.

"Just a few things to remember," she said. "When you go to the interview, don't wear makeup or nail polish. And wear something simple."

Really? I'm not supposed to look my best? I would think every family would want their kids to be around someone who looks good. I guess not. Why do I have to look plain? Even Lora looks surprised. But she's not saying anything.

"Most of the time the wife does the interviewing," Julia said, "and they won't hire someone young and attractive around the house. They don't want any competition for their husbands."

EIGHT

Julia was good at her job. The interviews were scheduled right away for the coming weekend. I was so excited and confident that at least one family would hire me. All I needed was one offer from all these opportunities. Since I didn't know how to get around, Lora and Viktor would have to drive me, which was great for me, but not so much for them.

The locations were far apart, so we were out all day, driving from one house to another. I went to a few interviews on Saturday, and the next day we did the same routine. I saw all kinds of diversity—big and small houses, some families with a bunch of kids and some with just two. No families had just one kid, which I was hoping for.

I had six interviews. All the people seemed nice during the interview. I thought I did well, and so did Lora. My confidence was high as we waited for responses. I tried everything to land a job. I even tried to expand my English, saying things like I love kids, so I had a better chance of getting hired. I agreed with anything they wanted me to do. I didn't expect to cook or clean the house when the interviews started but I was saying yes to all of it. I knew how to say yes very well in English, and I used it a lot those days. Some people got so greedy. When they saw I was agreeing to everything they started taking advantage, asking me to do more and more.

Sometimes if I would get confused about how to answer a question, I would pause and look to Lora, who would jump right into the conversation to help me out. Lora and I became such a good team. Some of them made me play with their kids to see if there was a connection with them. The kids were OK, and the moms looked pleased while I was playing with them.

As Julia instructed, I made myself look ordinary. I dressed in jeans and a simple blouse I had brought with me that I never wore because I didn't like it. It was white and in a boxy shape with no style. I also hated the jeans I was wearing, a gift from my aunt. They were a rough dark blue material, loose and high-rise. I remember my mother made me bring these jeans to make my aunt happy. I had argued about bringing them but good thing I gave in—it seemed like these jeans were popular in my interviews. Mothers do sometimes know best, somehow.

I didn't wear any makeup. My face looked pale and washed out. I even put some light-colored powder on my face to cover up my features. I covered up my naturally red color lips, so they didn't stand out, and put my hair up in a ponytail again. I scared myself when I looked in the mirror. It wasn't me, but I didn't care as long as I got a job.

"This is the way it works," Lora told me while we were driving home on Sunday afternoon. "Usually people are in a rush and if they want to hire you, they do it right away. I have no doubt you'll get some phone calls tonight, so you might want to prepare yourself. Get ready and pack your stuff so I can drive you tomorrow before I go to work," she said.

"OK," I said.

I feel great. I'm so excited to make a new start. It feels like I'm about to go on vacation. It doesn't matter who hires me. I just want someone to call and say I'm hired. I did like one family though. Somehow, I felt comfortable in their house. I met both parents. They were a young, pleasant couple, and the kids were adorable. They were year-old twins. It was good that I didn't need to speak much with them. I hope they hire me.

I undressed as soon as I got home. I was so tired of being in the baggy outfit. I took a shower, rinsed off my babysitter look and turned into the original me. The phone started ringing around seven o'clock, one family after another. Lora was answering most of the calls. Sometimes Viktor would pick it up from the kitchen and he'd tell Lora to pick up the phone. That's how I knew the calls were for me. I finished packing and sat down with a cup of tea as I tried to study my English.

What if I get a few offers? I wonder which family I'll choose. Some of them had a nice house, some had fewer kids, and some of the mothers were easygoing. It's hard to choose, but what a great problem to have! That family I liked the most had such a tiny place, which I didn't mind until I saw the big houses. It would be nice to live in one of those, even if I was working. That lady Julia. She's such a nice lady. I have to make sure to thank her for the good interview tips. She would've been so proud of me if she had seen my wardrobe and my look. I did everything she told me, and I tried so hard. I hope I'll be rewarded for all of this.

I was confident and happy when Lora came downstairs. The smile on her face made me even happier and impatient to hear what she had to say. She went straight to the kitchen, grabbed a glass of water and drank it without breathing—she seemed thirsty. She looked at me smiling; I smiled back at her.

"Alyssa, you were rejected by all of them," she said.

My heart started beating faster as I became even more excited.

Did I get rejected from all of them? Wow, I did even better than I thought!

I sat up straight, opened my shoulders, I put my head up and looked at her proudly. My happy face confused her, which made me confused.

"Alyssa," she said, "you were rejected. Understand? Rejected."

Why does she keep repeating the same word? Doesn't she know I got it? Wait … wait a minute. Did I get this right?

I quickly grabbed my dictionary to double check the meaning of rejected. And what I saw made me feel sick. I couldn't move or say anything.

Her smile. It's a nervous one, not a happy one. Or maybe she's happy that I wasn't going anywhere because she had some other plan, with her guns? My imagination is killing me.

"No one wanted to hire you because you're too young," Lora said.

Julia was right, once again.

"I'll call Julia tomorrow and we'll see what else she can do for you," Lora said, and disappeared, as usual.

I feel so down. Maybe I should call my family with that phone card I bought. No, I better not. Better to call them when I'm upbeat. I am so disappointed. I was so sure someone would hire me. And now I'm stuck in this house, with no end in sight. I just want to speak with Julia. She's my only hope.

The days started to fall into a dull routine, with no prospects. A whole week went by with no news about job opportunities. The couple seemed very robotic. They would get up, go to work, come home, have some dinner and go to bed. I had no idea what they were doing in the bedroom but sometimes I'd hear the TV. Sometimes it was complete silence. But the bedroom door was always open. That was for sure.

Daytime was easier for me since I was by myself. But in the evening when they were home? It was uncomfortable. They wouldn't say much to me. I didn't know if they were OK with me staying with them this long, or if they were frustrated. I'd get nervous when I remembered the shoeboxes. I never went back to their bedroom after discovering the guns. I was afraid of finding something else, which would terrify me even more, with nowhere to go.

Maybe I should look for my passport, figure out this address, and call Zachary and ask him to get me out of here. Something is a little off in this house. Aside from the guns, I never see any visitors come here. This seems rather strange to me. That's why the front door looks new, all bright white, with a nice shiny gold door-handle. The door is rarely used. Back home our house door is old and faded, with a discolored door-handle. That door is used all the time, opening and closing all day long. Sometimes we'd slam it so hard my mother would yell, "Don't you know how to close the door properly?"

We had so many rules to learn when we were growing up, but who would ever think there would be one about how to treat the door? All my friends and I would laugh and make jokes about it.

"Excuse me, door. I'm so sorry I didn't treat you appropriately." I guess some doors are busier than others. This couple's front door is so inactive it's almost useless. Lora and Viktor always come into the house through the garage. I never saw a garage attached to the house, but it's kind of cool. I can't wait to mention that to my family. I think I'm going crazy, making up stories about doors.

More than three weeks went by without any job news. I called home once, just to let them know I was fine. I wasn't honest with my stories and situation. I told them I was waiting for a job, which was supposed to happen soon. There was no point in telling them about all my worries and boredom. It would only make them worry, and it wouldn't do anything to help me. Finally, Julia called early one morning and said there was a family that had an emergency and needed help for a few days, maybe a week.

"Could you please drive her to the family today?" Julia asked. "Who knows, if they like her they might keep her on. You never know with these people."

"Yes, of course," Lora said to Julia as she turned to me. "Get dressed and pack your things. You've got a temporary job, but I hope they hire you permanently."

As we drove up, the house looked enormous, surrounded by woods. It looked like such a peaceful place. A woman opened the door and she and Lora had a conversation about me as we walked in. She just looked at me every once in a while.

"You're going to help her out for a few days," Lora said. "Don't worry about anything. Her name is Susan. She seems kind and she'll explain what to do."

"Ok, thanks," I said as Lora left.

I feel like a kid being dropped off at school by her mom.

"Hi Alyssa," Susan said.

"Hi," I said.

"I should tell you about our family and the help I need," she said. "We have three children. A six-year-old boy named Steven and four-year-old twin girls, Sara and Susa."

I guess she likes names that start with S.

"I'll need you to clean the children's rooms and do the laundry," she continued. "I'll be in the house, but on the phone."

"OK," I said.

She showed me the children's rooms and the laundry, which I started on right away. Then I made my way to the children's rooms. She was on the phone all day. Later she asked me to help in the kitchen, but the phone rang, and she was gone again. She seemed distracted. She came back, apologized for disappearing, and then asked me to check in on the children. The boy was in his room playing quietly, while the girls were playing with their toys in the den.

Susan seems nice. I feel comfortable here. The day went by so fast. I don't understand what she could be talking about for hours on the phone. Maybe she's a businesswoman?

I put my stuff in the basement where she showed me a room to sleep in. I went with her as she put the children to bed.

"Thanks for your patience today," she said as she closed the bedroom door. "You're free for the evening. Let's talk in the morning about tomorrow's chores."

"Ok, goodnight," I said.

It was 7:30. I went to the basement. It was too early to sleep so I watched TV. I flipped through the channels but there were only five of them. I found a show where pretty girls and guys were playing.

Well, even if I don't understand the dialog at least I can try to figure out what's going on. This room is right under the kitchen and I can hear Susan walking back and forth, like she's stepping on my head. Wait, is that another person walking? Great, now there are four feet stepping on my head. They sure do stop and start walking a lot. And that other person's footsteps are louder. Maybe it's a guy?

I assumed her husband came home from work. I heard a normal conversation at first, and then an argument, and then screaming. Then it went silent, and then she'd start screaming again. I got a little stressed, but I told myself not to worry about it. It was probably a typical wife and husband fight. When I heard her scream even louder, with slamming doors and breaking dishes, then I freaked out. But there wasn't anything I could do, so I just stayed where I was.

This is weird. Susan seems warm and nice. What's going on? She had such a kind, delicate voice when she was on the phone or when she talked to me. But now her voice sounds so loud and deep. It sounds like someone else. I hear steps. Oh, she's coming down to the basement.

I jumped from the bed as she came to my door.

"I'm sorry. You'll have to get dressed and go," she said.

What? I don't know what to say. What's happening and where am I going?

"Can you be ready in ten minutes?" she asked. "I'll meet you in the kitchen."

I dressed, grabbed my suitcase and went upstairs. She had her kids up and dressed. It seemed like we're all about to go on a road trip.

"I'm going to drive you to the train station," she said. "I'll call Lora and she'll pick you up OK? Don't worry, I'll explain it all to you in the car. Let's go now."

She was in a hurry. She grabbed the girls, I grabbed the boy and we left. I never saw her husband or whoever the guy was. She was shaking so much I was afraid she wouldn't be able to drive. She had a car phone and dialed someone. I heard some familiar words. She called her mother. It sounded like she had a fight with her husband and decided to leave. She was going to her mother's.

Why on earth is this happening now, at this moment? I'm not having any luck with this job thing. I finally get some work and the first day, I'm done and going back to Lora's place? The very first day?

Susan called Lora but she didn't answer. She tried a few times and she started to get nervous about it. She left a few messages. I had Viktor's office phone number and gave it to her. She called him and he picked up. She apologized, told him about the situation, and asked that he pick me up at the station.

"OK, I spoke with Viktor so there's nothing to worry about," she told me while she was driving. "I'll get you the train ticket and you just get off at Newark Penn Station. Here's a pen and paper. Just write everything down please. Go to the waiting area and stay there. Viktor will pick you up there. OK?"

"OK, but I've never been on the train and I don't know anything about it."

"You'll be alright. It's easy. It's just a train. Just make sure to get off at the right station."

Soon I was on the train with two male strangers. Just the three of us. One was sitting in front of me and the other was sitting a few seats behind me. As the train slowly started to move, I slowly started to cry.

I feel so sad, and lonely. It's so dark outside. I can't see a thing and I don't know where I am. The train is stopping already? The next station. I hope more people come into the car. I didn't know why I wanted more people around. Maybe for security? But it's not like I'm afraid. It's safe enough. It doesn't matter. No one came into the car anyway.

I was looking around constantly for the conductor. I saw him once when I got my ticket. I wanted to see him again, just for comfort, but I never saw him. I didn't even know what town I was coming from. All I knew was after eight stops or so I had to get off.

Finally, Newark Penn Station. I got off and walked so fast to the waiting area. I was in a hurry to see Viktor. I'd feel bad if he was standing there waiting for me at this time of night. He was usually in bed by now. I followed the signs and went to the waiting area. I looked around but couldn't see Viktor.

He's not here yet? I guess I got here before him. Maybe he has a long drive from his house, and it's longer than my train ride. At least there are a few people in the waiting area. See? Nothing to be concerned about. That makes me feel better.

An hour passed and I was still waiting for Viktor. Fewer people were waiting now. But I was confident and feeling a little proud of myself for taking the train and being by myself at the station. I waited, keeping an eye on the entrance doors.

It's three hours now, and I'm not so proud anymore. It's after midnight and I'm getting nervous. Hardly anyone is here, except the homeless, and some kind of weird looking people. It's not comfortable, but it's OK. I'm in America. I'll be fine. All I want to know is how much longer do I have to wait. Maybe his car broke down? Maybe he got into an accident? Maybe something went wrong. I hoped Viktor's OK.

I started to become irritated. I was sleepy but awake. I felt safe and unsafe at the same time. I was nervous and I was brave. I didn't know what to think. I never moved from my seat until someone sat right next to me, even though there were plenty of empty seats around. He was talking loudly, to himself. I was talking to myself too, but not out loud. He looked at me twice. He said something that I didn't understand, so I just slowly moved to the end of the bench. I didn't move fast because I didn't want to draw the attention of the others. Some of them gave me strange looks and were freaking me out. They looked like homeless alcoholics. When I looked at them, I saw glassy eyes. Who knows, maybe I looked the same way to them.

I put my head down and stopped looking. I was starting to hallucinate. I went to that place in your mind when you don't even know or care where you are. I didn't know the way to go and I had nowhere to go. I had zero energy. I had no emotion or desire. I didn't see anything or anybody. I was totally indifferent and exhausted, when I heard my name. I opened my eyes. Viktor was standing in front of me. It was 7:00 in the morning.

He just forgot about me.

NINE

It was a Saturday morning when Lora told me her relative Anna on Long Island might be looking for help. She had called and told her I was looking for a job. Lora told her I was experienced and promised she wouldn't regret hiring me. It was nice to hear that from Lora. Did she really think that, or did she just want this whole thing over with? Who cared? At this point I was willing to take any job.

Anna was anxious to meet me so she asked Lora if we could come by the next morning. I was so excited and nervous at the same time. Even though my previous interviews didn't go well, I was feeling confident about getting this one. But Lora told Anna she and Viktor had plans the next day, so they weren't able to take me.

I need to go there. I need to get this job. It's all I want.

Lora hung up the phone and sat down at the kitchen table staring out the window like she was thinking. After a while she went upstairs. She came down a few minutes later, grabbed her glass of water and went back upstairs again.

This is torturing me. I don't know what to do. I'm becoming irritated and impatient. I want to ask her if there's any way I can get there but now she seems distracted.

I was about to go upstairs when she came back downstairs. "My father, Alex, will pick you up tomorrow morning and take you to the interview with Anna," she said.

"Really?" I said as I jumped up and gave her a big hug. "Thank you for everything you're doing for me."

"You're welcome," she said with a smile. "It's all good. You'll be fine."

Her father, Alex? I'm not complaining but once again I'm about to take a ride with a stranger to some place I don't know? But it is nice to hear that Lora communicates with someone other than Viktor, especially a family member. I'm excited that I'll see someone new coming into the house. Hey, maybe I'll finally see the front door in action.

I was ready two hours early the next morning. Once again, I made myself look simple. I put on the same outfit, which made me laugh every time I looked in the mirror. The pair of jeans had become even baggier since I had lost weight over the last few weeks. It looked like I was wearing a man's jeans. Alex showed up exactly on time, which was nice. I heard him come into the house through the garage.

Even he comes into the house through the garage? I don't understand this system where everyone comes through the garage. What about the front door? Wait. I need to stop thinking about these silly little things. I'm going to leave this house soon anyway. Alex looks like a nice guy, maybe in his early seventies.

He had greeted me warmly and I hugged him. He said some things with a big grin. I thought he made some joke, so I smiled and pretended he was funny. Lora greeted her father with a nod. There wasn't much affection between the two of them. No hug or even an air kiss. Viktor came downstairs and said hi to Alex as he passed him on his way to the kitchen.

It seems strange that Alex and Viktor didn't hug or even shake hands but maybe every family and country has its own way. Maybe this is their way. I feel a little weird after hugging Alex, but he seems pretty delighted about it.

Lora gave him directions and told him what to do, so we were ready to go. His car was old and big, like the cars I'd seen in American movies. I got into the car and felt so tiny.

"Seat belt on please," Alex said.

"I'm sorry, what?"

Did I do something wrong? Was I not supposed to sit in the front?

I opened the car door to move to the back when he pointed to the seat belt, and I got it. The same thing happened with Lora when I got into her car. I kept forgetting to put my seat belt on because I wasn't used to it. No one used seat belts back home. They didn't even know they existed.

I put my seat belt on as I smiled at him. He was chatty as he drove. Since the radio was on, it was even harder than usual to understand what he was saying. He wanted to communicate, and I responded when I could. I always tried to be happy and friendly. I appreciated the ride, even though I knew he was doing the favor for his daughter and not for me. It was going to take about two and a half hours to get to Anna's house because of all the traffic. We were driving for about an hour when his phone rang.

"That was Anna," he said after a quick conversation. "She asked that we meet with her later because she has something urgent to take care of."

"Oh, OK," I said.

"It doesn't make sense to take you back to Lora's place since we're more than halfway there," he said. "I live about ten miles from here. We can just wait there for Anna's call."

"Alright," I said.

Like I have a choice? I really don't want to hang out with him, but this is what it is. I just have to deal with it.

"My wife just bought one of my favorite desserts, so we can have some cake and coffee while we wait," he said.

Well, at least he has a wife. Somehow that makes me feel better.

Their apartment was really small. A one bedroom with a tiny kitchen. It was clean and neat. The floors were shiny and there wasn't much furniture. The kitchen was also clean and well organized.

At least I can enjoy a piece of cake, which sounds good right about now.

I've always been a picky eater, even as a little girl. I wouldn't eat food from just anywhere, and especially not at somebody's house if it was messy or dirty. I always thought sloppy people in messy kitchens probably don't wash their hands much, so I'd be eating the food prepared by hands that have been who knows where. Gross.

One time a friend from school invited a few of us over to her house for dinner. We all went, and inside I saw a super messy house, and her mother sweating with what looked like dirty hair. I immediately lost my appetite. I'm thinking she was in the kitchen cooking this meal, standing over the stove, with sweat dripping down her forehead and onto the fried food. I couldn't eat anything when we all sat down for dinner. I made up a story that I wasn't able to eat fried food since I was taking some medication. It worked.

"Sit down. Make yourself comfortable," Alex said.

"Thank you," I said.

I was hoping to meet his wife, but she wasn't home. I went to the living room, sat on the couch and grabbed a magazine. I pretended to read but my mind was somewhere else. I couldn't wait for Anna to call so we could leave.

"Would you like some coffee or tea?" Alex asked.

"No, thank you," I said, even though I really wanted a cup of coffee.

"You're going to try one of my favorite cakes, right? Coffee or tea would go well with it. Come on, have some coffee or tea."

He was so kind. This time I said yes, and it felt great. I think I missed someone looking after me. He wanted me to feel comfortable, which was nice. He went to the kitchen and I heard dishes shuffling and coffee brewing.

"May I help?" I asked.

"No, no, you go back. Read your magazine and relax."

I remembered my grandfather. He used to like taking care of us too. Grandparents like doing that, I guess. I sat back down and continued flipping the magazine pages.

"Here's my favorite cake," Alex announced as he entered the living room, placing the tray with the coffee and a round cake with slices on the table. "This is a cheesecake. I like this variation because you can have a little bit of every flavor. This is the original; this is chocolate, vanilla, raspberry, caramel and blueberry," he said, pointing to different areas.

It looks like a bunch of colors to me.

"I'm sorry, what's the name of the cake?" I asked.

"Cheesecake. Do you know cheese?"

"Sure."

"And do you know cake?"

"Yes."

"So, this is cheese and cake. Cheesecake," and he laughed.

What's so funny? I don't understand if he's offering me cheese or cake? Whoever heard of combining cheese and cake?

"Here's your coffee. Please pick any piece of cake you want," he said as he sat next to me.

I was sitting in the middle of the sofa and there were a couple of armchairs near the coffee table. But Alex decided to sit on the sofa. Maybe it was his favorite seat, or he was just used to it. It was kind of awkward sitting so close to each other and having a conversation, so I slowly moved a little bit to the right. After a few sips of coffee, I noticed he moved closer. I moved again, and so did he. Then I stopped and grabbed my coffee again for a few more sips. He grabbed the plate.

"Go on, try a piece. It's really good," he said.

"Can we cut a piece in half? They look really big."

"No, no, it's not that big. Try it and you'll see. I bet you'll finish the whole thing."

This is getting stupid.

I just picked the chocolate one, which made him happy. Before I took a bite, I moved slightly to the right again, and then he did too.

What is wrong with this guy? Why are these weird things happening to me? I didn't give him any reason to act like this. I was just being friendly. He's the same age as my grandfather for Christ's sake. But I don't want to say anything to him. Maybe it's just a habit. I'm getting impatient for that phone call.

I ate a piece, and it was delicious.

"This is very good, thank you," I said as I moved to the right again. By now I was at the end of the sofa.

"See? I knew you'd like it!" he said, and now, he was right next to me.

This isn't a habit. He's just some old man who wants to be close to a young girl.

We were so close our legs and forearms touched. I froze and stared straight ahead, not looking at him. I didn't know how to react. He suddenly went quiet and put down his plate. I reached to grab my cup of coffee when I felt his hand on my thigh. I jumped up, spilling some coffee.

"Where's the bathroom?" I asked.

"Just around that corner, in the hall."

I stayed in the bathroom for a while, washing my face with cold water. I was blushing. I almost started to cry but then became angry.

I want to take that piece of cheesecake and smash it in his face and then pour that cup of coffee right on his head.

I came out from the bathroom with an attitude and sat on the armchair opposite him, without looking at him. I completely ignored him.

Sometimes when you try to be warm and friendly to another person, they misread it for flirting and try to take advantage of you. Just because someone acts nice and treats you well it doesn't mean there's an attraction. I knew this. I should've kept my distance from a stranger until I got to know them, but I had let my guard down.

Luckily the phone rang, and we had to go. He knew I was pissed, and he became quiet. His party was over. He didn't even ask me if I was going to finish the stupid cheesecake as he quickly cleared the table. He put it all in the kitchen and we left.

What about his wife? Did he even have one? No, he did. They had pictures of themselves in the living room, at different places. They looked like a lovely couple.

There weren't any jokes or laughs while he was driving now. I sat in the back and any conversation between us was over. I thought he was a kind grandfather, but he turned into a creep in a heartbeat.

When we had reached the house for the interview, I was astonished by its size. This wasn't a house. It was a palace. It was so big that I couldn't imagine just four people living there. I pictured myself living in this house and it made me excited, even though it was for work.

It was a Victorian style house with huge rooms. Inside was beautiful, with a big foyer opening up into a dining room with large windows. It had a long hallway with many individual rooms and a huge open kitchen at the end. I couldn't keep track of how many doors I saw. The house had a basement with a playroom for the kids and a gym for the adults. There was an upstairs with two individual rooms and a bathroom for house workers. A young woman opened the door and pointed to the large living room, which looked like an entire apartment. There, waiting for me, was Anna.

She seemed pleasant, right from the beginning. We sat down and she explained the job. I tried to understand but it didn't matter. I would agree to whatever she wanted me to do. She didn't spend much time with me. She seemed rushed. She walked with me as we made our way out of the house and told me she'd call Lora to let her know her decision.

I'm confident about getting this job, just like last time. I think she liked me, and we had good chemistry. I wish she would've just hired me right then and there, but she had to talk to her husband first. I don't get it. Why all the formality? It's just housekeeping, mostly.

She was a busy lawyer and her husband owned a business. He was around the house more often than her. They had a four-year-old girl and a five-month-old boy. They already had a babysitter for the two of them. She needed another person in the house who would do house cleaning, laundry, and help the babysitter whenever she needed it. It didn't seem too hard, and there wouldn't be much English needed.

She walked me to the car where Alex was waiting for me. He got out and said hello to her. They had a brief conversation while I was sitting in the car. I sat in the back seat again. As Alex drove, he kept looking back at me through the rearview mirror.

"She liked you," he said. "She just needs her husband to agree."

"Thank you."

I can't even look at his face. It makes me nauseous.

"Goodbye," Alex said as he dropped me off.

I left the car without a word, went inside and waited.

TEN

Leaving Lora and Viktor's house was a relief. I finally landed a job. Anna called the night before and told Lora she wanted me to start working the next day. Lora asked her father for help again. I didn't want to see this guy anymore, but I had no choice. I wasn't nervous or afraid of him. I just didn't want to deal with him. If he even so much as brushed up against me, I'd slap him. That I knew for sure. I sat in the back seat again and didn't even look at him. He acted as if nothing happened and was being chatty and sweet like before.

I had a contract with Lora and Viktor. Now and then one of them would drive to Anna's house to pick up my salary until I paid them off. After that, they would return my passport. I was now a live-in helper for six days with one day off. I didn't need any spending money during my workdays, so that was helpful. For my one day off, I asked Anna if I could just stay in my room, since I had nowhere to go. Fortunately, she agreed.

Alex dropped me off in front of Anna's house and drove away. He didn't even wait until someone opened the door. I rang the bell and waited for a while. I rang again and waited. The house was big so it could take a while for someone to walk to the front door. As I rang a third time and nobody answered, I felt a pain in my arm from holding my yellow suitcase. I put the suitcase down and sat on the stairs.

I just sat and waited. Somebody would show up eventually. I wasn't concerned or anything. It was just weird. When I looked around, I could just about see a neighbor's large house. There was a lot of land for each home. I ended up in the middle of nowhere again, but with better housing.

Where is the shiny, exciting, crowded, fun city that I saw on television? It must be around here somewhere. I hope I can go there soon and that it's like what I imagine.

Forty minutes passed. I was daydreaming when a mailman approached the house and said hi as he handed me the mail and some magazines. I looked at the mailing label. Anna and Michael Weizmann.

Nice names.

I rang the bell again even though I thought no one was home. But then Anna opened the door looking like she was half asleep, with her hair all messed up.

"Come on in," she said. "I'm so sorry. I fell asleep."

She was home by herself. No kids, no husband. The house seemed peaceful.

I happily grabbed my suitcase and walked into the house. She looked astonished that I was carrying this huge suitcase. I pretended it was light and fancy.

"I decided to work from home today," she said. "This way I can show you the house and explain the job."

What kind of work from home job includes falling asleep?

I followed her as she showed me the room where I was going to stay. It was up a narrow set of stairs and I had a hard time with the suitcase. I had to stop a few times to take a break and change hands. She didn't see me struggling up the stairs since she walked so fast and didn't look back. The room was small, clean and bright. The entire house looked brand new. There was one single bed and a small dresser. On the same floor was another bedroom that belonged to the babysitter, and a bathroom we would share.

"Make yourself at home and let me know if you need anything. After you get settled in a little bit come downstairs and we can get started," she said as she left the room.

I sat down on the bed. I had a room to sleep in, a job, and I could start paying off my loan. I closed my eyes and tried to relax, but I was too excited. I changed my clothes and went downstairs.

"The house is so beautiful," I told her.

"Thank you, it's brand new. It's a gift from my husband. He had it built for me. We also have a place in Manhattan, so we go back and forth. But we're mostly here. Do you know Manhattan?"

"Yes, I know Manhattan, or at least I've heard of it. I haven't seen it yet."

"You've never seen it?"

"No, unfortunately."

"You will," she smiled. "Here's a notebook and pen so you can write some things down. I'll show you around and explain the job."

She showed me every room and explained in detail what I was supposed to do. How to do the laundry, how to clean the rooms. There were a lot of instructions and as I was writing, I became completely confused. The laundry had all these rules. Which clothes to wash together and with what water and soap. Which cleaning products to use, depending on what you were cleaning. I never saw so many different cleaning products.

Her bedroom was huge, with a walk-in closet and a huge bathroom with a standing shower and a big Jacuzzi bath. The most complicated place was the kitchen. There were actually two kitchens in one area. There were duplicates of everything—appliances, sinks and utensils—because they were a devout Jewish family. She explained that dairy and meat couldn't be eaten together, so even the silverware and all the dishes were separate. They couldn't even touch each other so they had separate cabinets. She said I had to follow their eating rules while I was in the house.

My head was spinning. I didn't understand all the rules. But the most shocking moment was when she opened a door and took me into what she called the "food storage room". It looked like a big grocery store. Shelves took up all the walls, each stacked with food. I had no idea what was what, but there were boxes, packages, cans of foods, bottles of water and all kinds of juices.

I would never think of collecting this much food. I know they're rich people, but why? Why store so much food? Did they hear a war might be starting soon and they had to be prepared?

But I did love that room the most. I used to go there in my free time, like going to an art gallery. I'd look and try to make out the meaning on the labels. After all the instructions she told me to relax the rest of the day and meet her at 6:30 the next morning.

I met her in the kitchen right on time. She was all dressed and in a hurry. I already knew what I had to do that day, but she asked me to add one other thing. She asked me to make dinner for her and her husband.

Wait … what? She never mentioned cooking in the interview.

"I'm not sure I can cook," I said. "I don't know the products and I can't read the labels."

"Don't worry. I wrote down the recipe and all you have to do is follow the instructions. Thank you so much. I really appreciate it. I have to go now. Have a nice day. Bye."

She ran out so fast I couldn't even respond. I looked at the recipe. I could read some of the descriptions and the ingredients, but I didn't know what the products looked like.

Geez, I can barely read her writing. I guess I'll go to that food storage room and look for the stuff. I can't focus on anything else until I figure out how to make this dinner.

I grabbed the piece of paper and went into the food storage room. I stayed in the room looking at the writing and then tried to find the right product. I did this over and over again. I had no idea what ingredients to collect for this recipe. I became nervous. It was my first day and I wanted to do well so they would keep me on.

The babysitter was near the kitchen area taking care of the kids as she watched me. She could tell something was wrong as I went back and forth to that "food Disneyland". She was a Hispanic girl named Kalian. She came to me and asked me to give her the recipe and hold the baby. She took the recipe, and collected all the right ingredients. We kind of exchanged jobs for a little bit.

"Thank you so much Kalian. I really appreciate it."

"No problem. If you ever need anything, just ask. I'm happy to help."

"That's very nice of you. Thanks again."

She was a kind person. I got my notebook and started my work. I did some extra cleaning work even though Anna didn't ask me to, trying to impress my new employers. Then it was dinner time. Since I had all the right ingredients, I felt fairly confident I could prepare a nice meal. Kalian would stop by the kitchen now and then to make sure I was all right. She mentioned that the house had cameras recording everything, so I should try not to mess anything up.

By the time Anna and Michael came home I had finished all my work and the dinner. Chicken in tomato sauce with vegetables. It smelled delicious, and Anna thought so too. I didn't take a break all day. I felt a little tired, but the family had a couple of friends over for dinner, so Anna asked me to help.

I set the table and served them. While they were having drinks and dinner I stayed in the kitchen. Anna didn't tell me I could go to my room, so I didn't know what to do. I was shy to ask her if I was done for the day, so I stayed in the kitchen until all the guests left. That evening seemed so long. I was standing and hanging out in the kitchen like an idiot.

I'm starting to feel a little sad. Look at my feet. They're all swollen from standing all day. I've never been a servant before. I'd help my family or friends but that was different. It was my choice. When I serve others like this, I feel like I don't belong to myself. I can't believe my swollen ankles. I used to walk so much, and this never happened. What's different now? Maybe it's because I was up at 6:30 and now it's around ten and I had no down time. This is pretty brutal.

While I was hanging out, Michael would come to the kitchen for more drinks and just smile at me. Instead of just standing there, I'd pretend I was busy doing some work. There was nothing else to do. I did all the cleaning. The kitchen was ready to be closed and I was ready for bed.

It's no one's fault but my own that I'm too shy to ask to leave. I hate my shyness. They're busy with dinner and their guests so obviously they're not thinking of me.

I cleaned the kitchen area, again.

"Thank you so much for dinner," Anna said. "The chicken was more than delicious. Goodnight."

That's nice to hear that but somehow, I know I'll be getting "the cooking recipe of the day" from now on.

"Goodnight," I said.

"Yes, thanks again for everything," Michael said as he opened the refrigerator and grabbed a big carton of ice cream. He sat at the table eating the ice cream with a big spoon.

Well, this is new. I've been learning so many interesting things since I landed in this country. Having ice cream in the middle of the night? And he's scooping it out, like he's determined to finish it all? I would never think of having so much ice cream all at once. Back home, we only have it in the summer, and always during the day. Maybe in the evening on a hot summer day we'd have a scoop or two.

I probably look surprised, so he offered me some. I wanted to try American ice cream, but I said no thank you.

"No? It's delicious and this one? Mint chocolate chip. It's one of my favorites. You should try some next time."

"OK, next time. Goodnight," I said as I turned to leave.

All I want to do is go upstairs to my room.

When I got to the room, I was so tired I thought I would crash in a second. But instead I laid down on the bed and cried. I cried so hard. I looked at my swollen ankles and I cried some more. I felt sorry for myself. And I had the same questions that I had back home, standing and looking in the mirror.

Why? Why me? Why am I doing this to myself? At home I was poor, but at least I was surrounded by people I love, sleeping in my own house and my own bed. Is this what I want? Do I really want to work for these people and lock myself in someone else's house? My mind is going dark, where I had visited many times, and I don't like it at all. I always try to escape but I keep going back. I need to stop. It's not healthy or helpful at all.

I knew that. I was fully aware of it. But my subconscious mind was so powerful that it pulled me along.

I miss my house and my country. I miss my friends and having a good time. I wish I was with them. Maybe I made a big mistake coming here. I don't care about the money, or the future. Or do I? Wait a minute. What about all the bad stuff? Remember how hard life is there? Did I forget how I struggled financially, and not only me but my entire family? Did I forget that there's no path to success? Just a seemingly endless road of misery, disrupted now and then by the joy of being with family and friends, mostly fueled by alcohol. What I have here is an opportunity to change my life, and all I'm thinking about are the good times back home?

I even feel uncomfortable in this beautiful house and in this nice clean, brand new room. It would be nice to have this room back home. But I hate this room. I don't give a shit about the money. I want to go home, but I don't even have the money to do that. Or my passport.

I remember all the guys who were in love with me, or at least they said they were. The old ones and the new ones. I miss them all. I appreciate their love for me now. Not so much before. I miss my best friend, Nikki. I forgive her for what she did. She's so smart and lucky she stayed there. I picture everybody and everything as so beautiful over there.

The mind is remarkable. When it gives you a signal of your desire for something or someone, everything needed to make it happen feels so positive and beautiful, even when in reality, it's not. It can actually be worse for you. We just want it all. It's like a little kid who just wants candy, cake and oh by the way, that toy, too.

I have to stop torturing myself. Either I have to find a way to go back home now or just deal with this until I have my own money and then make a decision. I'm ashamed of myself, thinking like this. I was fine all day. I felt strong, motivated, positive. I learned a lot and the couple seems to be happy with my work. I have a job and at the end of the week, I'm going to get paid. I'm living in a beautiful house with nice people. What else do I want, my evil, subconscious mind?

Before I could answer I drifted off to sleep. The loud alarm woke me the next morning. I was in a better mood. More calm and peaceful. But I felt so sore. My legs were hurting, and my arms ached, especially the right one. I could barely get out of bed.

Maybe I didn't sleep properly? The bed felt pretty comfortable but maybe I slept on my right arm all night? Oh wait. I was sore from all the work the day before. I was working and moving around all day and my body isn't used to it. All I did the last few weeks was sit on my butt like a sack of potatoes, waiting for work.

The thought made me smile.

I went downstairs to make coffee for the homeowners before they got up. I didn't expect to see Michael standing in the kitchen. He was the last one to leave the kitchen, and here he was.

Does this guy ever leave the kitchen?

He made coffee and was having a cup by the glass door looking out into the backyard. I got confused.

I know I'm on time and making coffee is one of my jobs. Maybe I was supposed to start work earlier?

"Good morning, Michael," I said with a smile.

"Good morning," he said.

He seems agitated. Last night he was friendly, but this morning he's different. Maybe he isn't a morning person, but then, why is he up before anyone else?

"Let me show you something," he said.

He opened up the dishwasher in one of the kitchens and then the other dishwasher in the other kitchen.

"You mixed the dairy and meat silverware, and washed them together, which is unacceptable. See the difference in the designs? The dairy has this fancy ornament and the meat silverware has none."

I'm sure Anna told me about this but either I didn't understand or didn't remember. This is a big deal for them. He's not happy. I feel so bad.

"Oh … I'm … I'm really sorry," I said.

He's just staring at me, not saying a word. This is becoming awkward. Oh, here comes Anna. I'm sorry, but I'm kind of happy to see her. I'm not getting anywhere with moody Michael.

"I'm very sorry, Anna," I said. "I guess I didn't really understand the silverware rules."

"It's OK, you're still learning. We'll just have to buy new ones. Please grab all of them and put them in the garbage."

Really? Throw them all out? They're serious about these meat and dairy rules.

But I felt relieved. She was much nicer than her husband. She handed me my "to do" list and grabbed a cup of coffee.

"Have a nice day," she said as she hurried back to her room.

Over the coming weeks, I noticed she was always in a rush. She was a lawyer who worked in Manhattan. She left for work before her husband and came home after he did. She'd come home, have a quick dinner, quickly play with her kids, and then go to her bedroom, quickly. She probably even slept quickly.

I worked extra hard that day. I cleaned her office even though it wasn't on the list. I wanted to do something nice for her since she was nice to me that morning. When I saw her office, it was such a mess I couldn't resist cleaning it. There were three trash cans, all full. When she came home and saw her office, she thanked me.

The day went well. I was swamped and didn't have time to think of anything negative. Once again, my new best friend Kalian helped me find the right ingredients for preparing dinner. I would also help her if she needed me to hold the baby for a while. The baby boy, Aaron, was cute and quiet. He liked being carried. The four-year-old girl, Jessica, wasn't so friendly or happy. She didn't like to eat, so every meal was an adventure. She would cry and cry while Kalian would try to get her to eat. But she liked sweets, and she knew where to find them. She would try to sneak into the "food Disneyland" to grab some cookies or candy.

It was hard to take care of both these kids at the same time. I didn't know how Kalian was handling all this, but she seemed to manage. I guess she was a professional. When Kalian wouldn't let the girl have any sweets, Jessica would cry hysterically. I didn't like this little girl, and she knew it. She always gave me a nasty look. I wanted to give it right back to her, but I was afraid there might be cameras around. Kalian was patient with her. She would keep saying no until the little girl finally gave up. I probably wouldn't be so patient. Watching all this made me happy to take care of the house rather than the kids.

The house had five bedrooms and four baths. The kids had their own rooms. The couple had their master bedroom and there were two guest rooms. When Michael came home, I was doing the laundry and just stayed there for a while. Even the laundry room was huge. It was so easy and comfortable to hang out there. He came to the laundry room to make sure I wasn't screwing anything else up. He corrected me on how to wash and fold the clothes. He seemed to take an interest in how I was taking care of things. I was a little surprised by that. I didn't think a guy would care about house cleaning and stuff.

That day was long. I stayed in the kitchen until they finished dinner again. I made sure I studied the china and silverware designs and was fairly sure I put them in the right dishwashers, but I was still nervous. I didn't want to see Michael in the kitchen the next morning, waiting to tell me what I did wrong.

I went back to my room and realized I didn't eat anything all day but an apple. I focused so hard on doing a good job that I forgot to take any breaks. I thought I should eat, to keep up my energy for work. I thought about going to the kitchen to maybe grab something, but I had no energy to make the trip downstairs.

I laid down and again became sad and ended up crying—the same thing that happened the night before. I was fine during the day, but not so good at night. I hoped the sadness and all the negative thoughts were over. But they weren't. They hit me again, even harder than before.

I can't keep doing this for long. I can't do this job and be so uncomfortable. I want to give it all up and go home. I don't care. I want to leave. I've been crying for so long, and hard. I can't seem to calm myself down. How can I find a way to go home? My biggest problem is money. Again. Money was the problem with getting here and it's the problem with leaving here. What am I doing? Or thinking? I have no money to buy a plane ticket. That's a fact. Of the hundred dollars I borrowed from my neighbor to get here I have forty left. I spent sixty buying the phone cards to call home. The phone cards are damn expensive. They cost five dollars for five minutes. What's five minutes? It's like "Hello, Mom? It's me." And that's it. By the time she calmed down from being excited to hear from me, the five minutes were gone.

Of course, forty dollars won't be enough to escape. I know I have to stay here and work, to pay for my ticket, plus interest, and pay my neighbor back. She helped me so much. I know it was only a hundred dollars, but it made a big difference. At least I know I have a few bucks for emergencies. I need more than just ticket money. I have no chance to get away. I feel so sick and unhappy with myself once again. I don't even have anyone to ask for help. But I never like asking for money anyway.

I closed my eyes but couldn't sleep. Even all that crying didn't help me go numb and pass out.

ELEVEN

I slept for about two hours when the alarm went off. I hated the alarm. But then again, who doesn't? It's the worst. It reminded me of when I went to school and didn't want to get up, so I'd pretend I didn't hear it. I wouldn't move in bed. I hoped my mom didn't hear it either so I'd miss school.

Kids are funny when it comes to things like that. Yeah, like she would just forget about me. I'd lay there in silence until Mom would come into my room and say it was time to get up. Then she would scream from the kitchen, the bathroom and anywhere else she'd go until she heard me get up. Her voice annoyed me as much as the alarm. But we'd go through the same routine every school day. I think real success is when you get up when you want to instead of when you have to.

I got up an hour earlier than the day before to beat Michael to the kitchen. I wanted to get there before him so I would make the coffee. It was my job and I didn't want Anna knowing that her husband was making the coffee instead of me.

Good. No one's in the kitchen, so now I can figure out how to make coffee with this contraption. Everything is different here. Even the coffee pot is different. I'm learning everything, like a child.

After a failed attempt, the coffee came out right. I felt relieved. I got up way too early, so I was waiting for a while until they all came to the kitchen. Anna got her coffee and gave me all the jobs for the day and started to leave.

"Anna," I said. "May I use the phone to call my family? I know it costs money, but I'll pay for the call."

"Sure, you can. I don't know how much it costs but when the bill arrives you can pay me then."

"Thanks."

Nice. I found the courage to ask her. I lied about calling my family, but that shouldn't matter to her.

"Oh, by the way," she said as she turned around. "Is there any problem with the food? I've noticed you don't eat much. Are there any specific foods you like? I can get them for you."

"No, but thank you. I wasn't really hungry these past few days, but I'm fine. I'll eat today."

"And you can take a break at lunchtime," she added.

"Yes, thanks Anna."

How did she know I wasn't eating? Did she check everything on the cameras? Or maybe the babysitter told her I wasn't eating? I'm completely under their control in this house. It makes me uncomfortable and paranoid. I want to do everything right and perfect. But if I screw up, they'll see that too. I don't like the idea of them watching me all the time. I don't think anybody does. It feels weird, even when you don't do anything wrong.

Around lunchtime I decided to take a break and force myself to eat. Kalian took the kids downstairs so I was in the kitchen by myself. I wanted to sit and have a quiet lunch. I like silence when I eat. I like to focus on the food and not having a conversation at the same time. I was so sure Kalian would want to chat if she stayed in the kitchen.

I was still thinking about Anna's comment about my eating habits. I guess she cared about me. I decided to have a nice, solid lunch. I found a piece of bread, chicken and cheese. I made a nice sandwich with mayo and lettuce. I wasn't hungry but I ate anyway. I needed the energy, and I had to put on a show for the camera. It was a pleasant meal. Kalian and the kids came upstairs. Perfect timing.

"Hi Kalian. I still have some break time left so I'm going upstairs to my room."

"OK, did you have your lunch?" she asked with a smile.

"Yes, and it was really good."

The sandwich made me feel a little better, and happier. But maybe it wasn't so much the sandwich as the phone call I was about to make. It was a nice, sunny day in May. I went to my room. I rolled up the shade and looked outside. The warm sun felt good on my face. It felt chilly all morning, maybe because I didn't have much sleep the night before. I laid down and closed my eyes. I felt relaxed but excited about making the phone call. Suddenly, my eyes got big. I shot out of bed.

Crap. That lunch. Chicken and cheese together. Strictly a no-no in this house. Here we go again. I was probably recorded and would be busted! I wish I could find that damn tape and get rid of it. I can feel my face becoming flushed. I'm starting to panic. I need some fresh air.

I tried to open the window, but the handle was a different style.

Why the hell is everything so different here?

I finally opened the window all the way. I took a deep breath and just started to calm down when I jumped again, startled by a super loud siren. So annoying. I looked outside but didn't see anything. The siren was wailing non-stop.

Wait. Oh no ... no ... NO! Is that coming from inside the house? Are you kidding me?

I remembered. I was told not to open the windows or any outside doors. The siren was from the security system. My heart started beating fast. I didn't know what to do. I screwed up, again.

There are way too many rules in this house!

I ran downstairs so fast I almost fell. I sped down the long corridor like I was doing a hundred-yard dash in the Olympics. I saw Kalian in the den earlier watching television, but she wasn't there. The siren was so loud it could make you deaf. It was just like the sirens in the war movies. I ran into the kitchen and found her standing near the wall, pushing the buttons in a box attached to the wall. Her fingers were shaking as she pushed the bottoms. She kept trying but it wasn't going well. She was getting frustrated and stressed. She finally got it right and the siren suddenly stopped.

"Well, that was exciting," she said with a smile.

I ran over and hugged her.

"I am so, so sorry," I said.

"No big deal. It happens. Thank God I remembered the code and entered it in time. Otherwise the police would soon be knocking on the door."

I feel so bad. I made her do something to fix my mistake. It seems I can't get through a day without having to apologize. What is wrong with me? I'm distracted. I'm here but I'm not. Here physically but not mentally. That's what's wrong with me.

"Oh my God," I said. "That would be bad. Thanks again Kalian."

I was about to ask Kalian to do me a favor and keep this accident between us, and not mention it to Anna and Michael when the phone rang.

I hope it isn't one of them.

Kalian answered the phone. It was the security monitoring service calling to make sure everything was OK.

"Sorry, it was an accident," Kalian said. "Everything is fine thanks … The security code word? Paris … OK, thanks, bye."

I exhaled.

"Hey Kalian. Can you please do me a …" and the phone rang again.

"Hello?" Kalian answered. "Oh, hi Michael."

No! Please Kalian, don't tell him anything!

"It's all good Michael," she said. "Yes, the security company also called, and I told them it was all a mistake … Yes … thanks, bye".

"Thanks again, so much Kalian, for taking care of this," I said.

"No worries. Just another day," she said with a smile.

I don't want to see these people when they come home but there's no way to avoid them. This accident messed up all my happy feelings about the phone call I wanted to make. I know I have no choice. I have to deal with them. I have to continue this job and do what I have to do, but it's hard to focus. I'm too distracted by my thoughts.

I had to make dinner and thankfully I got help from my buddy Kalian. She helped me find the correct ingredients once again. Kalian even complimented my cooking. Who knew I would end up cooking and would be good at it? My mother would be so proud of me if she could see me. She's a great cook. She made meals almost every day. Even when she didn't have enough ingredients, somehow she would create a great dish with whatever was in the kitchen. Sometimes there wasn't enough money for food. I have heard that you have to have good hands to make tasty food. It's not all about ingredients and recipes. It's more of an art. Enjoying it and putting much love into it. I guess my mother had all of that.

I wish she could have seen the food storage room. There was so much choice it would be so easy to make just about anything. All I was doing was following Anna's recipes, which she printed out from a website. No creativity at all. But I still enjoyed making a nice meal. I made beef stew with vegetables and asked Kalian to try it. She enjoyed it. She thought she could finish the whole casserole.

I barely cooked back home but my mother would force me to watch her and learn. Cooking was mandatory for a woman from her perspective. So, I would help her prepare the dishes. I guess I picked up some cooking skills while hanging around her.

I did some extra work around the house to try to make up for the stupid alarm incident and the chicken and cheese sandwich. I thought it might help avoid the attitude I was getting from Michael, with his rolling eyes. I cleaned the stove and decided to take out the garbage, which was Michael's job. I didn't know why it was his job, but he seemed to do it every night before having his ice cream and going to bed.

When I pulled the bag from the garbage it was quite heavy. The bag was almost as big as me. Probably the same weight as me too, but I pulled hard and grabbed it with both hands as it came out. I walked toward the back door, the same one I saw Michael use when he took out the garbage. I unlocked the glass door to slide it open, grabbed the garbage bag and stepped outside, when I heard the familiar, unpleasant, most disturbing sound of the siren once again.

I did it again? What the hell? I can't believe it! Why am I having such a hard time remembering all the rules? Maybe I'm just not used to living like this. I never had to stop and think before opening doors or windows!

I didn't get mad at myself this time. I got mad at all these rules I was dealing with. I put the bag in a big garbage can next to the house. I hoped I put it in the right place but at that point I didn't care. I was so tired of this and I wasn't happy about going inside and apologizing to Kalian, again. I wanted to just run away but there was nowhere to go.

I saw Kalian running from the hall to stop the siren. She was running while pushing Aaron in the stroller, with Jessica running behind her, screaming. What a scene. The little girl's screaming sounded just like the siren. Kalian kept asking her to stop but that only made her scream louder. Then Aaron decided to join in the fun and started crying. It was a madhouse, and it was because of me.

I took the stroller from Kalian and started gently rocking it so maybe he'd stop crying. I asked Jessica to take my hand, but she resisted and cried even louder to leave her alone.

"This is all your fault and I'm not going to you," she screamed as she grabbed Kalian's skirt.

Kalian saved me again, with the same routine as last time, including taking the calls from Michael and the security company. Kalian looked at me as I stood in the kitchen. She didn't say anything but after a while she just smiled. I smiled back. I was even more embarrassed.

When Anna and Michael came home, I expected the first subject would be the alarm incidents. But my obsession wasn't theirs. When they came home, they didn't even mention it. But of course, I continued to overthink it.

Was it no big deal or were they mad at me and giving me the silent treatment? I always prefer to have a conversation to make things clear and avoid any misunderstandings.

Sometimes when we do something wrong, we think too much of it. We think others feel the same way we do but it's usually not true. Most of the time they understand and quickly move on, because they're more concerned about their own lives. As long as it doesn't affect them, your mistakes aren't their priority. They didn't do anything wrong; you did.

I still had some work to finish up before my day was over. I was headed to the laundry room to finish folding some clothes. When I was done and heading to my room, I passed the bathroom and I heard Anna call me.

"Hey Alyssa," she said. "Come on in. We're giving Aaron a bath. Do you want to watch?"

Not really.

"Look at him," Anna said. "Doesn't he look so adorable sitting in the bath?"

Anna was happily watching Aaron as Kalian washed the baby. Anna was kind of helping her, splashing water on Aaron, playing with him. He was so happy, laughing out loud. He really was adorable. I did enjoy watching him having fun in the bathtub with his toys. I stayed there until bath time was over. I wanted to leave and go back to my room but thought it would be rude. I watched Kalian dry Aaron, wrap him in a fresh towel and hand the boy to Anna.

"Well, goodnight everyone," Kalian said as she turned to leave. "Have a nice weekend."

She's leaving the house for the weekend? Oh right, she has Saturday and Sunday off. I only have Monday off. I can't picture myself being in this house without her. She gives me so much support. It's great having her around. But sometimes when we depend on somebody the learning process goes slowly, and it doesn't help us become independent and confident. Maybe it's good that she's gone for a couple of days, so I can figure things out on my own. Taking responsibility for myself and my mistakes would make me stronger, although the learning process will probably be painful.

"Come with me," Anna said as she headed towards the baby's room. "Hold Aaron, please?"

I gently took the baby from her.

"Since Kalian has the weekend off, I want to show you, I mean teach you, some tips, just so you know," she said.

I'm not sure I like where this is going.

"This is the baby's sleeping monitor. Take it with you. If you hear him cry during the night, you'll need to go to his room and take care of him. He usually needs to be fed or have a diaper change. Let me show you how to feed him and change the diaper."

She went on and on. Explained it all to me. Of course, by now I realized I was taking on Kalian's job. I couldn't say no, but I also didn't expect to be taking care of a five-month-old baby.

So now I'm the housekeeper, cook and babysitter. I have three jobs so far. It's like I'm getting promoted every other day, but without the pay raise. Maybe I didn't understand her English well enough, but I don't remember any of this from when she interviewed me. Was I that good at these jobs? She obviously trusts me enough to take care of Aaron. Maybe I should be flattered, but it seems if I'm doing more I should be paid more. But what can I do?

I took the monitor and went up to my room. Sadly, instead of having a relaxed place, my room was the opposite. Every time I was in the room, I got depressed. A downward spiral of emotions to a place I didn't want to be. Where I didn't see any potential or any future. Did all these emotions make any sense? I didn't know. What I did know was that my depression was getting worse as time went by. I knew I needed time to adapt to everything new. I thought I'd be getting better but instead it was getting worse. I was overwhelmed. Perfect time to make a phone call. The sooner I made the call, the sooner I'd get home.

I looked for my purse. I didn't have much use for my purse lately and I missed it. I missed carrying it with me and being a girly girl, going out with it. It was the only purse I had. It came with me everywhere I went, for everyday use and special occasions. This purse witnessed many of my dates and my hanging out with my friends and family. This purse was one of my best friends, knowing all my moods and secrets.

Girls and their purses are best friends. We can't be without them. But these days my purse and I don't need each other. Not with the life I'm living. No need to carry makeup or personal stuff. I hope one day, very soon, I'll be back in a place when I'll need my purse.

I grabbed my small, light blue, faded leather purse with the broken zipper. Only I knew the zipper was broken. It wasn't noticeable, and also wasn't fixable. It was irreplaceable since I couldn't afford a new one. It was me and my secret purse, together again. I grabbed it and held it tight. I held it up to my chest, and then to my face, to smell that leather. It reminded me of my past life. Only good memories.

Why is it that it's just happy memories? Where are all the bad memories? I have a bunch of them. I have more bad ones than good ones. Somehow, I only think of the good ones.

I took the small notebook out to find the phone number. I was going to call Tobi, the guy I met before I left home. The guy who liked me and begged me not to leave. He was the guy who offered to help me with anything, who told me I was making a mistake to come here, the guy who wasn't happy that I had resisted his offer to stay with him. I was sure when I called this guy, he'd be really happy to hear from me. This guy would be more than happy to help me, if I asked.

I'm going to call him, even though I'm not even remotely attracted to him. This phone call won't include a promise of any relationship between us. I'm only going to ask him for help to escape from here, a one-way airplane ticket back home. I'm sure he'll do his best for me. He seemed like that kind of person.

I flipped a few notebook pages and found his number. My savior's phone number. I grabbed the phone to dial. It was a perfect time to talk as long as needed, since everyone was asleep. I could talk all night. I noticed no one used the phone at night. It never rang after 8 p.m.

I heard my heart beating in my head as I dialed the number. It went through. I waited but didn't hear a sound. I hung up and tried again. Same result. No sound at all. I became more anxious about making this phone call. I dialed once more, waited once more, heard silence once more and finally I heard "The number you have dialed is no longer in service." I hung up and dialed a few more times and heard the same message.

What happened to Tobi? How is this possible? I have to reach him. The only chance I have is to connect with him. I need to find a way to get his contact information. My notebook! One of my friends will have his number. I can call and ask. They'll want to know why I need his number but I'm not going to tell them about my situation. I'll make up some story.

I liked my plan. I called one of my friends. When she heard and recognized my voice, she started screaming. I wasn't expecting such a happy reaction from her. We weren't such close friends, but she made a big deal of it. Her screaming and excitement went on for so long, and it was costing me a lot of money. I wasn't able to get a word in to let her know why I was calling. She assumed I was calling to speak with her. Someone calling from America was a big deal. I knew the next day more than half the city would know that she received a call from overseas. I felt bad to tell her the real reason for calling. So, I ended up making some small talk with her for a little while.

"Oh, by the way, how is Tobi?" I finally asked.

"He's OK. Same as always," she said.

"Do you have his phone number? I tried to call the number he gave me, but it didn't work. He must have a new one. I thought I'd call him to say hello."

"Sure, I'll get you his new number."

It never happened.

TWELVE

Life is like a dream. The past doesn't exist except as something in our mind. We meet people, make some connections, maybe have a relationship with them, or not. Our lives are like bubbles. One day you're here, and then … pop! You disappear.

That's the way I was feeling. It was like Tobi didn't exist anymore, just like his phone number. Maybe he existed for others, but not for me. People move in and out of our lives constantly, just like the earth rotating, unnoticeably. The tyranny of time. I remember reading that somewhere.

I took a deep breath and stayed in one position while looking out the window. It was dark and quiet. I didn't even see any moonlight. I never usually liked silence and moonless nights. It makes me sad. But this time it felt fine. I needed to calm myself down, relax my mind. I believe things happen for a reason. I needed to observe my thoughts and emotions. I wanted to find a way to separate my emotions from my rational mind. These two weren't playing well together. I needed to think differently, so I could become stronger, and keep going on the road I'd chosen, and believe in it.

As usual for the last few nights, I quietly sobbed myself to sleep. I had a nightmare that I once again opened the window and triggered the siren. I was trying to stop it, but it was going on and on. I was randomly pushing the buttons because I didn't know the code. The siren kept getting louder and louder. I woke up in a sweat.

The siren in my dream was the baby crying. He was crying non-stop just like the siren. I got up so fast that I felt dizzy, but I didn't have time to slow down. I got to Aaron's room so fast that I was out of breath. I took him in my arms, fed him, and he went quiet. Then I carefully put him down on the changing table.

Anna showed me how to change the diaper, but it wasn't easy on my own. First, it took me a while to hold Aaron's legs up and at the same time wipe his butt. That was some kind of process. Second, as I put his diaper on, I was worried he'd roll over and fall off the table.

Boy, I could really use another hand. There, all set. The diaper is on, nice and neat. Not too bad. Oh … oh crap. It's inside out! How the hell did I do that? Damn, I have to start all over.

I felt much better when that was over. Aaron liked to move, like a fish out of water. I was so nervous he would squirm out of my arms as I put him back in the crib. Babies have such positive energy. It's easy to feel it from them. I needed that good energy, but my mind wasn't receptive. My mind was tired from fighting with my emotions. I looked at Aaron and smiled. He smiled back.

He was just a little innocent human being who needed some care and attention. I looked at him and it made me think. We all need each other to survive. We can't survive for long if we don't do things for each other. We need farmers to grow the food so we can eat. We need people to make the clothes that we wear. We need people to work the utilities that deliver the water and electricity we use every day. We do things for each other to survive and we take it for granted. We're not even aware of it. Even this baby's mother needs some help, so she can get enough sleep to go to work, make money, and pay me, so I can take care of me and my family.

Aaron wanted attention, so I stayed with him longer than I really needed to. After some food and a fresh diaper, he was wide-awake and wanted to play. I played with him and made him smile.

This baby is an absolute stranger, but so what? Do we need to know each other well to help each other? The world would be a better place if people would have compassion for strangers. It doesn't matter who you are, your age, your financial status. We all need each other. We're all connected.

The past few days I was struggling to adapt to this new life. I was still adapting. I was upset with myself for letting my emotions get the best of me. There was a better way to think, and it was up to me to change. Better is always best.

It's okay that I never worked as a cook, housemaid, cleaner or babysitter. Any job is a good job. We can take pride in doing a high-quality job in any profession. You can be a doctor or lawyer and still perform your job poorly. Or you can be the best, most efficient and effective janitor on the planet. Here's the difference—it's a mindset.

I have an opportunity. If I take responsibility for myself and perform all my work in a high-quality way, I will reach all my goals. I now have three jobs, which I didn't expect. It isn't easy, but I can take it. I'll start to work with it instead of against it. I'll learn more and more. I'll gain more experience and go for it. From now on I'm going to take the high road. Every day, I'll do the best I can. That's it. I'm determined to realize the future I've imagined for myself.

Of course, my new mindset was tested right away. The weekends were harder than the other days. My buddy Kalian wasn't around, and Anna and "The Corrector" Michael were home. I gave him the nickname to lighten things up, at least in my head. The Corrector would follow me around, giving necessary (and unnecessary) instructions all the time.

Maybe that was just his personality. It wasn't personal. It made me feel better thinking this way. I was working for him and that was that. His personality wasn't my problem. He would tell me how to do things and would add "that's the way I do it." I would listen to his instructions and consider them a learning experience. It seemed like he had nothing to do in the house, so he got busy teaching me.

The way I would do it? That's a strange thing to say. Did he do all the housekeeping before they hired me? Or does he just know these things?

Anna could care less. She seemed to trust me. She was fine with the way I did things. She would explain what to do every once in a while, but then she would leave me alone. But, The Corrector? He would stalk me wherever I went.

They mostly wanted me to take care of Aaron. Feed him, change his clothes or play with him. I preferred taking care of the baby rather than Jessica. But there was no chance of that. They asked me to take both of them to the basement and play with them. The girl resisted for a while, but Mommy told her she had no choice. That was a real nightmare for me. It really was.

She didn't want to play with me. She gave me such an attitude, throwing toys at me. But once again, it was my job. I patiently dealt with her behavior without any response. I just smiled. I did my best to understand and learn all the toys. I had never seen any of them before and had no idea how to play with them. But I pretended it was enjoyable.

Of course, The Corrector came downstairs to check up on things. He looked around and then approached us. He acted like a policeman. It was weird. As soon as Jessica saw her father, she ran to him. She didn't want to throw toys at me anymore as she hugged her father. He stayed for a while. When he had to leave, she cried so much he had to take her with him.

This girl, Jessica. She's temperamental and cries—a lot. She isn't friendly to me, but I don't care so much. What I don't understand is why she's so moody and cranky most of the time. She has everything. She lives in a beautiful house. She has a separate, beautifully decorated room, with so many toys. She has people who take care of her. What is the problem?

Maybe she doesn't have what children want most. Her parents. She might be missing them. Maybe she wants her parents to be with her more than with Kalian or me. She'd probably trade a lot of the stuff she has for more attention and hugs from her parents. Her mother is gone from early in the morning until late at night, every weekday. When she comes home, she doesn't spend much time with them. What else could all the crying be about?

I guess we might get mad about people's behavior even though we don't know what they're going through. Children like Jessica probably don't even know why they're moody. They don't know what's wrong, they just know something's not right. They can't observe their mind, ask why and find the answer. They're not there yet. Hell, most adults don't even do it. They just react impulsively, out of habit.

Jessica's just acting out her frustrations. She rarely cries when her mother's around. When her mother asked her to go with me to the basement, it wasn't so much about me. It was about leaving her mother. Separation anxiety. The heartbroken look she gave her mother said everything. Why do people have children if they don't have time for them?

With the weekend ending, I was close to my day off on Monday. I was so excited. I wanted to sleep late and do absolutely nothing. I wanted to go out for a walk and explore. I hadn't been out of the house since I started working. I was starving for some fresh air and free time.

Monday came but I didn't have anywhere to go so I just stayed in my room. Free like a bird, in a cage. There weren't any sidewalks around the neighborhood, so I just sat in the backyard. Sounds boring but it was exciting to me. I thought I'd do some reading, maybe study my English. But unfortunately, The Corrector was home. He had some workers in the backyard landscaping. So, I decided to stay inside rather than seeing him on my day off. I didn't want to see any of them. I had no doubt if I hung around The Corrector, he'd find something to criticize. He'd probably correct the way I read a book or something.

But soon, the day became long. I became bored. I had too much time to think, so my mind was thrashing. My subconscious mind was working overtime on me. But this time, I wouldn't let it. I knew where I would end up if I let it take control.

I've made my decision. I came all this way to make something of myself. Now it was my responsibility to make it happen. I have choices, and I've decided. If I don't stay strong, if I don't keep going, I won't achieve my goals. I could give up and go back to my old life.

But then what? I'd rather be disappointed here than have regrets back home. I could never forgive myself for being weak. This is where I am. I need to remove obstacles. Despite myself, I need to do this. I want to do this to help my family, and me. This is more important than my freedom. They need me. I'm the only one who can give them a better life, a better future. I'm not going to let them down. I made a promise. I want them to be proud of me, not disappointed.

Of course, they would support me in any decision I made. But that wasn't the point. The point was that I said what I would do, and now I needed to do what I said. Yes, at my age girls just wanted to go out, party with friends and date guys. Go on vacation or just have fun being a girl. Put on a dress, some high heels, create a nice hair style, put on some sexy lipstick and flirt. All normal when you're twenty-something.

I'm not going to let all those desires get in the way of my priorities. I need to put myself second and focus on the things that are worth more than spending time having fun. I need to take this opportunity to work, like a machine. Learn things and save money. I'm young and I can do it. At this age we have so much energy and ability we don't even use it half the time. I've seen that since I started working in this house. I even surprised myself. I could be standing on my feet and running around all day, sometimes without even taking a break.

I should be taking advantage of my body and my energy while I have it. Sometimes we need to give ourselves a pep talk. I've been doing that since I was a little girl. It works so well. It feels like I become two people at the same time, talking to each other. I talk to myself, then listen to myself. It's a conversation. I ask so many questions, then I answer them. I agree; I disagree.

I determined my priorities and what to stand for. I asked myself, thought about my situation and then what the results would be. This was a turning point. I was the housekeeper of my mind and I cleaned it up. Keep the necessary things and throw out the unnecessary crap, the useless dusty thoughts. It was a great day.

I went back to work on Tuesday. It was nice to see Kalian again. She told me about her weekend. I didn't understand half of her story, but she seemed happy. As I made coffee, I noticed the silence. There wasn't anyone around and it was already after 9:00.

"Where is everybody?" I asked Kalian.

"Oh, they're probably sleeping in. It's a Jewish holiday. Something called Shavuot, so they take the day off."

I'm not happy to hear that. I'm going to be around The Corrector all day.

It was around noon when I saw Anna.

"Good morning, or I guess I should say good afternoon!" she said with a smile.

"Good afternoon," we both said at the same time.

"I'm going to order some food. What would you girls like?"

It was nice of her to ask us. I didn't care much about food lately. I was eating a banana or a slice of bread with turkey and cheese. I ate this way most of the time because I had no clue what the other stuff was in the fridge and the "mini-supermarket." I was eating that way even though I knew about the "no dairy and meat together" rule in this house. I'd make that sandwich behind the open fridge door to block the camera. I followed the rules when it impacted them, making dinners or cleaning the kitchen. But it had nothing to do with me and my choice of food.

"I'm thinking we should have Chinese food. Here's the menu," Anna continued.

"Thanks," I said as I took the menu.

This all looks strange to me. I can't even understand how ordering food works. We never ordered food in my country. We buy the ingredients and cook.

"Ordering food? How does that work?" I asked.

"It works very well," she said with a smile. "You call the restaurant, they take the order and deliver the food to your home."

That sounds so easy and smart. I like this idea. It seems luxurious. I like luxurious.

Anna looked at me as I stared at the Chinese menu without responding.

"Or maybe you want something else? Do you like pizza?" she asked.

"Yes, pizza," I said. "I like pizza a lot."

"Pizza it is," Anna said. "That's probably better anyway since we usually have dairy on Shavuot. That reminds me, I need to get cheesecake for dessert later."

Boy, lots of cheese today.

"You need to eat, you know. You need food for energy," she said.

"I eat," I said. "I really do. I just don't like to eat a lot."

I lied. I love food and I like eating. It just hasn't been a priority lately.

The pizza came and I forced myself to eat even though I wasn't really hungry. I was curious to try American pizza. It was completely different from anything I had before. The slice was so big I could barely finish it. Kalian joined us. She had two slices.

"I could eat another slice, but I'd better behave myself," she said.

This girl can eat.

"Thank you very much for the pizza, Anna and Michael," I said.

I almost called him Corrector instead of Michael.

"It was tasty," I said.

"You're welcome. There's more if you like," Anna said.

"Thanks, but I'm full now."

The lunch was almost over without any critiques from The Corrector. But just as I started to clean up from lunch, he couldn't help himself.

"You know, we usually eat pizza with our hands," he said with a smile.

He saw I was eating pizza with a fork and knife. My eating habits come from when I was a little girl. I was taught how to eat properly, with silverware. I think it's the most appropriate way to eat. I don't like to touch the food with my hands because it's healthier, and I don't like having the smell of food on my fingers after eating.

"Yes, I noticed," I smiled back. "But I like to eat with silverware."

"Alright then," Anna said. "We're going to my mother's, and Kalian is coming with us. We'll be back this evening. Here's the phone number of my mother's house just in case you need anything."

"OK, thanks," I said.

They were probably a little worried leaving me home alone given my history of mistakes. It felt nice to be in the empty house. I still had a lot of work to do. She wanted me to organize her closet in addition to the usual laundry and cleaning.

It was already evening when I finished working. It was getting dark outside. During the day when it was light out and I was busy I didn't feel alone in the quiet house. But now I did. I went to the kitchen and hung out for a while as I waited for them. I didn't want to go to my room until they came home. It was still too early. After a while, I felt bored. I had nothing else to do so I decided to try that ice cream. It was The Corrector's favorite thing to do at night, so why not give it a try? Maybe it does have some special taste at night. He told me I should try it, so I did.

Oh my God. This is the most delicious ice cream I've ever had! I can't stop eating. Having this ice cream at night really is magical. It makes me feel comfortable. Yes, this is comfort food. Maybe ice cream is more of a nighttime dessert.

I knew The Corrector would notice I had some ice cream. I was also sure he'd say something about it. After my private ice cream party, I felt like going to my room. It was getting late and no one was showing up. I went upstairs where there was a spot to hang out near a big wide window overlooking the road.

It's so dark and windy outside, and this house is so huge. It's starting to get a little creepy. I don't see any cars on the road. Ah, there's one. This must be them. Nope, it's not. Damn. I can't even see lights from other houses. I hope the security alarm is on so nobody can come inside.

I had all kinds of silly thoughts. It felt like I was in a scary movie. I went downstairs, looked around. I went back upstairs. I went up and down the stairs a few times. I became anxious when I looked at the time; it was already after eleven o'clock. I started worrying about them.

Why are they so late? I hope they're all right. I didn't expect them to come home this late. They're all usually in bed by now. She told me they'd be home evening time. Maybe I should call them at the mother's house? But then again, I don't want to seem silly and bother them. Oh, forget it. They should be here by now. I'm calling.

After a lot of rings someone picked up the phone.

"Hello?" she said, in a sleepy voice.

I think it's Anna's mother. Did I wake her up?

"Hello. This is Alyssa, Anna's housekeeper. I'm sorry to bother you but I was wondering if Anna and everyone left yet? I was starting to worry because it's getting late."

"Oh no my dear. They decided to stay over. They're all asleep already."

"Oh, I thought they would be coming back tonight. OK, thank you. Goodnight."

"Goodnight my dear."

She hung up. I was happy, but surprised. Happy that everything was fine with them, but I couldn't believe no one remembered me when they decided to stay over.

That's rather inconsiderate. Didn't they care? They changed the plan, didn't call me, and here I was, sitting for hours waiting for them, and worrying. Another lesson learned.

THIRTEEN

NOVEMBER 1996, LONG ISLAND

It was always a special moment when I got paid. I made $230 a week. It was double what I made in a month back home. Knowing that I worked and earned this myself made me feel proud. I was grateful to Anna and Michael. But it should've been more, given the long work hours and the two additional jobs.

The Corrector would call me to come downstairs and hand me the cash. Of course, he'd be in charge of paying people, because of his controlling personality. I thanked him and went back upstairs to my room. I had all these dollars in my hands. I counted it a few times, because counting money felt good. It felt powerful, even though I knew the money didn't belong to me, yet. But it was still exciting holding it for a while. Getting paid always made me ambitious to earn even more.

In September I extended my visa for another six months. Anna was happy to help me with the application. I was learning more every day. As I learned, the job got easier. But I still wasn't comfortable living in the house. Even though it was beautiful, and my room was nice and cozy, I just couldn't get used to it. I was here because I needed to be here. Usually the new and unfamiliar becomes familiar. We get used to it. But this was not going to happen to me in this place, that was for sure.

Kalian worked and lived here too, but she seemed happy and comfortable. She seemed to love the kids and enjoyed taking care of them. She was smiling and happy when she'd leave the house for the weekend, and she'd have the same smile and positive energy when she came back. She seemed happy in her skin. It doesn't matter what kind of job or lifestyle you have; it's all about finding happiness with who you are and in everything you do.

After five months of work without leaving the house, Anna made my day when she asked me to go with them to their apartment in the city. I got so excited. I'd finally be able to see the city. This was my dream since I landed. I felt like I was going on vacation even though I'd be working. It was still going to be exciting to be there. I'd be able to smell the air and hear the sounds of the city.

I was desperate to see lots of people. I wanted to see the lights at night and the yelling of drunk people in the middle of the night. I felt like a caged animal who was hungry for freedom. I couldn't wait. The days were going slow as I counted them down, and my excitement grew as the day approached. It would be nice to leave this big, quiet house for a couple of days.

Since Kalian had the weekend off, I'd have to take care of the kids. After breakfast and coffee on Friday morning we all got into the car. I sat in the back seat between the kids. Even in the car I had to work. But it was nice to go for a ride. It felt different and fun. I pretended I was on a family trip. It was interesting to see new things while we were on the road. It was good to see some life, some energy. It felt comfortable hanging with them, even though they weren't my friends or anything.

Michael turned on the radio. Hearing the music made me feel even better. I became so optimistic and positive about being there. The sun felt good as we sat in the car. We hit traffic. Anna and Michael complained but I sat patiently, looking at the passengers in the cars around us and enjoying the music. Aaron was sleeping and Jessica was playing quietly with her dolls.

Interesting. Jessica's quiet and not crying? She's happy when she's around her whole family.

"We're getting close to Manhattan. You'll be able to see a nice view soon." said Anna.

"I can't wait," I said.

My dream will be a reality soon. I'm the happiest person in the world right now. I'll have a story to tell my friends and family now that I'll see this magical city with my own eyes. The Manhattan that we only knew from movies and books. The city that never sleeps. And now it would be real.

Then I saw it. My eyes got wide. The most unforgettable, powerful and extremely attractive view of the city skyline. I could actually feel its energy. I was speechless. I looked from one end of the skyline to the other, and back again. The architecture and the size of the buildings were like nothing I'd ever seen. I stared in awe until the car made its way into a tunnel and the skyline disappeared.

"Are we going close to those tall buildings? Are we in the city now?" I asked.

"Yes, we are. This is where I come every day to work."

"I'm so jealous."

"Why? Because I come here every day?"

"Yes. I'd like to work here, but I'd really love to live here."

"I love Manhattan too. When I was single I lived here. But we moved to the suburbs for the kids. Plus, Michael doesn't really like crowds."

She seemed to want to chat more, but Michael interrupted, asking her a question. We came out of the tunnel and I looked at the streets, the people and the buildings. I watched as the taxis would get so close to us you could see the eyes of the people in the other car.

Even the people look different here. Their look, the way they dress, the way they walk. Everything seems eclectic and different. I want to be part of this crowd one day. I belong here.

Michael dropped us off in front of the building. Getting out of the car felt so nice. I could finally take a deep breath of the city air. I needed that. I needed city oxygen. The air in the city always smells different. Most of the air is probably polluted but I didn't care. I liked it. It's hard to explain. At home, every time we'd return from the countryside, I could smell the city as we got closer. It always energized me. I helped Anna get four large suitcases out of the car. It seemed like they packed for a long vacation.

I thought this was a weekend trip. How many clothes do they need for just two days? I'll find out soon enough since I'll be unpacking all the bags.

All I had was a shopping bag. I didn't want to bring my big yellow suitcase, and I didn't have any small travel bags, so I just put some clothes and a toilet kit in a shopping bag. That's all I needed since I'd be staying in the apartment, working. I collected Aaron. Jessica went right to her mom. I became so distracted standing on the street that it was hard to focus on the baby. I was astonished. Looking around, seeing the people and the vitality of the city. It pulsated. I didn't want to go inside, but the fun was over.

The building had five floors. Every floor belonged to one family, and the elevator would open into the apartment. Their apartment was on the top floor. When the elevator door opened, I was stunned. The apartment was something from a movie. I couldn't hold my excitement.

"This apartment is amazing, Anna," I said.

"Thank you. I like it too. I wanted to keep this even though we spend more time on Long Island. I didn't want to give it up because then we wouldn't come here so much, and that wouldn't be a fun thing for me."

Seems like she still wants a city lifestyle. She was from the city. Michael wasn't. She seems happy enough on Long Island, but probably because she still has this place.

"Do you work close by?"

"It's not too far from here. But the travel from the house is long and annoying."

"Why don't you all just live here? This is such a beautiful place."

"Yeah, I know. Maybe. One day. Maybe we should start unpacking."

She wants to change the subject. She even looks different since we walked in here. Her appearance and personality are brighter. Maybe that will happen to me? Maybe the city will help with my attitude and energy. I'm hungry. It's the first time I've been hungry since I left home. This is a good sign. I was worried about not having an appetite and losing too much weight.

I put Aaron in his room for a nap and knocked on Anna's bedroom door. They were all in there resting. I asked Anna if it was OK to have a cup of coffee. She came with me to the kitchen to show me how to make it. She made enough for herself too and went back to the bedroom. When the coffee was ready, I asked her if she'd like to have it in her bedroom.

"I'll be right there," she said.

The coffee tasted good and it killed my appetite, a little.

"Let me show you something," she said.

I followed her up a narrow staircase. When we reached the top, she opened a door. It was a rooftop living space that was part of the apartment. I was amazed.

"I love hanging out here and having coffee or a glass of wine. It's so beautiful isn't it? I prefer this small rooftop more than that huge backyard we have on Long Island. What do you think?"

I don't know what to say. Actually, I do know, and I absolutely agree with her. But I don't want to share my opinion. I've learned it's not always good to share your opinions, especially with the people you work for.

"It's interesting," I finally said, looking around.

The rooftop was small but cozy, with plants scattered about. It had an unfinished look to it. A nice place to hang out and relax. There were a couple of comfortable chairs and a small coffee table. I wanted to stay there, have my coffee and daydream about living like this one day. But I heard Michael calling his wife and it reminded me that I was supposed to be working. I followed Anna downstairs. I went to the baby's room. His diaper needed changing.

"Alyssa, the food we ordered is here," Anna said. "Can you please go downstairs and get it?"

I finished up and handed Aaron to her and started towards the elevator.

"Hold on," she said. "Let me give you some money. And this is the elevator code. You'll need to enter it when you come back up."

I know the food delivery process already, but having a code for using the elevator? That's impressive. So many new and interesting things.

I was so hungry and couldn't wait to eat. We all sat down together at the table to have Chinese food. Maybe it was because I was so hungry, but everything was delicious. I didn't know how to eat with the chopsticks but watched them. After a while I kind of got it.

It was around eight o'clock when Anna and Michael were all dressed up and ready to go out. They were going to some special event she mentioned earlier. She was wearing a long dress with high heels. Michael was wearing a suit and tie. They both looked so different that I almost didn't recognize them.

Jessica was in bed and Aaron was about to fall asleep when they left. I was still feeling energized. I didn't want to go to sleep yet. I wanted to feel the city. I was hearing all the city noises. Car horns, sirens. I was receiving such positive energy even though I was inside the house. It felt great.

I wanted to call home and tell them about my adventure. Tell them I was feeling fine and I was in the city that many of my friends and family dreamed of seeing. But I hadn't seen much of the city yet. I hadn't even walked on the streets, but it was a beginning.

I went to my room to "unpack" my shopping bag, which took me about ten seconds. This shopping bag was ancient. I brought it from home. I even used it back home when I carried small things. It was a plastic bag with some flowers painted on it, but they were faded. I knew it wasn't appropriate to use a shopping bag, but I didn't care. I was far away from spending any money on any convenient things.

As I folded the bag, I felt something. I opened it and found a pack of cigarettes from back home. I used to be a social smoker. Just for fun. It was so in style and everybody did it. There were three cigarettes left in it. Looking at it made me think back. Me and my friends, hanging out, smoking secretly so our parents wouldn't know.

Young people smoking cigarettes in front of their parents was unacceptable back home. It was especially inappropriate for girls to smoke in front of older people. It was considered bad form. So we respected the old folks and smoked in private.

I grabbed a cigarette and smelled it. I closed my eyes and smelled it again. It was so good. I wanted to go out for a smoke. I missed going out. I missed being a socialite and talking to people. My desire became even stronger as I listened to the city.

I remembered when I was with my boyfriend and a girlfriend and we were all smoking when her mother caught us. My friend and I put the cigarette down in the ashtray, and it was still burning when her mother walked into the room. She said the room smelled like cigarettes and we both looked at my boyfriend and blamed it on him. It was a little more acceptable if a young guy smoked. She looked at him. He was holding his cigarette. She looked at the ashtray, and then glared at us. But we kept insisting they weren't ours, fruitlessly trying to convince her.

I smiled. Then my mind drifted to the boy I was so in love with. Maximillian. I would think about him every now and then. We had so much fun together. We were so madly in love and extremely attracted to each other. I got so excited every time I went to see him. Being close to his body was epic. When he would take me in his arms and hug me so close, I'd get goosebumps, and hot. I missed him.

I started feeling sexual. I wanted to see and feel a man. To have some sex, or at least flirt and kiss. I closed my eyes and thought about Maximillian and me, kissing, exploring my body with his lips. I started to feel warm and excited. I was dreaming so deep, like he was right next to me, touching me. He kissed me as he touched my body, caressing my breasts. He kissed my lips, and my neck. I dreamed so vividly that I felt my heart palpitating and my face blush. I noticed my legs were crossed, tightly. I felt warm and wet between my legs. I peacefully opened my eyes.

Now I definitely want to light up and smoke this damn cigarette. I should just go up to the rooftop, sit down in that comfortable chair, have a cigarette and look at the stars and dream. I love dreaming. I've been doing it since … well … forever. What's the big deal if I go upstairs? It would be fine right? The kids are asleep. I could just go up there for five minutes. Out and in.

I checked in on the children. They both looked like they were in a deep sleep, probably tired from the trip. They even fell asleep earlier than normal. I grabbed my jacket, a cigarette and took the steps to the rooftop. It was cold but it felt good. The sounds of the city and the fresh air made me feel relaxed. It was dark around the rooftop. I didn't even want to turn the lights on. I could see well enough with the light coming from the street and other buildings.

I stood next to the wall and looked down. The streets were busy with cars and people. It was noisy, even from up there. I heard a police car siren and it reminded me of the security system in the house. It looked so lively even though it was a little cold outside. People were walking fast and in different directions. Some were going inside places as others came out. I loved watching and observing. I looked into the windows of a building so close I could even see the people in their apartments.

These people live here. They work and play in this city. How great is that? I want to live here. I want to be one of those people who has an apartment. I want to have a relationship and spend my life here. I want to meet someone, go out on a date and come home to this kind of apartment.

Sometimes I feel like I'm living a dream. I go so deep that it feels real. It makes me excited and positive about my future. I didn't know how but I knew my dreams would come true one day. I could just feel it.

I sat down on the chair. I knew I only had a few minutes, but I just wanted to relax with my cigarette. I lit it up and inhaled deeply. As a gust of wind put out the match flame, I heard the loud sound of a door slam shut. I looked back quickly. My heart started pounding. I threw the cigarette on the ground and stepped on it. I rushed to the door and tried to turn the handle. It was locked.

FOURTEEN

NOVEMBER 1996, MANHATTAN

Hundreds of thoughts were rushing into my head. How is it possible to have so many thoughts a second, especially when you're in trouble? The mind. It's like the ultimate search engine. It gives you a bunch of ideas while it continues to look for an answer.

I tried the door again. I held the handle and tried to shake it open. I didn't think this heavy metal door would close shut with a burst of wind. I didn't want to face reality and admit that I was locked outside, with the kids alone in the house. What was I supposed to do now?

What are my options to get back into the apartment? This is really serious. They were little kids and God forbid they woke up with no one around. And what if the parents come home and see that I'm not there? I don't want to think about it.

I was nervous. I needed to get back inside somehow. I moved away from the door, back to the walled edge of the rooftop. I looked around and down, over and over again. My breathing was heavy, and my heart was pounding. Adrenaline. I couldn't come up with a solution. I walked to every corner, looking for a way.

Maybe I should try to break the door?

I went back to the door to check it out, but it was way too heavy and thick to break, especially without any tools. I grabbed the handle and shook it again as if it would magically open. After a while I knew I was wasting my time. I went back to the front edge of the rooftop.

Maybe if I start screaming for help someone will call the police. No, not a good idea. There would be too much commotion. Everyone will know what I did, including Anna and Michael. I need to get back into the apartment without anyone noticing. I can't jump from here. It's way too high. I can't climb down either since there's nothing to hold on to. It's not like I'm James Bond.

I went to the right-side edge of the rooftop. Straight across I could see inside the window of a townhouse. In between our two buildings was a smaller, narrow house, with its roof about one floor below. I stood and stared at it. I noticed the other townhouse had a balcony with a railing, just above the roof of the house below.

Maybe I can jump down onto the rooftop and step up onto the balcony? But is that really only a step up? If it isn't that would suck. I don't want to go from one bad place to another.

I moved to the left side of the rooftop to see if there was any other way off. Nothing. Unless I suddenly grew wings and learned how to fly, I didn't have many options. I smiled at the thought, which probably helped prevent a nervous breakdown.

I went back to the right side. I looked at the townhouse again.

It looks like no one's home. All the lights are off, but it's too early to sleep. They're probably out. Maybe I can climb onto their balcony anyway, and try to open the door? Maybe the door is open? But if it's open, then what? I'll be in somebody's house without permission. I'm in enough trouble already. I could get shot or arrested.

The air was cold but I didn't feel it. I was generating so much energy nothing could make me cold. I didn't see any option except to wait for Anna and Michael's return. I couldn't bear to think about it. But all I really cared about was the kids. I prayed that they wouldn't wake up.

Please God, let them have a quiet and deep sleep. Please help. Please keep them sleeping. Please make sure they don't know they're by themselves.

I prayed with my eyes closed. What else could I do? Suddenly, I saw a light go on in the townhouse on the right side of the rooftop, where I stood before. Now that the light was on it seemed even closer than before. I could see through the window, but no one was there. I stared into the room, without taking my eyes off it for a second.

It looks like an office, with a desk and a lot of shelves with a lot of books. Maybe if it was a bedroom I'd see someone right away, but it looks empty. Does that mean someone came in and just switched the light on? Strange.

I didn't move. My eyes went back and forth from the office room to the rooftop. Maybe someone would appear in the window. I looked at the rooftop again and when I glanced back at the room, I suddenly saw a man. A naked man. A completely naked man, standing by the bookshelves. He was facing away so he couldn't see me. He was standing there for a while without moving, paging through a book.

Oh, please, please turn around. Turn around. Turn around and look at me. Don't leave the room.

By now I was speaking out loud. He dropped the book by his side, and slowly turned around. Now I saw a distinguished face, and a full frontal of his naked body. He was tall and thin. He had dark hair and darkish skin. He was wearing glasses. He put the book under his arm and picked up a glass of wine. He sat down in a chair in the middle of the room, where I could still see him.

Am I wasting my time with this guy? Maybe not. After all ... he is naked.

I shook my head and laughed.

He's naked, but who cares? I need help and this is probably the only guy who can save me.

"Hey! Hey, in the room over there!" I shouted. "Over here! On the roof! Hello! Hey! Hello! Look! Hello!"

I was yelling as loud as I could while waving my arms and jumping up and down like a lunatic. He looked up.

He sees me. Oh, yeah, he sees me. I saw his eyes looking right at me.

He got up and walked to the window and opened it. He didn't seem to care that he was naked, or maybe he just forgot. Either way, it didn't bother me.

"Hi. Sorry to bother you," I said. "I accidently locked myself out of the house and I'm stuck on this roof. If I jumped down on the roof below, would you mind if I climbed on your balcony, and came into your house, just so I can leave and get back into my house?"

All the words and sentences just flowed out of my mouth. Best English I ever spoke. Fluently. It was a miracle.

"Sure," he said.

"Thank you!"

He left the room. I was so impatient to see him again. I didn't want him to disappear on me. Or call the police, or worse, call Anna or Michael. My body started shaking uncontrollably. My face was frozen, and my heart was racing as I climbed onto the rooftop edge. I slid over, and hung down from the edge, held my breath and let go. A perfect landing. I carefully walked towards his balcony and waited for him. I was like someone waiting to see a loved one return from war.

And there he was. My savior. Standing on his balcony, with a robe on. He reached down.

"Here," he said. "Take my hand so I can help you up."

"OK."

I took his hand as I stepped up onto the building ledge, and he pulled me onto the balcony, as I almost fell into his arms.

"Thank you so much," I said. "I don't know what I would've done without you. I'm so sorry that I had to ask for help, but I didn't know what else to do."

"It's OK," he said, "Follow me. I'll show you the way out."

We walked down three sets of stairs to the front door.

"Here you go," he said as he opened the door.

"Thanks again. I really appreciate it. Goodnight."

I started out the door but stopped and turned around.

"If I could just ask for one more favor?" I asked.

"What's that?"

"Please don't tell Anna and Michael about this. Do you think we could keep this a secret between us?"

"No worries. I keep many secrets. Goodnight now," he said as he closed the door.

I ran from his house to the building, up the elevator, to the apartment and the kids' room. I saw them. Two angels sleeping peacefully. I looked at Aaron and Jessica and felt so in love with them. I rubbed the baby's head and then I stroked Jessica's curly hair. I fixed her comforter as she slept.

I just want to hug both of them. Jessica's always kind of cranky towards me, and I'm not so friendly to her either. But now I don't care. I see her as the most beautiful and adorable human being, who has no idea she was alone a little while ago. Otherwise she'd probably be crying hysterically.

I couldn't seem to calm down. My breathing was fast, and my heart was racing in the quiet and peaceful room. I left and sat down on the floor in the hallway feeling exhausted. I was surprised that I was able to get out of that trouble.

Life is full of surprises. The kids are safe. I'm safe. Everybody's safe. Thank you, God. Thanks to the naked, nameless neighbor. When it comes to helping others, you don't need to get acquainted. You don't need to know anything about a person to support them in a moment of need. We all care about our loved ones. But being kind and helpful to a stranger without expecting anything in return? That's high quality. That wonderful naked man will stay in my head for a long time. Not just because he was naked, although that was kind of cool ... he did look good ... but anyway, it was really because he helped save the kids, me and my job. I'm so lucky to have met someone like him on my first day in the city. It really impresses me. One day, I'll meet someone like him, and fall in love, in this city that I love.

I never heard Anna and Michael come home. It was the first time I slept through the night without even moving. I didn't want to wake up. I was so sleepy when I got up the next morning to take care of Aaron. Anna came into the room.

"I called last night, and you didn't answer," she said.

"I didn't hear the phone ring. What time did you call?"

"Around 10:00," she said as she tilted her head and her eyes narrowed.

"Oh. I was already sleeping. I was so tired. I think I fell asleep around 9:00."

She nodded.

"Yeah. That's what I thought."

We left the city Sunday afternoon. Before getting in the car I looked at the naked man's house and around the street. I took one more deep breath to feel this crowded, dusty and loud city. It was pure energy, with well-dressed, free looking people. I didn't want to leave.

Even though I didn't get to go out and didn't see anything around the neighborhood, I still wanted to stay. I felt this was the place I belonged, where my future would unfold, with someone I could share it with.

This city, somehow it motivates me. It makes me want to work harder, to make the best of myself. This is my dream, and I'm going to dream about it every night until it happens.

On the way back, I looked at the cars and the people in them. Some were by themselves, some with others. Old, young, men, women. They were all driving to get somewhere, with their thoughts and desires. Some were going fast, in a hurry. Some were just cruising, in no rush. It seemed like life itself, when we're in such a hurry to get somewhere yet it's like we're in slow motion. It's like a race to be first at the finish line. Constant movement.

I thought about my secret. Secrets can change your life for better or worse. My secret made me stronger and more ambitious.

I don't want to share what happened. What good would it do? Anna and Michael would probably freak out and fire me. It's in the past and there's nothing that can be done to change it. Better to leave it as it is and not let it happen again. They say it's not a mistake if you learn from it. Well then, I didn't make a mistake.

Last night changed me. Yes, overnight. What I want, my attitude and thoughts, are different. Now, I'm a fighter. A survivor. I'm responsible for myself and others around me. I'm more determined than ever to have a better life and have a house like Anna, Michael and the naked man. I went through the naked man's house quickly, but what I saw was impressive. It was the kind of place that I wanted, and now I'm motivated to make it happen.

FIFTEEN

NOVEMBER 1996, LONG ISLAND

Twenty-three years old. I didn't want to tell anyone it was my birthday. It was bad enough I had to work and didn't have any family or friends around to celebrate. If I said something to Anna and Michael they'd probably just wish me a happy birthday, which would be nice, but it wouldn't mean much to me.

Plus, I didn't want anything from them. No gift or even a cake. So, I didn't say a word. I just wanted to keep busy with my work. As the day went on, I'd remember it was my birthday and get a little sad. I was still young and silly about wanting a big birthday party. The day was over and I was lying in bed, staring at the ceiling.

There will be a day when I'll have a huge birthday party, with all my friends and family, in a house just like that naked man.

I smiled and quickly fell asleep. The next day I called home.

"Alyssa! Happy Birthday!" Mom said. "How come you didn't call yesterday?"

"I was really busy and just couldn't get to the phone."

"How was your birthday? Did you celebrate? What did you do?"

"We had a small celebration in the house," I lied. "It was really nice."

"Oh, I'm so glad to hear that. How are you doing?"

"I'm doing great. I'm really happy here."

I'm only going to tell them good stories. They still don't understand this new life of mine and I'm not going to get into the details. It's better for them and me. What's the point of telling them my birthday came and went without notice? All they'd do is get worried and be sad for me. I never like it when someone pities me. I hate that. Whenever things aren't going well for me or my family, I always pretend everything is fine. I never want to hear "Oh … poor girl, oh … poor family."

I was happy when I got a friend of a friend's phone number. Silvia lived in the city somewhere. I had never met her before, but it would be great to know someone from home. I called her and we made plans to meet. She lived here for a few years. Before I saw New York City, I thought most people would miss home and go back as soon as they could. I thought it was impressive that she stayed and built a new life for herself.

A few weeks later when Monday arrived, it was time to meet up with Silvia. It was exhilarating. She gave me detailed directions on how to get to where she lived in Brooklyn. I wrote everything down, but it all sounded so strange. I asked a lot of questions and she patiently explained how to travel to and in the city. I wanted to go so badly that I didn't care if I got lost. I knew I was smart enough to figure it out eventually.

I let Anna know that I was going and that I'd be staying with Silvia overnight. The travel plan seemed like quite a process. I had to get to the Long Island Railroad station, take a train to Penn Station, take a downtown train to 14th street and then change to another subway to Brooklyn. I stared at the directions.

No doubt about it, all this switching is going to be tough.

I called Lora and Viktor to let them know I was going to be in Brooklyn, in case they wanted to meet up so I could make a payment on the loan. Viktor answered the phone. He sounded happy to hear me. He couldn't make it that day, so we made plans to meet on my next day off. It was a good conversation. Since I wouldn't be paying them back that day, at least I'd have some extra money in my pocket, just in case. I'd only have forty dollars left over after paying them.

"Anna, what's the best way for me to get to the station for a train to Manhattan?" I asked.

I hope she offers to drive me there.

"Oh, it's easy."

So much for the ride.

"All you have to do is make a right on the road in front of the house, walk straight for about forty-five minutes and you'll see the train station on the right side. You can't miss it. Go inside the station, buy a ticket and then wait on the platform with the sign that says Trains to New York. If the station is closed you can buy a ticket on the train."

Walking forty-five minutes in the cold doesn't sound so easy but I don't care.

"OK, thanks," I said. "I'll see you tomorrow then."

I left early to make up for the rather long walk. As I left the house, I felt so free and happy. It felt good to walk. I was on the road with my pocketbook and middle-heel shoes. I only had one pair of nice-looking shoes so I had no choice for the long walk.

I was the only person walking on the road. There wasn't even a sidewalk, and the streets were narrow. It was a little scary walking, especially when a car passed. Some cars would pass so fast my fluffy skirt would blow up in the air. It felt a little awkward while I was on the road. I saw some people in the car just staring at me. It was like they never saw someone walking on the road.

These roads aren't built for pedestrians. The people who live here must drive everywhere. I guess that's one of the reasons Anna isn't especially happy living out here. She mentioned a few times that she misses walking. I didn't understand what she meant. Why wasn't she able to walk? Now I understand.

I kept walking as fast as I could. I couldn't wait to get off the boring road. It took me more than forty-five minutes to get to the station. The heels slowed me down a bit. I felt relieved when I finally saw the station. I was one step closer to the city.

The train station was closed so I just made my way to the platform. There were quite a few people there, starting their workweek. Soon I saw the train approaching. I got on and took a seat close to the exit door. Almost every seat was taken.

"Ticket please," the conductor said.

"I need to buy a ticket," I said.

He said the price. I didn't understand so I just handed him twenty dollars.

"Here you go," he said as he handed me the ticket and change.

"Thank you. Does this train stop at Penn station?" I asked.

"Yes, and... *blah, blah, blah.*"

In my short time in America I was impressed with how friendly and helpful everybody was. Almost anyone I asked would stop and help me. It made a big impression on me. It was a huge help to me as I got used to living here. But I still had a communication problem.

I understood the yes, but I had no clue what else he was talking about. I wasn't shy to ask for help. I just didn't understand the answers. Every time I'd ask a question, my eyes and ears would get big to absorb the answer, but it just wouldn't happen. Maybe it was because people would speak fast or with an accent, but either way, I just wasn't getting it. I was barely able to understand any of the announcements on the train, so whenever we stopped I'd look outside for the station sign. A well-dressed man sitting across from me must've seen me looking at all the station stops.

"Don't worry," he said, smiling. "Penn Station is the last stop on the train. You can't miss it. Just follow the crowds."

Now *that* I understood.

"Thank you," I said, smiling.

The train pulled into Penn Station and I followed the crowd. The second part of the journey was over. So far so good. Now I had to find the right subway. I followed the signs to the 1 train and bought a token and watched how people used it to enter the subway. Then I did the same thing and went through the turnstile, like I knew what I was doing. The subway was trickier than the train. There were so many people, and it was chaos.

I never saw so many different people in one place. There were Asians, Blacks, Whites, Hispanics, Indians and who knows how many others. I felt like I was on another planet. It felt great, like I just joined an international community. They all knew how to move around and what to do.

I want to be like them one day, traveling around the city with ease. I need to ask a guy if this subway is going downtown, so I don't get lost. I always like to ask guys for help. They're friendlier. Girls aren't so friendly to me. I'm not sure why. Maybe it's a girl thing.

I went up to a man. He looked like a local guy, reading a newspaper as he waited for the subway.

How can he read with all this noise?

"Hello, excuse me. Do you know this station?" I asked as I showed him my piece of paper with the station name on it.

"Yes, of course. That's where I'm going," he said with a pleasant smile. "Just wait here and follow me when the train arrives."

"Thank you," I said, flirting a little.

Wow. Either I'm lucky or maybe American men just like me. Everyone is so kind to me every time I ask for help. Maybe I'm attractive to them? Or maybe they're just good people? I like the former.

The subway came and I followed the guy into the car. I tried not to lose him. There were already so many people on the train, but people just kept pushing to get on. I pushed my way to a spot right next to him and firmly stayed there. No one could move me from his side even if they tried. He folded up his newspaper to read as the train left the station. I just kept an eye on him to make sure I didn't lose him as the train made a few stops. Sometimes he'd look at me and smile.

"We get off at the next stop," he said.

When the train stopped and the door opened, I moved aggressively to stay with him to get out. People were pushing each other to get off. Soon I was so far behind I couldn't even see him. Finally, I pushed one guy really hard and got myself out of the train.

I feel like I just left a battlefield. I'm a hero. I won and I'm free. Part three of the journey is behind me.

Silvia asked me to call before getting on the L train to Brooklyn. I found a public phone, but I didn't understand how to use it. It was different from the phones back home. I tried every which way, but nothing worked, and I became frustrated. I had no choice but to ask for help. A lady was sitting on a chair by the subway wall. She didn't seem happy about getting up, but she helped me and returned to her spot.

"Hello Silvia, how are you?"

"Hey! I'm great. How was the train trip? Are you safe?"

"I am. It's been an adventure, but I figured things out," I said with a laugh.

"That's good. Where are you now?"

Then … click.

"Hello? … Hello?"

We were disconnected. A voice came on the phone.

"Please deposit *blah, blah … blah, blah, blah*," she said.

I didn't understand what the hell she was saying. I hung up. I needed to redial, so I asked the same lady for help and she just rolled her eyes. I showed her the piece of paper with the phone number on it again. She just looked at it, dialed the number and handed the phone to me.

"Thank you so much," I said.

She didn't say a word. I watched as she walked back to her chair and moved it further away. I smiled.

"Hi Silvia. I'm afraid we'll get disconnected again so I'm just letting you know that I'm going to get on the L train now."

"OK, great. I'll meet you at the subway station. I'll be wearing a baseball hat so you can recognize me. The subway will take about forty minutes or so. See you soon," she said.

"OK, see you soon," I repeated.

See you soon? Another forty minutes of travel and she thinks that's soon? It doesn't seem that soon to me. And what the hell is a baseball hat? How will I know it's her if I don't know what a baseball hat is? Whatever. I just need to find the subway and start the ride. Why does it seem like every trip is around forty minutes?

I found the L train to Brooklyn. There were a lot fewer people on this platform. I asked a pretty black woman if this was the right train for the station I pointed to.

"Yes, baby girl, this is the right one," she said with a smile.

Baby girl?

"Thank you," I said, smiling.

The train came with only a few people on it. I sat down for the ride. When we reached the station, I followed the crowds to the exits. I looked for a girl in a hat, any kind. There were a lot of people with hats. Seemed like a popular thing. Maybe one day I'd wear one, but probably not. Most of the hats looked kind of boyish. Not my style at all.

I heard my name as Silvia called me. Somehow, she recognized me as I came down the stairs. But I guess I wasn't that hard to find.

When I looked around, I was the only white girl. Seeing Silvia standing at the end of the stairs, waving her arms at me, made me so happy and so proud that I made it.

Yes, I made it. Here I am, at the finish line. Of course, tomorrow I'd have to do the same trip in reverse, and I don't have a clue how to do that. But for now, I'm going to enjoy being in Brooklyn with Sylvia.

Seeing her was like being with family. She was everything to me. She was my friend, my sister, my mother. We could speak in our native language without thinking, without being worried about grammar or finding the right words. I couldn't wait to chat with her and share each other's stories. We got along right the way, like we knew each other for years.

"I am so happy to meet you," I said as I hugged her.

"Me too!" she said with a big smile. "I was so glad when I found out you were here. I've heard a lot of good things about you. Let's go have some pizza. They have really good pizza here. I hope you like it. There's a place near my house."

"I love pizza!"

I'm so excited. I'm outside, walking and going for a slice of pizza. This is so much fun. I want this day to go slowly.

We stayed at the pizzeria for a while. We each had a slice as we talked continuously, without breathing. Then, we repeated. Another slice of pizza, and we went back to chatting, and laughing at just about everything. We had discovered we had so many mutual friends and went to many of the same places back home.

She was renting a single room on the fifth floor in an apartment building. One room with a kitchen. The apartment was dark, with dim lighting and old bulky looking furniture. The room was full of furniture. There was her single bed by the window, and next to it was a small desk that looked like it was used as a vanity. On the opposite side was a convertible couch where I'd be sleeping. There was also a small dining table with four chairs, and a console with a small television on it. There wasn't a lot of empty space in the room. Every wall was completely occupied.

This room is a mash up. It doesn't seem possible to fit so much furniture in such a small space. It's not my style. I never like clutter or too much stuff. But it works for her so it's all good. I wonder who carried all this furniture up here?

"I had a chance to rent just this one room, so I don't have to pay much money," she said. "Renting a full apartment is expensive, and it's not easy. The landlords want all these legal papers and a stable paycheck. I get paid in cash, so I'd have to find a guarantor, but that's not easy either."

She went on and on.

Who is a guarantor?

I just listened and nodded.

"Also, this isn't such a great area of Brooklyn to live in. It's not safe here," she frowned.

"Why? What's wrong with this area?" I asked. "It seems like a great city crowd. I saw some guys walking with their cassette players on, singing along with the music. Seems pretty cool."

She smiled too but didn't respond.

"Really," I said. "Why is this a bad area?"

She just ignored me, like when a little kid asks a question and there's no way they'll understand the answer. She just changed the subject and went back to talking about the latest gossip from back home.

Time went quickly. It was almost bedtime when we felt like having some tea. We chatted more before finally getting into our beds around 3:00 a.m. Having fun makes me forget what I have to do, like sleep for a couple of hours before getting up early. She fell asleep as she was telling me some story about how she met some American guy. I had to be back at work by 8:00 a.m., so I set the alarm for 4:45. I had to leave by at least 5:15 to catch the 6:09 train to Long Island. I tried to sleep but it just wasn't happening. My head was full of the stories that Silvia and I shared.

I needed to go to sleep, but then I started thinking about the travel I'd have to do in a few hours and that kept me awake. I was trying to visualize the whole journey. Subways, trains and walking. I started to drift off to sleep. My eyes were so heavy. I peeked out from one eye and saw it was 4:25 a.m. I felt happy that I had a few extra minutes to stay in bed. I turned the alarm off and just cuddled up in the bed. A few minutes can sometimes feel like an hour.

I opened my eyes and jumped out of bed.

Damn it. I fell asleep. This has happened to me before. I think I have a few minutes and then I fall asleep, when I should just get up. I never seem to learn. I need to be right on time for my job. This is the first time I left the house and I want to prove I can come back on time, even when I stayed overnight somewhere.

I looked at the clock. It was 5:13 a.m.

SIXTEEN

DECEMBER 1996, BROOKLYN

If I didn't make the train on time, I'd have to wait a half hour for the next one. Not good. I'd screw up everyone's schedule if I didn't get back to the house by 8:00 a.m. I dressed and ran down the stairs, skipping a few steps along the way. I ran so fast with long strides that it seemed like my legs were punching up to my head. I was in the subway station waiting for the train when I looked at the time. It was 5:21.

I think I broke the land speed record getting from the apartment to the subway. But I was still going to be late. I couldn't think of a way to get back on time. I couldn't ask the train engineers to go faster. I couldn't stop time. The subway came quickly. I was looking at the time every other minute, like that would change anything.

I kept showing other passengers my piece of paper, asking them if I was going in the right direction. I switched subways and I was almost at Penn Station. I remembered there were only two stops left when I looked at the time. It was 6:09. I was late for the train. I was hoping beyond hope that the trains were running late. I didn't know how I would tell the family I'd be late if I missed the train.

I got off the subway and ran down the stairs so fast that my chest hurt. Running through the corridor was even harder now since I was going in a different direction than everyone else. I saw the sign for the 6:09 and ran down the steps to the track. It was still there.

My train is waiting for me? Are trains human? Or did the universe make it stop for me? It's a miracle.

I approached the conductor leaning out the train window to ask if this magic train was the 6:09.

"This is the one," he said. "We got into Penn Station late so we're a little behind, but you'd better get on board since we're leaving any minute."

I ran through the open doors just as they were closing. When the conductor came, I showed him my station stop and he gave me a thumbs up and I bought another ticket. As the train started moving, I started to calm down, and my mind wandered.

It was really interesting listening to Silvia about her experiences and opinions about this country and its culture, or rather cultures. She seems to know an awful lot. About their lifestyle, how they work, their dreams. What makes a country? It's the people, always. They have their own ways that make them feel comfortable living here and now. I carry my country's culture and traditions within me. They'll always be there. But just because we eat free-range chicken or meat from the countryside where I come from, that doesn't mean I need to bring cows or chickens with me. I want and need to adapt to this environment. I want to live free and easy here, without any baggage.

When Silvia heard about my six-day work week and long work hours doing different jobs, she said my salary was way too low. Anyone knows that, even me. All you have to do is look at my swollen feet at the end of a long day. The question was, what to do about it? Right now, I'm not going to do anything. It's still too soon for me to approach Anna or Michael about work and pay. I never responded to Silvia about it.

It was 8:02 a.m. by the time I walked from the train station to the house.

Two minutes late. Not bad, considering. I did it. I completed my adventure. Another learning experience. I am never, ever taking a few more extra minutes of sleep. That's always trouble.

I rang the doorbell and Michael opened the door, with Anna standing behind him. Kalian was approaching from the hallway. They all looked happy to see me. Even Michael gave me a nice, sweet smile and said good morning. Not the usual grouchy "Hey." I was a little flattered that they seemed to have missed me. Then I walked into the house and knew why.

What a disaster. As usual, after my day off, but this time was even worse. The entire house was a mess. The kitchen had piles of dirty dishes in the sink. The living room looked like a playground, with so many toys you could barely see the floor, or the furniture. The master bedroom had clothes strewn all over the bed and chairs. The main bathroom looked like they had had a wet towel fight. Aaron's bedroom smelled like crap, literally. Old diapers in the trash.

Jessica's room was the worst. I guess the parents let them run wild. No constraints. As long as they were happy. There was even half eaten food in her room. All the dresser drawers were open and empty, with the clothes strewn all over the floor. Anna came to the room and saw me standing there, staring into the room.

"Some mess, huh?" she said. "Sometimes Jessica likes playing dress-up with all her clothes."

She smiled at me, kind of expecting me to say, "Ah, such an adorable little Jessica."

"I see," I said.

How is it possible to make this much of a mess in a house in one day? I know it's my job to clean it up, but would they be this sloppy if I weren't here? How can they live like this for even a day? And I can't believe most Americans live this way. It's just these guys.

After an endless day of cleaning, washing, dusting and laundering, I was exhausted, but happy. I had so much fun with Silvia the day before that dealing with this madhouse didn't bother me that much. I crashed into a deep sleep.

I decided to visit Silvia every other week. She was more than happy to see me anytime, but I couldn't afford to visit every week. I was trying to save most of my money. I wanted to pay off the loan as soon as possible.

On one trip to Silvia's, I called Viktor to let him know he could meet me there so I could pay him. He said he'd stop by. He seemed anxious to get the money, but then again, who wouldn't be?

The phone woke me up. It was Viktor. He was parked right in front of the apartment building. I had no luck with napping. I hoped to get a little extra sleep on my day off but nope. I quickly got dressed and went outside to give him the money.

He rolled the window down halfway. He didn't even say hello.

"Do you know what neighborhood your friend lives in?" he asked.

"Yes, I gave you the address. You got here right?"

"No, I mean, do you know about this neighborhood? Do you have any idea?"

"No, I don't think so."

I feel embarrassed about not knowing something important about this area. Maybe it has some special history?

"Are you OK?" he asked with a slight frown.

"Yes, I'm fine. Why?"

"You're staying in a dangerous place. You need to be careful, especially at night. This is a black neighborhood. It's not safe for whites."

What's a black neighborhood? I'm confused. What's he talking about? Is he drunk? Black? White? What does that even mean?

I handed him the envelope with the money. He didn't even get out of the car. During the whole transaction, I was standing at the side of the car. He took the envelope, said goodbye and shut the window as he drove away. I stayed on the street for a little while and looked around.

What was Viktor trying to say? That it's dangerous here because it's black? I've been here a few times and it's never felt dangerous to me. Last night I got here around eleven at night. I walked from the subway to the building and I didn't see anything or feel any danger. I stopped by the supermarket and it was fine. I bought a pack of cigarettes and some water (yes, I decided on the pack of cigarettes instead of something to eat).

As I approached the building last night some guys were hanging out, sitting on the front steps. I passed them and didn't say hello or anything. As I climbed the stairs one guy got up and opened the lobby door for me. Another guy jumped up and asked if he could carry the water. I thanked him but said I was fine. And then I realized what Viktor meant.

He meant people. Black people. Why would anyone describe people by their color? That isn't even a notion to me. People are people. Why talk about their color? I still don't understand what he meant by a black neighborhood being dangerous. I think everyone is the same. I grew up listening to James Brown, Michael Jackson and Bob Marley. We loved watching Magic Johnson and Michael Jordan. My friends and I love all the music and sports. We never think of them as black. They're just people. The same people Viktor was talking about. I don't have a clue why he thinks they're dangerous. I need to talk to Silvia about this.

"I think Viktor is ignorant," I said. "And I don't mean that in a bad way."

"What do you mean?" Silvia asked.

"I mean he's just repeating what he heard or read somewhere," I said. "He doesn't know because he doesn't live here. He lives in the suburbs without any diversity, and he has some unexplained fears about people who are different. He doesn't have enough experience."

"That's probably true," Silvia said.

"The way I see it," I said, "good and bad things can happen anywhere because there are good and bad people everywhere. Not only in black neighborhoods. I have experience. I'm living it. I've never felt unsafe coming here. Hell, until Viktor mentioned it, I never even noticed there were mostly blacks living here. So what?"

"You're right," Silvia said. "I never thought of it like that."

By January 1997, I had a couple of more payments to make and then I was done seeing Viktor. I was close to being free. How great is the feeling when you don't owe anybody any money? I was already getting excited about the extra money I'd have.

I can help my family even more. That is one of the reasons I came here, to give them a better life. I don't want them to worry about having food on the table when they wake up in the morning. It's everything when a family has food every day and a place to call home.

The first time I sent money to my family it was one of the greatest feelings ever. I knew how much it helped. They were happy, which made me happy. I became even more motivated to work harder every day. I also wanted money for me. I wanted to earn enough money so I could be one of those sexy girls I saw walking on the streets when I visited the city.

Lora found a second job for me close to Anna and Michael's house. I could work there on my day off every other week. It was taking care of an elderly man in his house. He had a full-time person who lived in, but she wanted a day off every other week, so I would fill in for her, staying overnight at his house.

Peter was about eighty-seven. The right side of his body was paralyzed from a stroke. His mind was sharp, but his body was weak. He had problems getting up and down and dressing. It wasn't a difficult job, but it was emotionally hard. I could never be a nurse. I'm the one who would pass out if I saw blood. And I usually couldn't take care of someone like Peter because I'd feel so bad and anxious about him. But the job would bring me extra money.

I was getting paid eighty dollars for a full day. He would usually sleep through the night, so it was easy after he went to bed. But I could never sleep there. Not even one night. I was too afraid. What if he died in the middle of the night? It would freak me out if that happened. I was always afraid of dead people. Too creepy. So, I'd get up a few times during the night and go to his bedroom to make sure he was still breathing.

Martha, the lady who usually took care of Peter, was always happy to see me. She couldn't wait to escape. She was always dressed up with makeup on and ready to go. A few times I arrived there early, and she would just leave even though it wasn't time. I never said anything. I didn't blame her. I couldn't imagine living in this house and taking care of this guy all the time.

Peter was always happy to see me, too. He was hard to understand since one side of his face was paralyzed. I barely understood what people said under normal conditions. Trying to understand him was a nightmare. His son lived across the street and came over on my first day.

"Hi, my name is Robert," he said. "I just wanted to stop by to say welcome and thank you."

"Hi Robert, I'm Alyssa. It's nice to meet you and Peter."

"It's nice to meet you too. When are you leaving tomorrow?"

He speaks so fast.

"I'm living just down the road with the Weizmann's. I help take care of the house."

"What?"

"What?"

"Leaving," he said slowly. "I asked when are you leaving, not where you're living. I want to pay you before you go."

I laughed out loud.

"I'm sorry. Leaving and living sound the same to me sometimes. I'm *leaving* at 7:30 in the morning."

"OK," he said with a smile. "I'll come by early."

"That was pretty funny," Peter said. "I promise I'll help teach you English while you're here."

Well, that's nice, but I don't see how that will work.

"Thanks," I said.

During the day I sat with Peter at the kitchen table while he watched TV or listened to him talk. He loved talking. One time he fell asleep in the middle of a story. Just drifted into a nap mid-sentence. It was a nice break for me when he napped. He did like to get up once in a while to walk around, so I'd help him get up and hold his arm as we walked. And there were trips to the bathroom. The first time I got him to the bathroom I was about to leave him in front of the toilet when he pointed to me.

"I need you to help take my pants off and sit me on the toilet," he said.

What?!? Really?

I looked at him and sighed.

Oh well.

I undid his belt and unzipped his pants. I grabbed one of his arms so this six-foot man wouldn't fall, then I closed my eyes, dropped his pants and underwear at the same time, and guided him as he sat down. I opened my eyes as Peter laughed loudly.

"Well done, Alyssa!" he said. "Well done."

"Glad you liked it," I said with a smile.

When he finished, he called me in to help him get back up and get dressed. I did the same process in reverse and he laughed again. I helped him get in and out of bed as well, but at least he had his underwear on.

He was intelligent. He seemed to get everything right away. He knew I was shy taking his underwear off, so he would start to giggle to lighten things up. I also cooked dinner for him and sat with him, although I never had much of an appetite in that house. I hardly ate anything. Maybe some ice cream. The house was old with one floor, crowded with old furniture and other old stuff. Things collected over a lifetime. There was a living room, a kitchen, a master bedroom, one guest room and one bathroom. Old houses with old stuff seem to have a unique smell. They make me depressed. I never liked going to the country and staying in old houses. They make me think of scary stories and dying. I rarely used the bathroom, and I never brushed my teeth there. I just couldn't do it.

Peter wanted to talk all the time, but it was so hard to understand him. I pretended I understood most of it by shaking my head in agreement. He knew I was pretending. He told Martha that I didn't understand most of what he was saying. He liked to chat with her. She told me he would laugh a lot when talking about me. He told her he enjoyed watching me because I was pretty and had a nice body.

Men. It doesn't matter how old they are does it? I never got mad at him or anything. He was a nice man who just liked to chat and gossip. He was probably a player when he was younger, and now just looking at me was enough fun.

It wasn't long before Martha reached out to me to let me know she was leaving to take another job. She was in charge of hiring her replacement and of course, Peter would have to approve the hire. Both Peter and Martha thought switching care providers would be emotionally hard for him.

"I have a lot of candidates," Martha told me. "It's an easy job and they're paying good money."

"That's good," I said. "I guess you'll hire someone soon."

"Well, the problem is, Peter doesn't want any of them. He only wants you. It pays well. Do you want the job?"

I don't care about the money. I can't do it. I just can't.

"I'm sorry Martha, but I already have a good full-time job, so I'm going to have to say no."

SEVENTEEN

MARCH 1997, MANHATTAN

Silvia and I now had different work schedules. When I went to Brooklyn, I could only see her at night when she came home after work. I'd wait impatiently for her so we could sit in our favorite place in the kitchen to chat before going to sleep. But soon I wanted to start exploring on my day off before seeing Sylvia, so she showed me how to use the subway map to get around Manhattan. I was desperate to visit Manhattan and walk on those beautiful, crowded, lively streets.

My first stop was Times Square. I stepped out onto the street but couldn't move for a while. Everything was moving fast—except me. People, lights, cars, buses. The crowds and sounds made me dizzy. I was astonished by the energy. As I was standing in the middle of the city, I sensed some kind of power that made me feel stronger, and I was so grateful. I walked straight north on Broadway, taking it all in.

These streets are dirty, crowded and noisy, but no one seems to care. They just go about their business, walking quickly to wherever.

Look at these tall, beautiful buildings with large windows right next to some sleazy looking places with signs that say peepshow, with large XXXs everywhere. What does that mean? Oh, live nude girls. Interesting. How about all these men dressed in suits and ties hurrying past a man in ragged clothes, standing and muttering something. What strange contrasts. Looking down the streets I see theaters with big signs about the shows that are playing, while street musicians and dancers perform for some change. It's such a pleasure being in this city, with its crowds and interesting people. I like every single person I see. They each have their unique style and personality. There's the Ed Sullivan Theater. I've heard of that. I've never heard of David Letterman though. Must be someone important to have his name on the theater.

As I continued walking north, the city became calmer, with fewer people on the streets and what looked like either apartment or office buildings. I was amazed by the architecture of so many buildings. Each had its own character. They were different but compatible. On the ground floors were boutique shops, cafes or restaurants.

These high-rise buildings make me feel high and strong—like them. I've never seen so many stores, cafes and restaurants, all right next to each other, and all crowded with people. I wonder what's going on inside them? Next time I'm here, I'm going in.

I reached the corner of Broadway and 59th street and just stood there for a while, looking at a statue in the middle of a traffic circle as the cars buzzed by. Across the way I saw an entrance to a park.

"Excuse me," I asked a well-dressed man as he rushed past me.

"Yes," he said as he stopped.

"What is this area?" I asked, pointing to the statue and then at the park.

"This? This is Columbus Circle, and that's Central Park."

Ahh … of course. Central Park, I should've known.

"Thank you," I said as I turned to the man, but he was gone.

I walked along 59th Street as I continued staring at the park.

That must be a beautiful park, and right here in the middle of the city, surrounded by these buildings. How great is that? I definitely want to spend some time in there, but I should start to make my way back.

I turned right onto 7th Avenue. Every building I saw was more impressive than the next. There was Carnegie Hall, soft brown with its beautiful arch-shaped windows and inlays, and the tall and elegant Park Central Hotel, with people buzzing in and out, everyone in a hurry. As I went south back towards Times Square, the quiet and quaint cafes gave way to loud, dark dive bars, and more of those peepshow places.

I love it all. The beauty, the ugliness. The brilliance, the darkness. The beautiful people, of all shapes and colors. It makes this city what it is. It's alive. It makes me feel free and independent, in mind and body. This is the city where I belong.

I must've walked for about three hours. It was getting late, so I made my way to the subway. It wasn't far away but it wasn't easy because of the crowds.

It takes some kind of navigation skills to walk in this city. But I'll figure it out, with practice. Wait a minute. Why am I rushing? I'm free. No one's waiting for me to be home at a certain time. This is just an old habit, from when I had to be home at whatever time I promised my mother.

I had that happy, exhausted feeling on the subway ride back to Brooklyn. I couldn't wait for my next day off in the city.

Every time I went to Brooklyn, I'd buy *Vogue* magazine. When I went to Peter's I'd bring the magazine with me, and while he was napping or sleeping, I'd read it. I'd read every single article, with my helpful dictionary by my side. *Vogue* was my English textbook. It would take me such a long time to finish one article. I'd stay up late and read all night. I couldn't sleep in Peter's house anyway. Articles would teach me so much about fashion and fashion people. Other articles would tell me about Manhattan: the lifestyles and the places where people went for parties and charity events; the restaurants and bars, the museums and galleries, with various exhibitions. I was learning about restaurant dinner menus and cocktails. It was all new to me. I wanted to know about the high-end stores and where the wealthy shopped. I wanted to know about new, hot items arriving in stores. Every city has its own fashion and lifestyles. I wanted to learn about Manhattan's. I'd write down all the popular places. Any place where the Manhattan crowd would go socialize.

Now when I went to the city on my day off, I'd grab my list with the addresses to see the places, at least from the outside. I was learning about the city and how to move around the areas and streets. I was downtown, uptown, midtown and downtown again. I was all over the place.

I'm preparing myself to live in Manhattan. One day, when some gentleman asks me out, I'll know things. I'm not going to be some silly girl who just moved here, who doesn't even know what a cosmopolitan martini is, or has no idea how to eat sushi. Or where to go shopping for a nice pair of shoes or a handbag.

I was in a hurry to learn and live in this city. *Vogue* magazine was my teacher and my best friend. It gave me so much information about how to be fashionable. It motivated me to look pretty and stay slim so I could fit into one of those beautiful dresses I saw in the magazine.

Most importantly, *Vogue* helped me improve my English, which I still needed. I used to watch the fashion television channel a lot back home. I could watch for hours and would never get tired of it. I love fashion. I never had any high-end designer clothes or accessories, but I knew all about them. I even knew the annual designer collections. Reading *Vogue* and seeing familiar designer names was cool. There were also American designers that I never heard of before. It was interesting and fun to learn about them. *Vogue* inspired me even more to be part of the fabulous city crowd.

From *Vogue* I learned that Bergdorf Goodman sold high-end designer suits that a young Goldman Sachs vice president might buy, like a dark pinstriped suit from Giorgio Armani's Black Label collection. Or Purple Label by Ralph Lauren, or a suit from Ermenegildo Zegna, at about $2,000 a suit. I discovered that Barney's New York was a favorite store for busy New Yorkers, who hire personal shoppers to buy their clothes. I read about the famous Fifth Avenue, where there seemed to be an unending number of high-end stores, right next to each other.

I want to shop for a beautiful Dior dress, or extremely fashionable Prada clothes. I want to experience the distinct style of Chanel, or the sexy girly-girl style of Dolce and Gabbana. I want to feel so feminine in the La Perla store, buying the sexiest lingerie I can find.

I read about the Balthazar restaurant on Spring Street in Soho, where celebrities like Calvin Klein, Isaac Mizrahi, Spike Lee, Robert

De Niro and Steve Martin mingled with a stylish supporting cast. I stopped outside there once. As I looked through the window the entire place seemed to vibrate and glow, like the Folies-Bergère painting by Manet.

And there was the 21 Club, which started as a speakeasy in Greenwich Village and moved a few times before settling into its current 52nd street location in 1929. It was popular with the Wall Street elite, who would finish eating and then head over to the Oak Room and Bar at the Plaza Hotel for whiskey and cigars.

The more I read about these Wall Street financiers, the more I sensed their power—and money. All these smart, highly educated men taking risks and getting big paydays. I'm attracted to them. I admire the fearless, hard-working and fashionable man.

Vogue described the Four Seasons and St. Regis hotels, where rooms and even suites were booked all the time by Hollywood stars and executives. It made me want to stay at those hotels forever. I couldn't even imagine how beautiful they must be on the inside.

There were nightclubs like Tunnel, The Limelight and Twilo, where DJ Junior Vasquez was spinning. I wanted to hear him live. The hidden bar Magnum in SoHo was the best place to go on Mondays, when you might run into Lenny Kravitz. It was his favorite place in the city. Or the Pangea nightclub, where it was almost impossible to get in without being on the guest list.

I'll have to be creative to get my name on that list.

I read and read. So much information. I really believed that one day I'd put all this knowledge in practice. I became an expert about places without ever being there. My favorite place was downtown. I liked walking around the West Village and seeing the townhouses. They looked like dream homes, like you might never die if you lived in one. I loved looking through their windows, stopping for a second to look inside. I was so curious about who lived there, and what they looked like inside. I imagined the people who owned them were secretive, famous and interesting.

One day while walking I saw an old townhouse with wide, high windows that didn't have any shades. The lights were on even though it was still light out in the early evening. I could see inside. It looked enormous. Pale green walls in an open room, with old antique furniture, and a large painting and a big mirror on the wall.

Imagine living in a place like that, in a city like this? It must be magical. It looks huge, with that open room, old antique furniture and large paintings on the wall. I wonder …

"Hello, can I help you?"

I turned to see a guy standing on the stairs picking up a package. He came out of the house I was staring at.

Well, this is embarrassing. What the hell do I say?

"I'm sorry," I said. "The chandelier caught my attention."

I started to turn away as he came down the stairs and walked towards me. He turned and looked through his window.

"Chandelier?" he asked. "There's no chandelier in there."

I looked in the window.

He's right. There's no chandelier. Damn. I used the wrong word. It's a lamp. *Lamp.* Why is he staring at me? Am I in trouble? Maybe I should just …

"My name is Jeff," he finally said, extending his hand.

"Hello," I said as I shook his hand.

"And your name is?"

"Oh, sorry. I'm Alyssa"

Why am I nervous?

"Do you live around here?" he asked.

I wish. It's cool he thinks I could be from this neighborhood. Maybe I'm starting to look like a Manhattan girl?

"No. I live in Brooklyn, but I love Manhattan."

He was curious about my accent and where I was from. We continued talking, and it ended up being a long conversation. Me, with my broken English, and him with his super-fast talking. And I mean really, really super-fast. He spoke so fast it seemed like he wasn't even finishing one sentence before starting another.

Every time I respond to one of his questions, he becomes impatient and finishes my sentence for me. He does seem to understand what I was trying to say. He's always looking right into my eyes. It's kind of unsettling. He's staring at me as if he knows me. What is going on inside his head?

"Well, I really should be going," I said, trying to end the conversation. "My friend is waiting for me."

"Oh, OK," he said. "Hey, would you like to go out to dinner sometime? I know a place that makes great cocktails."

Wow, an invitation to dinner? He lives in Manhattan and wants to take me out, to some cool place? He seems like a good guy.

"Yes, that would be nice," I said. "But I won't be around for a while. Let me look at my calendar."

I took my notebook out to find out when I'd be in Brooklyn again. I pretended to be confident, like this happened all the time.

It is so nice that he asked me out. I miss being with a guy so much, how can I say no?

"I'll be back in two weeks," I said. "Is that OK?

"Yes, that works. Maybe I can get your number so I can call you before, to make sure we're good to go?"

"Sure," I said.

I gave him the Brooklyn phone number.

"Great, I'll call you around 6 p.m. in two weeks."

"Sounds good," I said as we exchanged goodbyes.

I walked away feeling both happy and confused. Happy to be asked out and confused that I said yes.

I don't even know this guy! Maybe it's the weather. It's a warm, sunny day in March. The air is fresh, and everything and everyone was coming back to life after the long winter. Maybe I have spring fever or something.

Whatever it was there was a smile on my face and a bounce in my step as I made my way to Silvia's.

"So, what does he look like?" Silvia asked.

"You know, I really can't describe him," I said, puzzled as to why I couldn't remember his face or body. "I guess he's not that memorable."

"Well I'm shocked," she said. "How is it possible that I've lived here for years and have never been out with an American man, and you go into the city a few times and meet someone, just like that? Are you making this up?"

"No, no. Not at all," I said laughing.

"Well I don't get it. What the hell?" she said smiling as she poured us both a glass of wine.

I worked hard for the next two weeks, hoping the time would go by quickly. I was getting excited about my next day off. Maybe my look changed as well.

"You look different somehow," Anna said one night.

"Yeah," Michael said. "You look … happier. What's going on?"

Why are they so suspicious? Maybe they're worried I'm planning to leave them for a better job or some other reason. They always seem to be asking if I'm happy. Even Kalian mentioned that I look and even sound different.

I just shrugged my shoulders.

"Nothing's going on," I said. "I'm the same girl as before."

But my intuition proved correct.

"We're friends so I feel like I have to tell you," Kalian said.

"Tell me what?" I asked.

"Anna asked me to try and find out what's happening with you. She's worried you might be quitting."

Nosey people.

"They shouldn't worry," I said laughing. "I'm not going anywhere, at least not for a while."

I'm still making payments to Viktor, so I need this job, more than they know. But it's not going to be forever. Let them think that one over.

Martha's replacement was hired but Peter asked me to continue working, and I agreed. My days with Peter were easy. I kind of got used to him but I never got used to his house and its atmosphere. As soon as I walked into the house my appetite went away. The house was my fasting place. Peter was chatting away, as always. But since I was in a better mood, I chatted with him. I told him my story about meeting Jeff. I was practicing my English while also making Peter happy. But I didn't tell him about my dinner date with Jeff. He had a big mouth. If I told him the whole neighborhood would know.

Lately, I was going to Brooklyn right after I would finish my work on Sunday, so I'd have a full day off. I got in late, so I'd go straight to the apartment and wait for Silvia. The next day I was always on my mission to go explore the city and learn more. By the time I returned home I'd be exhausted. I'd go to sleep as soon as possible since I had to get up at 4:30 a.m. (having learned my lesson). But I never really walked around the Brooklyn neighborhood. All I knew was the subway and supermarket.

I was expecting a phone call from Jeff later, so I decided to go around the neighborhood instead of going to Manhattan. I wanted to check out the stores where I might find a pretty but inexpensive dress for my night out. Silvia told me there were a bunch of low-cost stores in the neighborhood. I wanted to go to the stores I read about in *Vogue*, but I was still far away from that. Whenever I got paid, I had my loan payments to deal with.

It was a warm day, so I took a walk and ended up on a busy avenue, with very loud people and a lot of stores. I didn't realize in just a few blocks from the quiet apartment there could be such a lively place. It looked like some kind of festival. I kept walking, astonished. Right next to the stores was a barbershop with a group of young, big-muscled guys hanging out. They were wearing sleeveless shirts and white boxers, with baggy pants and cool sneakers. They were gathered around a big, portable stereo playing loud rap music, listening and shaking their heads. They moved like Eminem. It was like I was watching one of his music videos right there on the street.

A group of girls walked by with large gold jewelry on, wearing tight dresses. So tight it seemed like they could rip at any minute. They wore high platform heels or bright colored sneakers. They reminded me of the girls in music videos. Then I realized, I was in the middle of a black community. I was so drawn to all the activities that I stopped and watched for a while.

How do the girls braid their hair like that? Everything is so colorful and loud. It's energizing. It seems like I'm the only white person around, but I don't feel out of place. No one's paying any special attention to me. I'm just another person hanging out on the avenue. It's so alive. I could stay here all day. But I should get going.

I had no luck shopping. The prices were right, but the styles weren't. Most of the clothes I saw were vivid colors. I wanted something a little subtler. I did see and even tried on some black but dramatic dresses. I laughed out loud when I tried on a couple of dresses. I tried on a sundress that I thought would fit but it was two sizes too big. It looked like I borrowed it from a large neighbor. The dresses were either short and tight, or long, and still tight. I started walking back to the apartment.

When you wear those dresses, everyone knows what your body looks like. I might as well be naked. I'm not going to show Jeff all the details of my body the first night out. I'll have to go with my spring and summer dress I brought with me. I've had it for years, but it's still pretty.

EIGHTEEN

"Hello?"

"Hi Alyssa. This is Jeff, we met the other day?"

"Hi Jeff, how are you?"

Wow, the phone rang right on time. Not like the guys back home. They never called on time. I hated waiting for them. This guy is different. Maybe he's anxious to see me?

"I'm well, thanks. I'm even better since you picked up the phone. I hope you're still available for dinner?"

"Yes, I'm still available for dinner."

I'm starving.

"I can pick you up if you give me the address."

"Thanks, but you don't have to do that. I don't mind taking the subway. I can meet you in Manhattan. Wherever you tell me."

"Where would you like to go? What kind of food do you like?"

What? Why is he asking me? Aren't men supposed to figure out where to take a girl? Back home no guy would ask such a thing. They take you where they want to go. They were in charge. But I do like that he's asking. It sounds polite.

"Well, I like all kinds of food. Wherever you would like to take me will be fine."

"Ah, great."

He sounds relieved. He probably already has a plan.

"How about seafood?"

"Sure. I love seafood."

I have no idea what seafood is. I don't remember reading about that place in *Vogue*. Wait. Is seafood a restaurant, or is seafood ... food? I'm confused.

"Great. The name of the restaurant is Aquagrill. It's one of my favorite places. It's at 210 Spring Street in Soho. Let's meet there say ... 7:00?"

So, seafood is food. Good to know.

"OK. I'll see you there," I said.

It's 6:05 already. Why did I agree to 7:00? I could've said how about 7:30? Damn. Sometimes I'm too shy or too accommodating to others. I need more time to get ready. He lives in Manhattan. It's easy for him. The subway ride alone will be at least 45 minutes for me.

I never liked being late, so I just brushed my hair, put on some mascara and lipstick and left for the city. As I got closer to the restaurant, I could see Jeff standing outside with another man from across the street. They were having an animated conversation. The man seemed angry, or maybe he just looked like one of those angry guys? He was doing most of the talking.

Why would he come to meet me with another man? Was I going to dinner with two men? I don't want to do that. It would be too much for me. I never went out for a dinner date with anyone in the city yet and now, all of a sudden, I'm going out with two men? Maybe I should turn around and go back to Brooklyn. But I want to be on a date and have this dining experience so bad. I've been waiting two weeks for this.

It was 7:15. I just stayed, observing the two of them. I didn't want Jeff to see me. He was looking around the street, but the other guy just kept talking. At one point when Jeff looked around, I stepped behind the phone booth to hide. When I slowly took a peek from my hiding spot the other guy was gone.

Is he really gone? It looks like it. So, I'm not going to meet two men after all. Great.

I crossed the street and approached Jeff. He was medium height and skinny. He wasn't handsome but did have an interesting look. His face was thin with small dark eyes. His nose was a little big compared to his thin face and lips. He had a nice smile. His hair was light brown and cut short. He looked professional and polished. He was wearing a dark blue suit with a white shirt and a light blue patterned tie. He looked older than me. I would guess about thirty-two.

"There you are," he said as he smiled and gave me a big hug. "Let's go inside so we can talk. I hope you're hungry. I am."

I stayed quiet. I wanted to say something, but I wasn't sure what. He talked so fast it took me a while to catch up. By the time I thought of what to say, the moment had passed. So, I just smiled.

He was one of those people where you could just relax and listen since he would always find something to say. There wasn't any awkward silence between conversations because he was never silent.

He had a reservation and the host seemed to know him. I followed them and we sat down at a small square table, face to face.

"I'm so glad you made it," he said.

I smiled again.

I made it? What did I make? He said he was glad so at least he's happy with whatever I made.

The waiter came to our table and handed each of us a large menu.

"Would you like something to drink?" Jeff asked me.

Now this I understand. Thank you, *Vogue*.

"Sure, I'll have an apple martini please."

"That sounds good. And I'll have a vodka martini, very dry please."

"Excellent," the waiter said as he disappeared.

Everything seems so different here. I like this restaurant. Look at all these well-dressed people, chatting away. I feel happy and calm, like happy butterflies. So far so good. I'm doing good.

"You look very beautiful," he said to me as he stared at me.

This staring thing. I don't know what to do.

"Thank you," I said.

I put my head down to look at the menu and pretended I was reading.

Like I have a clue what this stuff is on the menu.

"So, you like martinis huh?" Jeff asked.

"Yes, sometimes."

"Why an apple martini?"

Just then the waiter interrupted our conversation.

"Excuse me. Unfortunately, we don't have apple martinis available at the moment."

Thank God. The waiter saved me from answering the question.

"Would you like something else?" the waiter asked.

I paused. I tried to remember another popular cocktail I read about many times in *Vogue*. I struggled. Now I had two men staring at me instead of one. I felt like I was in a police interrogation. I looked at Jeff. I looked at the waiter. Then I looked at Jeff again, then the waiter again.

They're no help. Wait. Ah, yes!

"A cosmopolitan please," I said with a smile.

"Great. I'll be right back."

"Let's look at the menu while we wait for the drinks," Jeff said.

"Sure, let's look at the menu," I repeated.

I looked and looked, from the top to the bottom and back again. I really was just looking. I certainly wasn't reading. I tried to find something familiar that I could order. I had no idea what the dishes were. I guessed there were a lot of seafood choices, but the names weren't familiar.

"I think I know what I'm going to order," he said. "It looks like you're still deciding?"

"Yes, still looking."

"Take your time. They have great appetizers too."

I wish the dishes were served family style. It's much easier. Everything's on the table and everyone can try whatever they want. I don't know what to choose.

"Do you like octopus?" he asked. "It's great here. Or maybe tuna tartar? It's also really good."

All those names sounded the same to me. I'm clueless.

"Tuna tartar," I said, just repeating him.

"Great. You'll like it," Jeff said. "What about the entrée?"

"Here's your cosmopolitan, and your dry martini sir."

Perfect timing for the waiter to show up again. Now I have more time to think about what to order.

"Cheers," Jeff said.

"Cheers."

We raised the glasses and I tried a cosmopolitan martini for the first time in my life. "How's your drink?" Jeff asked.

"It's very good. It's just how I like them."

As if I know.

"What are you going to order?" I asked. "Do you have some favorites?"

Maybe I can figure out what to have from his favorites.

"Yes, I do. I have a few. Tonight I'm thinking of the pasta with …"

"Are you folks ready to order?"

Damn. So much for the waiter's good timing.

"Yes, I think we are. Are we?" Jeff asked, looking at me.

"Yes," I said.

Jeff ordered the appetizers.

"What would you like as an entrée miss?" the waiter asked.

I looked up and they were both staring at me—again. I was out of time. I looked at the first entrée choice on the menu. Seafood casserole. The words were familiar. I now knew seafood was fish. And casserole? I think I know what that means. Maybe I can say it right.

"Seafood casserole please," I said, pointing to the menu, just to make sure.

"Very good," said the waiter. "And you sir?"

"I'll have the seafood pasta."

"Perfect. Thank you."

Jeff watched the waiter leave and then turned to me.

"I have to say, you're an interesting girl. You like martinis and seafood. You must like mussels as well?"

"Yes, I do. Mussels are one of my favorites."

What are mussels?

"That shows quality," he smiled. "You have beautiful eyes. And I like your dress. The color matches your eyes."

"Thank you," I said, looking down at my hands.

"Please stop me if I'm going too far giving you compliments so soon. I just couldn't help myself."

Where did he go too far? He's right here. I understand he likes my eyes and dress though. That's nice.

"I like compliments," I said with a smile. "I always take them. Thanks for mentioning my dress. I like it too. This is one of my favorite Prada dresses."

"Ahh ... you're a fashion girl. You like shopping?"

"Yes, I do, but not for just anything. Only the good things."

"I do like that designer," Jeff said. "I like Prada suits. Maybe one day you can come with me and help choose a nice suit and tie."

Selfish guy.

"What do you do here in New York?" he asked.

"Right now, I'm just studying English."

"That's fantastic. It seems like it's going well, based on what I hear. Is that why you moved here?"

"Yes, I wanted to learn English and put it in practice, so I decided to move here."

"That's great, and I completely agree with you. Being good at anything requires a lot of practice. Do you work as well?"

"No, I just go to school."

He looks like he's wondering how that's possible.

"I come from a wealthy family," I said. "I get an allowance, so I don't have to work."

I don't want to get into my story right now. I feel like acting wealthy tonight.

His eyebrows raised in surprise.

"Oh, I see. Wow, that's great," he said.

"What about you Jeff?"

"Well, I'm not as lucky as you are. I still have to work. I'm a lawyer."

"You're a lawyer? That's an impressive job. Do you do trials?"

"Not so much," he said. "I have my own firm. I mainly work for corporations."

I don't know what that's about, but he does seem like a smart guy.

"You look like a lawyer," I said.

He laughed.

"I guess that's a good thing? You've made me smile a few times. I like that."

"Pardon me," said the waiter. "Here are your appetizers."

We finished the appetizers as we continued to talk. It was the first time I had tuna tartar. Now it's one of my favorites. Then the entrées arrived. My seafood casserole looked colorful, and confusing.

I have no idea what I ordered. It looks like soup but the things floating around are making me nervous. I don't know how to eat it, especially looking at these half-opened shells. I can't eat the shells. That much I know. I'll just eat what's on the inside. How the hell do I eat these things? Do I pick up the shells and eat them? Or do I leave them in the soup? What's in Jeff's pasta? He has the same black shells with white small meat that I have. Great. I'll watch him.

"*Bon Appetit*," Jeff said.

"*Bon Appetit.*"

I ate slowly. I tried the liquid and the other pieces of fish. I didn't touch the shells. I was waiting for Jeff to eat them.

"How's your dish?" he asked. "Did you try your favorite? The mussels?"

Ah … those are mussels.

"Not yet. I always save them for last," I said.

He's finally trying the mussels. Mystery solved. Pick up the shell, take out the meat with the fork and eat it. Simple enough.

The cosmopolitan drink gave me a nice buzz. I became relaxed and chatty.

"Would you like another martini?" Jeff asked. "I'm having another."

"No, thank you. I'd like an espresso though."

"Sure. Do you like this place?"

"Yes, it's very nice. The food was so delicious. Thank you."

"My pleasure. I've enjoyed your company more than the place or the food."

"Thanks. You're very kind."

I sipped my espresso as he told me about the places he liked to go to. He's lived in NYC for a long time, and he travels a lot. He likes sports, movies and music. He was talking a lot. I liked listening to him and learning new things.

I just wish I could understand him better. I'm only catching a few words here and there.

"You know," he said. "I was watching you. Your manners and etiquette are impressive."

"Why, what do you mean?"

"It's just the way you sit and eat. You're a girl with great manners. It makes sense that you're from a wealthy and classy family."

"Thank you."

I didn't do anything special. Doesn't everybody know how to sit and use the silverware properly? Except for mussels maybe.

"I'm going upstate to Hyde Park next weekend to visit some friends. Would you like to come with me? It's a very nice town with some great restaurants."

"Next weekend? Maybe," I said. "I have some plans, but…"

"Please change your plans. Please come."

NINETEEN

APRIL 1997, LONG ISLAND

"Kalian is sick," Anna announced when I stepped into the house after my day off. "I need your help. Can you do Kalian's job until she gets better? Please? The kids love you and I trust you. I know you'll be fine. You can do less housework, and don't worry about dinner. I'll order something. I have to go now. I'm already running late."

She didn't even pause to take a breath. She handed Aaron to me, grabbed her handbag and went out the door.

"Thank you, I really appreciate it!" she yelled as she disappeared.

I just stood in the hallway, dazed and confused. The house-keeping job was pretty hard physically, but the babysitting was a nightmare. Then I heard Jessica's operatic voice.

This girl Jessica. What am I going to do with her? She can really get on your nerves and drive you crazy. I saw it many times. Two children and no Kalian? It's one thing taking care of them with the parents in the house or watching them as they slept while in the city. Taking care of them alone during the day? I'm not prepared for this. I don't know how to feed one while playing with the other. Or how to prepare a meal while holding a baby in my arms. What do you do with the kids when you need to go to the bathroom? You can't leave them alone. Do you take them with you?

I took them both with me. I didn't care as long as they both were with me and safe. Since the bathroom was the size of a New York City studio apartment there was plenty of room. I used the master bathroom. I didn't even care if there was a camera hidden somewhere.

Soon I got tired just from constantly focusing on them. Jessica was smart. Without Kalian taking care of them, she knew the routine would be different. Kalian knew how to say no and how to stop her bad behavior. Now Jessica could act wild and stubborn. Every time I'd say no to her she would cry hysterically. Why my "no" was unacceptable and Kalian's "no" was OK was beyond me.

I was told Jessica couldn't have any cookies during the day, and especially before dinner. Like all kids she loved sweets and her mother was worried about it. But Jessica wanted sweets and she knew where they were. She would head towards that food closet and try to open the door, but it was locked.

"No, Jessica," I'd say nicely as I took her hand to take her to another room. "You can't have cookies now."

"Yes, I want cookies," she'd respond. "I want cookies, I want cookies."

She kept repeating the words, probably thinking if she said them enough I'd give in or the door would magically open. She would go on non-stop until she became frustrated, and then she started screaming and crying.

I tried other ways to entertain her. I played with her. I sang with her. I watched cartoons with her, but nothing helped. She would get distracted for a few minutes but soon she was running to the food closet, banging and kicking at the door. All the drama and noise would trigger Aaron's crying. Then I'd be chasing Jessica while holding and trying to console the baby.

Aaron was easier to take care of. At least he couldn't run around. But he pooped, a lot. I was constantly changing his diapers. I couldn't take it anymore. Sometimes I'd even ignore his dirty diaper until the next poop. But then he'd start crying and I'd feel bad for him. One time I changed his diaper, put it aside, and Jessica grabbed it and ran down the hallway.

"Jessica, stop!" I yelled. "Come back here. Please don't run. Please put that in the garbage."

She was giggling and running, poopy diaper in hand, until she slipped on the floor. Now I heard crying instead of giggling. I grabbed Aaron to find Jessica, and there she was. Her light reddish hair covered in greenish baby poop. It was also on her face and all over the floor. A literal shitstorm.

Good Jessica, very good. You deserve it. See what happens when you don't listen?

I reached down for her and helped her up. She was crying as if she was so innocent. She stunk. She begged for a shower. She was the most humbled Jessica I ever saw.

By the end of the day I thought I was going crazy. I was praying to see Kalian the next morning, or the next, or the next. But I didn't see her for two weeks. It was hard work, and after all of that, I decided I didn't want to get married or have any children. That was my attitude when I stepped out of that house on my way to Brooklyn for my first day off in more than two weeks.

I got my *Vogue* magazine before getting on the train. I was way behind in my reading. I sat down on the train, took a deep breath and opened my private world of fashion and the good life, when a mother and her daughter about six years old sat next to me. This girl never stopped talking to her mother. It was getting on my nerves.

Why? Why is the universe doing this to me? Why now? I just got released from crazy kindergarten and now this girl has to sit right next to me and talk nonstop nonsense? This mother is even worse. She's so loud. Does she really think everyone on this train enjoys hearing her daughter's childish stories and dopey questions? Look at her. She's even looking at me so proudly, like, isn't my daughter special? Isn't she so adorable? No, not really. Some parents think everyone loves their children as much as they do. It's just not true. I'm so distracted by them that I can't focus on my reading. Am I getting punished by the universe because I said I don't want to have any children? Maybe so, but this certainly isn't helping to convince me I should be a parent.

I stopped by the supermarket for some food and went to the apartment to lay down until Silvia came home. It was late Sunday night. I never returned Jeff's phone call after he left me a message on Silvia's answering machine. I wasn't sure I wanted to see him again and continue lying. With Jeff it was just a date. I wanted to be a girl having a nice dinner with a good guy; that's all. The restaurant and atmosphere were perfect, and I just wanted to be there and forget about all my hard work and tight money for a little while. Just a few hours being the girl I wished to be. When we left the restaurant Jeff offered to get me a car service but I said no. I told him I get car sick and since I had a drink, I preferred to take the subway.

Sometimes I believe in my dreams. When I was acting out my dream with Jeff, I believed it was all so true, until I looked down at my pair of shoes on the subway on the way home. They still looked nice, but I knew they were old. I knew I was going back to a small, dark Brooklyn apartment, and not as a wealthy girl. Welcome to reality.

I was asleep when Silvia stepped into the apartment. She got home earlier than usual.

"Hey, since I'm home early tonight let's go out," she said. "Let's go to a bar. Maybe I'll meet some American like you did."

I'm exhausted. All I want to do is sleep. I can't even move from the bed.

"Silvia, can you believe Kalian got sick and I worked two weeks straight, with two kids? I had almost no experience but I handled it. At least the kids were good when I left them," I said, laughing.

"Really? They're not supposed to do that. That's so wrong. Working that many hours and days without a break? I hope they paid you extra so we can go out tonight."

"OK, you're right. I can always sleep later. Let's go."

"Where are we going? Do you know any nice places?" she asked as we approached the subway.

"You're asking me? I thought you already had a place in mind. You're the one who wants to go out."

"True, but I don't know many places in Manhattan. You're the one who goes there every other week with all your *Vogue* research," she smiled.

"I've never been in the places I read about. But I do know where they are, so let's check them out."

We went to a nightclub. We couldn't get in because Silvia didn't bring her ID. We walked a few blocks and found a bar and diner called The Coffee Shop. We went inside and sat at the bar. The place was pretty empty. It was around 2 a.m. I ordered a gin and tonic and she ordered a beer.

"Beer? Really? Who drinks a beer when they want to meet a guy?" I joked.

"Why? What's wrong with beer?"

"It's just not sexy."

Just then the bar got crowded. All sorts of guys and girls came flowing in. It was like they were coming in after clubbing, to continue the fun with more drinks and food.

"You girls came in just at the right time to get a seat," the bartender told us.

We hung out for another hour and had another round, but no one hit on us. Maybe I looked tired and boring, and Silvia was trying too hard. We paid the check and left.

"We had no luck meeting anyone, even though there were so many guys there," she said as we walked to the subway.

"I told you not to drink beer," I said. "And you even had a second one!"

We laughed so loud, people were staring at us. I told Silvia about the mother and daughter I sat next to on the way to Brooklyn and we laughed even more. We had one of the best times on the way home. Between the laughing and joking we became so hyper we weren't able to go to sleep until sunrise.

The gin and tonics and late night hit me hard. I stayed in bed and slept all day. I was so exhausted I couldn't even open my eyes. I missed my trip to the city. I wasn't happy about that since it was my first day off in a while. But my body couldn't respond to my brain.

On the way back to Long Island, I realized I was in a much better place. I felt happier, calmer. Perhaps because I got used to my new life. I was close to paying off my loan, I was speaking better English, and I was able to get around the city with relative ease. I still had so much more to learn but I was getting there. Things were good.

I was really happy to see Kalian. I felt relieved from the pressure of taking care of the kids. Babysitting is an enormous responsibility. Just watching them made me exhausted. If anything happened to them, I was the one responsible. No matter what it was. They're not like a piece of furniture or lamp that you break and can just replace. I never wanted to take care of the kids. It's too much. But my relief didn't last long.

"Alyssa, we're going to the city this weekend," Anna said.

The good news is I'll be in the city. The bad news is, no Kalian. I have to take care of the kids—again.

"When we get there would you mind cleaning the rooftop area? It's pretty messed up from the winter and it would be nice to get it in shape since we're having guests over."

"Sure, no problem," I said.

The infamous rooftop, where I had one of my great adventures.

"Anna, would you please help me fill out the application for a student visa? My latest visa will expire soon so I need to re-apply. This way I can stay and continue working."

I took advantage of asking for a favor since I had been extremely helpful to her over the last few weeks. I was proud to step up for myself.

"Of course," she said. "Remind me when we get in the city."

"OK, thanks," I said.

We made our way to the city and I went straight to the rooftop. Standing and looking around reminded me of that crazy night. I just looked and stared once again at the beautiful townhouse.

I'll never forget naked man. If not for him who knows what would've happened to me. I can't see him. But I remember him well. His face and ... other stuff like ... he had a nice robe.

I spent quite a lot of time on the roof, cleaning and organizing the place. Now and then I'd look into naked man's windows, but I never saw him. Anna, Michael and their guests were having drinks and dinner on the rooftop while I was in the apartment with the kids. Anna asked me to come up to help out. While there I peeked at the townhouse. It seemed like someone was home because the light was on.

In the early evening the guests left. Anna and Michael went to bed. Everyone started sleeping as I went up and down the stairs to clean up. On one trip I noticed another light on in naked man's townhouse. I went closer.

Not that I want to see him naked or anything. Well, maybe I do. I just want to see him. But I guess he's not around.

In the morning I went to the corner grocery store to buy milk, and there he was. Naked man. I recognized him right away. He was getting a newspaper and a cup of coffee. I felt a little shy to approach him. Maybe it was inappropriate, especially early in the morning. Some people want time alone until they have their coffee. I'm like that.

I grabbed the milk and got in line to pay. He must've sensed me staring at him because it wasn't long before he turned his head and looked at me. I quickly looked away. When he passed me on the way out, he looked at me again.

I think he recognizes me.

"Hello," I said.

He stopped, confused and pensive.

"Hello," he said. "Have we met before? You look familiar but I don't remember from where."

I can feel my face.

"Yes, we've met. I'm the girl you helped. On the rooftop? From the building, right next door?"

"Oh, that's right," he said. "Now I remember. You look different."

"That's probably because I'm not freaking out. You really helped me. I don't know what I would've done without you. Thank you again."

"Do you live around here?"

"No, I work for the owners of the house next to yours. Most of the time I'm with them on Long Island, but sometimes we come into the city."

"I see. Well, it's nice to see you again. Next time you're in trouble just give me a call," he said, smiling.

"Thanks, but I hope I don't have to," I smiled back.

He laughed.

"Well, have a nice day," I said.

"See you later."

"Bye."

I don't know why but I was happy to see him. We never introduced ourselves, so he was still naked man to me, even with his clothes on. I started walking back to the apartment.

What did he mean by see you later? Did he mean that he might see me on the rooftop later? Or did he want to see me later in person? If that was an invite, I feel bad since I didn't respond. But I can't see him later anyway.

We went back to Long Island on Sunday night. On my day off I worked at Peter's. That "see you later" comment was still on my mind. I couldn't understand why what naked man said was so important to me.

"Peter, when someone says, 'see you later,' do they mean they want to see you later?" I asked.

"Well, it depends," he said. "If they ask a question like 'see you later?', they're asking if you'll meet up later. If they say, 'see you later,' it's usually just another way of saying goodbye."

Well that's good. At least I wasn't rude to naked man, especially after everything he did for me. I really wish I knew his name.

TWENTY

The next day Anna announced we were going back to the city again on Friday for the weekend. I was getting frustrated about taking care of the kids, but I was also super happy going back to Manhattan. I wanted to see naked man again. Just the thought of seeing him made me happy. Just a one-minute conversation made me think of him now and then.

It's probably silly of me but he seems like an interesting person. He looked fashionable and handsome. Maybe his style attracts me? I remember the entire outfit he was wearing in the grocery. I looked him up and down so quickly he didn't even notice.

He was wearing soft, dark grey pants that were a little baggy. A light gray long sleeve sweater, with a patterned dark blue scarf around his neck. He was also wearing reading glasses. When he stopped to talk, he took off his glasses, and I noticed his eyes were greenish grey. His hair was dark but greying.

Anna and Michael were going shopping during the day on Friday, and they planned to attend some dinner event in the evening. I asked them if I could take the kids to the rooftop to play and they both said no. They were afraid Jessica might run around and get hurt, so I was stuck in the apartment.

While I put the kids in for a nap, I thought about going to the rooftop. I wanted to go and look around and get some air and hear the noise. But there was another reason, which I didn't want to admit to myself.

OK. I wanted to see the townhouse and if he was around. I went upstairs. This time I made sure the door was unlocked. I stepped out and took a deep breath. I missed the city. I missed walking around the last couple of weeks on my day off. I looked at the townhouse but couldn't see anyone. I stayed there for a while, looking into every single window. But no one was there. I went back inside to check on the kids. They were sleeping peacefully. I went right back upstairs and looked around once again. I looked out onto the city. It looked so beautiful, as always. I looked back at the townhouse. I noticed some empty bottles and boxes on his balcony.

Looks like he had a party last night. Why isn't he home? Where is he now? Maybe at work? Maybe he's not even in the city. I'm so silly, thinking about some old guy and wondering where he is or what he's doing.

I went back inside and didn't return to the roof. I dialed Silvia to chat.

"You know," she said. "Jeff has called a few times."

I have no desire to call him and hear his hyper-fast talk. I'm just not attracted to him.

"Again?" I asked.

"Well, if you're not going to call him back, maybe I will," she joked.

"Be my guest," I laughed.

On Sunday I had some chores to do before we left for Long Island. I took the umbrella downstairs from the roof. I didn't look at his townhouse once while I was working. I thought I was being ridiculous, looking into his house all the time. Now it seemed rather pointless.

In the city I had the additional job of a gardener. No extra pay for that either. So, I went back up to water the flowers. I was still thinking it was silly to look over at his place, but I did it anyway, and I saw him.

I saw him in the same room as the first time. I was trying to force my eyes to look away and continue to work, but my heart forced my eyes to stubbornly stare at him. He was standing by the bookshelf. I couldn't figure out what he was doing. I saw him but he didn't see me.

I'm not going anywhere until he sees me. I want him to see me. Come on naked man, look over here. He's turning around. Damn, he's not looking out the window. Maybe I should throw something at his window. You know? To get his attention? But what if I break it?

I laughed out loud. He left the room and I left the corner where I was standing. I started watering the flowers. I finished up and checked around the rooftop to make sure I didn't leave anything behind. As I looked around, I saw him on the balcony. He was just standing there, holding a rolled-up magazine in his hand, staring at me. When he saw me look at him, he smiled and waved.

"How are you," he said.

I felt so nervous and excited. I approached the rooftop edge and smiled. He climbed down from his balcony, crossed the rooftop between us and came close to the wall where I was standing.

"Hi there, my name is Gilles."

"I'm Alyssa."

"What do you say about getting together for coffee one day? Next time you're around?"

"I'm never available when I'm around."

"Oh, I see. Well, can I call you sometime? So, we can talk?"

"I … I … don't know. Well, OK, but I'd prefer to call you, when I have some free time."

I don't know why I said that.

"OK," he said, and he told me his phone number.

"Please call me when you can. I'll be waiting to hear from you."

I didn't have a pad or pen, so I had to memorize his number. We said goodbye and I ran into the house as I kept repeating the number. I ran past Anna and the kids in the kitchen, completely ignoring them, and into the kid's room where I found a pen but no paper. I wrote the number on my palm, so no one would see it. When I came out Anna stared at me.

"Are you OK?" she asked.

"Yes, yes. I'm fine. Just a small emergency," I smiled.

She smiled and rolled her eyes. I was really careful with my palm, all the way home. I wanted to call him, but I just couldn't do it. Over the next few days, every time I'd find the time and prepare myself to make the call, I'd stop. I'd grab the phone to dial and then put it back. I thought if I heard his voice, I'd become nervous, which would cause me to get confused, which might confuse him.

Damn, I wish I told him to call me instead of me calling him. After all, he's the guy. Aren't the guys supposed to call the girls? I know. I'll call him on a weekday during working hours. That way, he won't be home, and I can leave a message.

I even wrote down the message I wanted to leave and practiced before I called. I was well prepared. I dialed and left the message, asking him to call me back on the Brooklyn phone number.

My next Sunday trip to Brooklyn went quickly since I was lost in my thoughts about Gilles. I stopped by at the market to get some bread, cheese and ham to make some sandwiches. Silvia loved that sandwich and I wanted to make her happy. I called Viktor to schedule a time to meet him the next day to make another payment. I was so close to getting my passport back, and never seeing Viktor again.

On my way to the apartment something started bothering me on the bottom of my right foot. Maybe from the shoes I was wearing. I needed to get a new, lighter pair of shoes. That was on my to-do list right after I paid my loan off. My foot looked fine except for this small spot that felt itchy. I assumed it was a bug bite, from a mosquito or something. I put some lotion on and lay down.

It was dark getting outside. Silvia was coming home late, so I thought I'd take a shower. I went to the bathroom and tried to turn the light on, but it didn't work. I went to the kitchen and the light didn't work there either. I looked out the window and none of the buildings had lights on. It was a little scary.

I'm shocked. Electricity goes out in this country? I thought this only happened in my country. I didn't see or hear anybody say something was wrong.

I found a candle and lit it. A common practice back home. I sat by the window, staring at the neighborhood. It was really quiet and dark. Just what I hated the most. I started thinking about my family, my home, my past.

In the darkness, without anything to do, my thoughts consumed me. I was traveling everywhere. It felt good thinking about what I had accomplished over the last year. It was comforting to know that my family was safe, physically and financially. They didn't have much, but they had enough for a simple life.

I was close to paying off the loan. I had a place to stay on my day off, and I was able to explore the city. I had renewed my six-month visa as a student. Silvia's friend told me it was always good to have a bank account, even with just twenty bucks in it, so I opened my first bank account. Silvia had lived here for years and she didn't have a bank account. When her friend mentioned it, Silvia didn't pay much attention, but I did. I thought it was pretty cool having a bank card in your wallet. It made me feel rich. I was thinking about Gilles and when he would call when somebody knocked on the door.

Maybe it's Silvia. Maybe she can't find her keys in the dark?

"Hello? I own the apartment next door. Hello? Is Silvia home?" she asked.

I felt relieved that she was (probably) a neighbor and opened the door.

"Hi, she's not home yet," I said. "Do you know what happened?"

"Oh, hey there, girl," she said. "Yeah, there's some electricity problem in the 'hood. Hopefully, it'll be fixed soon. I noticed some light coming from under your door, and I see you've got a candle. Do you have an extra one? I wanna show this young man the apartment I'm renting out."

I went to the drawer but couldn't find any more candles.

"Here, just take this," I said. "It's all I have."

"Aww, thank you sweetie, but I can't take that from you. Maybe you can come with us into the apartment with the candle for a little while? It won't take long, it's just one room."

"Sure," I said.

I walked out and left the apartment door open.

"Thank you so much," she said with a big smile. "By the way, this gentleman speaks the same language as Silvia."

Really?

"Hello," I said to him in our home language.

We all walked into the studio apartment. It was dark, so I tried to help with the lighting. It was hard to see what the place looked like.

"I can hardly see but I don't have the time to come back when the lights are on, or during the day," he said in English.

He sounds a little tipsy.

"I guess it looks alright," he said. "I just need a place to crash."

"Did you just move here?" I asked.

"No, I've been here since last year. March 17th to be exact."

"That's funny," I said. "That's the same day I got here."

I can't see his face. The candle's reflection makes him look kind of creepy. I probably look scary too.

"We must've been on the same flight," he said.

"I would think so," I said as I moved the candle closer to his face. "Did you meet some girl on the plane?"

"Yes, I did, and I'll never forget her."

He definitely sounds tipsy.

"So," I said. "I'm that girl."

"What?" he said, as he stared at me.

He took my candle and moved it closer to my face.

Whoa, he's going to burn off my eyebrows.

"You?" he moved in even closer. "It *is* you!"

It was my travel buddy, Zachary.

"I'll take the apartment, here's my deposit," he said to the neighbor.

Soon the electricity came back on. I checked the phone, but it wasn't working. It must've been damaged somehow by the electricity outage. I got the phone company's number from the neighbor and ran downstairs to a small pizzeria with a payphone inside. I asked the pizza guy for three dollars in quarters for the payphone. It could take a while to get through to someone. I called and waited and waited.

Someone finally got on the line and I explained the situation. These conversations with my English and accent were always hard over the phone. It took some time, but she finally got what I was trying to say. She took my phone number to check things out while she put me on hold.

I was on hold for a while and I was running out of quarters. I let the phone dangle and went across the room to ask the pizza guy for more quarters, handing him the cash. He gave me the quarters with a smile.

I don't know what I'd do without these random people who are so nice to strangers. These people are on the streets, at the train stations, at the supermarket and subways. These strangers behave like your friends, always willing to help. I've come a long way in knowing how to live in this city because of them. And here I am again, being helped by a pizza guy I don't even know.

I had to get change a few more times. I was on hold for more than forty-five minutes, but I wasn't about to give up. I wanted the phone fixed so I could get the call I was waiting for. Someone much older than me, but interesting and attractive.

She finally got back on the line and said the phone was fixed. I wasn't impressed with the customer service but at least the phone was working. I was also proud that I made it through the phone conversation.

As I walked home the pain in my foot got worse, and soon I couldn't press my foot down at all. I needed some medication, or a doctor. I never had such a thing and I didn't know where to go. It seemed like a bite or some kind of allergic reaction.

The timing sucks. I'm about to have a whole new experience and now this? Why is this happening now? On Monday, my day off, I'm not able to walk at all?

I even tried to put my shoes on and tippy-toe around, but I just couldn't do it. I wasn't able to go to work the next day, or for the next week. I was devastated, unable to do anything. Silvia brought me various kinds of ointments in the first few days, but nothing helped.

Zachary moved into his new apartment on Tuesday. He worked all day, every day. After work he'd come by with fruit or some ice cream. He'd hold me by the arm so I could walk to the bathroom. He'd visit me every evening and stayed until Silvia came home. Sometimes he'd even stay until I fell asleep. He was so supportive. But I was impatient.

"I need to see a doctor," I said. "These creams aren't working. I'm just wasting time and money."

"OK, we should find a foot doctor," Silvia said.

She called one of her friends who referred a doctor and we made an appointment. Now I needed a ride because I wasn't about to walk.

"Why don't you call Jeff?" Silvia asked. "I bet he'd be more than happy to give you a ride. He keeps calling. Have you ever called him back?"

"No, I never did, and I don't want him to take me. I'd rather call a car service."

"Alright, but if you want the car to wait for you it's going to cost you a fortune."

After a few days my foot seemed to get even worse. I was in serious pain. I didn't know what to do. I wasn't getting any better, I was by myself and I couldn't get to a doctor. I missed my mother, but I didn't call her. I never liked talking to anyone when I'm not well, not even Gilles. He called and left a message. I was excited but I didn't want to talk to him or tell him about my foot. Who wants to hear that?

When Silvia came home, she took me to the hospital emergency room. We waited about two and a half hours before finally getting a room. An Indian doctor came in. Silvia was with me so between the two of us we were able to communicate with him.

He said he was going to make a small cut around the irritated area which would help speed up the healing, and he gave me yet another kind of cream for it. I had no choice. Whatever he wanted me to do, I would do. The cutting thing kind of freaked me out, but whatever. As long as it worked.

I was hoping to be back on my feet (or rather, foot) after a couple of days, but nope. I was still in bed without any improvement. By now I was into my third week of being in bed. I was desperate. Then the neighbor who rented the apartment to Zachary heard about my condition and paid me a visit.

"Girl, you need to go to a specialist, a good specialist," she said in anger. "You think all these doctors know what they're doing?"

"I don't know," I said. "I thought they'd all be good doctors here."

"What? Why? Because it's America?" she said, shaking her head. "Sugar, there are a lot of doctors out there you just can't trust."

Sugar? I like this woman.

"My sister had a problem with her foot not too long ago. The doctor fixed her right up. I'm gonna call her right now."

"Thank you so, so much," I said.

She had a few more doctor stories but finally called her sister.

"OK, sweetie," she said. "Here's the doctor's phone number and address. He's in New Jersey."

She continued telling stories and complaining about a lot of random things. She had some kind of accent that was hard to understand most of the time. I didn't have the energy to focus on her stories, so I just kept smiling as I looked at her face.

Her name was Rose. She was around sixty-five years old and originally from South Carolina. She even told me how she got her name.

"When I was born, some of my momma's friends visited her in the hospital and brought her these white roses," she said. "Then her friends were all like, oh, your baby is so beautiful, just like these white roses we got you. My momma loved the roses. So, she says to everyone, they are so pretty. Maybe we should name the baby White

Rose. And everybody kind of looks at each other, not saying a word, until my daddy says, that is a nice name honey, but I don't think it's gonna work. Well, why not? my momma says. What's wrong with it? So, my daddy, he looks around at my momma's friends, and then at my momma, and finally he says umm … because she's black? Like us? Let's skip the White and just go with Rose."

Rose laughed and laughed. Her laughing made me laugh. She loved telling stories. She stayed with me for quite a while. Zachary and Silvia soon joined in and we all stayed up until midnight. It was a good time. Rose gave me hope that maybe now I'd be healed by a qualified specialist.

"This doctor is in New Jersey?" Silvia asked as she looked at the address. "That's pretty far from here. How are we going to get there?"

"We'll figure something out," Zachary said.

"Like what? It's at least a ninety minute drive from here," Silvia said. "We need a car, and who has a car? Nobody."

Silvia's working herself up into a frenzy.

"And she doesn't even want to call the guy she knows who has a car," she said pointing to me. "Why don't you call Jeff?"

"Who's Jeff?" Zachary asked.

Awkward silence.

"Well, whoever he is we don't need him," Zachary said. "I'll find a way to take her there."

"Yeah, right," Silvia said, shaking her head.

"Don't you all worry 'bout nothing," said Rose. "My grandson can take Alyssa. He doesn't have classes tomorrow, so he has the time."

The next morning, I made an appointment and that afternoon Rose's nineteen-year-old grandson and I were on the way to New Jersey. Rose helped me find a doctor, and she volunteered her grandson to give me a ride. She was, like, everything to me at that moment. She was my mother, grandmother and good friend all in one. We can all take roles as brothers, sisters, mothers or anyone, and we don't have to be related by blood to be there for each other. She was from the human family.

I was getting a ride to New Jersey with my young brother from another mother. Rose's grandson Jordan. He played rap songs so loud all the way from Brooklyn to the doctor's office. By the time we got there I thought I'd need another ride to an ear doctor because I was going deaf.

TWENTY-ONE

MAY 1997, BROOKLYN

"Hallelujah!!!" as Rose might say. I was completely healed just two days after visiting the specialist. It was a bad infection that the specialist said I must've caught from walking barefoot.

I was so excited to walk and go back to work. I wouldn't say I missed my job so much as I missed being active. Three weeks without physical activity was not for me. Only my brain was active. Thinking and reading. I read *Vogue* and any other magazines Silvia would bring to me. I was learning more and more about everything. I missed walking in Manhattan. I couldn't wait for my next day off to go and immerse myself in the city.

Soon I was back into the same routine, but I needed to work even harder. I would've worked eight days a week if it were possible. I owed just two more payments to Viktor, and soon I'd be going to school to take a course in English, since I now had a student visa.

Everybody seemed fine when I came back to work. I expected a little more excitement on my return, but it was like I never left. Anna did call me a couple of times when I was out, which was nice. Michael just said hello, with a smirk on his face, like, "we were doing just fine without you."

But later Kalian told me they were both impatient for my return. You could've fooled me. I didn't see that from them. Maybe once they saw me, they just relaxed because they felt things would be back to normal in their world.

"Of course, she's back. What else?" they probably told themselves.

"Anna," I said a few days after returning to work, "with this student visa I'll have to attend classes for at least 16 hours a week. So, I'll need to have two days off."

"Oh, is that how it works?" she asked.

"Yes," I said. "I also won't be working at Peter's any longer. I'm happy to put in extra hours on the other five days to make sure the work gets done."

But really, how many more hours can there be? I already work more hours than I'm supposed to.

"To be honest, I'm not happy about this," she said. "There's a lot to do around here."

Tell me about it.

"But I understand," she said. "Let's try to make it work."

Going back to school was exciting. It also meant I was staying here longer than I originally planned. I did want to take English classes and then go back to my country. That was part of my plan from the beginning. I just didn't realize I couldn't get everything I wanted in six months or even in a year. Time went so fast.

But it was also true that I wanted to renew my visa. I was slowly starting to enjoy life here. Little by little. I wasn't ready to go back. Financially or emotionally. I hadn't been able to save any money yet. That was another priority.

I promised myself I'd stick to my original plan from the beginning. To go back home speaking English, with some savings, and to bring everyone fantastic presents. Often before I fell asleep, I'd visualize my arrival, including seeing everybody at the airport. I missed my family and friends so much but at the same time, I wasn't ready to leave the beautiful city that I fell in love with. At least not yet.

Sometimes I had dreams that I went back to my country and I wasn't happy. I regretted going home and wanted to go back to America but couldn't. That was a nightmare. I always felt relieved when I woke up and realized it was only a dream. No, it was best to be patient, stick to my plans and go back when I was ready. I was certainly having mixed feelings about my old and new lives. But I felt certain that in the end, I'd go back home, to my friends, family and culture.

The next time I was in Brooklyn I brought a bottle of champagne for Zachary. I used my last twenty dollars. I wanted to say thank you for being so kind and such a good friend over the last few weeks. I knocked on his door, but he wasn't home. I left a note, but he never showed up, that evening or the next day. It seemed strange but I didn't know much about his personal life. I left Brooklyn without seeing him.

It took me a while to prepare myself to return Gilles's phone call.

Why do I get so nervous every time I'm about to call him? Or even when I just think of him? Maybe because of the age difference between us? Maybe I think it's like reaching out to a person of authority, like a teacher, or a boss? When you have to be super-polite and respectful? Geez, I hope he's not a teacher. Not that it's a bad profession or anything. It's probably gratifying. I just don't think I could ever be attracted to a teacher. He's definitely not a teacher. Not the way he looks and dresses—when he has clothes on. Teachers don't look like him. At least not my teachers. And teachers don't have townhouses. Or do they? Maybe they do in America? Nah, can't be.

I finally called. I became even more nervous when I heard his voice. He sounded different on the phone. His voice was deeper. Even my voice sounded different. I didn't recognize it. It was like I was having an out-of-body experience.

"I'm going out of town on business the next few days," he said. "But I'll be back this weekend. I'd like to take you out to lunch or dinner if that's OK."

"Yes, sure," I said. "I'd like to meet but I work on weekends."

"Oh, I see. Well then, what days do you have off?"

"Mondays and Tuesdays."

"OK, how about Monday?"

"Sounds good."

"I'll call you on Sunday evening to let you know where to meet up," he said. "Talk to you then."

"OK, bye."

When I hung up the phone, I felt excited but also cautious.

I want to see him, but then, maybe not. I like him, and I don't. I shouldn't be with a man so much older. And I don't have time for distractions like this. I have to work. I even want to find another job to make things happen sooner. And what about school? There isn't time for Gilles or anybody else. Work should be my boyfriend. But it would be nice ... oh hell.

I listened to my heart instead of my mind. I thought about him day and night. I pictured him from when I saw him in the grocery store. I tried to remember everything about him. His look, his manners, his face. I thought I liked him since that day. Or maybe I liked him from day one, when he helped me off the rooftop.

I really do want to see him again. All my thoughts are so romantic, but I have to stop it now. I shouldn't be an unrealistic romantic. He's just a regular guy. There's nothing special about him. I'm not THAT attracted to him.

I got up and went for a walk to clear my head.

"Zachary!" I said, seeing him as I walked towards the house. "I was hoping to see you last week," hugging him.

"Yes, I just saw your note last night. I haven't been home for the past few nights."

"Where did you go?"

I'm being nosey.

"Are you hungry?" he asked. "Let's order some Chinese."

"Let me stop by the apartment first to get something, and then I'll meet you at your place?"

"Sure. I'll order. Let me guess. Chicken and broccoli?" he smiled.

"Yes. What else?" I smiled.

I ate a lot of chicken and broccoli when I was couch surfing. I went home to get the champagne I bought for Zachary but it wasn't there, and Silvia wasn't home yet.

She knew it was for Zachary. Maybe she gave it to him?

I went to his place but didn't ask about the champagne. He'd probably say something if she gave it to him. The Chinese food arrived.

"Let's have something to drink," Zachary said. "I have some high-end cognac."

"Sure," I said. "Let's find out how good it is."

No champagne around. It wouldn't go with Chinese food anyway, but then, neither does cognac.

"Cheers. Good to see you walking around again," he said.

"Cheers, and thank you so much for everything," I said.

We raised the glasses of cognac. It tasted strong but it felt nice going through my body. I needed it, to relax and stop having all my romantic illusions. But soon the alcohol triggered even more delusional thinking.

"I missed you last week," Zachary said.

"I missed you, too," I said. "I was used to seeing you every evening. You helped me so much. I don't know how to pay you back for all your kindness. I bought you a gift, but I don't know … "

"I love you, Alyssa," Zachary said.

He's staring at me, without blinking. How does he do that?

"I've loved you since we first met," he said. "When we spent so many hours together on the plane. Since then I can't stop thinking about you. I didn't know where or how to find you, but I did. That's destiny. When I saw you in this apartment, I couldn't be happier.

"Why didn't you tell me before?" I asked.

What I just said makes no sense, but I had to say something. This is weird.

"When I saw you every evening those three weeks, I realized my feelings were real," he said. "But I didn't mention anything because you didn't feel well. You know, you are so beautiful, even when you're asleep."

He poured another glass of cognac.

Yes, I need another drink. Quickly please.

"Cheers," he said.

"Cheers."

"I didn't intend to tell you tonight, while eating Chinese food," he said. "I was going to ask if I could take you out, in the city. I just couldn't hold it any longer. You look so beautiful."

He paused, "Excuse me, I need to go to the restroom. I'll be right back."

He sure is animated and chatty. I've never seen him like this. I'm feeling a little buzzed from the drinks. Maybe that's why I'm relaxed. I can't even think of anything to say about all this.

Zachary came back and sat right next to me. He looked at me and then hugged me so tight, and for so long. I felt his deep breathing and strong desires. His energy went right through me. He slowly started kissing my neck. It felt good so I let him kiss me more. I didn't move. He became more active as I felt his lips on mine.

I briefly kissed him back and then I stopped. I resisted him, but he resisted my resistance. He kept kissing. I wanted to kiss more, but I didn't want him. I was feeling a sexual desire that needed to be satisfied more than an attraction to him. It didn't feel right. I gently pushed him away, but he didn't stop. He came to me even harder, so I pushed him again, harder. He kept ignoring my defiance and continued kissing me until I pushed him so hard, he almost fell off the couch. He looked up at me, astonished.

"I'm sorry," I said. "I'd rather not do this."

He got up and filled our glasses. He sat down in silence. It was awkward.

"Let's move in together," he suddenly said. "Let's rent a place together. We can both work and build a life together. I have a good job. I can afford a bigger apartment and you don't have to stay on Long Island or with Silvia. You can find some other job nearby. We can get married and have a family. I'm serious about this."

He's animated again, and speaking very fast.

"I know we'd be a great couple," he said. "I know I may be moving too fast but why wait? We both like being together. What do you think? Let's start looking for a new place. Please say yes."

"I can't do it," I said. "I don't plan to stay here. I'm going back home as soon as I reach my goals. I like it here but not enough to stay. I just want to work, save money, and go to school to improve my English."

"Is that some kind of girly answer?" he asked laughing. "You're playing hard to get but will eventually say yes?"

"No, I'm serious."

"You can't be serious. Nobody wants to go back. You're not going back. You're just playing with me."

He was irritated. It was quiet for a while. He stood up.

"Let's have another one," he said.

He poured himself a drink and walked over to me.

"I'm good," I said. "I can't have anymore. I'm pretty buzzed."

"Just one more. Come on, drink with me."

"I can't, and let's not have any more cognac. Let's have some coffee. Do you have coffee? I can make it."

Look at his face. He's drunk.

"I don't want any coffee," he said. "I want another drink and I want you to have one with me. What's the big deal? One more and that's it."

He filled my glass.

"Cheers," he said. "Here's to our future."

I put the drink on the table.

"You're not going to have a drink to our future? I don't understand that. Have a drink."

He's slurring his words. He's a different person. His quiet and serious personality has turned loud and aggressive.

"I mean it," he said. "I love you. You're not going back. You're staying with me. I know you like me too. You're just not saying it. We belong to each other."

He grabbed me and started kissing me aggressively. It was uncomfortable and I couldn't take it anymore. I pushed him away and he pushed me back.

"What's wrong with you?" he asked. "I'm trying to kiss you and you're pushing me away? I just want to kiss you. What's wrong with that?"

"There's nothing wrong with that. I just don't feel like doing it. I told you already."

"But why not? Maybe you don't love me yet, but I know you like me."

"Who said that I liked you that way? I like you as a person and as a good friend. I really appreciate the attention and kindness you gave me but that's all."

"I don't understand you. What do you mean you don't like me? You were so nice and warm to me. I thought the feelings were mutual."

"But they're not. I never thought my being nice to you would make you think of that."

"I love you and want you. You can't just ignore my feelings."

He stood up, went to the door, and locked it.

"Now you can't go anywhere," he smiled darkly as he took another drink.

"Zachary, please don't drink anymore. This good cognac isn't good anymore. It's bad cognac," I joked, smiling as I tried to soften him.

"I'm fine," he said. "I'm not drunk. I'm just trying to explain my feelings to you. I was so sure you liked me, and you would say yes to my offer."

He sounds calmer.

"I know," I said. "I'm sorry, but I told you all I want to do is focus on my plan. I'm not staying here. I can't."

"You're just saying that," he said. "What don't you like about me? Or do you like Americans better? Do you like that American guy? Jeff?"

He's getting worked up again.

"What?" I asked. "Who?"

"You know. Jeff? Silvia mentioned him the other day? You're dating him and hiding it aren't you?"

Enough of this.

"I'm not answering your questions," I said. "Let's talk tomorrow. I'm tired and I want to go to sleep. You look tired too. You should try to get some sleep. You're working tomorrow remember?"

I smiled and gently took his hand.

"You're staying here," he said. "You're not leaving me. You're going to sleep here, with me."

"Please let's not fight, OK?" I asked. "We have nothing to fight about. We both left our country to come here so we can fight? I can't fight with you. I can't be mean to you. You're a good person. You helped me so much when I was alone and sick. And on the plane coming here. You got me through a long flight. It meant so much to me, you have no idea. I'll never forget that. And I'm not going to fight with someone who has a kind heart."

"Are you just saying that to make me feel good?"

He poured himself another glass.

"Yes, I am," I said. "I want you to feel good."

I got up and went to the door.

"I'm not a kind man," he said. "I'm a bad man. And you're staying here with me!"

He grabbed me again, this time so firm that I felt pain in my arms.

"Stop! You're hurting me. Stop it!"

I pushed him again as hard as I could. But he was stronger than me and didn't let go. He pushed me onto the couch and held me. His face was all over mine. His senseless kissing sounded like a dog drinking water. I don't think he even knew what he was doing. He was numb from the alcohol.

Every time I tried to push him away and stand up, he'd get up and shove me back onto the coach. It went back and forth, back and forth, like we were in an ultimate fighting ring. Finally, I pushed him so hard he lost his balance and fell. He just lay there, exhausted from the alcohol and the fighting.

Is this what he thinks I want? Really? I've escaped so many guys like him back home. I didn't come here to be with someone like him. Someone who makes quick, irrational decisions. I'm so over this immature bullshit. These so-called men who can't take responsibility for their behavior. Who treat women like crap because they have no self-esteem. If he really loves me, he sure has a bizarre way of showing it.

We don't even know each other that well. Fifteen hours on a plane and sitting together in an apartment doesn't tell you all that much about a person. We never went out. We never took a walk. We never exchanged our thoughts about life, relationships or our personal experiences. We never talked about art or books. All we did was joke and talk about movies and stories about other people. I don't know him well enough to even ask him any personal questions.

And that's fine, for a new friendship. But he doesn't seem to think so. Why can't a guy and a girl just be friends? Why can't they have a friendship without any expectations? I guess that's just the way it is. Maybe it's hard for many of them to be around a woman without taking some kind of action. Women, too. Either the road leads to attraction or the road ends. There's no pure friendship road. Being friendly to him doesn't mean I have romantic or sexual feelings towards him. I just don't feel that way. Even though I want sex, really bad, I just can't do it. He's got to be around my age, twenty-five. He's young, but he's supposed to be a man. He's not a teenager anymore.

There was knocking on the door. Zachary was still laying on the floor.

"Hello?"

It was Silvia. I had left her a note that I was at Zachery's.

"One minute," I said to her through the closed door.

It was a long, hard fight but the match was over. He got up from the floor and fell into the couch. I went to the kitchen and got a glass of water. When I got back he was out. I put the water on the table next to him. I took his shoes off and covered him with a blanket. Then I set the alarm for 6 a.m., at maximum volume.

There, that should scare the hell out of him when it goes off.

I smiled as I opened the door.

"What's going on? Did I knock at the wrong time?" Silvia asked, smiling.

"No," I said. "It actually would've been better if you knocked earlier. Where have you been?"

I closed the door behind me and we started walking towards her place.

"Yeah right, I know," she said. "I know you two like each other."

"By the way," I said. "I left some champagne in the refrigerator last week. Do you know what happened to it?"

She just looked at me and smiled.

TWENTY-TWO

The next day I stayed in Brooklyn. I wanted to go to the city, but I didn't have any money for the subway. I didn't hear from Zachary all day. I wasn't happy about last night but I wasn't mad either. What would be the point? It was just another experience, and there's always something to learn in every experience. Good or bad. You just don't want to have too many of the bad ones, and you certainly don't want them to be repeated.

I still believe Zachary's a good person. Maybe he has issues he's working through that I don't know about, and the alcohol just amplified them. If I agreed to his offer, I wouldn't have seen the anger. I wonder if you should see a person drunk before you start a relationship? And why do I seem to attract sexually aggressive people? Like Lora's father Alex? Why on earth did Zachery think he could force himself on me? Just because I was friendly towards him? Or is it a guy thing? They just go for it when they're horny, without permission? I don't even have what I'd call an overly sexual look. I don't have the big boobs, large hips or facial features that many men might get excited about. But I must be putting some vibe out there because they're attracted to me. It's nice to be desired. I just wish they weren't so crude about it.

I couldn't find the necklace that Maximillian gave me. It was a thin gold chain with a small diamond. I wore it all the time. I didn't even take it off in the shower. I think it came off in Zachary's apartment when we were wrestling. I didn't want to talk or see him, so I asked Silvia to leave him a note to ask if he had it. He told Silvia he found it, but it was broken so he was going to take it to the jeweler to get it fixed. I didn't want him to do that. I wanted back my necklace right away, even if it was broken. Silvia asked him for the necklace, but it was already at the jewelers.

I was excited about receiving the student visa. I was a little worried that I wouldn't be approved but it all worked out. It was much easier getting this one than the first time, when I stood on line in the cold, brutal weather back home. It was a simple and efficient process. I filled out the papers, submitted them and within a few weeks I received the approved visa by mail. Just like that. Now I was going to take classes in Manhattan. How cool was it to go to school in Manhattan? It was exciting. I'd have to pay for school, but once Viktor was paid off, I'd be fine.

After more than a year I finally had two days off in a row. It felt like I was going on vacation. I was leaving on Sunday night and I was free until Wednesday morning? That sounded fantastic. Gilles called me late Sunday.

"Good evening, Alyssa," he said. "How are you?"

"I'm good thanks, and you?"

"I'm well thanks. Are we still on to meet up tomorrow?'

"Yes, tomorrow is still good."

"How about lunch?

"Yes, sure,"

"OK, let's meet on the corner of 72nd and 5th. How about 1:00?"

"1:00 is good. Could you please repeat the streets?" I grabbed a pen and paper.

"72nd and 5th."

"OK, I'll see you there. Goodnight Gilles."

"Goodnight. Talk to you later."

My face is on fire from blushing. This is ridiculous. Look at my face in the mirror. It looks like a monkey's butt. I was proud that I understood him and I never had to say, "excuse me, what did you say?" It feels like when I passed the conversational exam for the English class I'm going to attend. He spoke slowly and clearly. Not like that guy Jeff. I had such a hard time understanding what the hell he was saying. Gilles is good. His words are clear, short and specific. But what's up with that talk to you later thing? Is he going to talk to me again before we meet? Oh, this is torture. Now I'm confused. Wait a minute. Maybe it's like that see you later he used in the grocery store? See you later, talk to you later. What other later things don't I know about yet? I have to learn all these expressions. And quickly.

I looked at a map to see where 72nd and 5th was. I had never been that far uptown. I made my way to meet Gilles. I left early just to make sure I'd have enough time to figure out where I was going. There were subway delays, but I had plenty of time. While I was on the subway, I felt calm and happy. I was independent, controlling my life and decisions. No one checking up on me or criticizing me. I was a free adult. It made me think of how different it would be back home.

There, everybody had to know everything about everyone. Any time you left the house all the neighbors knew when you left and when you returned. Sometimes they even asked where I was going and why I looked so pretty. Or my friends would wait for me to get home and give me a call. It felt like being under control twenty-four/seven. Here, no one cared. I liked that free lifestyle. I liked that I didn't have any time limits on my days off. I could take my time without anybody's permission. Sure, it's nice when people care about you and want to hear your stories. But you share when you feel like sharing, not because they want to know.

My family used to say I was so stingy with my words and sharing stories. When I'd come home from some party or something, they all wanted to hear everything about it. They wanted to know who was at the party, who wore what, or all about the food. They wanted all the details. But I'd just respond with a few words. Yes, it was fine; the food was good. My family would get upset. You never like to share, they'd say. We want details!

My siblings were energetic storytellers. They'd come home and as soon as they stepped into the hallway they'd start chatting away about their night, with all the specifics. All of them were like that. They'd even go on about it the next morning at breakfast, repeating the same stories from the night before. I never liked to chat that long, especially in the morning. I'd say "You guys already talked about that last night. We got it. How many times do we need to hear the same thing?" They'd look at me, frown and continue talking.

I miss them. All the good memories, and the bad ones. The past. I never like thinking about it. Maybe because there aren't that many good memories. But my love toward them is stronger than any unpleasant moments we ever had together. I love them and my freedom, at the same time.

"Next stop, 77ᵗʰ Street."

Damn it. I missed the 68th Street stop. I don't have much time. It's a quarter to one already. I never like being late, but especially with this guy. I'm not sure why, but I respect him.

I got off at the next station and started walking. I had heels on, but I walked fast. I was going to be late. I was hoping he would wait for me. It was only a few blocks, but the streets seemed to go on forever. I couldn't wait to see him. My heart was racing, from the cardio and the excitement.

It was a perfect day in May. The sun felt warm, but the air was cool. It was a day when the air smelled of spring, when everything feels new, like when you're happy but you don't know why. It was a feeling of great energy, the feeling of life. It was the feeling of existence, of being present. No past or future. It was at just this moment when I saw him. He was standing, leaning against a wall, with legs crossed, reading a magazine.

He looks like he's just hanging out. Enjoying his magazine without a care in the world. I wonder if he really wants to meet me.

As I approached him, I was hoping to catch his attention, but his head was buried so far into the magazine that you couldn't see his face. I was standing right in front of him when I tapped his magazine cover. He lowered the magazine in slow motion and looked deeply into my eyes. His eyes got smaller as he smiled. He hugged me and kissed me on the cheek. He embraced me as if he knew me for a long time. It felt so warm and comfortable.

"Sorry I made you wait," I said. "I missed my subway stop and I had to walk from 77ᵗʰ Street."

"You did? You must've been lost in thought on the train."

"Yes," I laughed. "That's exactly what happened. How did you know?"

"It's happened to me many times. No big deal."

He looks so energized and upbeat. I can feel his energy and happiness. It's contagious.

"So, here's the plan," he said. "Let's take a walk in Central Park for a while, and then we can go to lunch at the Boathouse."

"Sounds good."

Maybe I didn't talk much back home, but with him I became the chattiest person ever. I told him every detail of my trip. How I missed the train stop and that I walked so fast, but the blocks were so long, and the weather was so nice, and on and on. I became so lively and animated. I had no issue with my English or thinking of something to talk about.

We walked for more than an hour, but the time went super quick. Central Park with its beauty and open spaces made me dizzy. The richness of nature gave me goosebumps. It was pure joy.

"I've never been in Central Park before," I said.

"Really? Well, I'm glad I could be the first person to take you here. I love this place. I come here as often as I can, and especially when I want to be by myself. I do come here with my friends, but I'm selective about who I come here with."

"Well I appreciate you sharing your special place with me," I said, smiling. "This park looks so huge. I'm sure there's enough room for everyone."

"Yes, it's massive, and every area seems to have its own natural beauty. It's like you can never know the entire park, but I like to try anyway," he smiled.

The conversation was flowing. I talked more than he did. He was a good listener. He was curious about me. Who was I, where I was from, what I was doing here? All natural questions anyone would ask, but I wouldn't answer them for just anyone. With him? I wanted to tell him whatever he wanted to know. I didn't have any barriers. I felt absolutely comfortable and I didn't mind sharing my stories.

I gave him a short version of my past and why I was here now. I shared some of my crazy experiences at work as a babysitter, house-keeper and cook. We laughed, a lot. I hadn't been this chatty and happy for a long time. I sounded weird, but a good weird.

"You're very charming," he said. "You keep making me laugh. I like that. You have a good sense of humor."

"Thanks, and I like your style."

"My style? What do you mean?"

I stopped walking and pointed to his whole outfit.

"Oh," he said. "Well, thank you."

He said he had to make a phone call so we sat down on a bench. While he spoke on his cell phone I checked him out, top to bottom, and back again.

He does look good. He's wearing a nice pair of leather shoes, dark blue jeans and a blue sport jacket. His tailored blue-striped dress shirt is perfectly complementing his beige Burberry soft fabric scarf. He must like scarves. He's medium height, slim and fit. He must hit the gym a few times a week. He's so well-groomed and smells so fresh. That's important. I can tell by a close look at his face that he's way older than me. Maybe too old. He's got to be around 47. I'm 23. Maybe I shouldn't be here. But I do feel some kind of chemistry with him. He's interesting, and handsome.

"Sorry about the phone call," he said. "Should we hit the restaurant?"

"Should we what?"

"Are you ready for lunch? Should we go?"

"Oh, yes. Of course. I just didn't understand what you meant by 'hit the restaurant.'"

We both laughed as we started walking again.

"I'm sorry about my weak English language skills. It might be hard for you to understand me as well."

"No worries. I'm used to it. I meet with foreigners all the time and seem to be able to tune into their accents after a little while. And by the way, you have a cute accent. It's easy to listen to."

He meets foreigners all the time? At his job? Or does he like to date new immigrants?   I smiled.

"You're smiling," he said. "What's so funny? Tell me. I like to make you laugh."

I shared my thoughts.

"No," he laughed. "I don't stalk immigrants. I work with a lot of foreigners."

"I just got a student visa and I'm going to take English classes. I start next month. I'm so excited. I'm going to be very busy with my job and school."

"That's great."

"Yes, thanks. I want to learn English really well so I can go back home and have more job opportunities."

"So, once you finish school you're going back to your country?"

"Yes, that's the plan. Besides, I can't stay here once my visa expires.

"I see."

"How about you Gilles? I hear an accent. Are you French?"

"You're perceptive. Yes, I was born in Paris but I've lived here for a long time."

We continued to walk and talk. Or more like, I continued to talk. I couldn't shut up.

"Did you say the restaurant is called the Boathouse?"

"Yes, have you ever been there?"

"Never, but I've heard of it. I mean I've read about it. It's a place where a lot of famous people go."

"I guess. "

We walked into the restaurant, the host greeted us and took us to our table. It seemed like the host already knew which table Gilles wanted. We sat outside. The place looked beautiful. The sun shined off the water and we were surrounded by beautiful plants. It was romantic and sexy.

"It's beautiful here," I said. "No wonder famous people like coming here."

"What famous people?"

"I don't know. You know, just some famous people I've read about."

"What do you read?"

"*Vogue*," I answered.

I'm so proud.

"You like fashion?" he asked.

"Very much."

"I like reading *Vogue* sometimes. If the articles are good."

"You do? I love that magazine. What do you think of Anna Wintour? I'm sure she's intelligent and good at what she does, but how come she never changes her hairstyle? And what's with the sunglasses all the time? Do you know? And did you know Miuccia Prada is a fun person to be around? Who would think? But her designs are unique. The colors she creates are so deep and rich. The style, with precise lines and perfect fit, really shows how professional she is. Maybe because …"

I took out my notebook.

"This is one of her quotes. 'I had no fun. My family was way too serious.'"

We both laughed,

"Am I talking too much?" I asked.

He just stared at me in silence.

"No, no," he finally said. "Not at all. You've made some interesting observations."

I don't know why I want to share all my fashion opinions with him. Maybe I assume he's interested because he looks so fashionable? Or maybe I'm just comfortable with him and I can talk about anything.

"I never thought about Anna Wintour's hairstyle but you're right," he said. "It's the only one I've ever seen on her."

"Wait. Did you say, 'Have seen on her?' You mean in person?"

"Yes, at a few charity events. I don't know much about women's fashion, but I know a little about men's. I do like Brioni and Cucinelli suits, and Zegna's cashmere coats are the best for dealing with New

York City winters. I also like Ferragamo shoes and Hermes ties. And that's the extent of my fashion knowledge."

He smiled, looking even friendlier.

"You have gorgeous blue eyes," he said. "They're so bright. I've never seen a color like them. Are they real?"

"Actually, no. I can take them out so you can take a closer look if you want."

I slowly moved my fingers to my right eye but couldn't hold it in when I saw his eyes get big. I giggled.

"I'm joking. Yes, they're real."

We both laughed. We were having so much fun we forgot to order. We looked up and the waiter was patiently standing there. As he was telling us about the specials, we looked at each other and started laughing again. We couldn't stop.

"OK, OK. Let's get through this. No looking at each other while this gentleman tells us about the menu. Sorry, please," Gilles said, looking at the waiter.

We paid attention. All the choices sounded so good. We were both hungry.

"And, we also have a caviar spec ... "

"Caviar?!" I said.

They both turned to look at me.

"I'm sorry," I said.

The waiter finished with the specials.

"I guess you like caviar?" Gilles said.

"Yes, but ..." and I started looking at the menu.

"Why don't you try the special caviar dish?" he asked.

"Thanks, but that's OK. It's just that I haven't had caviar since my father died. He left, and so did the caviar."

We looked at each other and smiled.

"Well," he said. "Unfortunately, I can't bring your father back, but I can bring back the caviar."

TWENTY-THREE

I like the way he speaks. Everything seems so smooth and easy. No drama. I'm not used to that. Why do so many people make so much drama? What's the point? I like that I mentioned my father and he didn't say, "Oh, I'm sorry to hear that."

I'm so tired of all the heavy, dark comments since my father died. All the neighbors, relatives or whoever knew him would go on and on. From their conversations you'd think it was the end of the world. How tragic that he's gone. How hard it must be, losing such a great person. What are you going to do without him? Life is so cruel. You poor, poor people. You poor kids. They kept saying the same thing over and over again, for years.

Yes, it was sad. Yes, we lost a great person and a kind, loving father. Yes, it was painful, and yes it was a hard life after he died. But no. No one wants to hear this endless stream of negativity. It was depressing and unfair for adults to say this in front of us. Instead of making us live the sad event over and over again with their depressing comments, they should've lifted us up. Life is still beautiful. You'll be all right. You're young. You have the future ahead of you. But no, they said the exact opposite. And now I tell Gilles about losing my father, and somehow, he respects my father and me with one simple sentence.

"Thank you, Gilles," I said. "I heard 'caviar' but didn't hear about the rest of the dish."

"He said it was an angel hair pasta with caviar. It sounds delicious."

"I never had caviar that way. I'm not a big pasta fan but I'll try it because of the caviar."

"How do you like to eat caviar?"

"With toasted rye bread, butter, sliced cucumber, and a whole bunch of caviar," I said smiling.

"Wow," he said. "Now that's a serious caviar dish."

"Yes," I laughed. "It's *all* about the caviar."

I excused myself to go to the restroom. When I returned, he was on the phone, and what did I see? A wooden braided basket with sliced toasted rye bread, partially covered in a white cloth. There was a large round white plate with small cubes of rich yellow butter, thinly sliced cucumbers, peeled, and a decent-sized, cute jar of black caviar. It looked like a work of art, with all the colors and beautifully shaped food. My mouth was watering but I waited until he finished his phone conversation.

"Thank you, Gilles. This is so beautiful, and very thoughtful."

"Of course. Please, let's eat."

I enjoyed every taste of the caviar. I ate slowly and with joy.

"I'm guessing you know your caviar," he said. "How is it?"

"It's excellent, very fresh. I can't stop eating it. Would you like some?"

"No thanks. I'd rather just watch you enjoying it."

After lunch he ordered dessert wine.

"This is one of my favorite dessert wines. It's a French Sauternes. I have one every time I come here."

It was tasty: sweet and light. It went well after the salty caviar.

"I'm just curious," I said. "I read in *Vogue* that in the 21 Club restaurant some wines cost $1,500, or even $2,000. Is that true?"

"Yes, it's true. Some wines cost even more than that. Have you ever been to 21?"

"No, I've never been there. I haven't been to many places, besides a few museums. I just read about them."

"Well, you seem to know a lot about a lot of things. Maybe more than me," he smiled.

"Yeah, right," I said and we both laughed.

"I don't understand how wine costs that much," I said. "How is that possible? I know it's all about the age, where it comes from and the quality of the grapes, but still."

"I think you just answered your own question. Those are the main reasons why."

We left the Boathouse. I was satisfied. I didn't ask any more questions. I had enough air time with Gilles. I didn't ask him any personal questions. If he wanted to tell me his story he would. If not, that was OK too.

"Would you like to walk some more in the park?" Gilles asked. "I can show you some other pretty areas."

"Yes, let's see some pretty areas."

It was a beautiful day for walking. We laughed about the time he helped me escape from the rooftop. I knew one day I'd laugh about it, even though it wasn't so funny at the time. Well, maybe it was. After a while we sat down. He apologized because he had to return a couple of phone calls. He was on the phone a lot longer than I expected, but I enjoyed the people watching and the nice spring air, up to a point.

"I think I'm going to head home now," I said when he finished one of his calls. "You seem busy, plus it's getting late."

"Oh, I'm sorry. Please don't go. I have to make one more call and it won't be long. These are just a few urgent calls that I didn't expect today."

It was hard to resist so I stayed. We were in the park so long I felt like I was back on Long Island with all its nature. Parks are so beautiful with all the plants and flowers. We all need that once in a while. But I wanted to get back to the energy of the city streets and crowds. And once I've had enough, it's enough. He finished his calls.

"I'm so sorry," he said. "I had to take these calls. It's work, you know?"

"I understand. Work is work. I had fun looking at the people and the park, but can we go? I should be heading home soon anyway."

"Sure, let's go."

We walked towards Fifth Avenue.

"What kind of work do you do, Gilles?" I asked. "You seem like a very busy man."

"Business. It's all business. I'll tell you about it another time if that's OK."

"Of course."

"But, because you waited so patiently for me while I made those calls, which I appreciate by the way, I'd like to take you somewhere. Wherever you want to go. Can you stay out a little longer?"

"Wherever I want? Are you sure? Don't change your mind when I tell you."

"I won't," he laughed. "I promise. Where do you want to go? You seem to know a lot about this city."

"Hmm, let me think ... I'm thinking ..."

He was looking at me, without moving.

"I don't know," I said.

"That's where you want to go?" he asked, smiling.

"Yes, I don't know. It's a great place. Two Michelin stars."

We laughed as we continued walking.

"I'm kidding, obviously," I said. "I really had a great time today. Thank you so much for everything, but I think I should head home."

"Wait," he said. "You're not telling me where you want to go because you want to go home?"

I do want to stay with him longer, but I don't want to tell him that.

"OK," he said. "If you're not going to tell me where you'd like to go then I'll take you where I'd like to take you. What do you think?"

"That sounds much better," I said.

"OK, let's grab a taxi."

We headed downtown to the Meatpacking District. It looked like an abandoned and eclectic area. He told me it was the new trendy area that was growing into one of the cool places to hang out.

We approached a building without a sign. He told me the name was Lotus. The place had a big, heavy wood front door with curtains. There was a big muscular guy and a beautiful girl holding a notebook at the front door. It was impossible to see inside because the large glass windows were covered with velvet.

Where am I going with this older guy? It looks like a secret, illegal place. I'm happy to be with him, but why here? I'm not feeling any bad vibes. I'm dying to see the inside of places like this. I'll just follow my older man.

As we approached the door, he grabbed my hand. He said something I didn't understand to the pretty girl. She smiled at him and asked him for my ID. He said something else to her that I didn't understand. She smiled and nodded her head, and the muscular guy opened the heavy door to let us in.

Inside there was a bar and lounge area, with a dining area a few feet away. We went straight to the bar. The bartender came over right away. He looked like a model. He seemed to know Gilles since they shook hands and started a conversation. I felt like I was in a movie. There were beautiful people all around us. Men, women. They all looked so attractive and fashionably dressed. I was wearing a plain, knee-high blue-laced dress with shoulder straps. It was simple but elegant.

"These people look so beautiful here," I said. "Very stylish. I don't think I'm dressed well for this place."

"You don't need to be," he said. "You'd look beautiful no matter how you dressed."

We drank our champagne. The music was playing so loud it was hard to hear each other.

"Champagne always makes me hungry," he said. "Are you hungry? You had such a light lunch."

"I had a light lunch?" I asked, smiling. "I ate a jar of caviar."

"Come on," he smiled, "let's go to the dining room. I know I'll be hungry later, so I'd rather eat something now. I don't like to eat late. It's bad for you."

I never heard of a man not eating late. I remember my mother saying the same thing, but nobody listened to her. He does look healthy though.

The dining room was beautiful. We sat at a corner table.

"They serve Asian Fusion here," Gilles said. "It's very good."

I nodded my head and looked at the menu.

What the hell is Asian Fusion? I only know a few Chinese takeout dishes, like chicken and broccoli or fried dumplings. I don't see those on this menu. What is Hamachi Kosho? Or Dragon Tail Spareribs? Dragon Tail? Really? I'm so confused.

"Gilles, I'm struggling with this menu. Would you mind ordering for me? I trust your taste," I said.

"Sure. Are you in the mood for anything specific? Fish, chicken or meat?"

"I think I had enough fish today. Maybe chicken? Wait, no. Maybe some vegetable dish?"

"Good call on the fish. You don't want to grow gills," he smiled.

"Grow what?"

"Gills. You know, gills. On fish?" he said as he waved his hands next to his ears.

"Oh, gills," I smiled. "Actually, I'm aiming to be a mermaid."

We laughed.

"Why not chicken," he said. "You don't like it or ..."

"I like it, but I had a lot of Chinese delivery last month. I only ordered chicken and broccoli."

"Do you order Chinese often?"

"Not usually. But I didn't feel well for a few weeks, and Chinese food was my best friend."

"Oh, you didn't feel well. I'm sorry to hear that."

"That's OK. It has nothing to do with you."

"No, I said sorry to hear."

"No, no. Don't be sorry. You didn't do anything."

"This is too funny," he said.

"What?"

"When someone says, 'sorry to hear' it's not an apology," he smiled. "It's a just way of showing sympathy, like it makes me sad that you were sick."

I laughed so hard I had tears running down my face, and then he couldn't stop laughing. We shared a few appetizers. The conversation and champagne flowed. It was a great time. When it was time to go, he put me in a taxi and paid the driver.

"I had a great time, Alyssa," he said. "Please call me when you get home?"

"Yes, I will," I said as I hugged him. "And thank you so much. It really was great."

While the taxi driver raced on the highway, my mind was racing.

What a great day. Full of fun, warmth and beauty. It was the most interesting and classy day I've had in a long time. It was like the days I had with Maximillian back home. It was just being who you are and, in the moment, forgetting everything as you experience pure pleasure. I didn't get tired at all around Gilles, but I'm not sure I want to see him again. Sure, he was fun and comfortable to be with, and the places he took me were fantastic. I felt so free with him, which doesn't happen often. I'd love to do it again. But wait. Why? Why do I want to see him again? Because he's kind? Because he takes me to nice places? Because when he holds my hand, I get goosebumps? Did just that little touch make me feel, sexual? Maybe that was it. The reason doesn't matter. I do want to see him again.

"Hi Silvia, I'm glad you're home."

"Hey Alyssa. I was just about to make some tea. Do you want some?"

"Yes, please."

"Where did you go? I'm sure you did your city tour."

"Yes, I did a city tour, but a real one this time. I never had a chance to tell you ... do you remember naked man?"

"Who?"

"You know, naked man? When I was stuck on the roof and the next-door neighbor helped me? And I saw him naked?"

"Oh yeah," she laughed. "I remember. What happened? Did you see him naked again?"

"Very funny. No, I didn't see him naked, but I did go out with him today. I spent all day with him."

"Really? Tell me more."

As she poured the tea, I told her everything about my great day in the city with Gilles. I shared every single detail, from the beginning to the end. She listened carefully, with wide eyes. I talked so long our tea turned cold, but neither of us cared.

"The most important part?" I said. "I felt so comfortable with him. We got along so well. It was an instant connection. He's like one of those close friends who you can talk to about anything. No barriers you know? I also felt protected by him. Like there was a real man right next to me. An older, mature man with power. Like a father."

"Like a father?" Silvia asked. "What do you mean? Do you like him like a father? That's just weird."

We laughed so much that I accidentally spilled my tea on the table, which made us laugh even more.

"No, no, I mean, like when you're a little girl and your father protects you. You're being cared for by a smart, mature man."

"Oh … I know what you mean. How much older is he? Five or six years?"

"I should really say no if he asks me out again."

"Why? I like him already. For you of course," she smiled.

"Dating takes time. Time that I have to use for other things. I have a student visa that could be extended, but it's questionable. He seems to be high class. With good manners, good looks, and he's stylish. It doesn't seem like good timing. I'm super busy with my job, school will start soon, and my plan is to go back home. Why start a relationship now? It was a great day with him, and I loved the places we went, but it's a distraction. It should just be this one day out and that's it."

"How old is he?" she asked again.

"He's forty-seven. I don't care about his age. I like older men."

"What? Did you say forty-seven? I think that's too much. I would never date someone that old."

"Why not, if you liked him? What's the difference? If you feel happy with him that's all that counts, right?"

"You know, I've heard that some older man can be strange. They might ask you to do some bizarre stuff. Especially if he's rich. They like to do strange things with younger girls."

"Yeah, but younger guys can be weird too," I said, thinking of Zachary. "By the way, did you ask Zachary about my necklace?"

"Yes, he said it's still at the jewelers."

The phone rang and Silvia picked it up.

"It's for you," she said covering the mouthpiece. "It's the old man."

We both started giggling.

"Hello?" I said, still laughing.

"Hi Alyssa," Gilles said. "I hope you got home alright."

"I did," I said, trying to compose myself. "I'm sorry. I forgot to call you."

"That's OK."

"My roommate and I have been chatting since I got home."

"Girls … I hope you weren't chatting about me."

"Actually, yes, we were. I was telling her that I had a great day and … and you … and you showed me a really nice time."

We were on the phone for an hour. We talked about everything. Neither of us wanted to hang up. I usually don't like talking on the phone. But with him it was easy. We finally said goodnight.

"Right. Like you're not going to see him again," Silvia mumbled from her bed. She was sleepy.

"I'm not. Goodnight Silvia."

She didn't even respond. She was fast asleep.

TWENTY-FOUR

I slept late and didn't even hear the alarm. I had to meet Viktor and I was going to be late. It was an important meeting. I was making my last payment. I would get back my freedom and my passport. I borrowed it for a day when I applied for my student visa. You'd think they would have let me just keep it with only a few payments left, right? Nope, they took it back.

"Sorry I'm late Viktor. I slept through the alarm," I said as I handed him the envelope.

"You slept through the alarm? Who sleeps past noon? I missed my lunch. But here's your passport. Good luck."

"Thank you, and to you too, Viktor."

On the way home I stopped by Zachary's apartment. I didn't think he'd be there during the day, but I thought I'd try anyway. I wanted my necklace. I always felt like something was missing, something from Maximillian. He wasn't home so I left a note that I wanted the address of the jeweler so I could pick up the necklace. I never heard from him. I called a few times, but he never answered his phone.

I know it's just a necklace. I shouldn't let it ruin my day, but I'm getting frustrated. Why is it taking so long to fix? And why doesn't he answer?

The phone rang. I thought it was Zachary so I rushed to pick it up, but it was Gilles. I was happy to hear his voice, but I wasn't happy about being happy. I was trying to suppress my desire to see him again. I wanted to focus on my goals. I didn't want any distractions, and that was that. I was preparing myself to say no to him, in case he asked me out again.

"I'd like you to join me for dinner," he said. "Can we meet at seven-thirty?"

He seems rushed.

"No, no…. I can't… I can't meet you tonight."

My heart is pounding so fast, again.

"Oh. Why not? I thought you said you were free tonight."

"No… I know, I am, but…. I have to go to work tomorrow and I need to wake up at five."

"That is early. I have to catch an early flight tomorrow as well, so we won't be late. It's just dinner."

What is he catching? A flight? Oh, never mind.

"I don't know… really, if I can, but … where is dinner?"

As if that matters.

"You'll see."

"I don't think I can. I didn't bring enough clothes with me.

Yeah, my big wardrobe is on Long Island.

"Don't worry about the clothes. Just wear whatever and tell me yes."

I heard a female voice in the background, but I didn't understand what she was saying. I understood Gilles though. He told her "He's on his way."

Where was his way? What's that all about?

"Sorry" he said. "You still there?"

"Yes."

"Yes to dinner, right?" he asked.

"No, I said yes for…. that I was still there. Not the yes that you want to hear."

"Yes is yes. I'll see you?"

I paused, and then said yes. I wanted to say yes all along. I was just being stubborn, but then I gave in to my desire. I became who I really was. A girl who wanted to be out on a date with a guy.

"Great. Just wear something casual," he said. "Let's meet at seven instead of seven-thirty. 58th and 5th."

So, I said yes again, to the old man, just as Silvia said I would.

Wear whatever? Something casual? I'm confused. What am I supposed to wear? The same dress? Or just pants and a top? No, pants and a top would be too casual. Better to wear the same dress. At least it's a dress.

When Gilles saw me crossing the street going towards him, he smiled. Then we both jumped when a loud and long car horn started honking at me. I ran to him. He grabbed me and squeezed me so tight, without saying anything, like we hadn't seen each other for a while.

"You look beautiful," he said.

"Do I? Thank you."

I was self-conscious about wearing the same dress, so I put some accessories on to camouflage it.

"Let's go," he said. "We don't have much time."

He took my hand and I followed him like a little girl. He walked so fast I had trouble keeping up. And he kept speeding up as we went. I was too shy to ask him to slow down so I had to walk even faster. He was walking fast, and I was jogging, like a girl.

Bergdorf Goodman. I saw the building we were approaching. I knew that place. I passed it many times. I stopped to look at those beautiful window displays for a long time. I looked at the windows while I was jogging. There were new, beautiful collections, in all colors.

How often do they change these window displays?

I wanted to ask him but didn't since I was out of breath from the cardio. I kept jogging as we took a left turn.

We're going inside? Why? Maybe he has to pick something up. Or there's a restaurant inside? Who cares? We're going in!

As we went into the store, he held my hand even tighter; it almost hurt. I thought he wanted to avoid the crowd and keep up his pace. I didn't ask any questions while we waited for the elevator. I was too busy looking and he was busy with his cellphone. It seemed like his mind was elsewhere. There was beauty all around, the fashion and the people.

"Hello, Gilles. I'm glad you made it," a woman said, waiting for us on the floor.

"Hi, Caroline, how are you?" he asked as he kissed her on the cheek. "This is Alyssa."

"It's so lovely to meet you," she said as we shook hands. "This way please."

I had no idea what was going on as we followed her into a private room.

"Please, have a seat," she said.

"Caroline, I'm afraid we don't have much time," Gilles said.

"Of course not, Gilles," she said with a smile. "You're always in a hurry. We'll get you out of here quickly. From your description of Alyssa, I've already chosen a few dresses and shoes. The dresses are popular with young women. I think you'll like at least one of them."

She walked over to a rack with three dresses and on the floor below were three beautiful pairs of shoes.

"Please, this way to the fitting room."

Is this happening?

"I've already paired the shoes with each dress, but you can experiment. Try them on and come outside so we can have a look," she said as she closed the door.

My face is numb. I think I'm in shock. I need to calm down and focus since we're in a hurry.

I put on each outfit and stepped out where Caroline and Gilles were sitting judges. I tried on a Giambattista Vali sleeveless black midi dress with Valentino lace slip-on style, pointed toe high heels. A long Oscar de la Renta poppy-print satin dress with Prada pump suede upper low heels. And a Giorgio Armani sleeveless floral mini-dress with Yves Saint Laurent metallic leather pointed toe high heels.

"I like all of them, but my favorite is the Oscar de la Renta, even if she didn't follow my advice on the shoes," Caroline smiled, as she looked at Gilles, with an attitude.

That's right, I didn't.

"What do you think, Gilles?" she asked. "Which is your favorite?"

"I like all of them," he said looking at me. "Which one do you like, Alyssa? Why don't you choose the one you like the most? You're the one who's going to wear it. But please hurry. We need to go," he said as his phone rang.

I went back to the changing room and put on the Giambattista Vali midi dress with Yves Saint Laurent shoes. I felt bad I didn't go with Caroline's suggestion. Well, not that bad. I loved the dress and shoes. I walked out, and Caroline smiled.

"You have good taste, seriously," she said.

Gilles looked up from his phone at us and said nothing. He came to me and took my hands in his. He looked at me from head to toe, and then into my eyes for a few seconds.

"Ready?" he asked. "Thank you, Caroline, as always. You're the best."

"Anytime," she smiled as she gave him a kiss.

"Yes, thank you, Caroline," I said.

Do I have to give her a kiss or a hug too? That would be kind of weird.

I shook her hand. Walking in high heels has never been a problem for me but keeping up with Gilles's fast pace while holding hands wasn't easy. Looking back, that's the day I became a professional high heel walker.

We left the magical store and went to another magical place, 21 Club. We quickly walked the six blocks without saying a word. We entered the restaurant where the host was waiting for us. We were following him until Gilles stopped at a round table where a bunch of guys were dining.

I was still following the host when Gilles grabbed my arm and pulled me back, and next to him. The men at the table were all dressed well, like serious business people, and they all seemed to like meat. I stood behind Gilles as a few of the guys stood up to shake Gilles's hand. As they shook hands they'd look up and down at me with a big smile.

Well, this is kind of awkward, although I do feel fantastic in my new outfit.

After all the handshaking, I felt Gilles's hand touch my body as he spoke to all the men at the table. He put his arm around my waist and held me close. He was serious, speaking with authority. He went around the table and introduced me to each of the men. They would nod their head, smile and say hello, or nice to meet you.

Gilles was discussing something with them that I didn't understand. He was still holding me tight, his body close to mine. I felt his hot energy coming right through my body, into my blood and up to my face as I blushed. I felt so warm and distracted.

We finally said goodnight to the men and walked to our table. With the high heels I was almost as tall as him. We sat face to face and I silently looked at him as he looked around the room. He looked serious and tense and then, suddenly, he relaxed. He looked the way he did yesterday, in Central Park. I continued to stare at him until our eyes locked, and we just sat there for what seemed like an eternity. Then he took a deep breath and smiled.

"OK, now I feel better," he said.

Yesterday Gilles is back. This is the Gilles I like.

I guess some of us have different personalities. We can be nice, friendly and happy or we can be the complete opposite. But the personality we are most of the time is the one the matters. The personality that's dominant shows who we really are. I saw another side of Gilles today. He was unfriendly and indifferent, like an arrogant businessman. I hope the Gilles I saw yesterday is dominant.

"Now we can relax and talk," he said as he put his hand on mine. "So, how are you? Tell me, how was your day?"

I felt that hot energy from his hand. It made me blush again, which I didn't like. I moved my hand away from his and reached for the water.

"Did you buy this outfit for me?" I asked.

Everything happened so fast. I'm not sure what's going on.

"No," he said. "I borrowed it and we have to take it back after dinner."

"I see," I said. "Well, I hope she kept my dress, the one that I left there."

"I'm sure she did," he said. "You look so beautiful in this dress. You chose well."

"Thank you," I said.

He took my hand again as we sat quietly.

"I'm just kidding, Alyssa," he finally said. "Yes, I bought the dress for you. It's a little gift, from me."

"A little gift?" I laughed. "It's very generous of you. Thank you so much."

I stood up, walked over to him and kissed him on the cheek.

We had a good laugh over how naïve I was. It was the same, laughing-over-nothing that we had all day yesterday. Just silly happiness.

"Maybe I don't know much about a lot of things," I said, "but I do know about high end fashion designers and value. Thank you again for the gift."

"I can tell you do. You even did better than Caroline. She has a great fashion sense, but I was happy you didn't follow her advice. I like that."

"You like what? That I didn't follow her advice just because she said so or you like the outfit I put together?"

"Both."

While we had dinner, another meat-loving-looking-man approached him to say hello. It was the same handshake and small conversation. He didn't introduce me to him.

"You seem to be popular here," I smiled.

"They're just business colleagues. I'm leaving tomorrow morning on business for a week. Can I call you from there?"

"I don't use the family phone where I work. I don't think they would like that."

"They wouldn't mind a quick phone call, would they?"

I need to change the conversation.

"Probably not but work is work," I said. "I don't think I can give you their phone number without their permission. You know them, right? They're your neighbors."

"I know of them, but I don't know them. I see them occasionally on the rooftop. But I don't look there often."

"You might not be looking but others are looking at you. I saw you naked."

"You did? When?"

"That day you helped me, on the rooftop."

"Really? I don't remember. But I'm sure you saw me. I do like being naked."

"I named you naked man. That's what I called you when I chatted with my roommate."

"Seems about right."

We laughed and laughed. The food and the company were great. He had a car waiting for me to take me home. He kissed me on the cheek as we said our goodnights. I stared out at the East River as the car headed south on FDR Drive.

What do I like about him? Do I even like him? Maybe. No … no, I can't like him. I do love this dress and these shoes. I can't believe I have them on and they're mine. Where am I ever going to wear this dress again? I would feel bad if this dress would just hang in the closet all the time. No, it won't. I'll wear it again when I go out with Gilles. With Gilles?

Did I say with Gilles again? Do I like him because I think of him? OK, maybe I do. But why? Why do I like him? Maybe because he's handsome? No, no, that's not the reason at all. First of all, he's not *that* handsome. I'm not blind. And what about his age? He's so much older than me. Yes, but maybe that's exactly what I like about him. Maybe I like that he's older. Because of the comfort I feel around him. Maybe I like that he's self-assured and powerful, and it makes me feel safe. Maybe because I didn't have enough quality time with a man after my father's death, and I'm missing that? Maybe I like his generosity.

Wait, I know. I just like being there. I like being around him because I just miss having a social life. That's why I feel happy with him. Plus, he's fun. I laugh all the time and I feel free with him. Otherwise, there's really no attraction to him. Well, maybe there is. What about every time he touches me? I get goosebumps, and I feel hot and nervous at the same time. Why do I have butterflies in my stomach every time he looks at me? Probably because I miss being with a man, and sex. My body is starving for sex. OK, but if my body is starving for sex, why didn't I have any desire to see Jeff? There would've been sex with him, after another date or two. Or what about Zachary kissing me and I didn't want to keep going? Because I don't like them. Exactly! I don't like them, but I do like Gilles. I didn't realize just how much I do like him until now. I have to admit, I can't wait to say hello to the man I just said goodbye to.

When I got home, I discovered that Zachary had moved out. He was gone and so was my necklace. I felt sad, like I lost a connection with Max.

TWENTY-FIVE

JUNE 1997, BROOKLYN

School and Gilles, Gilles and School. That's all I thought about the next week while I was working. I was thrilled to start school on Monday. I wanted to see Gilles and I wanted to see the school. I was so curious about everything. The school, the teacher, the students. I was late getting to Brooklyn because of train delays. I was sure Gilles would leave a message on the answering machine, but he didn't.

I'm surprised he hasn't called. How is that possible? Was he into me? Is he married? If he was, how could he be comfortable taking me to public places? He even introduced me to those guys at the restaurant. Or maybe he does that with girls? Uses them as eye candy? Maybe it was just a couple of days of fun? And actually, that would be fine. I'd almost be relieved. I don't need a relationship. I like him, but then I could focus on my studying and plans.

"Silvia," I said, "since I'm going to stay at your place more often because of school please let me pay some rent money."

"Oh stop."

"No, really. I want to. It would make me feel better. It would be good for both of us."

After a little more resistance, she agreed. The first day of school made me forget about all Gilles. It was exciting to meet the teacher and all the students. It was a joy. The teacher had a way of explaining things so everyone understood. I spent eight hours at school, and I couldn't wait to go back the next day.

That evening I did my homework, stayed at home and went to sleep early. I was wiped out, from school and from trying not to think about Gilles. He never called, which made me even more ambitious.

I had new friends from all over the world. There were about twenty students in the class. I became friends with Columbians, Asians, Argentinians and Mexicans. It was a high energy, fun class. It was like we were all the same, but with different languages. We helped each other, as friends do. We were spending all day together with just a few breaks. Some of them would go out for lunch; others would bring food. I didn't do either because I didn't want to spend any money. I sat next to a guy who didn't eat lunch either. He was doing his homework. His name was Franco, from Argentina. He was around my age, skinny and hyper. Even while he was sitting, he was still moving, like tapping his legs or his fingers, or spinning in his chair. Watching him made me dizzy.

"Where do you live, Franco?" I asked.

"In Jersey City, with four guys," he said excitedly. "I moved here six months ago. I live with my cousin and his three friends. I can't afford to live by myself yet. I'm still looking for a job and I have to be at school because of my student visa. Have you done the homework for the next subject?"

"The grammar class? Yes, I did," I said. "I'm not sure how good it is, but I finished it."

"Do you mind if I copy it from you? I didn't have enough time to do it last night. I had a few beers with my roomies," he smiled, as he continued his tapping.

This is a troublemaker, but he seems like a good guy.

"Sure, here," I smiled. "But don't blame me if the teacher says your homework is full of mistakes."

"I won't. I don't care about mistakes. As long as I have the work done—to show him."

After a long day of school, everyone's face looked worn and tired. The minute the class was dismissed, everyone bolted from the room so quickly. Franco and I were the last to leave because he couldn't find his MetroCard. I was thinking his MetroCard must've flown out of his pocket from all his moving around.

"Here it is!" I said, picking it up from the floor by the window.

"Thank you!" he said. "You saved me. I don't know how I would get home without this."

We left the building and walked towards the subway.

"Are you taking the subway to Jersey City?" I asked.

"No, the subway doesn't go there," he said. "I take the PATH. You go by subway, right?"

"Yes," I said as we walked past a hot dog cart.

"That food smells so good," I said. "I'm starving. I haven't eaten all day."

"Me neither," he said. "I'm so hungry. All I have in my pocket is my MetroCard. I hope I get home first so I can have the leftovers from last night."

He smiled and started walking faster.

"I love pizza," I said. "It's my favorite food. I'd love to have a slice right now."

"I can eat pizza anytime. Especially now, but...", he shrugged.

"Let's have some," I said. "There's a pizza place right on this corner."

"I can't. I don't have any money. Not even a penny in my pocket, look."

He turned his pants pockets inside out and we both laughed.

" "But I do. Let's go," I said. "I'll pay for your slice."

"Thank you, but no. Another time, when I have money, after I find a job."

"Come on, let's go," I said. "I'm starving."

I grabbed Franco's arm and pulled him into the pizzeria. After two slices of pizza and a can of Pepsi, we were both happy as we headed home. I had to borrow some money from Silvia for the train the next day, but the pizza was worth it.

I was back on Long Island around 8 a.m. The kids were visiting their grandparents, so I thought I'd give Anna and Michael some private time. I finished all my work, said goodnight and went to my room.

It wasn't long before I heard knocking on my door.

It's probably Anna with more work for me to do.

I opened the door and Michael was standing there with a box.

"Here you go, someone found your book. You left it on the grocery store counter." he said as he handed me the box.

"My book? What book?"

"You know, your English vocabulary book? When we went to the city and Anna sent you for some milk or something that day? I don't know. Anyway, you left this on the counter. Who goes to the grocery store with their vocabulary book?" he asked, shaking his head.

"Thanks, Michael."

"Don't thank me, thank our neighbor. He's the one who found it. It was nice of him to return it."

I said goodnight to Mr. Corrector. I returned to my bed and opened the box. Inside was another box and a letter:

Dear Alyssa,

I hope you're well.

I bought you this cellphone so we can stay in touch. And don't worry about your bosses. I made up a story so they would just hand this to you. Please dial my number when you can so I know you received the package.

Hope to see you soon,

Gilles

I didn't call him that night, but I did sleep well. After work the next day I took a shower and went to bed. I got my new cellphone from its hiding place and I called Gilles around ten o'clock.

We talked about everything. Food, movies, everyday life. We laughed—a lot. As usual. I'd laugh about my English when I misunderstood what he said, and he had to explain it. By the time we hung up it was one o'clock in the morning. He told me he was in Chicago and then he had to go to London. The next day we spoke even longer. I should've been doing my homework at night, but we just kept talking, like best friends.

After three weeks I became much better at communicating on the phone. Studying English was one thing, putting it into practice was another. It was the best. I was on my way to Brooklyn when my cell phone rang.

Who could that be? Oh ... Gilles. Who else?

"Hello?" I said, laughing.

"Hello, Alyssa, how are you?" he said.

He sounds serious. He must be in that mood I don't like.

"I don't have a lot of time," he said. "I wanted to let you know I'm back in the city and I'd like to see you tomorrow. How about lunch, around one o'clock?"

"I can't do lunch. I have school all day."

"Can you skip school?"

"I can't. I have to attend for a certain number of hours."

"I'm super busy tomorrow evening or else .... ok, let me go. We'll talk later."

He hung up. My cell phone and I were lonely all evening. But everything brightened up the next morning when the phone rang.

"Good morning, Alyssa," he said. "I rearranged things for tonight. Let's go to the King Cole Bar, in the St. Regis Hotel. Can you meet me outside, at the corner of 55th and 5th at ten o'clock?

"Sure," I said. "See you then."

I went home right after school. It was getting dark as I dressed and put my beautiful high heels on. I was so happy to wear them again. I put on eyeliner and mascara. I covered my face with a natural colored powder and my lips with light red lipstick. I looked in the mirror, and I liked what I saw. My heart was soaring as I left the apartment. But I struggled to ignore the negative thoughts in the back of my mind.

I saw him right away as I approached 55th Street. He was standing with his serious look. I started walking faster when he saw me. He watched me the whole time. I felt like I was on his personal runway.

I reached him. He looked into my eyes. I tilted my head and looked at him. Neither of us said a word. I moved closer to him, to his face. My heart was pounding. I looked into his eyes, then at his lips, and I kissed him. Deeply. He pulled me close and kissed me back. I closed my eyes. I felt high from kissing him. We kissed more, and more, until we both needed oxygen. We looked at each other. He hugged me so tight. My entire head was covered by his arms. I felt so warm and sexual. I could've had an orgasm just kissing him. We kissed again, and then took a breath.

"I put red lipstick on for this evening. but you ate it," I smiled.

"Yes, thank you for that," he said. "Delicious."

He smiled and took my hand as we went inside. We had a lovely evening. He never mentioned anything about his feelings. We never talked about what we were thinking.

Between our jobs and my school, it was hard to find time to see each other. When he had time, I didn't. When I was free, he couldn't always make it because of his business. We talked on the phone almost every day, sometimes two or three times a day. I was learning a lot from our long conversations. On one call he invited me to his house for dinner. I always thought there was a big difference between dinner at a restaurant and dinner at home. I felt trusted and respected by him. I was flattered.

"I'm looking forward to seeing you tonight," he said. "I can show you my home."

"Yes, and thank you for inviting me. I remember it as a lovely place," I smiled.

"I promise I won't greet you naked," he said.

"You can, if you want."

"Hmm ... well ... maybe," he said as we laughed.

"Would you please wear your new dress and those shoes?" he asked. "Another good friend of mine will be joining us for dinner. Actually, he's a friend and he works for me. He's an interior designer and he's done a lot of work on my house."

"That's nice. Sure. I can't wait to wear that dress again."

I rang Gilles's doorbell and he opened the door. I wanted to kiss him badly, but the friend was standing behind him. I walked in.

"Hello, you must be Alyssa. My name is Mark."

He already knows my name?

"Hey wait," Gilles smiled. "I was supposed to do the introductions."

"Hi, Mark, nice to meet you," I smiled as we shook hands.

A woman in a white apron came out from the kitchen. She walked over to Mark.

"Hello," I said to her.

Who is this woman? His mother, or an aunt? Or maybe his wife is cooking dinner for us?

I giggled at my thoughts, and the others gave me a surprised look.

"Let me at least introduce her," Gilles said. "This is our great friend Mona. Mona, this is Alyssa."

"Very nice to meet you, Mona," I said.

"Mona's going to make us a fantastic dinner tonight, right Mona?"

Mona just smiled and shook her head yes.

"Mark, before we sit for dinner, do you mind if I show Alyssa the house?" Gilles said.

"Not all," Mark said. "I'll join Mona in the kitchen. Cocktails for everyone?"

"That would be great," Gilles said. "What would you like to drink, Alyssa? Or would you like to try his specialty. It's very good."

"If it's very good then I'll have that one," I said.

They all smiled. Gilles took my hand to give me the tour. The first floor was a big open space with a living room, a separate lounge in the corner with a fireplace and a dining room. There was a large gourmet kitchen. The modern looking staircase led to the second floor with Gilles's office and three guest rooms, each with a bathroom. On the third floor was his master bedroom, with a big walk-in closet and wide double doors that led to the balcony. The entire house had a contemporary French style. Most of the furniture was European influenced. It was all tastefully furnished and well organized, with clean lines. There was a small fireplace in the master bedroom and heavy dark green curtains pulled back from the windows and balcony doors.

I can imagine it being very cozy in this room on a rainy day.

Gilles led me outside to the balcony. He put his arm on my shoulder, pulling me closer to him as we looked around.

Damn, I'm feeling sexual. I need to control myself and not blush. I think he wants to kiss me but with Mark and Mona downstairs he probably doesn't want to start what he can't finish. Look at Anna and Michael's rooftop over there. That was a crazy night. I remember being afraid and mad at myself at the same time. But then again, if I didn't lock myself out, I might never be here.

We went back to his office on the second floor. He wanted to show me a magazine. The office looked more like a library. There were a desk and chair. In the center of the room were two armchairs looking toward the windows. The other wall had built-in shelves, with books and magazines of all shapes and sizes.

"Have you read all these books?" I asked.

"Most of them," he said as he looked for the magazine he wanted to show me.

"Ahh ... here it is," he said.

"How do you know which books or magazines are where?"

"I don't know. I just start looking and somehow, I find them. You know, when you're looking for something, you always seem to find it, right? It may take time but eventually you do," he said as he turned to look at me.

"Here's the magazine I wanted to show you. This is a *Vogue* issue published on April 1, 1923."

I stared at the magazine, not saying a word.

"This is so beautiful," I finally said. "I love the cover. This is art."

"I'm glad you mentioned that. Do you like her look and style?"

"Yes, of course."

"This cover is a George Lepape fashion illustration. It was for the springtime issue's Paris openings. Look at the woman, so delicately dressed in that pink gown and white scarf."

He paused for a few seconds.

"Well, if you look at her closely," he continued, "she's admiring her jewels, and not the Paris streets outside her balcony."

He paused again.

"There are a couple of reasons I wanted to show you this," he said. "First, I know how much you like reading *Vogue*, and I thought you might find this interesting. But also, remember our first date in Central Park?

"Sure I do," I said.

"Seeing you reminded me of this cover," he said. "Looking at you I thought of her."

Now I blushed. Big time. I could feel my face heating up. I looked at him, and then at the magazine.

"I'm flattered. She's very beautiful," I said.

"So are you," he said.

"Who was George Lepape? I never heard of him."

"He was a French designer. He was one of the world's most groundbreaking fashion illustrators, and his work was in-demand by the top haute couture houses in France. I got this magazine from a special person in France. It's very valuable to me but I can lend it to you, if you'd like to have a look inside," he smiled and handed the magazine to me.

"Thank you," I said. "Of course, I'll return it in the same condition as it is now, I promise. I would love to look inside."

"I thought so," he smiled.

We went downstairs where Mark served us his specialty, French martinis. We made a toast and sat down. The table looked so beautiful. The table cloth and all the china were white; each setting had a small vase with a dusty pink rose and a small round white candle. At the center of the table was a flat round vase with a mix of flat-shaped white flowers and taller round candles.

"The table is decorated so beautifully," I said as Gilles offered me a chair.

"Yes, it always is. From our interior designer, Mark," Gilles said.

Mona came out from the kitchen to announce what she would be serving. The first course was French onion soup, the second, duck breast with baked potato, covered with melted cheese and garlic. Dessert would be a napoleon pastry.

"Mona makes the best French onion soup in the world," Gilles said.

Soup? Again? And what is onion soup? That doesn't sound good. But I'll have to eat it, if only out of respect for Gilles and Mona.

Mona served the soup and returned to the kitchen. Gilles and Mark looked excited. I was like the sad child at the table who didn't want to eat. I got even more depressed as I looked at its strange color. Both of them were about to dive in when Gilles paused.

"Please, eat," he smiled. "I want to know what you think."

"What about Mona?" I asked. "Aren't we waiting for her?"

Gilles looked at me and smiled. Mark already had his face buried in the soup.

"That's kind of you, but Mona is doing her job. She's the cook, and the waitress tonight."

"I'm sorry, I misunderstood. I thought she was a friend and guest like us," I smiled.

"Well, she is our friend. She's just working tonight."

Gilles turned his attention to the ugly soup as I forced myself to eat. After what seemed like hours, I finished, and gulped down the rest of my French martini.

Nope, still taste the onions.

Gilles poured some red wine for everyone. Soon Mark became super friendly. He had a great sense of humor. He started telling stories about his crazy city life. Everything was crazy around him, but in a funny way.

"One day, I had this crazy subway experience," Mark said. "I was standing on the platform waiting for the train, and this homeless man comes up to me. He was really ragged, razor thin and tired looking. So, he asks me if I can spare some change so he can get a cup of coffee. Any amount at all he said. Now, sometimes I give money but sometimes I don't. It depends. This time I definitely would've given him something because he looked so down. But I didn't have any money with me. I had my wallet, with my MetroCard and credit cards, but I keep my cash separate, and I ran out of the house so fast I forgot to grab it. So, I tell him, I'm sorry but I don't have any money. He looked at me with these big sad eyes, shook his head back and forth, then reached into his pocket and handed me a dollar. I look at the dollar, and then at him, and tell him no, no, no … I have money, just not with me. He patted me on my shoulder and said 'That's OK, son, you shouldn't be walking around a city like this without any money.'"

"Wow, that's something," I said. "That's generous."

"Right?" Mark said. "But now I'm chasing him on the platform trying to give him his money back, but he refused to take it. Is that crazy or what?"

"That is crazy," I said, as Gilles and I laughed.

I felt so comfortable with these two even though they were older. I didn't feel any awkwardness. What I liked most about Mark was he never asked me about my personal life. He never asked where I was from or what I did. All those annoying questions. He did most of the talking, and we did most of the laughing.

Mark had his own interior design business. He did all the decorating work for Gilles. He also did some kind of house management or coordination of repairs. He was currently working on changes to the two second floor guest rooms. That's all I wanted to know about Mark. I usually don't like to go too deep into people's personal lives when I first meet them. What's the point? But I do observe people.

In one story he mentioned he was about the same age as Gilles. But physically, and with his style, he looked much younger. He was thin, and about 5'10", with light facial features. He had thinning, brown greyish hair, and used hair gel to shape a fashionable style. He wore a mix of formal and sporty styles, all high end.

Mona served the duck. It was cut into small, thin slices (three each), with a small baked potato. It wasn't a lot, but it tasted rich, and heavy. Gilles put on some classical music and Mark continued with his stories as we ate. By the time dessert arrived I was so full. But then I saw the light and crispy four layers of puff dough that looked like clouds, with heavy white cream in between, and my eyes got big. I never saw a napoleon that tall.

"I asked Mona to make the napoleon especially for you," Gilles said. "I know it's one of your favorites."

"Thanks," I said. "I've never seen one like this. I'm sure Mona makes the best."

"Absolutely," Gilles said. "She makes it better than they do in France, right Mark?"

"Hell yeah," Mark said, smiling.

Gilles seems a little fanatical about Mona's cooking. According to him, anything she served was the tastiest ever. The onion soup was the best in the world. He said he's tried duck everywhere he's traveled, and the best is here at home, because of Mona. And this kind of napoleon is better than any in all of France? Really? Do all employers get obsessed with their cooks? Or is she the best because she's the one who cooks for him, so she must be the best?

I ate the napoleon.

I must admit, I have no experience to judge what's good or bad when it comes to onion soup. And I don't want to. I hate soup. But this napoleon? I wish Mona lived with me. I would never get tired of eating this delicious, fluffy and fresh napoleon. Each bite just melts away in my mouth, leaving a fantastic taste. I want more of this. A lot more! It's probably a good thing Mona isn't around me all the time. Otherwise my body will become as big and fluffy as this napoleon.

We finished our dessert and coffee, and soon after, Gilles called a car service and I made my way home.

What a lovely evening. Everything was great. Mark, Mona, and Gilles. The drinks, the dessert. I'm feeling so satisfied, except I have a lot of pent-up desire. For sex.

TWENTY-SIX

JUNE 1997, LONG ISLAND

"I'm in Washington, D.C. this week," Gilles said. "You should come down and stay with me. I can show you around the city."

"I'd love to see Washington, but I can't," I said. "I have work and school."

Silence. Whenever I say no to him he goes quiet. How come he never says, "I know," or "I understand?"

"Why don't you just take off?" he finally asked. "Tell them you're taking a few days off. Better yet, tell them you're quitting. You should just quit your job."

This is starting to irritate me.

"I can't do that," I said. "I have to work."

"OK, don't get irritated," he said. "Let's talk when we meet."

"I'm not irritated," I said. "You're saying I am, but I'm not."

We hung up.

I can't believe he can tell how I feel over the phone. I am irritated. Who is this guy? I want to know who he really is. I've never asked him any personal questions. I don't like prying into people's lives, but still. The phone rang again.

"Look, please come to Washington," he said. "I'm here mostly for business but I also want to take you to a birthday dinner party I've been invited to on Saturday."

"And why me?" I asked. "Why do you need me there? I won't know anybody."

"You don't need to know anyone. You know me," he said. "And don't worry about your job. Just call out sick for two days. It's a weekend and they probably won't mind. I'll get you back Sunday night. I promise you won't miss school on Monday."

What am I going to do? I want to be with him, anywhere he wants to take me. Who wouldn't want to go with him to D.C. rather than work? I'm tired of my job but I have responsibilities, to myself and my family.

"Alright," I said.

"Great, I can't wait to see you."

I can't say no to him. I'm becoming so weak to his charisma. It's hard to resist. This will be interesting. It'll be the first time we spend a weekend together.

It was early Friday afternoon. I had to leave the house, but I didn't know what to say to Anna. I've never been that good at lying. I just couldn't do it. I went to Kalian for advice. I told her the situation, then I asked her to take my place.

"It's just one weekend," I said. "Plus, you can make a little extra money."

"I would but I can't this weekend," she said. "Just leave the house before they come home so you don't have to deal with them. I'll tell them you had some personal business to deal with in Brooklyn. They can take care of their kids and the house for a couple of days."

"Kalian, you're one of the best people I've ever met. Thank you. I'll never forget your kindness and support, from day one."

"No problem. We're friends. You did the same for me. When I called out, remember? You did my job. Otherwise they would've fired me. Anna told me that."

"I didn't know that. I'm glad to hear I did something meaningful for you."

"If you get married to that man, don't forget about me," she smiled.

"Yeah, that's not going to happen," I smiled.

"You never know."

"I'll see you soon. Thanks again!"

I left the house for Brooklyn, feeling as light as a butterfly.

"I'm glad you went to Brooklyn," Gilles said when he called that evening.

"Me too," I said. "I'm excited about going tomorrow."

"I'm glad to hear that. Are you excited to see D.C. or me?"

"Hmm … both."

"Good answer. Mark will meet up with you tomorrow. You remember Mark, right?"

"Sure, I remember him."

"The two of you can fly down here together. He has some business here as well. I'll meet you at the hotel."

"That's great. I'm sure I'll hear more of his funny stories. I like him."

The next morning, I did as Gilles asked and went to meet Mark at 61st and Lexington Avenue, just outside of Barneys.

Is Barneys one of Mark's clients? Or does he live around here? Oh, there he is now.

"Hi, Alyssa," Mark said. "Gilles asked me to take you shopping for the trip. He said you might need some clothes for the dinner party."

"I've heard about this store, but I've never been inside."

"It's one of my favorites. Let's have some fun before we take off. Shall we?" he smiled, grabbed my hand and we were off to the races again.

What's up with the hand holding and pulling me along like a little kid? I thought Gilles holds my hand because he's attracted to me, like a couple. But Mark does the same thing. Is this what people do in crowded city streets, or do I look like a confused kid?

"Should we start in the shoes or clothes department?" he asked.

Look at all this stuff. I feel lightheaded.

"Mark, I want you to dress me. Whatever you think would look good on me. I like your style and I want to look like a New York City girl. I'm sure you know what's in fashion now."

After a successful shopping adventure with Mark, we piled into a waiting car and made our way to the airport. As Mark and I chatted it suddenly got dark as we entered a tunnel.

"Where are we going Mark?" I asked.

"New Jersey, Teterboro Airport," he said.

"Oh, I've never heard of that."

After about twenty minutes we pulled up to a small building.

"This is the terminal?" I asked. "It's really small."

"Indeed," Mark said.

We gathered all the bags and entered the building.

"Do you have my airline ticket?" I asked.

"You won't need a ticket," he said smiling.

"What do you mean? How will I know what seat I'm in or get through security?"

"Don't worry," he said, still laughing. "Let's hurry. The plane is waiting."

The plane is waiting, for us?

We stepped outside and I followed Mark as we made our way to a small, beautiful, white jet.

"Well this is our ride," Mark said.

"This?" I asked.

"Yes, it's just you and me, and the crew of course."

As I scanned the plane my eyes got wide.

"This is amazing," I said.

"Yes, it's the only way to fly," Mark said. "Shall we?"

We boarded the private jet, carrying a bunch of large shopping bags. It looked like we bought the whole store. Mark and I settled into the plane and as we were drinking a glass of champagne, he started chatting away.

"I have this crazy guy I work with," Mark said. "You know, one of those eccentric types? A fantastic designer, but he can be super moody. You never know from one day to the next what his attitude will be. Just this past Tuesday I'm in the office and I hear him going crazy. 'Son of a bitch,' he says, 'why the hell is everything so god-damn difficult?' He's yelling, slamming things down, just making a real racket. So, I go over and say to Larry, 'What's going on, is everything alright?' He looks at me and slumps into his chair. 'Sorry, I just had a really bad morning,' he says. 'What happened?' I asked. 'Well, you know my apartment near Lincoln Center, on the 32nd floor, with the row of windows that you pull so they slant to the inside, and they have the opening on the top? Well my cat was jumping along the ledge and he jumped right out the window.'"

"Oh my God, that's horrible," I said, but then I started to smile.

"Yeah, see?" Mark asked. "I see you smiling. You're doing exactly what I did. I know it's bad, but I just couldn't help visualizing the scene he just described, and I had to try really, really hard to stop myself from smiling. I had to go to my office and shut the door so I wouldn't lose it in front of him. So crazy."

"Can you imagine?" I asked as we both giggled and shook our heads.

Gilles was waiting for us in the St. Regis hotel lobby. It was beautiful. He looked excited to see me. I was still in shock from the shopping and the private jet ride. It was all a little overwhelming.

"Gilles, thank you," I whispered to him when I kissed him.

"I can't wait to see you in your new clothes," he whispered back. "I'm glad you two are here, safe and sound. Here's your room key. We're on the same floor."

"Oh … OK," I said.

I smiled as I entered my room with all my shopping bags. The large suite was beautifully designed, with soft colors and elegant furniture. I opened the curtains to make the room brighter. I looked around.

I'm here with him, in this beautiful hotel with these beautiful clothes, which belong to me.

I opened the large French style window to let the air in and took a deep breath. I returned to my shopping bags to look again at all the beautiful colors and high-quality fabrics. Soft leather shoes and bags. I only dreamed of having things like these. I had blouses and pants, a few dresses, and a couple of bags, all by high-end designers, an ensemble of Marni, Nina Ricci, Prada and Lanvin. I was in love with all of them.

I admire Mark's taste. He dressed me well.

I was filled with happiness. I couldn't wait to dress. I was so excited, and suddenly, I wasn't. I sat down on the couch. I became sad. I was thinking about my family. I wanted to share everything with them. I wanted them to experience being in a fancy hotel and unlimited shopping and flying on a private jet. I wanted to pack up all my shopping bags and send them to them, right away. I was only helping them with money, for a simple life. Food and the basics. I wanted to do more. It made me cry.

Gilles asked me to be ready an hour before going to the party. He wanted to spend some time with me. Just the two of us he said. After a shower I put on some light makeup and a small amount of mascara with pale red lipstick. I pulled my hair straight, so it was laying over my shoulders. I put lotion on my entire body, and no perfume. I wanted to smell fresh. I was wearing a Marni light green, shoulder strap, wrap cocktail dress, with Lanvin high heeled, open toe summer shoes. The dress felt so soft and light, like I wasn't wearing anything. It just flowed on my body. I felt so sexy. I was ready on time and waited for him.

The knock on the door knocked my entire body. I opened the door and saw Gilles standing there, so handsome. He was wearing a light grey dress shirt with a dark blue sport jacket and dark grey fitted pants. He smelled fresh and looked fantastic. He was standing there for a while as I held the door, and we stared at each other, speechless. I smiled and blushed. My heart was racing.

He stepped into the room, came close to me, hugged me and kissed me on my lips, for a long time. It felt like he was holding that in for a long time. I melted. He held me tighter and pushed me against the wall. He kissed me more and touched my breast through the soft fabric. He kissed my neck slowly and went down to my breast. The wrap dress with an open cut collar was perfect for easy access. I felt his lips on my breast. I felt warm and high as he kissed me. He was hot when I touched his hair and felt his face on mine. He was back to my lips, and kissing me slowly, until he stopped and moved back.

"I couldn't help myself," he said. "You look beautiful. Those lips, your breasts, your body. You're so sexy. The dress you're wearing. It's quite sexy too."

We sat on the couch. He made a phone call as my heart's pounding started slowing down. Room service arrived with champagne. When the waiter left, Gilles softly kissed me again. I was losing myself in him. He stopped and picked up the champagne glass.

"Cheers," he said, taking a drink. "Are you happy with your shopping?"

"Very. I got beautiful clothes, shoes and bags. Thank you so much, Gilles."

"My pleasure. I hope I'll see more of them tomorrow."

"Yes, of course. I can't wait to wear them."

He became serious, but he still had a smile on his face.

"I love being with you, Alyssa. You're such a beautiful girl and have such a great personality. What I really love is that you give me some kind of energy. I can't explain it. But ... I want to be honest with you," he paused. "I'm in a relationship."

"You are?" I asked, searching for the right tone and questions. "Are you married?"

"No, no ... I'm not married," he said with a smile. "But I've been in a relationship with someone for many years. I'm truly in love with him."

"I thought I was the one who needed to go to school for English," I smiled. "But maybe you need to join me?"

"What do you mean?" he smiled, taking my hand.

"You said you're truly in love with him, instead of her," I said, so proud of my English.

"It is *him*. And you know him."

What? I heard it, but it's not sinking in. My heart is pounding so hard. All these emotions. I'm so happy being with him, and with the intimacy between us. Look at him. His face, his eyes. They look better than when we first met. I don't want to talk about anything. I don't care about anything. I want him. Now. I want to enjoy the joy of life. And the love he feels for me. Right now.

I sipped some champagne and put the glass down. I took both his hands in mine and moved closer to him. I kissed him slowly. He kissed me back, more passionate than ever. He relaxed, becoming free to explore his desires with me. He touched the dress, unzipped it, and touched my body.

I think we're going to be late to the party.

We made love, and it was beautiful.

We were both calm and high as we sat together on our way to the party. We didn't continue the conversation we started in the hotel room. After the champagne and burning so many calories from our long love-making, we were both looking forward to the party. We arrived at the house. The dinner party was outside in the backyard, with hundreds of people. We missed the cocktail hour and people were on their way to the tables for dinner.

"What a perfect time to arrive," Gilles said.

"I'm starving," we both said at the same time, and we laughed.

Gilles was holding my hand once again. He was introducing me to everyone as his girlfriend.

I'm his girlfriend?

It was a lovely evening with interesting conversations and delicious food and wine. We went back to the hotel bar where Mark was waiting.

"You look so beautiful in this dress," Mark said. "Wait, no. Actually, the dress looks more beautiful because you're wearing it. I love it."

"It's because of you, Mark. You chose for me."

I gave him a big hug. After a couple of drinks, I said goodnight and went to my room.

My head is spinning from … from … I don't even know. I don't want to think about anything. I don't care about anything. I'm numb. My mind is disconnected from me. I just love it. My heart is full of joy, love and honesty.

I felt a tingling in my entire body as I fell into a deep sense of gratitude. I drifted off to sleep in the big comfortable bed and had the sweetest dreams ever.

The next morning, I skipped breakfast with Gilles and told him I'd meet up with him later. I had so many questions I wanted to ask him, and myself. I stayed in bed, thinking. I tried to understand what he told me, but it was hard.

We met in the hotel lobby. He looked fresh, energized and happy. He kissed me and complimented my new outfit. I was wearing jeans and a white T-shirt with a blue linen jacket.

"Where's Mark?" I asked. "Isn't he joining us?"

"No, Mark wanted to see a friend who lives nearby. He left right after breakfast. But he'll be flying back with us."

We walked around the city. He showed me the White House and the Capitol. We went to the Museum of Natural History and visited the Lincoln Memorial. It was all so interesting, and great to see them with him, since he explained everything. We were out all day. We kissed and hugged. It was a day of love, knowledge and pleasure. I didn't want it to end. I wanted to stay with him, to be with him, in love. We went back to the hotel and up to my room.

Flying back to New York was bittersweet. I knew my mini-vacation was over, and I wasn't sure where things would go with Gilles. But seeing that lavish lifestyle? It motivated me to work and study harder.

Monday morning was rough. I stayed up late doing homework. I was so sleepy at school. I wore my usual clothes at school. I didn't want to wear my new clothes and stand out from my classmates. At lunchtime, we all went out to see an exhibition nearby. Even our teacher joined us, and we all had a good time. I was making great progress with my English. I was becoming more confident that I could understand whole conversations, most of the time.

Gilles wanted to see me Tuesday night. Kalian never called me, so I thought (hoped) everything was all good with Anna and Michael. I met Gilles downtown. It was just one day, but I missed him. When he kissed me, I missed him even more.

"You must be hungry. Did you eat today?" he asked.

"I'm OK," I said. "I had some lunch at school."

"Some lunch? What do you mean 'some?' What did you eat?"

"I had coffee and a banana."

"That's it?

He sounds like a parent.

"Come on," he said. "Let's go have a good meal."

I held his arm as we made our way to Balthazar. I've never been to France, but from the pictures and movies I'd seen, it felt like we were suddenly in Paris. Like most people, I dreamed of seeing Paris one day, but only in a romantic way. I didn't want to go there with my family or friends. I only wanted to go there with someone I loved.

"Does France look like this?" I asked, "I mean Paris cafes? The atmosphere?"

"Pretty much," he said. "I love this place. I come here whenever I miss Paris. Have you ever been here?"

"Never, although I've stared through the window a few times."

The food and wine were so delicious. It felt like home cooking. It was so cozy, especially with him.

"Are you going back to work?" he asked.

"Yes, tomorrow morning," I said.

"You didn't get fired, did you? That would be fun."

That's annoying.

"Fun? What do you mean? I hope I still have my job."

"I'm only joking," he said. "I meant it would be fun if you could just stay and not leave for work."

"I have to work."

What kind of joke is that? And why are we even having this conversation?

I wanted to say more but I didn't. I just put my head down and continued eating.

"Please don't be mad at me," he said, touching my hand.

"I'm not," I smiled.

"Exactly what do you do at work?"

Now I'm getting annoyed. What's wrong with him? This place is so comfortable and romantic. I don't want to talk about my shitty job here.

"I clean, iron, do laundry, cook. I take care of the kids once in a while. Why do you ask? And why do we have to talk about my job right now, especially here, together, in such a beautiful place?"

"You're right, and that's exactly why I asked. All those jobs you do at work? I don't want you to do them anymore. You don't have to."

"Oh really? Why is that?"

"I'll provide for you."

What is he talking about? I thought I was honest with him about my life situation and plans.

"Thank you, Gilles, that's very generous, but it's not just about me. There are people I need to take care of back home."

"I know, so let me make this clear. I'll give you the money, so you don't have to work. That's what I mean when I say I'll provide for you. For you and your family. This way you can go to school full time and focus on your studies."

I put my knife and fork down and stared into his eyes, not saying a word.

"Please, let me do this," he said.

"And who are you, Gilles? What exactly do you do?"

TWENTY-SEVEN

The next morning was tough. The alarm rang at four-thirty in the morning, as usual.

Why does the morning come so fast when I have to go to work?

I jumped out of bed and ran to the bathroom. I moved so fast I felt woozy, probably from all the wine I drank the previous night. I was tired and sleepy, but I ignored all that and kept moving. I furiously brushed my teeth to finish quickly. I looked in the mirror, saw my face and I slowed down. Slower and slower, until I stopped brushing my teeth, and smiled.

Ah, I don't have to go to work. I'm done with housework for others. I'm free.

Soon I became a full-time student. Throughout the summer and fall of 1997 I was seeing Gilles more often. I was becoming closer to him and learning more about his character, and we learned to trust each other. We were socialites at dinner and various charity events. Sometimes we would have dinner at Gilles's with Mark, which always included too much wine and many, many laughs. I never stayed over at his place. It didn't matter what time it was, I always went back to Brooklyn.

It was a fun but confusing time with Gilles. He was a great lover and companion, but I knew he was in love with someone else. I never went deep into that subject with him, until we talked about my school situation and I told him that my visa would expire soon. I would have to leave and go back to my country. My English had improved, and it would give me a huge advantage for a new career back home.

"I want you to listen to me carefully," Gilles said.

He held my hands as he spoke to me on a crisp November evening at the Bubble Lounge in Tribeca.

Time for the breakup. I knew this day was coming. My heart is sinking, but I'm going to face him bravely and hold my emotions. Actually, this is good. It will motivate me even more to go back home. It's OK. Really. I can do this.

"I want you to marry me," he said.

He paused without moving his eyes from mine. He looked at me for a while, like he was trying to see through me, to read my thoughts.

"I know we haven't spoken about my personal life," he said. "You've been very respectful in not asking me anything about anything. But I want you to know the truth, and I want to be honest. I want you to be the closest person in my life, in my everyday life. I adore you and love you. You have changed me. You have no idea what you've done to my life, and to me. In an incredible way.

"I want to marry you. I know we can be very comfortable together. I need a marriage for my business and career, and for my family and other people I need to be around. Mark and I have been together for about seven years. It has always been secretive, and we've tried our best to be discreet so that it wouldn't be known. Unfortunately, this is still a controversial thing today, and some people are prejudiced against a relationship between two men. It can be quite emotional on both sides. I don't like to live this way, but I absolutely cannot announce my love for Mark because of my business. My career would end badly. My family is nice, but conservative, so I'm not honest with them either.

"Anyway, rumors have started to spread around town about me and Mark. The looks we've been getting from others lately have been bizarre. It's suffocating and uncomfortable. I screwed up a couple of times when I drank too much and showed affection to Mark in public. I've been denying it, but no matter how much I do, some people don't forget and are likely to talk. Unless I can effectively cover up my orientation with a marriage, the rumors, gossip and insults will overwhelm us. If you and I get married, it would help eliminate this drumbeat of gossip. It would provide some evidence that I'm straight.

"But this is not just about me and Mark. I want to help you. You can stay here and live freely. Because we'll be married, you'll be eligible to apply for papers and become a permanent resident. I can give you a wonderful life. You and your family will be worry-free. I guarantee it. We'll live together like a husband and wife in my house. You'll come to dinners, events and some business trips with me. You can go to school and enjoy the city. I'll continue with my clandestine life with Mark. I will always respect you, Alyssa. And we will have a faithful, straight marriage. You'll never hear gossip about me or ever see me out with anyone else. I promise."

He was confident and passionate. He was smiling, waiting for me to say something. I looked at him, my mouth open, astonished. I picked up his glass of Macallan scotch, drank the whole thing and put the glass down. My hands were shaking.

"I don't understand," I said, "I don't understand many things. I'm not sure what to say. Are you serious? Does Mark know about all this?"

"Yes, and he's fine. He's fine because he loves me and will do whatever is best for me. He's very supportive. He doesn't want to lose me, and I don't want to lose him. This way, we can be freer in our relationship. Why would anyone view me with suspicion when I have you? Mark said he's fine with the marriage because it's with you. If it were anyone else, he probably wouldn't be happy. He loves you. He loves being around you. Please try to understand. I only ask that you take me seriously. We can have a wonderful life together."

I left. I was shocked, confused and excited. Somehow, I was smiling and frowning at the same time. It's like when you watch a movie and something suddenly scares you and your face freezes—eyes and mouth wide open. I think my jaw was open for three days.

I don't know why but November always seems to go by quickly. It was now Christmas time, when the most beautiful colors, decorations and feelings of warmth surround the city. It was a feeling of love, life and freedom, and there I was, at City Hall.

I was standing next to a man who was a great lover, a good person, intelligent, generous, lovable, weird and happy. A handsome, stylish, high-quality gentleman, who was one of the wealthiest people in the city. This was the man I was about to marry. We got married privately, with Mark as the witness. Gilles decided we'd get married first and announce the news later.

My husband, Gilles? He's originally from France and his parents still live there, in Paris. His family has been wealthy for as long as Gilles can remember. He has two sisters who also live in France and are married to French guys. His family is steeped in French culture and traditions. I mean they are very, very French. It was a huge concern for them that Gilles wasn't married, and it would be a huge disappointment to them that he didn't marry a French girl. Their other worry was that Gilles was the only man left to carry on the family name. The parents were obsessed about Gilles getting married and having children, especially a boy.

Gilles's father was a diplomat, and when he was given an American assignment, the family lived in New York, where Gilles received his education. He fell in love with Manhattan and never left.

Gilles is the founder and C.E.O. of a successful hedge fund. He is well connected with wealthy people. Businessmen, celebrities and socialites. His company is rather small, relying on a few smart people and technology to run the business. They create various economic models that are used to generate program-trading algorithms. The company's models and funds have made a lot of people a lot of money over the years.

Gilles is always busy, at his job and in his personal life. He is the kind of guy who is hyperactive and always doing something. He loves traveling, good food and great wine. He enjoys going to the movies and off-Broadway shows. He's always reading, and taking long walks in parks. Any and all parks. I was all over New York City's parks with him. The only thing he loved more than the parks was coffee. He was a coffee maniac. Parks and coffee. All very French.

I moved in with Gilles the day after we got married. A driver picked me up in Brooklyn. Silvia cried. I promised her we would see each other often. Me and my yellow suitcase were at Gilles's front door when I rang the bell. The door opened to a big warm welcome home for me. Party music was playing loud, Gilles and Mark were drinking champagne and dancing around. Mona was in the kitchen preparing dinner. French food, of course. I saw all the love and fun and joined the celebration. We soon wore ourselves out.

We sat down at the dinner table and drank more champagne while we waited for Mona to finish her works of art. Everyone was happy. After dinner, Mona brought out the *pièce de résistance,* the napoleon. She baked it especially for me. She also made French macarons to celebrate the marriage.

"She only makes macarons when she hears happy news," Gilles said.

Mona is like family. She cares about Gilles—a lot.

"Did you make the announcement to your parents?" Mona asked.

"No, not yet," Gilles said. "I will. Next week ... I think."

"What are you waiting for?" Mona pressed. "You know your father. I hope he doesn't get upset that you didn't tell him right away."

"He'll be fine," Gilles said. "I'm just wondering if I should call or write a letter to my entire family and send a picture of Alyssa and me. When they see I married this beautiful girl they'll all be satisfied. I really don't want to hear all their questions. 'Why not a French girl?' or 'Does she at least speak French?' Those kinds of things."

"That's right," Mona said. "Always do what's best for you."

"Come on, I respect them," Gilles said. "I just don't want any drama, you know?"

Mona sighed and looked at me.

"Well, it's time to learn French my dear," she said.

"I'd love to!" I said.

We all laughed and kept the party going. After dinner I offered to help Mona with the dishes and stuff.

"No, no, no, but thank you. I'll do my job, you go sit down," she smiled and waved for me to go back into the dining room.

"Cheers," Mark said as he poured more wine for me.

Gilles was in the kitchen chatting with Mona while she cleaned things up.

"Cheers, Mark," I said.

"I'm really happy today. I'm so glad you did this. I want you to know that I'll always respect you and your privacy. Please feel open and free with me and think of me as your close friend."

"Thank you, Mark, same here."

"After all, we both love the same man, right?"

Mark stood up and hugged me.

On his way back to his chair Mark noticed my yellow suitcase standing just outside the dining room. He walked over to it and studied it closely. I was feeling a little embarrassed.

"It's just an old suitcase from back home," I said. "It was the only one available when I came here."

"I think it's unique," he said as he continued staring at it. "It's like a work of art. You know, I like to do photography, as a hobby. Would you mind if I took a few pictures of it?"

"Sure, if you want to," I said.

"Hey, Gilles, come here," Mark said. "Look at this piece."

"Yeah, so?" Gilles asked.

"Look at the style and design. Look at these large heavy stitches, and the leather. It's so thick. And the color. That yellow."

Oh yeah, it's definitely yellow. We all know that. I want to move on from talking about the suitcase but Mark's going on and on. He thinks it's "art worthy?" That's a surprise, but kind of cool. This poor suitcase. It went unnoticed for years back home and here it is now, so popular and interesting. Beauty is in the eye of the beholder, so they say. Here's the proof.

I was buzzed from the wine and the good vibes as the night wound down. Mona had left. Mark stayed a little longer but was gone right after midnight. He had an early business flight.

"Welcome to your new home, Alyssa," Gilles said as he hugged me. "From now on this house is your house. Thank you for everything. I love being around you. You are my beautiful girl, and wife."

We kissed each other and said goodnight. I had my own bedroom on the second floor. It was newly renovated in the style I loved, thanks to Mark. Every piece of furniture was brand new. The dresser, nightstands and armchair were all French, with faded beige colors. The walls were a light rose color with light and dark grey shades and curtains. There was a queen-sized bed with a few white fluffy pillows and a white down comforter. Even at night, the room looked bright. Dark rooms and furniture make me depressed. Good thing Gilles and Mark know my taste. It felt warm and relaxing.

The bedroom windows looked out onto the street. I opened the windows to breathe in some fresh air and to hear the city, and then jumped into bed. Literally. The bed made me feel like I was laying in big, fluffy clouds. The fresh air made me awake, and the sounds of the city gave me goosebumps.

This is where I live. I'm living in the city that I fell in love with from day one. Living in the city I was dreaming about every single night. I'd imagine myself here and walking on the street, a city girl. I'd imagine walking in and out of a house, and living a simple, everyday life here. And my imagination came true. Tomorrow, I can get up and walk in and out of this house. My family. I always think of them at night. I haven't even told them the news yet. I want to share every single moment. My stories and my new life, but I just don't know where to start or what to say. I don't want to lie to them, but I'm not ready to be honest with them either. Maybe they're not ready either? Who am I kidding? I'm just rationalizing. It does make me feel better that they're all doing well. I know they have good financial support, now more than ever. I know they can have more than they did before. I know they're happy and healthy, like me.

Over time, Gilles and I learned how to make a happy house. I tried to understand what pleased him and what irritated him. I knew when to leave him alone and when to reach out. I knew about morning and evening Gilles—two different guys. I'm always flexible. I'll change my plans if he needs me to be with him. Sometimes he'll call about an unplanned dinner or he just wants to go out for drinks. I always dress up and meet him on time.

He loves hanging out in his bedroom, especially on a rainy day with a fire going. But then, who wouldn't love that? Or when the weather is nice, he hangs out on the balcony, another one of his favorite places. We sit there having cocktails, look at the sky and talk. I make him laugh with my broken English or stories from back home. Sometimes he tickles me. I scream but he doesn't stop. I hate being tickled and he knows it. That's why he does it.

We spend hours in Gilles's bedroom. Just being lazy, watching stupid TV or reading magazines and books. I join him when I need help with my homework. I only ask him when he isn't busy, which isn't often. Sometimes I fall asleep in his bed while watching a movie or reading but when I wake up, I go to my bedroom. I love sleeping next to him, but I also love sleeping in my fluffy bed.

Most weekend mornings I make coffee and bring it to him along with fresh croissants. I lay down and enjoy breakfast while he reads his newspapers. When he isn't home, I still go to the balcony, but I never stay in his bedroom. I've never been nosey, so I don't go through his drawers or anything like that. I always respect his privacy. I don't think he has anything to hide, and I have nothing to look for. There are no secrets, which is a wonderful way to live.

Since he announced our marriage to the public, my life has become much busier. Now he receives invitations that include both of us. I'm always proud to go with him. There are so many people that I never met before. His friends and some of his relatives invited us over to their houses for dinner, to celebrate our marriage.

There were an awful lot of people who were happy about the news. Happy and astonished at the same time. Many of them wanted to get to know me and they'd ask so many questions, some of them rather personal. It's hard to avoid them, and I always try my best to represent him, since he deserves it. I'd rather be quiet and let Gilles do all the talking, even for me.

You know how these dinners are. Sooner or later the girls separate from the guys, and then it's question time for Alyssa. Or people are staring at me like I'm an alien with three heads and a tail. I like to think I'm unique, but not that much.

I'm glad I attended classes. My English improved dramatically, and I'm able to answer many of their questions. At least the ones I want to. I remember when I started dating Gilles and he would have all these questions, and I'd get frustrated, and he would laugh.

"Don't ever worry about what anyone asks you," he said. "Their curiosity is not your responsibility. They can ask or say whatever they want. Your responsibility is to choose how to respond, or even if to respond. Just because someone asks a question it doesn't mean you have to answer."

Now I'm part of Gilles's social network, and I've become one of the more prestigious girls in the city. I'm receiving personal invites from ladies I've met at various events. I've been invited to fashion shows, charity dinners and gallery receptions. I'm in the city's high society circle. I've tried to avoid being in that circle for a while, because once they get you, they don't let go. They want you everywhere and follow you everywhere. As much as Gilles is so private with some of his life, he also leads a public life, and now I'm part of it.

When Gilles has free time, he likes to spend it with me and I'm always ready. It's a joy to spend time with him. We live on the Upper West Side, just steps from Central Park. It feels like our personal backyard. We take long walks. I listen to his opinions and ideas while we hold hands. We walk, sit, walk again and sit again, as we talk and laugh about everything, just like our first date. Sometimes we stay there until the sun goes down, and then we make our way home.

"Oh, I needed that," he says often. "I needed you and this laughter after the day I had!"

He kisses me and hugs me so hard it hurts. When Mark is around, I'm a little quieter because he dominates the conversation— in a good way. He always has some story, and no one can compete with his energy. Mark is one of those natural born storytellers who can mesmerize a room full of people with his animated monologues. I always enjoy his company.

I never feel jealous of the two of them when they spend time together. Before I said yes to Gilles's proposal, I thought about it. Would I be able to accept their relationship, their love? What if I can't? Would I be jealous? No, I don't think that way. I don't judge. I accept people and situations as they are. Love is love is love. I'm completely free of jealousy, because I'm completely free.

When Mark comes over, I greet him happily, just as I do with Gilles. I want to make him comfortable when he's here. I don't want him to think I'm trying to take the place over, and that maybe one day I'd take Gilles away from him. We both know we love Gilles. And that's fine. There's enough love for everyone. Why resist it? If Mark is jealous of me, he never shows it. What he does show is respect, and kindness.

I'll never forget when he told me about his parents. He was an only child growing up in Austin, Texas. He was always outgoing, and high school came easy to him. He got an art scholarship to NYU. After finishing his first semester, he went home for the Christmas break. Mark and his parents were driving home from a midnight church service when they were hit by a drunk driver who ran a red light. Mark was unconscious and beat up, but alive. When he came to, he was devastated to learn that both his parents had died at the scene. He was in shock, and numb, but he took care of business. He made the funeral arrangements, buried his parents, and spent a month hiking River Place, thinking about his future. Then he sold his parents' property, moved to New York and never went back.

When I heard this story, I had so much compassion for him. I knew something about what he was going through. As happy and energized as he was most of the time, I could imagine how much pain he had inside him from that tragic accident. I lost one parent; he lost both. He loves chatting and spending time with Mona in the kitchen. Maybe he wants that motherly, family feeling.

Many times, I'll go away and make myself busy when Mark comes over. Gilles and Mark were together long before I showed up, and I'm sure they're fine without me around. They announce they're going to the balcony, and that's usually a cue for me to quietly slip away. I know the balcony leads to drinks, which leads to the bed, which leads to…well, you know. It doesn't bother me. Well, at least not that much.

TWENTY-EIGHT

APRIL 1998, MANHATTAN

Gilles told his family about our marriage, but it took a couple of months before they agreed to meet me. I guess it took a while for them to process the news and face reality.

Are they worried about meeting me? Who would ever think I was such an important person that people would have to prepare to see me? I have zero worries about meeting them.

"Mother and father are nervous about meeting your wife," Gilles's sister told him.

After Gilles stopped laughing, he told her they have nothing to be nervous about. Gilles and Mona would chat about the family conversations. I never got involved in those. People are nervous because they're afraid. Gilles's parents are afraid that I'm not fit to be his wife, or I'm not attractive enough.

"She looks pretty in the picture," Gilles's mother told him. "But some people are just photogenic, so I can't say anything until I see her."

"I understand, but you'll see," Gilles said. "She looks even better in person."

"Beauty isn't everything," she said.

I wasn't able to travel overseas yet because I was still waiting to get my permanent resident card, so they made arrangements to come to New York, and we made plans to entertain them. Gilles wanted to have a special dinner at home the first night, and then go out to a few of their favorite restaurants and the opera.

Gilles was excited to see them. With the travel dates set, he became the serious Gilles, which means he is happy on the inside. He called his secretary and asked her to clear his calendar on the dates they were coming and gave her the restaurant list to make reservations.

In between school and my social life with Gilles, I was now taking introductory French lessons with a tutor who came to the house three times a week. I tried to learn as much as I could until they arrived, but there wasn't much time. Even though the teacher kept telling me I was doing great, I knew I wasn't making much progress. It was so hard to pronounce the words. I wanted to at least learn the basics, to greet the family and make them happy. Mona said it would be respectful.

"You know, you're such a good girl," she said. "It's the right thing to do. I'll tell you, in Paris, we always appreciate when visitors at least say hello or thank you in French. At restaurants, waiters are happy to hear diners speak even basic French, you know?"

I agreed with her but thought since they are visiting New York, how about they speak English? But I didn't say that to Mona. She was one of those French people who didn't smile so much. I loved her attitude.

To provide the illusion of a traditional marriage, I moved into Gilles's bedroom. My bedroom was transformed into a guest room. They were all staying in a hotel, but when they came over, they'd be snooping around the house. I was kind of sad to say good-bye to my bedroom for a few days, but I was excited to say hello to Gilles's bedroom.

The day of the dinner arrived, and Mark took care of the preparations. The dining area was decorated with white roses and candles. The table was set up for eight people with white and faded pink antique porcelain china, with vintage silverware and Baccarat glassware. Mona was working in the kitchen with two other assistants, including a white-gloved bartender who was going to greet everyone with champagne.

I had returned from the beauty salon, and Caroline arrived with a new dress, which she helped me with. It looked great, but it was so tight there was zero space between me and the fabric. I could barely breathe, and I was afraid to eat. Gilles seemed nervous and excited.

"Look at her," Caroline said to Gilles as I carefully walked down the stairs.

"Wow," Gilles said. "I love this dress. Thank you, Caroline. You always come through."

"Any time, Gilles. Congratulations once again and have a wonderful evening. Goodnight."

"Goodnight."

"You look very attractive tonight, my husband," I said. "Did Caroline help you with this beautiful new suit and bow tie?"

"You look so beautiful," he said. "This is such a French look. Chanel. I'm sure my family will love your style."

I was wearing a long sleeve, open back, long white lace dress. I had my hair up, with light makeup on, and red lipstick. I wore no jewelry other than my diamond wedding ring. Gilles offered to buy me a diamond necklace that Caroline showed us, but I refused. I wanted them to see me, not the diamonds. The dress was enough of a statement.

The guests arrived. Gilles and I were standing next to each other to greet them and he could introduce me. I was greeting the guests in French with a small smile that I had practiced all day in the mirror. My heart was palpitating, but I pretended I was fine. I was really worried about blushing. I covered my face with a natural-colored powder that I hoped would help.

Gilles's father, Rámy Durand, was about seventy-five. Slim and tall, with a deep and smart look behind his tiny blue eyes. His mother, Jeanne-Marie, was a couple of years younger than her husband. She was also slim, but petite, with straight shoulder-length brown hair. Her pink lipstick and oversized round glasses made her look extremely fashionable. Her style was simple but high-end, with a great mix of colors. She had a Hermès look.

His sisters, Françoise and Clara, looked alike. They were both wearing long dresses with beautiful diamond necklaces and earrings. Their husbands also had a similar look, and definitely French. Françoise and her husband had a three-year-old boy. Clara and her husband had twin six-year-old girls. When they came in, all of them were wearing scarfs. I guess scarves are mandatory if you're French.

After a champagne toast, we sat down for the first course. There was some small talk with awkward silences in between. With the second course and more wine, the family members became chattier. Half the conversation was in English and half in French. Every time someone would say something in French, Gilles would gently remind them to speak English as he looked at me with a smile. They would pause with a forced smile and switch to English.

By the time the third course arrived, the wine was flowing and the entire family was immersed in long conversations in French, without even thinking about speaking in English. They found their comfort zone and became even louder. After unsuccessfully trying to stop them a few times, Gilles just looked at me and rolled his eyes. I smiled.

"Pouvons-nous parler en anglais?" Gilles said, once again asking them to speak English.

They all just looked at Gilles and started to quiet down.

I'm feeling really good from all this alcohol. Ah, what the hell.

"Ça va bien avec moi, Gilles, s'il vous plaît. J'aime entendre parler français." *It's okay with me Gilles, please. I love hearing French*, I said, as I put my hand on his.

Well, that made an impression. Now there are seven pairs of eyes staring at me. I might as well keep going.

"Salutations pour la famille, je suis plus qu'heureux de vous rencontrer tous." *Greetings to the family. I'm more than happy to meet you all*, I said.

"Cheers," I said as I raised my glass.

"Cheers," they said slowly, eyes wide.

After dinner, we moved near the fireplace where dessert was served, along with more drinks. Gilles's mother sat next to me and Gilles and his father were standing as they had a conversation over drinks. The sisters were a little buzzed and chatty with their husbands.

"I'm so glad to meet you," Jeanne-Marie said.

"Thank you. I am very happy to meet you as well," I said.

"I hope you and Gilles will visit us in Paris sometime soon," she said. "You can improve your French," she smiled.

Did she just criticize my French?

"Gilles used to come to Paris often, but not anymore. I miss him," she said.

"I'd love to visit Paris and see you and all of his family more often," I said.

"Thank you," she said, nodding her head. "Gilles is always busy with his business. And now he has you. He used to visit us and bring Mark. Mark is Gilles's good friend and personal designer. I see Mark more often than Gilles these days. He is such a talented guy. Have you met him?"

"Yes, I have. He's great."

"Once my husband and I hosted a dinner for the French president and his wife at our chateau outside of Paris. There were around eighty people. I asked Mark to decorate the chateau and the dinner table. Since then, Mark is well known around Paris. He's got a great business there. Whenever he travels to Paris, he always comes to visit."

After dessert and coffee, and a few more conversations, we said our goodnights.

"I'm looking forward to seeing the children tomorrow," I said to Gilles's sisters.

Gilles's mother came up to me and said goodnight with a handshake. His father kissed me on each cheek. Very European. I was exhausted because of my tight dress and from controlling myself, trying to look calm and glamorous.

Right after the guests left, I went upstairs to unleash my body. The dress was so beautiful, and it made me so pretty, but when I took it off it was a relief. I made myself comfortable in my robe and went back downstairs looking for dessert. I grabbed a slice of the meringue almond cake and indulged myself. Meanwhile, Gilles came downstairs and joined my party.

"I'm so glad this dinner is over. I'm so tired," he said. "May I have a bite? Watching you makes me want something sweet."

He sat closer to me and I fed him a piece of cake.

"I hope your family had a good time," I said.

He was quiet. After having a few more bites he calmed down.

"They all seem like nice people." I continued to probe.

"My father liked you, that's for sure."

"How do you know? Did he say something?"

"No, he never says things like that. I just know."

"You just know?"

"Well, when he said goodbye, he kissed you. That's how I know. He only kisses people he likes. I know his mannerisms. But he doesn't know I know," he smiled.

"What about your mother? Do you know her mannerisms?"

"My mother? She's funny... she said she was glad you have small breasts. It's a French thing."

I laughed.

"She speaks highly of Mark," I said.

"Oh really?" he smiled. "She's such a good actress."

Gilles launched into stories about his childhood with his father. None about his mother. As I listened, I mindlessly ate and fed Gilles with the cake. When he finished his stories, I went to the kitchen to get more cake, but it was gone. We laughed about how much we had eaten and went upstairs.

"We were like a real husband and wife tonight," he said. "We even shared the plate, and now we're going to share the bed. You know what happens next?"

I think we had too much sugar.

TWENTY-NINE

JANUARY 2000, MANHATTAN

We had been together for two years, and most of the gossip about Gilles had faded away. He was a happily married man.

One evening, I was invited to a charity dinner by Kaley Wainwright, the wife of one of Gilles's friends. Gilles never liked me going by myself to these dinners unless it was for a worthy cause. Too much potential for drama. We were already going out to so many events that it was fine with me to skip it. None of the women were near my age and I had zero in common with them. Despite all that, Gilles asked me to go to Kaley's event. He felt the need to be respectful to his friend, so I agreed.

It was a small, selective crowd. After a few drinks and chatting with many kinds of women on many different subjects, I felt bored. I went to the bathroom to freshen up. While I was in the toilet, I heard two women come in, laughing loudly about something. They sounded drunk. Then one of them mentioned me, asking the other who I was.

"She's Gilles's wife. You know him. You know his story, don't you?"

"I've heard of him from my husband."

"Between us, he married this girl to distract everyone about the rumors about him. They say he's really attracted to men."

"Really? How is that possible if he's married and sleeps with a woman?"

"I don't know if it's true or not. For years my husband was one of Gilles's most successful traders. But after a big disagreement, Gilles let him go. You know Charlie. He can get so angry and he just doesn't let things go. He's going after him."

"What is he going to do?"

"Oh, I shouldn't say. But Charlie told me the paparazzi will be chasing him down tonight. You know, with Charlie's new job we have a lot of contacts with the media. His wife is here alone, so where is her husband? You'll see. We'll destroy him," she laughed.

I stayed in the stall until they left. I called Gilles but he didn't pick up. I knew where he was. He was attending a dinner for French actors at the Carlyle Hotel and he was with Mark. I was worried he might drink too much and lose control. I left for the Carlyle. I ran into the hotel and found the private dining room, but a waiter told me all the guests had just left. I kept calling Gilles, but he didn't answer. I went to the front desk and asked them to make a phone call to the room under the name Durand. Gilles answered.

I went up to their room and told them what I heard.

"Well, I guess Charlie never got over getting fired," Gilles said. "Good thing you were there and came here. Thank you, Alyssa."

"Of course, but what are we going to do now?" I asked.

"Well I think you should stay here with us, and help us finish all this champagne," Gilles said smiling. "What do you think Mark?"

"Sounds good to me!" Mark said.

"But what about the press?" I asked.

"Oh, I'm sure they'll get tired and go home after a while. Here, have a drink," he said, handing me a glass of champagne.

I took the glass as I looked at both of them, shaking my head and smiling.

"You two," I said, as we all laughed.

Architectural Digest called Gilles a few times requesting an interview with the two of us about our life together, and to take some pictures of the house. He would say no, but then he finally gave in. Gilles was a private person, but in this case, he thought it would be a good way to showcase his faithful marriage and counter any lingering gossip.

It was organized chaos that day. There were reporters, photographers and designers running every which way. The house was decorated by Mark and his team while Gilles and I were decorated by costume designers and make-up artists. We had a full day of interviews and photoshoots, with a few breaks. The shooting started in the dining area with the table set for dinner. We moved on to the office with all the books, and then to the bedroom where they asked us to sit next to each other in a romantic pose. We took some shots on the balcony, playing with a dog that Mark hired for the day. We finished in the living room on the couch by the fireplace as a loving couple. On this last shoot my attention was drawn to Mark. He did such an excellent job, as always, but something made me sad.

Mark should be sitting next to Gilles instead of me right now. Why can't these two people be free, together? Who decides what's right or wrong when it comes to love? Two adults should be able to choose for themselves, to be themselves. What difference does it make who loves who? As long as we don't harm others, we should be able to express our love any way we want. Isn't it important to just be kind and to respect one another? Then why can't we respect people's choices about who they want to be with and love, and be kind to them?

I was so distracted with my thoughts until I heard the photographer.

"We need you to smile, let's see a happy smile."

About a month later, Gilles came home holding an issue of *Architectural Digest* with us on the cover. I followed him as he went to the living room, poured a glass of scotch and sat down. I took the magazine from him as he stared at me in silence. Because of his serious look I quickly went through the pages, trying to find something wrong with the pictures or the articles. But it all seemed fine. We looked like a happy couple. I couldn't wait to spend some quality time with the magazine.

"You look so damn beautiful," he said. "I'm so proud to call you my wife. I wish I didn't have to do these things but maybe now they'll leave me alone, especially that bastard Charlie. I'm so done with him."

He's satisfied and angry at the same time.

"Come here, darling. Sit next to me," he said.

I moved to his side and sat quietly. He hugged me and took a deep breath. Then he squeezed me so tight and long I thought I was going to pass out. He put his hand on my face and kissed me.

"You're so feminine, and so considerate. You've made my life so much easier with your love and warmth. How can you do all these things so naturally? What am I going to do with you?" he smiled as he looked at me.

His look always makes me blush.

"Why don't we celebrate this tonight? Let's go out and party all night," he said.

Fun Gilles has arrived. How can I say no? I love going out with him. More than just about anything.

"Is Mark coming with us?" I asked.

"Maybe he'll join us later. I think he's having dinner with one of his clients."

After dinner at the Four Seasons restaurant, we went out to a nightclub where Mark joined us. After clubbing we were all wide awake and energized. We stopped at Joe's Pizza in the Village. It's so good. Sometimes a slice of pizza tastes better than high-end restaurant food. We went home and went to the balcony. It was a cold March night but thanks to the heater lamp we were able to have drinks there.

"Look what I got from an old friend I ran into at the club," Mark said as he took a joint out of his pocket. "He said it's pretty strong."

"Let's see if your old friend is right," I said.

After passing the joint around a couple of times we all got the giggles. We laughed and laughed, about anything and everything.

We even laughed about laughing. Tears rolled down our faces and my jaws were sore from laughing.

It was about noon when I woke up. I was alive but I couldn't move. My body felt so heavy. I thought the pain was from all the dancing at the club. I slowly turned my head to the right and I saw Gilles, sleeping peacefully. He looked like he wasn't going to wake up anytime soon. I then moved my heavy head to the left and I saw Mark. He was also in a deep sleep with his mouth open.

Am I awake or am I dreaming?

I opened my eyes wider and looked straight at the ceiling. I tried to remember but nothing came. I just kept staring. After about ten minutes I squeezed out from between these two, wide-shoulder bodies and quietly disappeared. I went to my bedroom and took a shower. I felt dizzy and sleepy. I crashed until the phone rang.

Why is it so damn loud?

I thought about getting up but instead rolled over and went back to sleep.

It was now April, and I had invited Kalian and Silvia to brunch. I felt bad that I hadn't seen them for a while. I planned to take them to brunch and then do some shopping. I wanted to treat them the way I liked to be treated. They were both special to me, and always will be. They were there for me when I went through some hard times. Kalian helped save my job and Silvia helped save my sanity.

We met at Rue 57. It was a beautiful spring day. We had so much to talk about. Kalian was still working for Anna and Michael. Her goal was to save up enough money to go to nursing school. She had a boyfriend and she was hoping to get married.

Silvia lived in the same apartment with a new roommate, whom she complained about. She said she hadn't planned to have a roommate, but she desperately needed to save up some money for a trip to see her father, who was seriously ill. She wanted to be in a relationship, but it seemed to me she wasn't really trying that hard.

After lunch we took a walk to Saks Fifth Avenue to do some shopping. I wanted to buy them gifts, and the best gift is when you get exactly what you want. I told them to buy whatever they wanted. Well, every girl loves pocketbooks and shoes. It's typical. It was a wonderful day for all of us. When I got home, I found Gilles by himself, reading in his office. We kissed.

"Gilles, you remember my friends, Kalian and Silvia? They're the girls who helped me so much when I first moved here."

"Sure, I remember."

"Well ... uhh ... I'm not sure if ... umm ..."

"Alyssa, what is it? Just say it."

"OK ... well ... both of them are trying to save money. Kalian for nursing school, and Silvia to go see her father, who is very ill. I know what it's like to try to save money when you're living paycheck to paycheck. I would really like to ..."

"Yes," Gilles said, taking my hand. "Of course. They're like your family so they're important to me as well. Let me know what they need and I'll take care of it."

"Thank you, Gilles, this means so much to me" I said as I hugged him. "You're so generous. One of the many reasons I love you."

Silvia was with her father when he passed away. She stayed there with her mother for a few months. She called me when she returned. She wanted to see me and give me some gifts. Kalian became a full-time nursing student, and she called to say she was engaged.

"Congratulations Kalian! What great news! I am so happy and excited for you."

"Thanks," she said. "I think that pocketbook brought me good luck."

"It wasn't the pocketbook," I said laughing. "It was you."

THIRTY

MAY 2001, MANHATTAN

Spring always makes me excited. It reminds me of the day Gilles and I met in Central Park. I can even remember the smell. I remember I was in such a hurry to meet him. And when I saw him, I just liked him, for no reason. It seems like yesterday.

It's been more than three years since I started living with him, and sharing his crazy, busy, lavish, intense, weird and sexy lifestyle. Sometimes it's hectic, but most of the time it's fascinating. With constant meet-and-greets, dinners and events, with interesting, and not-so-interesting people. With lots of walking and talking in Central Park, in hot or cold weather. And lots of traveling, which includes more dinners. Dining out happens a lot.

I was always attracted to Gilles, but today I'm more in love with him than ever. It sounds crazy, but he's the man with the character I admire. I've learned so much and had so many life experiences with him. He's given me everything. He's made my life easy, in so many ways.

Life is like a roller-coaster. We just need to hang on, hold tight and don't fall off even when it's difficult. I started life as a carefree child in a wealthy family. Then my father died, and we plummeted. I fell into a life of poverty, where every day was a struggle. Now, I'm back on the high road again, and it's even better than before. Now I'm grateful, and I don't take anything for granted. And today I became a student of international and public affairs at Columbia University. I couldn't be happier, thanks to Gilles.

"If it weren't for you, I'd never have this opportunity to attend one of the most prestigious universities in the world," I said to him once. "Thank you."

"Why do you think that way?" he asked.

"How else to think? You're the one who opened the door for me and gave me a chance."

"You would've found a way to open the door, with or without me. When you desperately want something, believe in something and work on it, then it happens. It has nothing to do with me. It's you, all you."

Maybe he's right. It's true that when we intensely desire something and hold it in our thoughts, we get it—eventually. Especially if we behave like we already have it. But I still think it was more him than me.

I haven't seen my family in years. For more than a year, whenever I asked Gilles about going to see them, he'd have some dinner or another event where he needed me to be with him. He would politely ask me to push the travel to a later date. The interesting thing was I didn't mind the delay. Mostly I was relieved, and I wouldn't try to persuade him. Before, I was counting the days to go back. I was dreaming every night about going back to my country. But lately I haven't felt it was so urgent.

In the not so distant past, the constant delays in going to see my family would upset me. But I was different now. I had become more aware, more present and less emotional. I observed my reactions to situations and instead of becoming emotional, I accepted them and thought about how to respond. I'm not sure what caused the change. Was it the lifestyle that Gilles provided, where I didn't have to worry about pure survival? Or my internal evolution? Or both?

One day that spring I got an email from a woman named Rachel Beasley. Rachael wrote that we had a mutual friend from my home country. She owned an art gallery in Scottsdale, Arizona, and she wanted to get to know me. I didn't reply to her email. But as I was thinking about a trip back home, I began to wonder who she was. How did we both know the same person? I started thinking about my family and all of my friends who I hadn't kept in touch with. I missed them. I even dreamt about seeing them one sunny morning. It felt so real I didn't want to open my eyes. I had these great feelings rising in my body. I felt warmth, love and joy. I saw how much fun it would be spending time with them. I could see my friends and explore my home city again, with them. I wanted to see them.

"Gilles," I said that evening. "When school is over this semester, I plan to go see my family. Of course, you're more than welcome to come with me."

He looked at me, and then looked out the window.

"Thanks," he said. "That's great, but you know … when exactly are you planning to take this trip?"

"I was thinking sometime this summer."

"Summertime? Hmm…" he moved to his desk. "We have so many events this summer. I need you to be with me."

"I will be with you, but I'd really like to go, for at least a little while. At least a month."

"A month? I don't think so. Listen, my darling, I need your help with the Hamptons house. You know, we need to prepare it for summer and make some changes to it. We're going to be there for most of the summer. We're booked almost every weekend, entertaining a lot of clients and friends. You know how important this is to me and my business. How about we plan on going a little later, perhaps in the fall. You haven't seen them in years so you can wait a little bit longer, right?"

He smiled and gave me that look.

Damn. That look. I always say yes.

"How about we send your family somewhere on a long summer vacation? As a gift from us. Anywhere they want to go?"

"Thank you, that's very nice and maybe we should do that," I said. "But that doesn't mean I get to be with them, and it's not just about seeing my family, it's also about all my friends. And in the fall, I'll be busy with school and won't have time to travel."

He just stared at me, not saying a word. I left to go to my bedroom and sat down.

Am I sad? Upset? Yes and no. I don't get why he doesn't understand my feelings and the importance of seeing my family and friends. Why does he act like that? Whatever the reason, that's what it is, for now. No point in making a problem out of it.

I just went to sleep.

THIRTY-ONE

Rachel Beasley. She popped in my head right after I woke up. I found her email and out of curiosity I replied. She responded right away, and we started a conversation over email. She seemed nice and interesting, simple and funny. I liked her responses, so when she asked if we could speak, I didn't hesitate, and we exchanged phone numbers.

I had become a rather private person, but I also thought you could take that too far. It's good to be cautious but also open to meeting new people. Over the past few years I've met so many people from events with Gilles, hundreds of them. I know a lot of people, but only a few friends who I can talk to and trust on a personal level. I try to keep the right balance with them. But exchanging emails with Rachel was different. I felt a connection.

She called me the next day. It was awkward in the beginning but soon we were chatting easily, like typical girlfriends. We talked about New York, fashion, movies and just about everything.

"Well, we've been talking for a while," I said. "If you don't mind, please tell me why you reached out to me?"

"You're right, there was a reason," she said.

"So, who is this mutual friend?" I asked. "I'm just curious."

"I met Jasmine Ho recently," she said. "We were chatting, and she mentioned you, which reminded me that I saw you and your husband on the cover of *Architectural Digest*."

"Ah yes, Jasmine. I've seen her at several events."

"Those are beautiful pictures of you and your husband. When I looked at the pictures, I recognized you right away. You look the same as you did when you were younger."

"Thanks, but wait. How do you know what I looked like back in the day?"

"I've seen your high school yearbook pictures."

"Excuse me?"

"I went to college with our mutual friend."

"That can't be. None of my friends came to America to go to college. Are you sure you've got the right person?"

There was a silent pause.

"Yes, I'm sure. You know him well. Maximillian."

Maximillian? Of course, Maximillian…. Yes, high school. I was shocked. My mind lit up with so many questions.

Hey, calm down. Take a deep breath and get your act together.

"Yes, of course. Max," I said. "How is he?"

"He's doing well. He's Chief Technology Officer at some eCommerce company. He's married with one child. A four-year-old girl."

"Wow, that's great. I'm happy to hear he's doing well. Where does he live now?"

"It's funny but after college we ended up living near each other here in Scottsdale. It's a big reason we're still friends."

"What a coincidence. Wait, how did you find out he knows me? You recognized me from a picture? I'm confused now."

"When we were in college Max showed me pictures of when he was growing up and there were a few pictures of you. When I saw your pictures in the magazine, I recognized you right away. I have a good visual memory. He told me so many stories about you. I feel like I know you."

"Interesting, I'm impressed with your memory."

"I just thought it would be nice to connect with you since we both know Max, and I also thought we might have a mutual interest in art, since your home is so beautiful."

"Of course, yes. I'm glad you contacted me. I'm always happy to meet interesting people, especially artists like you. I always admire creative people. I wish I could do that."

"I come to New York every now and then. Maybe we can meet up?"

"Sure, sounds good."

"Great. I'll give you a call. Talk to you soon."

"OK, bye."

Maximillian. My first love. Someone I'll never forget. What a small world. Someone was able to connect us, here in this country? I guess so. Nothing would surprise me after what I've been through. Even now, look at me. Most of my life has been full of surprises. I wonder what he looks like now, or what kind of person he's become.

Who's his wife? Does his child look like him? I remember when I thought I couldn't live without him, and all the pain I felt when we broke up. I thought my life was over. I have so many happy memories of when we were together. He was so crazy—happy crazy. I wonder if he still has that personality.

When I think of him, I miss him. I've thought about him now and then, just wondering where he's living or what he's doing. Maybe the universe took my questions and just sent me the answers. I'm glad to hear he's doing great, but I don't think I want to hear more about him. We live separate lives now. We're both doing well. If Rachael calls again, I'd rather not know any more details about him.

"Gilles, would you like some coffee before we leave?" I asked one morning.

"No, thanks," he said. "Let's grab some outside. Are you ready? We really need to go."

Need to go? We're only going across the street to Central Park. He's Type A, even when it comes to going to the park.

After reading the newspaper and having a cup of coffee, the beautiful weather made me so relaxed and comfortable. I put my arm in his and my head on his shoulder and closed my eyes for a few minutes. But I had some things on my mind.

"Gilles, can I ask you something?" I asked.

"You just did," he said.

"Why is it that every time I try to plan a trip to see my family you always want me to reschedule it to a later date?"

"I do? How many times have I done that? It's probably just a coincidence, you know, with scheduling conflicts."

"Coincidences? I don't think so. What is it? Why don't you want me to go? I think you should at least consider it. You know my feelings towards my family, and I haven't seen them in years."

"Of course, I'm considering it."

"So, what is it then? We can tell each other anything."

"Tell you what? There's nothing to tell."

"I only want to go for a month. I thought I'd spend some quality time with them. Is a month too long?"

"A month is a long time for any trip, regardless... but the truth is ... it's just that ... I'm afraid you'll go and won't come back."

"What? Oh Gilles, that's absurd."

"I know, I know. It sounds silly. But I've had thoughts you might go and feel so comfortable and happy with your friends and family, and maybe see your ex-boyfriend or who knows. Something or someone might stop you from coming back here."

"Gilles, you have Mark. Even if I did stay there, which I won't, I'm sure you'll be just fine. It's funny though, I thought something similar. What if I come back and you don't want me anymore?"

"Don't be silly."

"But it will happen. One day ... we will go our separate ways. One beautiful day ..."

I hugged him so tight and spilled the rest of my coffee on his brand new, light blue scarf.

"Cheers!" I said as we laughed.

Rachel Beasley called and left a message. She said she just called to say hello and would like to chat again. I was glad to hear from her but at the same time I wasn't interested in doing this best friend forever kind of thing. I just spoke with her a couple of days ago. She seemed rather aggressive. But after a couple of days, I called her back.

"I'm so happy to hear from you," she said.

"Sorry, I've been busy the last few days and didn't get a chance to call you back sooner."

"It's all good. I just wanted to call to say hi, but another reason is … I thought you should know that Maximillian still has feelings for you. He still loves you. I thought you should know."

I paused, my heart accelerating.

"I don't know what you're talking about Rachel. It's been such a long time since…. and… you said he's married."

"Yes, he is, but he loves you."

"And I'm married. Remember?"

"I know, but this has nothing to do with marriage. It has to do with love. Marriage can be one thing, one story, and a happy marriage can be another."

"Of course, but why are you telling me all this?"

"Like I've said, Max and I have a great friendship. I know him. He regrets losing you. I asked him if he still thinks of you and he said yes, every day. As much as he's a good husband and father, and a great person, we all want real love. I don't know anything about your personal life, except what I've read, but I know about his. I wanted to share this with you, that there's another person in this world who thinks of you, and who has feelings for you."

"I appreciate that," I said. "I appreciate every single person who has given me even a tiny bit of attention. It's so wonderful to hear that but … I wish him much happiness. I really do. I'm sure he'll find real love in some way, with someone else. Thanks Rachel, I need to go. I'll talk to you soon."

THIRTY-TWO

SUMMER 2001, SOUTHAMPTON, NY

My head and body were aching. It took a lot of work, but the Hamptons house was ready to go. Ready for a busy summer with lots of guests and parties. The large house looked beautiful, with fresh paint, beautiful decorations and surrounded by colorful fresh flowers. It smelled like summer and felt lively.

The twin gabled house was white on the outside, with dark blue trimming and a dark grey roof. The first floor was all open, with a large foyer flowing into a sitting area, and a staircase to the right that led to the second floor. A step down from the sitting room was the dining room, which looked out on large paneled glass doors that opened onto a large outdoor area with more than enough space for entertaining. At the far end of the outdoor area, it was a few steps down to the infinity pool, which overlooked the ocean near the edge of the property. To the right of the sitting and dining rooms was an open, large gourmet kitchen with all the latest appliances, and to the left was a large living room with all the electronics and a Steinway baby grand. The living room also opened up to the space outside. All the walls were painted with soft pastels, some with wide, two-toned strips that looked like wallpaper. The floors were finished with a light beige Italian stone from Tuscany. All the furniture was modern chic, with an emphasis on simplicity and comfort.

As you reached upstairs, there was another sitting area, with large glass doors that opened out to a balcony, with a view of the outdoor area and the ocean. All five bedrooms were upstairs, each with its own bathroom.

Summer in the Hamptons was all about fun. All the Type A personalities seemed to soften around here. Maybe summer does that to them. Maybe the weather warms their hearts and minds. Maybe the free time makes them calmer, at least for a little bit.

These wealthy people could easily afford to take the whole summer off and completely relax but they didn't. While they're kind of vacationing in their beautiful houses, they still take business calls and travel here and there on business trips. That's their lifestyle. They never relax completely. It would be boring for them. It's fascinating that they want more. More business, more money, more power. There's never enough.

We scheduled all the events. Cocktail parties, dinners and some charity events. One of the largest events was a big family dinner, when Gilles's entire family visited for a few days. Other events were with friends and business colleagues.

One Friday evening I got a call that no one ever wants. Mark was in a car accident while driving out to the Hamptons. All they told us was that Mark was in the hospital. I didn't know his condition. I was on my way to the hospital when I thought about his parents' car accident.

I saw Gilles sitting in the hospital lobby with his head down. I was afraid to reach him. I didn't want to hear any bad news. I sat down right next to him without saying anything. He didn't say anything to me either, for quite a while.

"He's alive, thank God," he said finally. "He's going into surgery. He has internal bleeding and a broken arm and leg."

"Thank God. They can stop the bleeding, and broken bones can heal," I said as I hugged Gilles.

I saw his tears on the floor, and I cried.

We stayed at the hospital until they let us see Mark. Mark's right arm and left leg were wrapped in casts. While we were standing at his bedside, Mark slowly woke up and looked at us through glassy eyes.

"Hey, are you two OK? "he whispered. "You both look so scary. I'm not dead yet. Am I?"

"No, not yet," Gilles said. "But if you ever do that again, I'm going to kill you."

Mark started to laugh but it hurt too much.

"Stop," he said. "You're killing me now."

Mark stayed in the city all summer. He wasn't able to get around much and he needed a lot of help. He stayed home with his housekeeper, who helped him during the day. She took great care of him, like he was her son. I visited him at least twice a week. I needed to be there for him. He was family. We would have lunch or dinner, and of course, he would tell his great, funny stories. I'd comb his hair and give him a homemade facemask so he could still have a fresh and healthy look. Gilles stopped by whenever he could.

One weekend we hosted a dinner party in the Hamptons for business friends and their spouses. Drinks were flowing, and the crowd became louder as they hung out by the pool. I thought about Mark and felt sorry for him. He had to spend his summer in those heavy casts mostly by himself while we were enjoying ourselves on a beautiful summer evening.

"Are you OK? You seem a little out of it," said Tom, one of Gilles's business friends. Before I could even answer, he took his phone out and turned away.

I saw Tom a few times here and in the city. He rented a summer house every year. He was much younger than Gilles, I'd say around thirty-five. But he looked mature for his age. His face and eyes had that sad, old look. He was one of those Wall Street guys who were always stressed from work. Always checking his phone for the latest crisis that would divert his attention, and he'd make a call with a gloomy face.

Tom and Gilles seemed to get along well. Gilles would have long conversations with him. It seemed like smart, older people like to hear from smart, younger people to take in their energy and get new ideas about business.

"I'm sorry," Tom said. "I had to make an urgent call. I have to leave shortly after dinner since I promised some friends I'd stop by their party. Can I get you something to drink?" he asked.

"Thanks, but no, not right now."

Tom would always approach me at these parties to say hello and ask if I needed a drink. If I had a drink he would watch until it was almost gone and ask if I needed a refill. I think he's always been friendly with me because his age was closer to mine than others in the crowd. He would joke a little and give me compliments. He was kind of like, "stay closer to me than any of these other dudes."

"You look great, as always," he said.

Another compliment, right on time.

"Thanks."

"This summer the house looks even better because of you. You make it look better."

"Thanks. I do love the summer."

"Yes, summers are great, especially out here. It's so much fun. Are you having fun? Are you enjoying the suburbs?" he said.

"Yes, it's fine, in small doses."

"Well, if you ever get bored, you can always reach out to me. You can join me and my friends. It's a younger crowd," he smiled.

"That's nice of you. Thanks."

"Girls like you are always a pleasure to be around."

"Thanks. Speaking of girls, the girl you were with at the party last Sunday. She was nice. What was her name?"

"Sally. She's just a friend."

After cocktails by the pool it was time for dinner. Then it was back to the pool for more cocktails and desserts. People were having fun, laughing and dancing.

"That was a great dinner, thank you. I'm going to grab another drink. Would you like something?"

Ahh … my buddy Tom again, my personal bartender.

"I thought you'd be gone by now since you mentioned you had plans elsewhere?"

"Yes, I did, but there's a change in plans. I hope you're not upset that I'm still around?"

"I'm glad you stayed, of course. It's always fun to be around you."

"You know I've been wondering ... Well, I think you should know that you're so beautiful, and young, and you always look so sexy. I wish I could be next to you instead of ... I mean, do you like me? I can be a real gentleman to you, and a real man."

"What do you mean? I don't understand."

"I like you Alyssa. A lot. And I can make you happy."

"And who told you I was looking for happiness?"

"We all are; we're all looking for that. And we both know—and I'm just being honest here—Gilles, your husband? He can't give you complete happiness. You know that. You know what I mean. You don't deserve to be without sex."

"You know, Tom, thanks for your honesty. It's nice that you're able to express yourself and your feelings towards me."

"I really want to be with you. Let me show you what it can be like."

"Really? Hmmm ... Have you ever had sex with him?"

"With who?"

"With my husband."

"Who me? Oh, no ... no, no. I'm straight."

"Well, too bad you haven't. Because I have and it's fantastic. Have a good night, Tom."

Rachel and I became good phone friends during the summer. While I was in the Hamptons, she was vacationing in Lake Tahoe. When it was late and I couldn't sleep, I'd take advantage of the time zones and call her. We'd chat for a while and talk about our summer. She said she liked being surrounded by nature. She was inspired by the silent beauty. It was like a detox for her mind and soul. She seemed rather Zen anyway. I wasn't sure how much calmer she needed to be. Most of the time on the phone she would talk without emotion. She would never raise her voice or laugh loudly. She even made me calm.

We got along so well and the more I talked to her the more I became interested in meeting her. We decided to meet up after the summer. It was interesting knowing someone over the phone but it's nothing like seeing them in person. I didn't know what she looked like. Was she tall or short? Skinny or chubby? What was her style or manners? She knew me from all the pictures, but all I saw of her was a tiny picture on her website, where she was a natural, pleasant-looking blond.

She mentioned she was married. She never mentioned any children and I never asked. If she wanted to share, she would. She mentioned her husband, but just a little. It seemed she was on her own. Every time we talked, she would always find some segue and mention Max. She would speak about him so easily, and in such an unassuming way, that I couldn't resist. She was a great conversationalist. The last time I spoke to her we were talking about the beauty of Japanese cherry trees and that Max's job had him living in Japan for a few months.

Mark was healing slowly, patiently going through physical therapy, but it was a lengthy process. He tried his best to be grateful that he survived and keep his spirits up, but he was often lonely. Sometimes when Gilles arrived in the Hamptons after visiting Mark, he seemed tired and moody. At times it was hard to figure him out. I left him alone and went outside for a swim. When I came back, I saw him sitting pensively.

"Is everything OK?" I asked. "Can I get you something to drink?"

"I'm fine. Just come sit next to me. Tell me, how was your day?"

"I was thinking of … you know, I had a moment at the party the other night when I thought about Mark. I felt bad he was by himself and we were here, having a good time."

"Yes, it's hard. I'm so tired of it. But I can't imagine how hard it is for him."

"I was thinking … why can't he stay here? He can stay with us and then he wouldn't be alone in the city."

"Stay here? He needs a lot of help you know."

"So? He can bring his housekeeper. What difference does it make for her where she takes care of him?"

"It's not just about her. It's also about him. Aside from the help, he just can't stay here."

"Why not? At least he could be around us. It would be good for you too, no?"

"No, absolutely not. What the hell are you talking about? It wouldn't be good for me and you know it. We're finally in a place where no one gossips about us anymore, at least as far as I know. I'm not going to light that up again. No, he can't stay here."

We sat quietly for a moment, alone with our thoughts.

"But so what if people talk about it?" I asked. "And so what if you two want to be together? Aren't you tired of hiding your personal life? Why can't you just be free? Both of you, just be free and be together? How long are you going to live like this? I know you've done all this because of your career, your family and the people around you, but maybe it's time for a change. Time for being you. Just be you, with him, the one you love.

"Why do you care anymore about what people say? Whoever really loves you will do so unconditionally. They'll support you no matter what. The people who won't? That's their choice, and their problem, not yours. Your parents made their own choices in life, and so should you. You can't live your life for them. No one should ever sacrifice their personal life and happiness for the sake of others.

"Mark is going through a difficult time and you need to be with him, so you can help him. Mark needs you right now, needs to sleep next to you, and wake up next to you. I'm sure you want to support him completely, but you don't. Why? Because of what people might say? Do other people's opinions matter more than the person you love?

"Everything you've worked so hard for, your career, power, wealth … you have it all. You don't have to prove anything to anyone. What you're doing now is only hurting yourself, and Mark. You're a free man. You can do whatever you want. You can just quit your job and spend time with your loved ones. Just travel, have fun and enjoy each other. You can go anywhere, move to a beautiful island or in the mountains. You can leave your crazy city lifestyle for a quiet place, or just stay here. You have the power over your life. Do whatever you want, for yourself and Mark.

"One day we will leave each other, you know that. I can only hope I'll be able to find the love of my life, as you have. You're a very lucky man. You've found real love, and that love is returned. Don't you want to enjoy this beautiful feeling for the rest of your life? You deserve to be in love, without hiding. You can be a great example to others who are in the same situation as you and Mark. People who are afraid to be open about their love.

"Of course, you can do whatever you want. But just be real, free from the secrets and the lies. Be who you are, not who others want you to be. When you're free, and in love, that's real success, real happiness."

He was staring straight ahead, not looking at me. There was a loud silence.

He's always been a good listener. It's hard to read what he's thinking about from his calm facial expression. Is he just politely listening to me or is he interested in what I've said? Is he mad because I got too personal? Maybe he's not ready to hear the truth. I'm not going to press him for a response.

I left and went upstairs.

It wasn't long before the summer was over. It was a lot of fun, with many great memories. It was tiring, but in a good way. Now it was time to turn the page. Autumn in the city.

"Are you almost ready?" Gilles asked. "The driver's outside. We should go so we can beat the traffic."

"Yes, I'm ready," I said.

I was standing by the window, looking at the beautiful ocean view one more time. I turned around to leave and Gilles was in front of me.

"Alyssa, I have to ask. Are you mad at me?" he asked.

"Me mad? Why would you ask me that?"

"I mean, are you disappointed in me? That I didn't take the high road and step up for my love? What you told me a few weeks ago made me think. I've been doing a lot of thinking lately, about my life. All this time, with everything going on, I always wanted you to be proud of me. I never want to disappoint you. Are you upset? Is something going on between us that I don't know about? Are you leaving me?"

"Did I sound upset or mad?"

"Well … no. You were calm as you were speaking."

"I wasn't talking about me. I was talking about you and your life, remember?"

"I know, I'm just confused."

"Shouldn't we leave now, so we don't hit traffic?"

I grabbed my bag and started to leave. I turned to look at Gilles. He just stood there, motionless, with a sad expression. I dropped my bag, walked into his arms and hugged him. He smelled so fresh and felt so strong, with great energy. I took a deep breath to inhale him. It was like recharging my body and mind.

"How could I ever be upset or mad at you?" I asked. "You've changed my life. You've given me attention, support and opportunities, without conditions, like a parent would do. You've given me the greatest advice, as a smart professor would do. You've always trusted me and are always there for me, like a great friend. You've shared beautiful sex, like a good lover. You've treated me like a woman, like every gentleman should. Gilles, you're a great man, and I will always be appreciative that you're a part of my life. I'm always proud of you, and I could never be mad at you."

He stared at me, then he smiled and hugged me so hard, as usual.

"The pleasure has been all mine," he said. "You're so wonderful I just can't take it. OK, come on, let's go. Hurry up, we have to leave so we don't hit traffic."

Now it's hurry up? Is he something or what?

THIRTY-THREE

SPRING 2002, MANHATTAN

It took Mark about six months to recover from his injuries. The physical therapy he endured was easy compared to what he first went through. While he was injured, Mark had a lot of time to think about his photography. He was ready to share his hobby with the public. He announced he was going to exhibit his photography collection. His portfolio was all about physical objects, anything that didn't breathe.

It took him a few months to prepare his collection and choose the gallery, but he finally set May 9th as the date for opening his exhibition. As it turned out, it was right in the middle of when I was planning to see my family. I couldn't believe the coincidence, and I had to change my travel plans—again. Then I got an idea and decided to send an email.

Hi Rachel,

Hope all is well with you and your family. Sorry I haven't been in touch lately. I've been studying a lot and have little free time. I'm really enjoying Columbia University. The subjects and the teachers are great. This is my second year and, as you know, it gets busier each year.

I'm not sure if you've ever heard of the interior designer Mark Miller, but one reason I'm reaching out is that he's having his first photography exhibition, and I'd like to personally invite you. It would be great if you can attend, since we could also meet in person.

Please let me know if you're able to attend and I'll send you the invite.

Warm regards,

Alyssa

She responded the next day.

Hi Alyssa,

Many thanks for the invite, and yes, I've heard of Mark—he does such creative work. I'm sure his photography will be interesting as well, and I would be thrilled to meet you! It's been so long since we talked about meeting each other, but now it will finally happen!

Thanks for thinking of me and I look forward to seeing you!

Rachel

Soon, the opening day arrived. The Miller Gallery in Chelsea was newly renovated, and it wasn't structured in a traditional way, with big square rooms and pictures on the walls with small spotlights aimed at the art. It was a large, round, white room. In the middle was a circular walking space, and then three concentric circles with free-standing beige panels spaced evenly around the circle, with enough room between for people to move about the gallery. The photography was hung on the panels. Mark had a hard time finding a gallery that was designed to his taste but this one was right.

"I have something I'd like you to wear tonight," Gilles said, handing me a Van Cleef & Arpels box. "Please open it."

It was an Oiseaux de Paradis, Bird of Paradise necklace, with white gold, and round diamonds. I put the box down and stared at it, astonished.

"Do you like it?" he asked. "Let me help you put it on."

"You didn't know which dress I was going to wear tonight," I said. "How did you know the necklace would go so well with it?"

"I just know things, darling, I just know."

"Thank you so much, Gilles. Why did you decide to buy a diamond necklace? You know me, I'm not one of those girls who loves diamonds."

"I wanted you to be like one of them tonight," he smiled.

"Well, then you know, just a necklace won't be enough," I said as I hugged him.

I wore a long J. Mendel blue chiffon see-through evening dress, and the diamonds sparkled as they draped my neck. Christian Dior shoes were caring for my feet, and my head was dazzled by the champagne as I watched this lovely event with a high energy crowd.

Uptown meets downtown. Diversity. Classy, conservative styles meet hippy and chic styles in fashion. Older people with champagne and scotch meet younger people with vodka martinis. The DJ meets the piano player. House music meets classic jazz. I was meeting and greeting people I knew and didn't know.

Gilles was happy and busy having drinks with his friends. After a while most of the guests gathered in the center and started looking at Mark's photography. The noise sounded like a bunch of birds hanging out in the park. I took a break from greeting people and went by myself to look and enjoy every single one of Mark's photos.

They were all black and white. There were twelve standalone walls and each one had three or four photographs. I looked carefully, without rushing. Every time I looked at them, I discovered something new. There was a picture of an old wooden chair, abandoned on a Manhattan street corner, that somehow looked proud. Another of a narrow five-story Lower East Side building with a water tower on top—old but majestic. And one of the north side of Central Park in the winter, with snow on the ground, and large, cold rock formations with icicles. It made me cold just looking at it.

I moved to the second and third circles of the walls, which had fewer photos than the first. I did the same thing, slowly walking around, until I got to the final photo, where I spent a long time staring, without moving. It was also black and white, except for one piece. It was the only picture on the wall. It was a picture of my old suitcase, titled *Yellow Suitcase*.

There was a time when this piece was unnoticeable, insignificant and abandoned by everyone. Then I took it to America, even though I never liked it. I thought it was the ugliest, roughest, and most uncomfortable thing I ever had, and it caused blisters on my hands. But the picture had something to say. Something to make you think as you looked at it. I used to hate that piece, but now, as a work art, I liked it. It looked unique. Yes, it was unique and interesting, as a photo. It looked tired and old, with rough and heavy wrinkled skin. It looked like a human who once was young and beautiful, but life didn't treat it well, and it was all reflected in the photograph. It looked used, well-traveled, but abandoned. It was dead.

I'll never forget when I came here years ago with that suitcase. So many memories. New Jersey, Long Island, Brooklyn. Nikki, Lori and Viktor, Anna and The Corrector, Kalian, Silvia, Jeff, Zachary. All the loneliness, the doubts, all the strangers who helped me. What an incredible journey. I should write a book.

My eyes began to tear.

OK, hang on. This evening isn't about me. It's about the man who created all these beautiful works of art.

Someone gently touched me on my shoulder.

"I didn't want to tell you about this picture. I thought I'd surprise you. I hope you like it."

"Mark, I see so many stories in this picture. I see the suitcase with a tired and old expression, like a human being. How can you turn objects into living beings? Every picture seems to come to life with some story. I'm so impressed. Is this art? Or is this something else?"

"Thanks. I just try to capture the essence of things," he said. "Nice necklace by the way. I've seen that necklace. Now that's a work of art. No doubt about it, Gilles is a very generous man. You know, I wish I could just make a big announcement right here, to let everyone know how generous he is."

Wait. What?

"Announce what?" I asked. "My necklace?"

"What? No, no. Not that. You are too funny," he said. "Gilles bought this gallery for me, as a gift. I thought you knew about it."

"Oh Mark!" I screamed as I jumped into his arms and hugged him.

I felt bad that my scream caused a scene. I looked around and several people were staring at me. I smiled and stared back at them, and they slowly turned away to continue their conversations, but then I sensed someone staring at me, to my right. I turned to look, staring at his face and looking into his eyes. Eyes that were ... familiar.

Maximillian?

Now he was standing right in front of me, looking at me with a dry expression. It was hard to believe he was the same person I knew from years ago. He looked wise, with mature facial features. The young man I knew had transformed into a man. The man I once loved so much. He was looking at me, observing me, just like I was doing to him. When he smiled, his eyes had the same sparkle, except with a few lines. I felt I knew him and at the same time, I didn't. He was the man I had known so well, and now he was someone I just met.

"When I heard your voice, it sounded familiar and then ... I saw you," he said. "I can't believe my eyes. You haven't changed at all. How are you?"

"I'm very well, thanks. How about you?"

Rachel must have something to do with this. She sends him over instead of coming here herself? I'm not feeling too good about her right now.

"I'm shocked to see you," he said. "I feel like I'm dreaming."

I hear him but I'm a little disoriented. I'm not sure what to say. Oh …

"You look so different," I said.

"Yes, I got older."

"Yes, but it's a good older look."

"Thanks, I think."

"So, what brings you here? Do you know Mark?"

"Mark? Oh, you mean the artist of this exhibition?" he smiled broadly, and I saw the 17-year-old Max. "Honestly? I don't know much about art. My wife asked me to come with her and surprisingly, she's late. I just spoke with her. She'll be here any minute."

While we talked, his eyes would wander around, looking for his wife. I followed where he looked. I wanted to see who she was, who was chosen by him, and what she looked like. But it was tough looking through the crowd. Finally, his eyes locked-in. He waved to her and went to greet her. He kissed her on the cheek, took her hand and walked towards me.

"Here she is, finally!" he said. "Darling, I want to introduce you to someone. This is Alyssa. Alyssa, this is my wife Rachel, Rachel Beasley."

Rachel?

THIRTY-FOUR

It was early the next morning when I kissed Gilles goodbye and got in the car. I was on my way to the airport, taking a flight to visit my home and see my family and friends. I was happy, nervous and excited. After the plane took off, I pulled out the letter from Rachel, to read it again.

Dear Alyssa,

I'm writing to you to be honest, as a good friend would do. Maximillian and I have been married, living together and raising our beautiful daughter, who we both love very much. But it's not about a child or anything else when it comes to two people together in what we call marriage.

I believe it's all about love, trust and respect, and together they equal happiness. If one of them is missing, then there is no happiness. I love Max as a person, but I'm not in love with him. We are completely different people, in many ways. We are good friends, but not good lovers.

I have found my love. It's a beautiful feeling which every human being wants, and I hope everyone will experience it in their lifetime. I want to see Maximillian happy and so in love, as I am today. We had many great times together. Fun days and sharing our thoughts and supporting each other. But I have known for a long time that he can't give me true love because he's always loved you. I thought about leaving him, for my own love and happiness, but I want to leave him as a happy man, and in love.

We both tried to make it work but there's no human being on the planet who can convince someone to change how they feel. When I randomly found you, I became so happy that I could do something that would give him a chance to be with his real love again.

It wasn't a nice thing that I did, with my acting, and playing all the games with you. But I did what I thought I had to do. I hope you can forgive me.

Warm regards,

Rachel

In early 2003, Mark and Gilles announced they were a couple. They had a beautiful celebration of their love in Lake Como, Italy, at Gilles's new summer villa. It was just like a wedding, but without the marriage license. Max and I arrived a few days before the wedding and stayed in Milan. He wanted to take me there so we could have a fashion experience together and see all the sights like the Milan Cathedral, Leonardo da Vinci's "Last Supper," and an opera at La

Scala. We stayed at the Four Seasons, which is one of his favorites. Not only was it a beautiful hotel, it's also a magnificent work of art.

When we were kids, he hated it when I watched fashion TV, but I always tried to convince him to watch it with me. He used to say I should just move to Milan to see real fashion instead of watching it on TV. I'm not sure how he knew about Milan's fashion style, but he was right.

Milan was impressive. Walking on the Monte Napoleone on a Saturday afternoon was like attending many fashion shows by many high-end designers, all at the same time. Living in Manhattan with Gilles, I had an expensive, high-end wardrobe, and I saw many wealthy people dressed fashionably. I would never think that I'd be amazed by fashion somewhere else, but I was. Milan was pure fashion. You wouldn't even consider leaving the hotel without looking your best.

"Let's go see a movie tonight," Max said while we had breakfast in the hotel restaurant.

"See a movie in Milan?" I asked. "It would be hard to understand. I don't speak Italian. Do you?"

"No, but it would be like old times, when we used to go to movies. Remember? We wouldn't even watch the movie completely. We were too busy kissing."

"Yes, let's go for some kissing then."

"It would also be interesting to watch a movie and try to figure out what's happening, without the translation."

"OK, is this a new experiment or something?"

"It's a new life."

Space Cinema was the name of the movie theater. It was old and small but beautiful. The seats were a little uncomfortable, but it had a cozy atmosphere. Of course, the movie was in Italian without subtitles. Only the name of the movie was easy to understand. *Primo Amore*. Everyone knows primo and amore right?

"I can't believe you found a movie with this title," I said.

"When I was searching the movies, I saw the name and I couldn't believe it, so I just bought the tickets. I have no idea what the movie is about though."

We sat in the middle of the last row. The place was crowded with loud Italians. They would talk to each other even during the movie. But we didn't care. We couldn't understand a word anyway. We tried to watch, then we snuggled, and I closed my eyes.

Max woke me up and told me it was rude of me that I wasn't taking the movie seriously. We laughed for so long I had to leave the auditorium for a while to calm down. I went back inside and we both became quiet and romantic. He held me, and I put my head on his shoulder, like I used to do. I got chills when he kissed me, and this was it. I closed my eyes again.

I hope the guy doesn't kill that girl. He seems weird.

Then I heard loud screaming from the actor, and I thought I should see what was going on in the movie.

Why bother. I won't understand anyway.

When the screaming got even louder, I raised my head and watched the movie. She was standing naked in front of him and he was screaming at her. Who knows why?

"This is the movie that you chose?" I whispered. "It's a little disturbing. Can we leave?"

"Only if you marry me," he said.

"Really, do you mind if we leave?"

"Really, will you marry me?"

"What? Are you serious?"

"Yes. I love you. I always have and I always will."

Now we became like the chatty Italians, talking louder until we heard "shhh" from all sides. We left the theater, taking a long walk as we talked about our childhoods, our more recent adventures and our future, together. That night we stayed up until sunrise to celebrate our love, which had never died.

More than two hundred guests were invited to Gilles's and Mark's celebration. It was an unforgettable day for all. It was the celebration of the love, trust and respect that brings happiness to human beings. We were all together that day, to salute and enjoy life.

Max and Rachel's daughter Lola was a flower girl. Rachel's new boyfriend Santiago Cano, a Spanish painter, was one of Mark's ushers. I was just a guest with my fiancé.

"I'm so happy that you've been so understanding about Gilles and me," I said to Max. "You've shown him respect. Thank you for that."

"If it wasn't for him, I wouldn't be standing here right now. He helped you in so many ways, and it led to us finding each other. So why wouldn't I respect him? And thank you for your respect and friendship with Rachel. I appreciate that."

"Well, if not for her, I wouldn't be here either. She's the one who discovered me and reconnected us. Why wouldn't I respect her?"

Like I said … people? We're all connected.

ABOUT THE AUTHOR

"I live where I truly belong. I will never leave this unconditionally loved, and most beautiful island called Manhattan."

- L.W. Clark